THE CONTINENT OF

RUYN

Yule

Shiv

Fern's Rest

NORTHERN WASTES

Beaton City

BEATON

Grandun-Krator

Kaz-Curma

Dun-Filda

Mountain Pass

THORAN

Fanged Ones

Red Suns

River Head

Thoran

GOBLIN MAW

Liaf

Sharp Claws

Dun-Gaza

Luran

Ingur · Talgel

Dread Cliffs

Breyland

SOUTHERN REPUBLIC

Everstand · Good Harbor

Weysfield

Conny

Seagate · Cardun-Addush

Kaz-Ulum

N

SWORD OF RUYN

First Edition. February 10, 2018

Written by RG Long

RG LONG

SWORD OF RUYN

LEGENDS OF GILIA

BOOK 1

1: The Silver Wolf

S now fell heavily between the trees. The ancient oaks and pines typically shielded the forest floor from the powder of white.

It was a testament to how great the winter storm was.

The far mountains were no longer visible through the dense blizzard. On a clear day, from this spot in the northern wastes, one could make out the east and west mountain ranges that formed the borders of this hard, cold land.

On this day, however, it was a challenge to see the trees of the forest from twenty yards away, which, of course, was exactly why she had chosen this spot.

Normally to see the woman now standing at the edge of the mighty forest, if she didn't want to be seen, was quite the feat. She had a talent for disappearing, even in a crowded tavern. But today, between the hard snowfall, the trees of the Saliderian Woods, and the whitened cloak of wolf skin she wore, to see her would mean she was less than an arm's length away.

The wind was cold and bitter. It was these types of winds that had bothered her so when she first arrived here. No longer. Now she was accustomed to the wind and snow. So much so that she considered them her partner, always aiding her and allowing her to use them to her advantage.

What little of her face that was exposed stung in the fierce gale. Her silver hair was braided into a single plait that ran the length of her back, trailing from the heavy fur hood she wore. The hood was fashioned from the same skull of the beast whose fur she wore on her back. His face still struck terror in those who saw it now, though the life of him had bled out some five years ago.

She was of a slender build and medium height. Underneath the furs, skins, and double blades, she had strapped to her back was a beauty that was unparalleled to most of fairer lands. To see her without her hunting gear would cause most men to crane their necks to get a second glance.

If, indeed, their necks had not been broken before they could try to catch those enchanting blue eyes.

The wind was slowing now, but the snow was falling harder than ever. A new layer of snow would add another arm's length to the depth of what was already blanketing the ground. She had no fears of being followed and no worries about anything being found this far out in the wastes until spring.

Perfect conditions to claim a bounty.

She had been stalking her prey for three days, waiting for the right opportunity. He headed east for a while, which most travelers in these parts do after trekking through the southern pass. That path led to the first relief from the cold winter in a three-day walk in any direction.

Those who traveled east without first stopping to rest and resupply were either foolish or determined, or perhaps a combination of the two.

This man was the latter.

He now approached in his slow and steady pace, which he had kept for ten days. His heavy jacket and pack were covered in snow, and to any other man the two arm-lengths of powder he was blazing through would be enough of an excuse to turn back.

But not for a foolish and determined man headed east in the northern wastes.

Her eyes narrowed to ensure this was the same man she had been tracking for the last few days. The previous night she had gone ahead of him, anticipating the direction he was heading so that he might pass by her. Only once had she ended the life of someone whom she had incorrectly thought her bounty. Not this time.

Yes, this was the man. The military coat still showed some of the dark green color through the white powder. His stature was certainly that of a warrior. He was taller than the average male, certainly had a much broader chest, and his arms were the size of tree limbs. The wind gusted unexpectedly, knocking off the soldier's hat. His auburn hair flashed as he made a grab for the soaked and worn head covering. After tugging it back onto his head, he resumed his trek.

Though she cared less for the reason and more for the gold she would soon claim, it unnerved her to think of someone headed east after the rumors of the growing unrest down south.

She needn't lose much sleep tonight, however.

Her first knife found his chest before he had comprehended the whirl of the steel through the air. Clutching the handle now protruding from his heart, he staggered. It was only a breath before she was on him, blade drawn and brought to his neck.

"You're the most expensive bounty I've had in a year. It's been a pleasure."

For a moment, he struggled to reach around himself and grab this assailant. And in that brief moment, she feared he may have been able to draw his sword and do damage to her. But only for that moment, as the very next, her second blade made its cut: deeply and effectively.

His lifeless body sunk to the ground.

She cleaned her blade carefully and returned it to its sheath. Her knife received the same treatment before it was fastened to her calf. The number of blades she wore, both concealed and in plain sight, outnumbered her own fingers.

Her instructions were simple. Return the book and the necklace and she'd have her reward. Both of these he had kept in a satchel hung around his shoulder for the entirety of his time spent in the wastes. Anything else of value found on her kill was hers for the taking.

When she eyed the beautifully crafted spear with its azure gem set into the base of the tip, she hungrily relieved it from its former owner and took hold of it. A weapon so fine had not been seen in the wastes for many years.

Quickly, she looked up from her business of looting and sniffed the air.

This smell was new. Not one she had encountered while tracking the man who was now nearly covered in snow. She breathed in deeply, then spun around on her heel.

He was only a stone's throw away. How he had avoided her for so long made her wonder if he had come from the forest as she had. She dropped the spear and drew her blade, swearing under her breath for letting him see her.

He would not have the gift of sight for long.

2: Ealrin Bealouve

There was nothing but fog. It was all he could see.

He could still hear the screams. He could still taste the salt water in his mouth. But all he could see, all he could remember, was fog.

Sensations played in his head.

Falling darkness. Ear splitting screams. Water. Fog.

Suddenly a new sensation reached his senses.

He was on fire.

No, not on fire. But burning. In a moment he realized his eyes could open. In raising his eyelids a hair's breadth he immediately regretted it. The sun was burning down on him. He closed his eyes. The light was blinding compared to the darkness and fog.

His arms were only sluggishly responding to his desires to move them. His feet were soaked, along with most of his legs. He realized that half of him lay in water. Not still water, but a tide. It was at this same moment he realized the terrible pain in his abdomen. He slowly brought his fingers to his ribs and felt the torn cloth that was his jacket and his shirt. The warmth of his own blood contrasted the cool sea water.

As he touched his bare ribs the familiar darkness came back, threatening to engulf him again.

More screams.

And yet, these voices were different. These were not the ones in his head.

These were running down the beach.

"I SEE YOU'VE DECIDED not to die after all."

The throbbing in his head was immense. The pain in his chest was still quite real. The screams and the fog vanished a bit as he began to become aware of his surroundings.

Instead of a sandy beach, he lay on a bed. Instead of a burning sun, there was a ceiling above him. Instead of water at his feet, there was a blanket.

He lay in a room, dimly lit. The light was easier on his eyes than the burning sun he last recalled seeing.

But not much better.

It took him several moments of blinking to understand that, in the corner of the room sat a man. The one who had apparently just confirmed what he had been wondering during his dreams of fog and voices: he was alive.

Finally, his eyes were usable and he leaned forward to glance about the room.

It was sparsely furnished. He lay in one of the two beds that were separated by a small table at the head of each. The wall to his left was barely an arm's breadth away. At the foot of the two beds was a space slightly larger. Two chairs framed the small fireplace that provided low light in the room. To the right of the fireplace was the door. A few pegs on the wall beside held his shirt and coat.

An inn.

The idea came to him as he laid his head back down on the pillow. His ribs still burned with the small effort of looking at his surroundings.

"No. I'm alive," he finally said.

His voice was harsh, unused. There were suddenly several questions he had to ask, but the fog lingered in his mind, preventing him from forming any.

"You've been laying on that bed now for half a moon," said the man in the corner chair.

Instead of trying to ask, he looked at the seated man, investigating who he was.

Straining his neck a little, without moving his chest, he could see who was dimly lit by the fire.

The first thing he noticed was a grimace on the man's face.

He sat comfortably in the chair, as if he was accustomed to spending time in it. As if it were made for him. He was pleasant in appearance, save for the look on his face. His brown hair was not long enough to hide his green and narrowed eyes but stopped above his eyebrows. His expression didn't seem to be narrow out of menace or strife. His eyes spoke about the life he had seen lived out before him.

He wore a simple green shirt with a leather vest and pants. His black boots looked well-worn and traveled on. From across the bed, his stubble was visible. Some gray hairs betrayed him as older than 30, yet there was something in his eyes that Ealrin couldn't quite place. Like a father examining his son after seeing him fall from a tree.

"My name is Holve, in case you were curious."

He was curious.

"And yours is?" asked Holve.

But now his first coherent question came to mind:

"What is my name?"

The words escaped his lips alongside his thoughts.

The wrinkles on Holve's face shifted as his expression changed. Was it pity?

"Eh, that part I may be able to help with. Your coat had in it the name 'Ealrin Bealouve.' It's sewed into the collar quite nicely actually. Someone with a skilled hand had done it."

Ealrin.

The name floated in amid the fog. It sounded like a name he had heard many times. Could it be his?

He wasn't sure.

He didn't have any better suggestions either.

"Ealrin Bealouve."

Again his voice was harsh. He was overcome with a thirst at the moment.

"Water. Please. A drink." he managed.

Instead of a word, Holve gave him a wink and left the room. He soon returned with a wooden cup and a pitcher full of water. He poured some into the cup and offered it.

At first, Ealrin tried to sit up to accept the drink, but was overcome with pain in his head and his ribs as he made the attempt.

A very real groan of pain escaped his lips.

"Now don't work too hard, Ealrin. You've had it pretty bad."

Holve moved over to Ealrin and helped him drink the water. It was almost cool and certainly refreshing to his overly parched mouth. He gulped down every drop that was in the cup and wished there were more. But then it hit his stomach and he wasn't sure if he wanted to throw it all back up or just lay still a moment.

"Thanks," Ealrin managed as he licked his lips to spread the moisture on his chapped mouth.

Holve placed the cup and the pitcher next to Ealrin's bed on the table and returned to his chair. Resuming the same look of comfort, he began to speak.

"Well, I'd say welcome to Good Harbor, but seeing as you've already been here for the better part of a month lying in that bed, you ought to be feeling pretty welcome already. You sure gave us all quite the intrigue in your coming. This is a fishing and trading community. Not many boats occupy these waters without the knowledge of the general public. Yours sure snuck up on us, though. There was a pretty terrible storm the night before we found you lying on the beach, about a day's walk east of here. Your vessel was smashed to pieces. Most of it went down to the depths."

With this he paused.

"You're the only one we found alive among the wreckage."

He was looking for a response from Ealrin, but Ealrin had none to give.

A shipwreck?

A storm?

Others?

None of these brought any memories to his mind.

Only fog.

Hearing no response, Holve continued.

"We thought for a time we'd lose you, too. You had lost a lot of blood. Fortunately for you, a healer of some talent was traveling through this harbor. He was able to patch you up nicely before sailing on. Then, with Elezar's cooking and a room to rest in, it seems you'll pull through."

Ealrin saw that Holve had allowed himself another moment to examine him. His expression was stony. It didn't seem like the man smiled much. Ealrin felt odd as Holve continued staring at him, as if he had more to say and definitely more to ask but was pondering whether he ought to speak.

Holve sighed.

"Though, your fever certainly gave you some odd dreams. You fought those blankets pretty hard the first few nights."

For the next few moments, there was nothing but silence, broken only by the occasional crack of the logs in the fire as they turned to embers. The room had paint peeling off at certain spots on the wall and smelled of the sea. The hearth above the fireplace held a vase of long-dead flowers that were stiff and brown.

Ealrin looked up at the ceiling, staring at the wood he saw there to keep from feeling uncomfortable as Holve glared at him.

Holve asked the question Ealrin was wondering as well.

"Can you recall anything, Ealrin?"

Nothing Holve had said provided a picture in his mind. It was as if he was hearing a tale that he played no part in at all.

"I can't," replied Ealrin.

There, in his mind, was only fog.

For the second time, Holve gave a big sigh.

"Hmm. Well, I was hoping to find out some things from you. Like I said, boats here don't normally surprise us at Good Harbor. And the pieces of yours that washed ashore aren't like any I've seen in many winters."

"Good Harbor?" asked Ealrin.

"That's right," replied Holve. "Though, the only truly good thing about this place is the bed you're sleeping in. We're the only human island in-between the civilized portion of Ruyn and goblin-owned lands known as the Goblin Maw. They've sailed from time to time to the mainland, always landing here first to set the place to fire and stock their boats before turning on more populated areas. Though, it's been some time since they've set their ships to sea. I reckon they've been arguing among themselves. Better for us if they keep in-fighting."

Holve shifted in his chair to glance out of the window into the night. The small opening had four glass panels set into a wood frame. It was the only thing that decorated the otherwise bland, plastered wall.

"This island isn't the home of the willing. The ones who live here either want to get away from the eye of more civilized areas of Ruyn or can't afford to leave."

Holve adjusted his gaze back to Ealrin.

All this talk of Ruyn, goblins sailing, and fishing was so foreign to Ealrin. Nothing could fight through the fog that so clouded his mind.

He was only halfway sure of the name he was hearing.

But now, his present situation was beginning to register in his head.

"Who's been caring for me?" asked Ealrin.

Though he was sure he'd felt better at some point, he certainly wasn't starving. Nor was he unclean. In fact, save for the wound in his ribs that still hurt when he moved despite being healed, Ealrin felt well taken care of. His belly was satisfied and his skin felt as if he had had a bath.

Well, except for the feeling that he wanted to throw up again due to his headache and the water.

"We've been taking turns watching over you, Elezar, and myself. Well, us and the maid. Though, she refused to wash you up. Bit modest," Holve said with a wink. That seemed a little out of character for him, though Ealrin had only known Holve for a few minutes.

Ealrin was overwhelmed. If he truly had been lying here for a month or more, then he owed his caretakers much.

"Thank you," he said. And he meant it.

"Don't mention it," replied Holve, with a bit of gruffness to his voice. It sounded as if he truly wished Ealrin wouldn't mention it.

"And welcome to Good Harbor. And the Rusty Hook. Best inn on the island."

3: Stinkrunt

S tinkrunt sneered as he walked onto the goblin ship. He was doing his best to look fierce today, but, as always, it was hard to
look fierce standing next to old Grayscar. Grayscar was the big doyen
of the Sharp Claws. He had three scars running down his face, starting from his forehead, down his snout-like nose and going all the way
to his opposite cheek. The beast that had given him the scar lived just
long enough to admire his work before Grayscar skewered it with a
spear. He had returned to their goblin tribe with that great wolf
around his neck as a trophy and he had been the doyen, or leader, of
the Sharp Claws ever since.

Stinkrunt, who was one of the smallest goblin leaders, always felt
like he was in Grayscar's shadow. Of course, in a literal sense, he tried
to be as often as possible. The sun hurt his eyes and today was no exception. The goblin tribes were loading the boats and sailing toward
human lands, something they hadn't done in a generation.

Grayscar took a big sniff from his off-centered nose.

"Smells good. Smells like the sea. Smells like war. We'll stop fighting other tribes. We'll fight men instead. Dwarves and elves, too."
Grayscar looked over the goblins who were loading weapons and
barrels of supplies into the ship and chuckled. Stinkrunt could tell
the thought of war with the other races pleased his leader. He always
felt important whenever Grayscar talked with him.

"Stinkrunt!" Grayscar shouted unexpectedly and nearly knocked
Stinkrunt over as he turned around, searching for him.

"Oh," he said as Stinkrunt tripped over some rope, knocking over
a barrel and falling into its contents: a pile of fish. "There you are."

Grayscar lifted him by his ankle out of the fish and set him down. Stinkrunt looked up at him from the deck of the ship.

"You wanted me, Grayscar?" he asked, now knowing that Grayscar had been talking to himself.

Grayscar snorted as Stinkrunt got to his feet.

"Stinkrunt, you're clumsy," he said as he began to walk away towards the front of the ship. Grayscar was always calling Stinkrunt names. Mostly because he was disappointed with Stinkrunt in some form or fashion. That Stinkrunt hadn't brought him his sword fast enough, or caught a fish for him to eat yet, or hadn't been able to deliver a message to another doyen without getting beat up in the process.

Stinkrunt quickly got to his feet, slipped, and nearly fell, but ran after him.

Stinkrunt was always running after Grayscar. For the last two years the goblins had moved away from their ancestral lands and hidden themselves in the mountains to the north. They had been breeding there; increasing their numbers well beyond what was sustainable in their lands. A goblin was typically ready to bash some other creature's head in six months after it took its first breath. At two years old, it would be fighting fit.

But, if a goblin tribe grew too large with young goblins ready to prove their strength, there would be infighting without end. Rival doyens would challenge the tribe's leader, goblins would take sides, and then an all-out civil war would breakout until enough of one side had their skulls cracked in.

But this was not to be the fate of the goblins this time.

Grayscar was the leader of doyens. It was he who had convinced the other goblin tribes to sail east to raid the civilized lands. It was he who had been able to tell the others about the fertile plains and forested mountains that held fat humans who were lazy and stinking elves who were always lost in their own thoughts. These were the lands the goblins would take. Generations ago, they had tried and failed. Not this time. This time Grayscar would lead them all to victory. This time, the Sharp Claws would take the biggest cut of the loot.

And where had Stinkrunt been while Grayscar was off drinking goblin brew with the other clan's leaders? Following him around, carrying his banner, doing his dirty work, and making sure the daggers never found Grayscar's back like they had so many other doyens who tried to unite the clans.

Stinkrunt was the lowest of the goblin leaders and he knew it. But he wanted a chance and would take anything he could get. He knew that this was the moment to make his claim.

"I'm small. I'm weak. I'm clumsy. You never say I'm a good doyen." Stinkrunt came up beside Grayscar as he continued to bully around goblins who were loafing. Most at least pretended to work when he walked by. A good sneer from Grayscar would send the smaller goblins scurrying off to either pretend to work somewhere else or bully someone smaller than them. This was how the goblins worked. The bigger ones bullied the smaller ones into doing whatever they wanted. And Grayscar wanted to sail east and fight. He was the biggest among all the clans and knocked around whoever disagreed with his great plan. "Give me a chance," Stinkrunt said, almost whining to his boss. "Let me lead in a fight. I'll show you. Small isn't bad. I'm sneaky. I'm cunning. I'm..."

He was cut short as Grayscar shoved a goblin overboard who was eating a fish out of the barrel, instead of packing the barrel below the deck.

"You want to show me you can fight?" Grayscar asked as he continued surveying his ship: the *Big Scar*.

It was the biggest in the fleet of goblin craft, which was saying something because all the other clans had tried to outdo one another with their flagships. It stood nearly thirty goblins tall. Grayscar himself had laid down the goblins to measure it when it was being built. Its boards were black and its sails had the Sharp Claws' symbol emblazoned on it: three black scars running down the yellow canvas.

Stinkrunt knew Grayscar was pleased with his ship. It had three decks, the lowest for goblin slaves to row their oars, giving the ship a speed greater to the others around it. Grayscar was always the first to a fight.

"Our ancestors sailed east to raid. They brought down a whole city. I want to bring down more. Goblins don't have room for weak doyens."

Stinkrunt stomped his foot on the deck, hard. It hurt a little, but he wasn't going to let Grayscar know that.

"Give me ships! Give me goblins! I'll bring down a city myself! I'll show you I'm not weak!"

Grayscar looked down at him. Stinkrunt knew he didn't look big or scary like other goblins. But he had become a doyen, a goblin leader. Sure, he had stabbed a few other goblins in the back to get here, but he had stayed alive a lot longer than most of the others. He was always checking his back for daggers. He knew that some of the smaller gubbins were taking bets on how long he could keep his post.

Grayscar scratched the back of his ear with a finger and looked up at two goblins fighting on the rigging of the ship. Stinkrunt wanted his attention back on him, but he didn't want to be tossed overboard either.

Stinkrunt couldn't swim.

He leaped up and pointed to a smaller boat that was also being loaded with supplies. Unlike Grayscar's own three-mast ship, this little boat only had one mast. The *Big Scar* could easily carry three hundred goblins. More if the little ones packed in tight. Stinkrunt could see that this boat could only carry a hundred without sinking.

"That one," he said, knowing that his request wasn't outlandish. "Give me that ship. The *Fish Bone*. I'll bring down a city with it!"

Grayscar looked at the boat and then back at Stinkrunt. He paused for just a moment, and then let out a big long laugh. His mouth, wider than most of the others Stinkrunt had looked into, showed all his teeth bared and ready to bite into humans, dwarves, and elves. Even if there were only twenty left.

"Stinkrunt. You want to bring down a city? Good! Show Grayscar you can! Take the *Fish Bone* and four others. You'll be the captain. Show Grayscar that you are a strong doyen. Maybe small goblins are tough!"

Stinkrunt's heart leapt. Five ships! This was his chance to prove that he was a big, mean, scary doyen! He would make all the other doyens jealous. He'd find a city and bring it down. They'd loot the place clean and he'd take all the good stuff!

He turned around to run off of the ship when he felt himself jerk backwards. Grayscar had him by the collar. He felt his feet come off the ground and himself being turned around. Grayscar grasped him just underneath his chin with one hand.

"Stinkrunt," Grayscar said in a quiet voice and he knew that what he was about to hear would be important. That and he couldn't breathe.

"Don't make Sharp Claws look bad. Come back with a lot of loot. Or don't come back."

Stinkrunt was still massaging his short throat when he stepped off the ship. He could still smell Grayscar's breathe, too.

He wouldn't make the Sharp Claws look bad. He'd make them feared all over the big lands, not just the Goblin Maw. He'd show all of them.

Stinkrunt practically ran off the *Big Scar* and towards the *Fish Bone*. He saw it and the four other ships beside it that Grayscar had pointed out. These would be his to captain. So what if Grayscar had twenty to his name? Stinkrunt would take these ships and find a city.

He'd bring it to the ground. He'd send in every goblin that he led if he had to.

Goblin vessels lined the coast of the Goblin Maw. For the last month they had gathered here from all over the rough lands of the west. Hidden in caves along the coast or in the Big Sea in the middle of the Maw, ships had come here, right next to the grounds claimed by the Sharp Claws, to supply and get ready and mostly show off.

While running to the *Fish Bone*, Stinkrunt could clearly see two clans, much smaller than the Sharp Claws, trying to make a bigger show than the other.

The Red Suns had adorned all of their vessels with as many war trophies as they could. This was standard among the goblins. The small *Fish Bone* had a couple of goblin heads hung out at the front of it to make it look important. More than likely it was just some crew member that smarted off to the captain.

The Red Suns, however, were different. They had dwarven helms, shields, axes, and skulls hung all over their ships. The lands they claimed lay at the base of the mountains many dwarves called home. The Red Suns were always fighting with them over this cave or that. It kept their clan sharp. Their doyen, Gobber Dwarvenbane, was a brute of a goblin and an excellent fighter. Too bad he was as dumb as a rock. The only thing that kept him in power was that no one could ever get a knife to sink deep enough into the armor of defeated dwarven warriors that he wore.

That, and he'd crush your skull for trying.

The Fanged Ones, on the other hand, were always fighting one another. Their doyen changed three times on their journey from the west of the Maw to the eastern coast. Vicious goblins. Crackedtooth was their current leader, at least the last time Stinkrunt cared to check. He was always ready for a fight. In fact, he was the most willing to sail east and have a reason to fight someone else. Better humans than some other smaller doyen trying to climb up the chain of command a bit.

Finally, Stinkrunt came to the planks leading up to his future ship. He stopped just for a moment to catch his breath.

Yes, he thought to himself. *This is my chance to show them I'm not small and clumsy!*

He then suddenly slipped on some fish guts a gubbin had left on the dock as it scampered away from Stinkrunt.

Stupid gubbins, he thought as he climbed up the plank.

Gubbins, of course, were the smallest of goblins. They were the immature and not yet fully formed goblin young ones. Nasty boogers with full sets of teeth and a normal sized goblin appetite. It was best to avoid the things until they were matured.

Stinkrunt climbed on board the boat, puffed up his chest as big as he could, cleared his throat importantly and began his speech.

"Hey! Fish brains!" he called out to the crew. A few looked up at him. Most ignored him and kept working (or at least pretended to). Then Stinkrunt took one of the smallest gubbins he could find by the throat. He shook it harshly and watched the little gray thing's eyes bulge a bit. He yelled again.

"Listen up! I'm captain now! I'm the doyen in charge! You sail with me! We're gonna go beat up some city!"

He threw the gubbin into a barrel of fish, where it was quite content to stay, and then looked around at the crew. A few had actually looked up at him. One or two almost shook their heads in agreement.

There, Stinkrunt thought. *That'll do.*

He stepped up to the front of the boat and pushed off a goblin that was sitting on the side railings studying a map. The map fell into the water with the goblin and he felt pretty important already.

Stinkrunt, the goblin pusher! he thought as he listened to the little goblin struggle in the water. *Stinkrunt, the big and scary!*

Or something like that.

4: The Rusty Hook

E alrin would soon learn that the Rusty Hook was the only inn on the island.

It was an old two-story building. The second floor had rooms that could be rented out by the night or longer if you wished. Some rooms had beds crammed next to each other and others offered a more spacious experience. It all depended on your coin purse.

The ceilings were the same at both levels: parallel wood beams that held either the floor above or the ceiling in place. The walls were the same plaster as it was throughout Ealrin's room. Though originally white, the salt from the sea had yellowed it over the years. The furniture, linens, and most of the people shared the same smell of the sea. If you lay quietly in your room, it was easy to hear the birds calling over the harbor and the waves charging to shore, causing all manner of ships and boats to bump against their docks.

The Rusty Hook was indeed aptly named, for the salt in the air had managed to add at least a small measure of rust to every metal surface. There must have been finer inns in other countries, but it was the only choice in Good Harbor.

That didn't seem to make a difference to those who would come and go, spending a few nights and then returning to the sea.

Ealrin's use of his legs and body returned slowly. At first it was a chore to leave his bed and sit in the chair by the fire as Holve told him more about the island.

Yet after a few days rest and eating real food, instead of the broth they fed him while he was recovering, Ealrin began to regain his strength. He had begun to walk around the town of Good Harbor a bit, exploring his temporary home.

Instead of taking his meals in his room next to the fire, Ealrin began to sit in the common eating area that served as both the dining and welcoming area of the Rusty Hook. All who came and went through the little inn made their way through here.

Some of the tenants only stayed a night or two, just long enough to rest and eat a meal. Or perhaps they lingered long enough to share in a conversation with someone they had arranged to meet. These discussions would take place in the shadiest part of the dining hall with hushed voices and hidden faces.

Others visited for a greater duration. In fact, the longer a tenant meant to stay at the Rusty Hook, the more they would be inclined to make their presence known.

Their dress and manner varied as much as the shapes of the clouds over the harbor. One pair wore pelts and skins as their only clothing. They were dressed for a much colder climate than the mild spring Good Harbor was experiencing. Another came in robes and veils so thick that it made it impossible to distinguish who they were or any of their physical features.

Two things all visitors had in common: very seldom did any travel alone, and every one of them knew Holve. For the shadowy ones, a nod of the head in his direction would suffice. Sometimes he was invited over to the shadows in order to hear the news that was being discussed. With others, the greeting was more like seeing an old friend. Like the man who came a little more than a week after Ealrin begun eating his meals out in the open.

He was dressed in similar clothes as Holve: a leather vest and pants with a simple cloth shirt. A navy cloak covered his body and a hood lay unused on his back. He was much broader than either Ealrin or Holve and, as a breath of fresh wind from the east, much more jovial than any other visitor had been up to this point, especially Holve.

When he saw Holve, he ran towards him and picked him right off the ground in an embrace, letting loose a hearty, genuine laugh.

"Easy Roland, you'll crush me to pieces!" said Holve as Roland put him down, nursing his sides and giving him a stern look. Ealrin couldn't help but notice that Holve had a small twinkle in his eye.

Maybe he has a soft side down there somewhere, Ealrin thought.

"We'd all be better for it, Holve. That way, you could be in more places than one. I've much to tell you," replied Roland as he sat opposite Ealrin.

Elezar came over to the table and Roland let out another shout of joy. He had begun to rise, but the innkeeper and cook raised his old hands to stop him.

"You hug me like you did Holve and you'll certainly break my bones. What are you eating, Roland?" said Elezar in good spirits.

He was indeed older than many other people Ealrin had set eyes on. His gray hair was long, but tidy. Both his eyes were green, but only one was able to see. He playfully kept reminding Ealrin his left one was his good one and not to look at the right's playful jumping about. His hands were wrinkled and burned from many days and nights of keeping up the old inn and cooking for the tenants there.

"Your biggest plate full of your best catch. Whatever is left of it anyway. Po tells me that the fish haven't been biting like they used to," said Roland, looking hopefully at another patron's plate.

"That's because Po's not fishing like he used to," said Elezar, rolling his eyes. "I swear that boy will never make a living with his head in the clouds."

With that Elezar headed back to the kitchen.

Roland took off his cloak and laid it next to him on the bench. Ealrin could see Roland's eyes matched his scruffy brown hair well. He was a handsome man, but perhaps would have been more so if he didn't carry with him all of those scars of battle. A cut across his cheek and another across his forehead denied him a polished look. Yet still, his smile was such that it could make you forget your troubles and enjoy the company of one so jovial.

Roland shuffled around so that the assortment of weapons strapped to his back wasn't in the way of his seat. A menacing battle-ax, two swords, and a few others that were difficult to keep track of. Ealrin was sure there were at least eight but decided not to stare, just in case.

"And who might your young friend here be, Holve? I've never seen him around, nor have I known you to travel with a companion," inquired Roland, looking inquisitively at him.

Somewhere in Ealrin's mind, he took offense to being called young.

Since he hadn't a clue as to how old he might be, being offended felt odd. He ignored it.

"Well, Roland, I'll trade you tales since you say you have news for me," said Holve, reading Ealrin's face. Ealrin really had no desire to share his story.

He didn't know it. Holve told it instead.

As Roland's meal of three pieces of bread and some unidentifiable fish came to their table, he was just wrapping it up.

"And so he's been gaining back his strength here at the Rusty Hook. Though, I fear he'll need cooking of a different sort soon. He hasn't said whether or not he likes the fish," finished Holve with a rare smile at Ealrin. In fact, it may have been the first Ealrin had seen.

Ealrin thought for a moment and then realized he had only eaten fish or some variant of it for the last few days. His stomach rumbled a bit in agreement with Holve's statement.

"No memory, eh?" said Roland through a mouth full of food. "No worries there, young Ealrin. There are things I'd much rather forget myself if I had the chance."

"Like that time you went off searching for a dragon, eh Roland?" Holve said it with a bit of irritation in his voice.

"I've just met this young man, and here you are wanting to show off my most embarrassing tale," said Roland with mock remorse. "Fine. A story from me and then my news, Holve."

Roland wasn't embarrassed by his story. In fact, he seemed to be relishing in the chance to tell it. Ealrin noticed that a few of the Rusty Hook's patrons had taken a break from their meals and had begun listening to the tale.

Roland took another bite out of his fish, chewed and swallowed, then started on his tale.

"I was venturing through the villages and towns in the northern rim of the republic. There were rumors of a cleric who had been rounding up some followers and asking for all their gold. Normally religion doesn't bother me, but this one felt odd. I found the cleric and was able to expose his lie pretty easily. What I couldn't shake were the rumors I heard after the cleric. Dragon. One living up in the high mountains somewhere. He got himself a stash of gold and was killing anyone who came within a few leagues of the place. So, naturally, I went looking for it. I have to say, adding "Dragon Bane" to the end of my name seemed pretty tempting. Well, all the signs pointed to one cave up on the Morath Mountain. But what I found wasn't a dragon. It wasn't a stash of gold either. Just some troll shaman trying to act all-important. He burned down most of the trees, and what wouldn't burn he snapped in half just to add to the story. I figure he was trying to scare everyone away because he thought he found some Rimstone in the area. Well, taking on a troll shaman wasn't near the adventure I was hoping for, but he turned out to be pretty tough. Seeing as how I'm standing here and he's not, you can guess who won. But I still hold a grudge against all trolls because of what he did to me."

At this, Roland leaned in for dramatic effect. As a result, everyone else in the end also leaned in a little closer to hear what the troll had done to him. The inn's patrons held their breath.

"He turned me into a chicken."

Roland waited just a moment to let the absurdity of his statement sink in before throwing his head back and roaring with laughter. For good measure, he began clucking like a chicken and actually threw up into the air a handful of real chicken feathers.

It wasn't long before the entire inn was laughing, Ealrin included. It was the first time he'd laughed since he arrived here. It may have been the first time he'd smiled as well.

"I can't believe after all these years you still carry around a pouch of chicken feathers," said Holve through a half-stifled chuckle.

He does have some humor then, Ealrin thought.

"And I can't believe you still set me up for that story every time we meet," chuckled Roland, wiping away tears of his own.

Most of the patrons at the inn went back to eating their meals, breaking out into small fits of laughter as one or two retold Roland's joke.

"So, how much of your tale is true?" Ealrin inquired.

"The cleric and the troll are real. I checked those out myself, after I heard his version of it the third time," said Holve. "But, to my knowledge, our friend Roland has never been a chicken."

"In manner of speaking or in reality?" asked Roland, finishing off his supper. He was obviously pleased with himself for telling his story so well and for the reaction he'd received from the other patrons.

"Still, the only thing I got for all my troubles was a scar that won't heal on my neck from that blasted shaman," he said, rubbing it with his hand. "It's funny to tell it my way, but as it happened, I'd much rather forget. As I said, Ealrin, some things are fine for forgetting."

"I'd rather know who I am, and clear the fog in my head," Ealrin replied.

"Ah, but perhaps the man you were wasn't who you truly wished to be?" Roland said as he swallowed his fish and bread. "Like that cleric who used religion as a selfish means for himself. Suppose you used to be like him? Perhaps fate has granted you the chance of a better life than you lived before, hmm?" Roland said through half a mouthful of fish he had just purloined from Holve's plate. "Now, Holve," Roland said, turning his gaze back to his old friend with a wink. "I've been watching the goblins in the west..."

The thought Roland offered up hadn't occurred to Ealrin.

Would he be glad to remember his old life, or be shocked at the revelation? Was he a good person? He felt as if he was. But what if his feelings were wrong? Perhaps he was someone who was ruthless, uncaring, and unsympathetic towards others. What if the life he had forgotten was, indeed, worth forgetting?

There wasn't much time for consideration. Because Elezar came crashing out the kitchen, shaking a butcher knife at a man dressed from head to toe in brown cloth. The odd attire obscured his features.

"Thief! Brigand!" yelled the old man as he chased the man out the door. "Give me back that locket!"

5: The Stolen Locket

R oland and Holve were the first out the door behind Elezar. Ealrin quickly got up and followed the group out of the inn.

Elezar stood, cursing the north and throwing a wooden spoon
as the thief made good his escape. Roland and Holve were standing
next to him.

"What did he take Elezar?" asked Holve, putting a hand on his
shoulder.

At this, Elezar began to weep.

"He grabbed my locket, Holve! That's the most precious thing in
the world to me. I don't know why he'd take it. It certainly wouldn't
fetch a good price at market," he said through fits of sobbing.

"Doesn't seem to be interested in selling it," said Roland, still
looking in the direction the thief went.

"Either he's desperate or stupid. Both are dangerous," Holve said
as he adjusted the sword in his hilt. "Feeling up for a bit of adventure,
Ealrin?"

Ealrin wasn't sure. He'd only made a few short walks around the
town of Good Harbor. This didn't seem like it was going to be anything like those trips. Trekking after a thief who already had a good
head start on them and was heading out of town towards the forests
and small mountains of the island seemed more than a little taxing
for him.

But, then again...

It was hard to put a finger on it. Just like when Roland had called
him young, the thought of going off on a chase like this, an adventure, made sense to Ealrin. Perhaps the man he couldn't remember

used to do things like this all the time; chased down thieves, climbed mountains, did for others instead of himself.

Something in it was natural.

"Let's go," said Ealrin.

"Now, there is a little fight still left in you," said Holve. "Let's see if you can put it to any good use." Holve was almost glaring at him as he spoke. Was he daring him to run after the thief after just recovering from his injury? It certainly felt like it to Ealrin.

"Are you sure, old friend?" Roland said cautiously. "Ealrin here may not be up for it."

At this, Ealrin knew actions would speak volumes when his words would fall short and he set off at a jog in the direction of the thief.

"Are you going to let him keep his head start?" he shouted over his shoulder.

The chase had begun.

GOOD HARBOR WAS CONCENTRATED on the shore. Most of the businesses were built as close to the water as earth would allow. Ancient stones shored up the water as to not allow the soil to be washed out to sea by the tides. Looking down into the depths would allow you to see the murky water of the Forean Sea, the eastern side of the island.

The various shops and businesses that made up Good Harbor's commercial district could be visited with a morning walk. Each was made of wood and fairly plain, save for the painted signs that dictated whether you were walking into a baker's store or a fish market. The paint was peeling off the front and sides of most of the buildings due to the sea air. Each was closely packed next to the other, to be close to the shore and in sight of any traveler who stepped off of the docks. The stores all had some sort of glass front or window to show off their wares and several had their wares laid out on tables. The effect was four or five streets that split out from the docks to do your shopping on, with each having its own flavor of things to sell: metal and leather, fruit and other grown food, meat and animals. The five streets made the city of Good Harbor look like the fingers of a hand outstretched, with the palm being the docks and the water.

The docks themselves were a maze of old, sun-bleached, and slightly warped wooden paths that allowed small rowboats to be tied to them. Piles of goods were stacked onto every available space. Not that they stayed there long. Either they would go to the shops or the residents, or be put onto the ships that were anchored out further at sea. The water close to Good Harbor was too shallow to allow for the bigger ships to sail too close.

The residences that came after the shops, further past the shore, could all be seen with a walk during the afternoon. Though the Rusty Hook was a good place to stay if one didn't wish to be seen, you could hardly walk around the city of Good Harbor without being noticed by the general population.

Not a good place for a thief to run and hide. The people were too proud to be a refuge for thieves intentionally.

So, it was no surprise that the thief passed the walls of the city as quickly as possible. Though the town was small, an ancient wall protected it from outsiders and invaders.

"A city without a wall is like a chest without a lock. Easy pickings," Holve would later say.

The wall was the only thing made of stone in the whole city. Everything else was wooden and made from the trees that were closer to the city than the far mountains. Holve said that the wall was older than Elezar.

The trio jogged past the town and down one of the dirt roads that ran from Good Harbor to the outside farms and small villages. A man who was guarding the door to the city had seen the thief run past the door and pointed the direction out to the three. It was not yet fully dark and the gates weren't closed. He reminded them, as they ran by, that he would be closing the gates behind them and to expect not to be let in during the night unless they made a big racket trying to get someone's attention.

Apparently the city guard was understaffed.

Holve knew every farmer and villager by name. Ealrin was certainly impressed. Not just with Holve's uncanny recollection, but also by the sheer time and energy it must have taken the man to learn such small details.

The first house belonged to a farmer and his family. After asking if they had seen a man who fit the description, the farmer replied "He went running like he was a demon being chased toward the Lonely Pass!" Holve had thanked the man and promised to return to catch up later, but for now the group was quick to resume their pursuit.

Holve's mind was a treasure trove of information about the island and its inhabitants.

Ealrin's mind was an island in and of itself: one shrouded in fog.

The island could be covered from coast to coast in two days' time at a jog. Both Holve and Roland had done this on several occasions. As they ran, Roland was relating the stories to Ealrin, who was thankful for an excuse not to say much and only let out a grunt every once in a while. His body was still not fully recovered from being injured, and his ribs, though sufficiently scabbed over and healing, were still sore and bruised. Currently, they were screaming at the abuse he was inflicting on them.

How in the world can you run and talk at the same time? Ealrin thought as he listened to Roland speak without hardly any difficulty at all.

"...of course, that was after we had to round up that group of dwarves who claimed an ancient stronghold on the mountains. Ha! I've seen those mountains and the only living thing inside them are rocks. Ancestor's hall my foot! They were looking for an excuse to settle and mine for gold without going through the Republic's paperwork. They only put up a little fight when they saw my posse and me coming after them!" relayed Roland. Ealrin was jealous beyond measure. Roland had hardly stopped for a break from the jog. Yet he was still relaying past stories from adventures in and around Good Harbor. The man had yet to break a sweat, let alone become short of breath.

Though he ached with every step now, Ealrin certainly took in the beauty of the island as they pursued the thief. All of the villagers or farmers who had been watchful of the roads had pointed them continually towards what they referred to as "Lonely Pass." Spring had come beautifully for the island. Trees were exploding with the colors of their blossoms and the ground was giving forth life in all directions. To look in one direction would give you a fantastic view of a small mountain ridge rising up to meet the majestic reds and oranges of the setting sun in the west. The other would show you the land as it gradually sloped down to the sea. Night was beginning to fall in earnest and the deep blues and purples of the night sky were taking the place of the daytime's burning sun.

It was truly beautiful here.

Not a bad island to crash land on, Ealrin thought.

Holve finally stopped them upon coming to the entrance of what Ealrin guessed was Lonely Pass. It certainly looked lonely. At the base of the mountain grew a forest coming to life in the spring. Two of the mountains split ways at some point long ago to form a pass between them, covered in trees yet still allowing for a path to grow between. Only the desperate would take such a route in the night. Again, as Ealrin thought of the creatures of the darkness, some fog in his mind cleared. Traveling through a forest without light would not be ideal; least of all for someone who was as tired as he must be.

"If we head a bit to the east we can see if Old Soltack will allow us to stay the night with him. I wouldn't want to travel much through the woods while..." Holve cast a quick look at Ealrin, who was desperately trying not to breathe as heavily as he wanted to through his burning ribs. "Well, while we can't see our hands in front of our faces."

Ealrin knew they were truly going to stop for him and he was grateful for the break, but a small bit of pride was stirring up inside of him, pushing him to protest.

"Suppose we lose our man?" he asked through gasps of air. He wished he would start breathing normally again so he could seem like he was better fitted for the chase.

"With all the kindness Elezar has shown me I would certainly like to retrieve this locket of his to repay him. Don't you worry the thief might..." Might what? The island was, in fact, surrounded by sea. No land was visible from Good Harbor. Was there something within swimming distance on the west side of the island? Or a boat waiting for him?

Roland finished Ealrin's thoughts for him.

"I doubt the thief plans to steal away from the island. He'd have had a better chance of that slipping onto a boat in Good Harbor. No boats sail from the west either. Much too dangerous. Goblin waters."

"I think we'll be safe letting him sleep in the woods tonight," Holve continued, brows furrowed as he surveyed the landscape ahead of him. "If we're well rested, I'm sure we'll have the advantage over him tomorrow."

Ealrin thought the best way to have the advantage on the thief would be to sneak up on him while he slept. Yet, knowing his body had taken enough punishment from the chase so far, he conceded.

"So, who is old Soltack?" asked Ealrin as he followed Holve along the edge of the mountains. The trio was now walking off the beaten road and onto a narrow path that led to a house, just visible in the failing light.

Holve and Roland exchanged sly smirks. Roland answered.

"'Crazy old coot' doesn't quite do him justice. He's dependable and quite good company. But let's just say he's lived by himself 20 years too many. He's full of odd stories and rants every now and then."

"Has anyone turned him into a chicken?" Ealrin asked Roland, smiling a bit himself.

Roland let out a laugh that was much too loud for a group trying to hunt down a thief but was genuine and rang over the field and off the mountain.

"Holve, I've met many a man in my adventures and half of them were those that you've introduced me to in our many years. Some I haven't thought much about or like, but this one is growing on me!"

6: General Rayg

In the coolness of the dawn, he could see his own breath mist in front of him, as well as the breath of the four hundred souls behind him. The bursts of fog were the only telltale sign that they occupied this spot, covered as they were by several barriers of protective magic.

The mountain of the dwarves loomed before them. For generations dwarves had dwelled in and mined the mountains of the Southern Republic without fear of their precious bounty being claimed by another, thanks to the treaty of peace signed nearly one hundred years ago.

That treaty ends today, thought Rayg, general of the Mercs.

He stood taller than any other man around him. He was broader as well. The sword he carried was nearly the same size as his own body. It would have been impossibly heavy to lift for any other man, but not Rayg. He was more than just a man.

"I don't like the idea of raiding the dwarves," spoke Gileon in his ear. Typically, the short, squat man would not be able to whisper to him so because Rayg would simply ignore the words coming from the height of his torso. As the company was kneeling down to remain in the barrier, Gileon could talk directly into Rayg's ear.

This displeased Rayg greatly.

"You heard how they plan to attack Conny and usurp power from the elders so that they can mine the plains!" Rayg directed back to him in a harsh tone. "They must be dealt with swiftly if we are to maintain peace!"

"Peace," the word echoed in Rayg's ear. Yes. All would be done for peace. Or so the common man would believe.

Preparations for this day were four years in the making and all players had to be in the correct spot, ready to pounce as one. Some of the lesser races would play their own role. But it would all be for the rise of man.

"The age of man is come," said Rayg out loud, yet barely audible to any but himself and possibly Gileon. No matter.

The morning sunlight would cast out any doubt or darkness from their plan, Rayg thought.

He rose above the protective barrier, effectively breaking it and revealing the four hundred men in red robes under battle armor standing at the base of the mountain. A dwarven horn blared in the distance.

It begins, thought Rayg with a smile.

"Torch the mountain!" he yelled as he felt the energy around him begin to condense and burn hot.

In unison, four hundred fireballs shot from staffs bearing precious stones and blasted the mountainside. As expected, war machines cranked to life along the cliffs, but as they had not used them in such a long time, several groaned and protested.

The pause was all the Speakers needed.

Rayg mumbled the language of the stones. His sword began to emit a purple light that shone oddly around the red and orange flames near him. Fire erupted from where the war machines were creaking, and the screams of dwarves echoed along the mountain.

"What sweet music," said Rayg. "Advance!"

As one, they began to march up the mountain. Using the ancient road constructed by the dwarves themselves, the men advanced towards the stronghold known as Cardun-Adush. This dwarven city would fall before first light.

———✝✝\\\✝✝———

AS RAYG LOOKED AROUND the great hall where the dwarven leaders kept court, he smiled at the devastation. Bodies of dwarves littered the halls. Every now and then, a Speaker's words would echo throughout the cave turned into a city, signaling another burst of orange or red light, a scream, and then silence.

The dwarves had for too long mined the mountains and kept their bounty as their own, thought Rayg.

Now it would be put to good use. A noble cause. Not made into any crude sword or ax but fashioned into the rod of magic needed to bring peace to Ruyn.

"Peace," spoke Rayg as he surveyed the destroyed great hall and bodies strewn all about. He chuckled. Yes, peace would come in time. A peace that would surpass all expectations.

"By the blessed gods of light," Gileon shuddered as he walked into the ancient hall.

He and three others had emerged from a side room. Gileon was pale and ashen, adding to the impression Rayg always got that the man resembled a gourd more than a man.

"All dead, Rayg," he said through trembling lips. "We've checked every room we could find. Every dwarf is slain. By the gods, it didn't need to be like this."

Gileon was surveying the damage done with wide eyes. Rayg looked at his feet and saw a dwarf, or at least, the charred remains of one, still clutching his ax. He bent down and wrestled it from its former owner. It was a beautiful ax, though now the fire of the Speakers blackened it. The handle and blade were one magnificent piece of metal, shaped with care and the skill of a master craftsman. Rayg, who detested the dwarves, could tell that this was a great weapon and that its owner must have been someone of importance. At least to the dwarves. He kicked the carcass for good measure and turned to face

Gileon, who was still rambling about the needless shedding of blood and violence.

"Where was the council that was sent to bring about a peaceable agreement for the dwarves? Is this really what the elders had asked of us and our order? Are the Speakers meant to burn the mountains down to appease the leaders? This isn't putting down a rebellion. This is genocide. This is..."

His words were caught in his throat. More specifically the dwarven ax Rayg had hurled at him was caught in his throat. Rayg had heard enough from the sorry excuse for a man.

Gileon tumbled to the ground in a pile of robes and blood. The three speakers around him backed away as they watched their master twitch as he slowly died. Rayg allowed his blade to glow intensely as they recovered and turned their gaze at him.

"To the mines, Speakers. We still have work to do," he said as he turned from the great hall. These Speakers would follow him for sure, for they feared him above all else. But Rayg would not allow them to tell of how their master died. He would ensure an 'accident' claimed them while searching the mines for what they sought. The dwarves would be blamed for the death of the Master Speaker of the Southern Republic.

The golden inlaid columns were stained with blood and ash. The floors were charred and dented. As he walked from that place, Rayg could feel an elation rising up within him. This was why they had come. To end the dwarves. To take from their mines that which would serve men in the coming struggle.

This was his purpose.

To cleanse the world of the blight of the lesser races.

There was still much work to do.

7: Old Soltack

As the last few rays of the double suns faded into the mountains, Holve, Roland, and Ealrin came upon the house that Ealrin assumed belonged to Old Soltack.

The house looked older than the hills themselves.

The thatch roof had holes that could be seen in this fading light. A window with a pane knocked out of it long ago had several faded rags stuffed into the hole to keep out the critters and the wind. What may have once been a garden was now overgrown with weeds that threatened to move right into the old house, should the walls ever collapse due to the weight of plants crawling up its mud and log siding.

A dim light could be seen from the crack in the door, as if a single candle was all the light that was on inside the home.

Holve approached the door and knocked hard.

"Don't bang the door down! I saw you coming from a league away!" said a voice from the shadows of the side garden. "I may yet be 70 winters, but I'll not be snuck up on by the likes of vagabonds and pickpockets."

Ealrin nearly jumped out of his skin. The old man stood behind a bush to the right of the doorway. He hobbled out on a cane, hunched over, yet still demanding attention. His beard grew all the way to his navel, perhaps to compensate for the hair that no longer resided on his head. He walked up to the trio and looked each of them in the face.

There was a fire behind those old gray eyes.

"Holve Bravestead, I'll be waggered if you think you can come calling at this hour expecting a feast and wine!" he said as he opened the door and motioned for them to come in.

Three men followed the old one into his home. Holve came last and closed the door tight as he replied to Soltack.

"Your hospitality hasn't changed much in the last year, Soltack! We're chasing a thief, old friend, and simply need a place to lay down our heads tonight. I've brought some provisions for us in my pack, and we'll not intrude on your stores, you old greedy guts."

Holve's tone was sarcastic and harsh, but Ealrin could sense a playful tone in the gruff man's voice. All it warranted from Soltack was a simple "Bah!" as he led them into the first room of the house and then disappeared into another. A cloth that served as a door fell behind him, signaling to Ealrin that they were not to follow.

The floors were rough and uneven wood that may have once been straight and fine. Years of erosion under the house and what looked like much abuse had caused them to bend and warp.

A single candle stood on a table in the center of what could have been a common room for cooking and eating. Ealrin wasn't sure what anything was, as there were books, clothes, and all manner of odds and ends stacked to the ceiling. Everything was a shelf to Soltack, though for most it was not its original purpose.

The old man returned to the room with a loaf of bread, a pitcher of water, and a small wedge of cheese set upon a wooden plate. He threw it down on the table (on top of various books and parchments) and let out a "Humpf" as he seated himself on a crate that was over-turned next to the table.

"Sleep where you can, you and your friends. Just keep any thief you chase far away from my house!" Soltack said as he placed both hands on top of his staff and stared square at Ealrin. He felt uneasy as he moved a book from a chair in order to sit down himself.

Roland stood at the window and watched the night sky as Holve also moved to sit next to the old man.

"You're too kind to allow us some floor and a roof, Soltack," he said as he tore off a piece of bread, spread a bit of cheese on it and offered it to the white-bearded fellow. He then did this again and handed a piece to Ealrin.

"And since you won't stop staring at the boy here, I'll be the one to have manners and introduce him. This is Ealrin Bealouve. I believe you've met Roland before?"

Soltack grunted a response, which Ealrin supposed meant yes. Roland threw Holve a smile and a wink, and then went back to looking out the window.

"I doubt we need a watch tonight, Roland, as the man would be outnumbered three to one."

"Four!" interjected Soltack through a mouthful of bread.

"My apologies," said Holve giving Soltack a mock salute. "And if you continue to stare at the boy like that, Soltack, you'll burn a hole right through him. Come on, you suspicious old goat, he's trustworthy."

Boy. Ealrin wanted to fume at Holve for calling him young again. He wasn't young! Well, at least he didn't feel young. He felt experienced and... and what? Some other word tugged at him, but he couldn't quite call it to mind. But then Holve had also called him something else. Trustworthy. What on earth had Ealrin done to earn that kind word? Sure, in the last week he had stolen no food from Elezar and made small talk with Holve about the various visitors to the Rusty Hook.

Did Holve already consider him someone worth trusting?

"Perhaps if I told you my story you could try to enlighten us, Master Soltack," said Ealrin meeting his gaze.

At being called 'Master', Soltack's eyes softened a bit and the slightest turn of his mouth indicated a smile on his bearded face.

"So far, I like him," he said as he finished his bread and returned his hand to his staff.

The tale took Ealrin only a few moments to tell, but then Soltack began asking questions to which he didn't know the answer. Holve would fill in where he could, but every now and then he himself couldn't find an answer to the old man's questioning.

"Which direction did it appear the boat was headed? How many bodies did you find along the shore? Were there other things that washed ashore that could help ascertain the origins of the vessel? Did any scrolls or parchments appear as well? What did the sails have on them? Were there any signs of a battle? Had the magic gone wrong? Storms? A mutiny?"

Several questions to which Ealrin had not given much of a thought to. Holve, who had been unable to answer the last round of questions entirely at one point, said "We found little else on the shore save for Ealrin, some debris from his vessel, and a few other bodies. Whatever caused his ship to sink, it must have been catastrophic."

After some time, the man relaxed a bit on his old crate, satisfied with the tale.

"You say you're chasing a thief, eh?"

"Stole something off of Elezar," said Roland, speaking for the first time in a while. His gaze was fixed outside and he had not yet sat down to eat. He seemed determined to watch the darkness for any signs of the thief.

Or is he looking for that man at all, Ealrin thought.

He had said he had news of goblins. Was that his concern as the darkness enveloped the land before him? Ealrin could not remember anything about his past, but he remembered goblins.

Soltack interrupted his thoughts.

"It's been far too long since I've had visitors, so you'll have to pay me for spending the night by hearing one of my stories."

"Which one will it be this time, old man? The Dark Comet? The troll king who rallied the goblins? Or some other rambling we have heard at least a hundred times?" asked Roland, not looking at the old man, but still gazing out the window. "That comet's been in the sky for several years now and done nothing but inspire fear and dooms-day prophecies from crazy old men with nothing better to do than make people frightened of their own shadow."

"Boy, you'll hear my story or you will sleep under the stars," Soltack said as he pointed his staff at Roland.

"Easy, Roland," Holve said with a grimace. "I've heard just as many of his stories as you have."

Ealrin wondered if the old man would truly kick Roland out of the house for not listening to a simple story. But given Roland's play-fulness, he was sure that at least he was kidding. The old man, how-ever, he was less sure of.

As for the comet outside, Ealrin craned his neck at the window to see what Roland was talking about. The night had fallen now and, indeed, in the sky, there was a star greater than all the others, brighter and more intense. Its tail stretched over a large portion of the sky and its head was a deep orange, becoming an odd color of purple at the tip. What was that comet?

Ealrin didn't have much time to think it over, as Soltack started talking. He did notice Holve, however, who raised an inquiring eye-brow at him looking out the window.

"No. I'll tell you a story I know you haven't heard before. The oth-er day, I was reading through an old journal of mine, from when I was sailing as a merchant for the republic."

"I've heard several of your tales of adventures on the high seas..." Roland began, but Soltack cut him off abruptly.

"One more word from you, and I'll have you out of this house!"

Ealrin was now certain the old man was serious about Roland sleeping under the stars.

Turning his gaze back to what he probably considered his politer audience (Holve and Ealrin), Soltack began his tale.

"I've traveled far and wide in my younger years. I was never much for the sedentary life. I took several jobs working cargo ships that sailed from the continent of Irradan to Ruyn. The voyage was treacherous and sometimes meant goblin invasions."

"The other day, I was looking through my journals to remember some of the adventures we had as we traded goods from the two very different lands. We were a day's good sailing from the coast of Irradan when I heard a voice in the cargo hold. Not just a voice, but crying, whimpering. I went to investigate and low and behold, in a barrel, bound and gagged, was a young boy no more than ten. He was handsome, but pretty banged up. He had been through a pretty big ordeal.

"I took him out and tried to bandage him the best I could. He took to me rather fondly, perhaps like a father. I also made sure to save him from the glances of the more unsavory characters we took with us. Adventure sometimes calls the sick and twisted along with the good hearted.

"In the month that we were at sea, he barely talked at all, though when he did it was with the respect and poise of a knight's page or the most skilled magician's apprentice. He was no commoner! He refused to be bathed like a child and only washed himself in privacy.

"He told me that he had not come willingly on the boat and of course that much he was sure of. He had been kidnapped in the hopes that his father would pay a royal sum for his return. His captors learned that his father had been killed the very night he had been kidnapped! Figuring that without his father, he was worthless, they bound, gagged, and put him in a barrel to ship him off to his death, and have their names be cleared. He never got a good look at his kidnappers. Thank the stars they didn't sell him into the market to be used like a rag doll. As I said, he was handsome for his young age, and would have fetched a fair price. I assume they weren't the smartest bunch.

"The boy was determined to find his father's murderers and avenge him. I tried to talk him out of it. Perhaps he could sail with me instead. He would have nothing of it. His heart was consumed with the thought of revenge. He begged me to practice sword skills with him. He was already quite talented and by the end of the trip he could beat every man on the ship with ease. Not many threw him unwelcome glances after he had defeated them in a duel. Though, they may have held a grudge for being beaten by one so young.

"After we made it to Ruyn I offered to set him up with a decent paying job at a metalworker's workshop that I was familiar with, but when the time came for us to meet the head blacksmith, the young boy was gone. Vanished. I tried asking about his whereabouts, but no one knew what had happened to him. The idea of working for a blacksmith must not have been what he had in mind. I can only hope he's well. It's been twenty long winters since that fateful voyage when I ran into the wealthy man's son. I wonder whatever became of him. Eric Silverwind, the boy I found in a barrel."

After his story was completed, the bread eaten, and the single candle that had lit the messy and cluttered house was extinguished, three of the four occupants of the house went to sleep.

Ealrin, as he laid his head down on what may have been a couch for sitting before it had become a library shelf for three dozen books, thought of Soltack's story and wondered: How much control does one have over their fate? And how much is decided by chance? A little boy being kidnapped and nearly killed, then fleeing any care he may have received. Was fate to blame for his family's death? Was he in charge of his life's goal to avenge his murdered father now?

And what of Ealrin? Was it fate that brought him to Good Harbor? Did fate cause a man to steal a locket?

As he eyed Holve, who was sitting at the table, keeping watch in the night, he wondered what decisions he had yet to make that would be his own. And which would happen to him by chance? And he wondered, if just for a moment, what that comet in the sky meant also.

8: Thief Tracking

The morning suns had not yet spread their light on the house when Roland shook Ealrin awake.

"You snore, my friend. Quite impressively so." Roland moved to gather the rest of his belongings and his pack, as well as an assortment of weapons. After stowing everything into his pack or his harness he turned to Ealrin again. "We'd best get a move on before we lose track of our man's trail."

Ealrin tried to rise quickly, but his body protested at every move. He was still not completely well, and his soreness was trying to remind him of that fact. Stubbornness would not allow him to give up so quickly and he soon found himself outside of the house, taking in the morning air.

Holve was standing outside, surveying the hills, the forest, and the mountain range as Roland and Ealrin came up behind him. He handed Ealrin a piece of bread and a cup of water.

"Breakfast. Best be light if we are to keep a good pace today."

Ealrin ate quickly, and before he was quite awake or ready, they were on the move.

Perhaps it was because he was too tired to notice, but Ealrin's bones and muscles didn't seem to scream in protest as much this morning. It could have been the coolness of the spring air, but his ribs didn't seem to bother him as they had yesterday. He knew it had nothing to do with the stacks of books he slept on last night as his back was letting him know that his mattress had been made of uneven leather-bound volumes.

As Holve and Roland jogged silently beside him, Ealrin began to think out loud the thoughts that had kept him from wanting to stop the pursuit last night.

"Suppose the thief has had ample time to escape? Or has found some hiding place that will take us weeks to discover?"

Roland answered him, "Ealrin, I've known Holve here far longer than I'd care to admit, for it would betray my winters. If there is a man who can escape his keen sense of tracking, then he is no man, but a demon or a lesser god!"

Well then. Roland obviously thought much about Holve's abilities. But would he truly be able to find a man who had a full night's time to run and hide, and perhaps dispose of his treasure in order to claim his innocence?

Ealrin kept these thoughts to himself. He supposed that he would just have to see how able of a tracker his new friend truly was.

WHEN THEY REACHED THE Lonely Pass, the light of the morning had just begun to pierce through the darkness. Ealrin's eyes had adjusted to the dim light around him and he could see the path that led through the forest.

Presently, Holve was bent on one knee, investigating a particularly interesting patch of dirt. Or so it seemed to Ealrin. After a moment or two of study, Holve stood up and declared,

"He's definitely gone through the pass. Perhaps to hide in Everstand or the caves on the northern side of the mountains."

"We'll know soon enough," said Roland.

And the three men began to jog through the shaded pass, a dirt trail flanked by trees and mountains. The trees were tall and provided excellent cover from the sky. With ease their mighty branches covered the path so that if a rain had come over the pass, one could be well sheltered from it for an afternoon at least. The trees stood thick as well. It was impossible to see further than a stone's throw into the dense brush. Ealrin assumed that at some point the rocky mountain rose out of the forest, but the only evidence of this was that mountain that rose above the forest from the outside. Now that they were in the pass, there was no way to tell that a mountain stood on both the right and left.

Ealrin thought that any place along this path would have been an excellent place to hide for a thief. But he could also understand the reasoning for not going through the pass last night. If the thief had wanted, he could have waited in ambush for his pursuers. Being so outnumbered, he could never hope to face them alone. However, the forest would have given anyone an advantage to either losing someone following you or ambushing a potential attacker. Considering this, Ealrin became uneasy about their pursuit through the woods.

Yet Holve and Roland blazed on, neither speaking much. Both had the expression of determination on their faces. They were hunting someone who had wronged a friend and were not going to let him escape without being brought to justice. He was glad to have such men beside him now, but he still wondered.

What if he was a thief who had stolen away on a boat? Or perhaps stole a coat of a man named Ealrin Bealouve and was now parading himself as him? Could the loss of his memory have affected his character in some way?

He felt that now he desired to do right and find a thief to repay the kindness shown to him. Would he have done so before the shipwreck that left him without a past?

Again, his thoughts were interrupted when Holve stopped abruptly. He held out a hand to signal that Ealrin and Roland should stop as well. Holve sniffed as if trying to pick up a scent. He breathed the air in deeply.

Ealrin breathed deeply through his nose as well. He smelled the pollen of the trees, the flowers that were coming into bloom in the early spring. He smelled the morning breeze moving through the pass. The dirt that was packed down on the path invaded his nostrils and a bit of animal that may be close by wondering why these intruders were so close to its home.

Ealrin smelled nothing that would tell him a thief lurked nearby. "He stopped here last night." Holve said in the stillness.

And the stillness is what grabbed Ealrin. Though they were in a forest, which should have had any number of wildlife in it, there was almost completely silence. No songbird made its cry heard. No animal scampered in the underbrush. It was completely still.

Holve moved slowly over to a tree that was just a few steps off the path. He knelt down to examine the grass as well as the trunk of the old tree. He felt the ground with one hand, smoothly touching the grass with his fingertips.

"He's not far ahead. He overslept."

And with that the three were on the move again.

How could a man sense the presence of another just by observing the ground where his body lay? Nothing about that particular patch of brush and grass told Ealrin anything other than that the forest was alive there. To Holve, however, it spoke wonders.

And so the chase continued.

THE THREE SOON CAME to the end of Lonely Pass, and indeed it had been lonely. Though they had traveled for the entire morning through the forest and trod their feet on every length of the path, they had not encountered another living thing. No animal had crossed their path and no person had walked on the road going the opposite direction. From what Ealrin could tell, there were no others coming up behind on the road either.

What caused this path to be so lightly traveled, Ealrin wondered.

As they broke free of the canopy of trees, the three found themselves looking down a path that continued on to the sea. The windy road made its way down hills and over the plains, finally coming to an end at what Ealrin thought may have once been a mighty city.

What lay there now were the ruins of many buildings and, in the center, a tower that was standing by a sheer act of defiance. The walls of the city stood only in certain places. There were several places with breaches that exposed the ruins within. This city had not given in to the never-ending fight of time and erosion.

This city had fallen during a time of war.

Roland walked forward from the tree a bit, staring at the ruins, then turned to face Ealrin.

"Welcome, to the proud ruins of Everstand and the Tower of Pallum."

9: Everstand

Everstand. The arrogance and irony of the name were not lost on Ealrin. Certainly, whoever had built this city had been certain it could withstand any attack. That it would stand the test of any army that came against it and prevail for ages after. And why shouldn't it have? The mountains from which its rock came from stood close by and would provide a near limitless supply of materials to repair and continually add to the city.

Now Ealrin could see that a road had once existed that was flat and would have made transporting the stones easy. The city was built upon a cliff that overlooked the sea. It would have been easily defensible, for its massive wall only needed to protect its eastern side. All other parts of the city stood on the cliff, which would have been nearly impossible to scale without being mercilessly attacked from above.

The lands before them were fertile and good. The plains were green with the new spring. Ealrin guessed that crops would have easily grown and been able to sustain a city of its size. In fact, the land was abundant and could have provided stores of food and supplies should the mighty city come under siege.

Yet the city had fallen.

As the three approached the ruins, which Holve believed now housed their thief, Ealrin was lost in thought about how the walled and stoned city could have fallen. The Tower of Pallum stood tall, but the battle that had brought down the city had left its mark on the staggering tower. Ealrin guessed it stood taller than any tree they had passed in the forest, though it was blackened and charred by a fire that had also consumed a large portion of the city. Parts of the stones were cracked in areas, and in some parts of the tower there were large holes, not caused by any storm or natural causes, Ealrin knew.

"What calamity could have happened here to cause such a city to fall?" asked Ealrin after they had passed through what was once a mighty entrance.

The huge metal gates that would have served as a strong deterrent to any invaders had fallen to the side, mangled in a heap. The wood of the mighty doors that would have been the more decorative, and yet quite sturdy, barrier to the city lay fallen and charred. In some places there were massive holes where a catapults' rocks may have smashed it to splinters.

It was Holve who answered Ealrin's question. Roland's eyes were constantly surveying the path on which they walked, looking for the signs of any recent passing of the man they still hunted.

"Everstand was a mighty city once. The stories about it say that it was a bustling trade center for the Southern Republic. It heralded merchants from Redact, Irradan, and as far as the Holy Empire itself. It was a beacon of light; a wonderful place of ideas being shared and the bounty of the land blessing those who came to visit.

"And then the goblins came."

At this Holve's face went dark. His furrowed brow deepened and his eyes became narrow. Ealrin tried to place what that face meant. He guessed the only thing he could think of. It was the face of one who had seen great death. One who had known a great tragedy.

"Everstand was built to resist attack. Its founders knew that the goblin lands were close to its borders. But the Southern Republic at that time had expanded into the Goblin Maw. The city was not the last fortified city between The Elders of the Republic and the gray beasts. But the goblins had united under a new leader. A shaman who had learned about the deeper mysteries of Rimstone and its power. It was said that he was in control of a demon host, a mystic artifact that was possessed by a legion of demons that desired destruction and death.

"By the tens of thousands, the goblins came through the Maw. Their numbers were vastly underestimated by the Republic. They had hidden in the mountains, breeding like insects in the darkness. Under their new leader, they attacked. The expeditions into the Maw were wiped out in less than a month. Having stolen the boats and vessels that had once brought explorers and merchants, they added to their fleet of goblin-made craft and came across the waters of the Forean Sea.

"With numbers like they had, it made no difference how thick or how high the walls had been built. From the Great Tower, they watched the goblins sail towards them. They sent word as quickly as they could to the Elders, but to no avail.

"The ships that came to aid the city found only bodies, both goblins and men alike. After the great city had fallen the goblins turned on themselves, made with hate and a lust for violence from the demon host. Their great leader could do little to quell the rage of his army. They destroyed themselves on the island after having destroyed every person they could. The only reason Good Harbor stands today was due to the Lonely Pass. Men were able to cause an avalanche large enough to block the goblin advance. With no one left to kill, they turned on themselves. For some reason they didn't get in their boats and sail to the mainland. I've never been one to understand the goblin mind. All they wanted was death on this island and the presence of man wiped from their lands."

Holve's tale ended with his teeth gritted in anger, as if he had actually been there to witness the slaughter. Ealrin could tell that his friend had no compassion for the gray ones. Those who face the horde of gray hardly ever do.

The three had walked through the city streets while listening to Holve's tale of its destruction. Ealrin saw at every turn some efforts to clean the city, but not to restore it. Goblin weapons lay in charred piles. The metal had rusted and pieces of wood that had not completely burned were rotted from exposure. There were no bodies lining the streets now, as Ealrin supposed there must have been when the siege had actually taken place. A mass grave lay less than a stone's throw from the city walls. Humans, elves, and dwarves were buried with dignity. The goblins were piled and burned.

As the three came close to the tower, Ealrin peered into the door of a house that once must have been a beautiful building that could have held several families in its walls. He walked up the path to the door that was still on its hinges despite the damage time and the battle had done.

The dagger that planted itself into the wood of the door sailed so close to his head that he had felt the very air split as the thud resounded throughout the house.

For all their searching, instead of the trio finding the thief, he had found them.

10: Justice

As Ealrin spun on his heel, he saw the thief dart into another abandoned house across the road. Holve and Roland were already in a dead sprint, refusing to let him escape. It would still be three on one, not two as the thief had obviously intended.

Ealrin burst through the doorway of the house the thief had ran into. He saw a stairway leading up to a second level and heard scuffling above him. Without hesitating, he ran up the stairs. As he came to the top of them, he caught a glimpse of Holve with his dagger drawn, running out a door that led to an upper patio of the house. Ealrin could see Roland and the thief were already fighting outside. Roland had his sword drawn and was furiously exchanging blade hits with the thief who had a short sword. He was no older than Ealrin himself. His blonde hair was wet with perspiration, and his eyes were narrowed, not in hate, but something else. Was it fear?

As Holve ran to them the thief saw that he, again, was going to be desperately outnumbered. He deflected a swing of Roland's sword with his own, and then charged Holve, as if to tackle him. It was then that Ealrin could see what he was not sure Holve had: another blade the thief had drawn from his side and was aiming to throw at Holve before he crashed into him. Holve had his dagger drawn and was ready to receive the tackle, but not the second knife.

It wasn't more than a moment in which Ealrin reacted. Lacking a weapon, he threw the only thing he had at the thief: himself.

As the man leapt into the air to drive at least one knife into Holve and perhaps take a sword into himself as well, Ealrin came and rammed his side with his shoulder. Hard.

The thief was hit off his course, giving Holve the space he needed to jump aside and avoid the dagger that nearly cut his side. No longer in control of his body, the thief went crashing into the wall of the outside of the house and crumpled to the ground, unconscious.

The trio stood over the thief. He lay in a crumpled mess against the outside wall of the patio. Ealrin knew the man was breathing, he could see his chest rise and fall in rhythm. And yet he also knew that when he came to, this man would have a terrible ache in his head.

"He's a young one," said Roland, who had sheathed his sword.

"No more winters than Ealrin here," added Holve, who was now bending down over the man, removing the daggers from his limp hands and any other weapons he could find. Holve also saw that a small satchel was around the thief's neck.

"Oh, what have we here?" inquired Holve as he opened the small bag.

Sure enough, Elezar's locket was inside it, still whole and seemingly unharmed from its adventure. Ealrin was relieved.

"So, what do we do with our criminal here?" questioned Roland as he took a step closer. Holve stood up and examined the man. He seemed unsure.

"It'd be an awful lot of work to bring him back to Good Harbor. Plus, we would need to tie him up somehow. What do you think Ealrin?" Holve asked, turning to him.

Hmm. Well, he's obviously a thief, Ealrin thought.

And he had stolen from a friend. How would he make sure the man faced justice for what he did? And, Ealrin wondered as he surveyed the man, what reason did he have for stealing the locket in the first place?

"There must be a wagon or cart of some sort here to carry him back to Good Harbor in. I'm wondering why he took the locket in the first place. Maybe Elezar would recognize him if he got a good look at him. At any rate, I think he should face justice."

Ealrin paused. What does justice look like in Good Harbor? He had seen no jail or stocks, let alone any type of justice hall or court.

"My friend, I believe that you are right and that he should face justice, but bear in mind: many people in Good Harbor are good people but who are so with a price. They find little reason to offer mercy. Thieves are treated no less than one who murders. Depending on what the city council decides upon, this man may face the noose for stealing this locket."

Holve spoke the words without hinting at what he believed was the right or the wrong course of action. In fact, he spoke with an air of being removed from the situation. Was he trying to gauge what Ealrin's response would be?

At that moment, Ealrin decided that justice was right, but that mercy was needed in measures. He walked back into the house and looked around the second floor. Surely there must be something with which to tie up the thief? There! In an open trunk were several different looking tools, perhaps discarded by the previous occupant of this house when the goblins came to burn down the city. In it was a length of rope. More than enough to tie up someone with so that they couldn't get away.

Ealrin returned and offered the rope to Roland.

"Tie him up well so that he can't escape. I'll go find a cart to put him in so we can transport him back to Good Harbor. I'll speak with the city council if I must. He stole, yes, but we've retrieved the locket and there's no harm done."

Well, save for to his head, Ealrin thought.

"Maybe Elezar will be satisfied to have him work for him for a period of days? To repay him for the troubled mind he gave him."

Roland and Holve exchanged a glance and then looked back to Ealrin. Both were examining Ealrin in a different way.

Holve spoke first.

"Very well. Roland, tie up our thief. I'll go help our justice seeking friend here find a wheelbarrow."

And for the first time since meeting him, Holve gave Ealrin a true smile.

The effect on his face was instantaneous. It was as if Holve had grown thirty years younger in a moment. His face was bright and cheery.

For a moment.

He looked down at the man and the furrowed brow came back, along with his years.

Roland spoke and broke Ealrin from the thoughts of Holve he was having. Who was this man, apparently so angry at life, yet who hid something within himself?

Was it joy?

"Fine with me. But know that if he should decide to come to on my watch I'll take the honor of returning him to his current state of consciousness!"

IT WAS HOLVE WHO FOUND what was left of a horse cart. The bed of it was badly burned, but would hold the weight of one without fear of breaking. The wheels were slightly uneven, but as it had two wooden poles jutting out to go on either side of a horse or other beast of burden, two of the three could pull the cart along while the third kept watch over the still quite unconscious man in the back.

It was slow going and the suns had already disappeared over the sea when they emerged from Lonely Pass. There was still just enough light to see the path they were to walk to return to Good Harbor. Roland joked as they came out from under the trees that perhaps punishment enough for the thief could be to listen to every story Soltack wanted to tell him.

Perhaps.

The trio arrived back in Good Harbor long after the night had set. The city guard was right. They had to make a fair amount of racket to get someone to open up the gate. The lights from the various houses and businesses in the city gave them light to see as they brought the man to the city council. A weary looking man addressed them at the building and took them around to the rear, where he opened one door with a key, which led to a small hallway with six or so smaller doors leading off it. This was Good Harbor's jail.

They lifted the man off the cart and set him into the first room on the right. The room itself had no window. The only opening was a small barred rectangle high in the door and a swinging door in the bottom of the door, which Ealrin assumed was for food and water. The only furniture to speak of in the cell was a bucket. Before they left, Ealrin insisted the guard leave the man a pitcher of water and some bread from Holve's pack.

The thief had woken up several hours beforehand and refused to speak. Well, perhaps it would have been better to say he was unable to speak. Roland had taken the opportunity to also tie a bit of cloth around his mouth to gag him. He didn't strain or try to get free of his ropes. Though doing so would have been quite a feat, Roland had used the entire length of rope and wrapped the man several times as well as made secure his arms, feet, and legs. He didn't struggle now that they laid him down in the cell.

Ealrin himself bent down and cut the rope holding him quickly. He undid the cloth so that he could eat and drink. Standing up, he walked out of the cell and allowed the guard to close and lock the door.

"We'll come back in the morning and let you know what we've decided to do to you," Ealrin spoke through the barred window.

No response.

The three left the man where he was. Ealrin noticed Holve put a few coins into the guard's hand and whisper something to him.

The guard grunted and nodded his head. They turned to walk to the Rusty Hook and the guard resumed his post at the front of the council building. It was only then that Ealrin had a thought: Who else lay in one of those cells in the jail of Good Harbor? And what was their fate?

The walk back was made in silence. Holve had taken the locket out of his own bag and held it in his hand. Ealrin had seen the two interact a lot and knew that Holve would be glad to return this treasure to the old man. He was glad he was able to help retrieve it to help pay back the kindness of the innkeeper.

Heads turned when they opened the door and stepped inside the inn where several patrons, though it was late, were sitting at tables drinking or around the fireplace staring into its warmth. The spring night had turned cold.

When Elezar spotted them, he was across the room, attempting to stir a sleeping man whose grip was solidly on a wooden mug he had apparently been drinking out of a little too heavily. On seeing the trio, he left the man and walked over to them.

Holve held up the locket to him.

Elezar, despite his age, did a half skip to get to Holve quicker. He let out a laugh of happiness and hugged Holve around his chest. He then turned to hug Roland, who stretched his arms out wide and broke out a big smile as well. Elezar playfully pushed him aside and turned to Ealrin.

"Many thanks to you three for returning my locket. It's the most valuable thing on Ruyn to me! Though, I've still no idea why any thief would try to steal it," he said smiling at Ealrin and company.

"Perhaps you ought to quit calling it the most valuable thing on Ruyn, eh Elezar?" said Roland with a grin.

"Bah. Anyone who takes a second look at it would know that it's just a picture locket, barely worth a day's wages! It's the inside that holds value to me."

With that Elezar opened the locket. Inside were fashioned two small portraits of two women, one older and one just coming into marrying age.

"It's the only likeness I have left of my wife and daughter. They were killed in a goblin raid back twenty years ago. I miss them terribly, but because of this wonderful gift, I'm able to remember them as they were and carry them with me everywhere I go." He offered it to each in turn and Ealrin took it and held it gently in his hands.

Both women were plain looking, but both were smiling in a way that told Ealrin that they were content. Elezar had given nearly none of his looks to his daughter, save for her nose and smile. The rest was a carbon copy of the other woman in the locket, Elezar's wife.

It was then that something strained Ealrin's chest and would occupy his thoughts that whole night.

What had become of his family?

11: The White Wind

Elezar didn't recognize the thief. Their best guess was that he smuggled aboard some recent ship that had come to Good Harbor. Though he never offered a name, he agreed to work for Elezar for half a moon as punishment for stealing the locket. His nights would still be spent in the cell.

He never apologized for his thievery, but nor did his heart seem so blackened that he was beyond remorse. Whether he was trying to escape some worse fate in the Republic, Thoran, or Beaton, he was potentially just seeking refuge like others who come to Good Harbor. It couldn't have been his preferred choice to live. Probably just hungry and wanting to sell the locket for a meal. As Holve had said earlier: desperate.

The morning after the ordeal was over, the trio had woken early for breakfast. Elezar proudly wore his locket and showed with renewed passion. Every patron heard of his wife and daughter. Several times Elezar had to stop telling his own story, being so overcome with sadness for his departed family, or gratitude for his locket's safe return. Meanwhile Holve, Roland, and Ealrin ate their breakfast at a corner table, and received several pats on the back for a job well done. Holve was not in a talkative mood, so Roland and Ealrin did most of the talking about their adventure. It was after they had finished their meals that Holve finally spoke.

"My work here on Good Harbor is done for now. I'll be needing to make my way to Thoran. Roland is coming with me. The question is, what will be your course of action? You could stay here in Good Harbor. I could try to secure work for you in the city, in one of the shops, or out on the farms of the island if you wished. Maybe get you sailing again. Several merchant ships pass through here and they are always looking for honest sailors. Or..."

Ealrin contemplated his prospects. There was the chance to stay here in Good Harbor and to work. He wasn't sure about any craft that he knew much about. While walking through the stores, he had waited for one of them to trigger a memory. No matter if he was at the blacksmith's or the fisherman's docks, with the merchants haggling or the traders, nothing could clear the fog that prevented him from remembering who he was or what he had done before his crash. Spending time on a boat had not made him recall much. It had only made him sick.

"I want to come with you," Ealrin had said before giving Holve the chance to finish. "This island holds nothing for me, save for the kindness of you and Elezar. I want to come with you. I don't know what I'll find, but I know that Good Harbor won't help me remember who I am."

Holve looked to Roland, and then back to Ealrin. His face held a little less of a grimace.

"I had thought you'd decide on that."

"Hoping he'd decide that more like it," said Roland as he prodded Holve. He rose, adjusting his cloak over his back and picking up his harness of weapons. "Grab your things, Ealrin. We're sailing out before midday!"

Of course, Ealrin's things were easily put on his person. All he owned in the world was his clothes. His white shirt was tucked into his brown leather pants and the coat rested on top, which bore the only identifying thing about him: his name. After the crash site had been cleaned up and picked over, nothing more of value could have been garnished from the wreckage.

Eight small patches of overturned and uniform earth were the only things that remained of the wreck, and each of those bore a wooden sign that simply said:

"Shipwrecked in Spring, Imperial Year 1001."

EALRIN LOOKED BACK over the ship's railing at the city of Good Harbor, shrinking away in the distance. It wasn't home, he knew that well. Yet at the same time, it was the only place he could remember so it pained him, if only a little, to be leaving. Instead of trying to remember what the place looked like and boring the image into his mind, his hands were busy sketching roughly the scene he saw now: Good Harbor at the edge of the sea with the mountain range stretching behind it. The forest covering the space between the grassy farmlands, and the mountainous rocks that reached out for the clouds. The Lonely Pass that they had traveled only yesterday to return to the Rusty Hook. Yes, the Rusty Hook must be drawn as well.

Elezar had sworn that the pack had been left by some traveler many moons ago, and it had cost him nothing. He had pleaded with Ealrin to take it as payment for returning the locket. No matter how much Ealrin had tried to reason that it was he who needed to be paying debts, Elezar wouldn't budge. So Ealrin had taken the simple traveler's pack from Elezar, as well as the hug he had offered him.

Elezar let Roland hug him as they departed; as long as he promised not to crush his bones or pick him up off the ground.

Roland had happily indulged in only one of those requests.

Inside the pack, Elezar had put what Ealrin knew was not simply left by any traveler. A bound leather volume with blank pages and a writing tool lay in the bottom, as well as a fine dagger that was not meant to be worn around the waist or the ankle, but instead was fastened to the inside of your forearm. With practice, it could be released with the proper motion so that at any moment a knife could be in your hand within a blink of an eye. Ealrin was still trying to get it to work, no luck so far.

It was in the leather-bound book that Ealrin sketched Good Harbor on the second page. The first had one note:

"Remember from this point on, Elezar."

After writing a short passage about being found, Holve, Roland, the Rusty Hook, the thief, and Everstand, Ealrin began to write about and sketch the *White Wind*, the boat on which he sailed currently.

The *White Wind* was a fine vessel, nearly thirty paces long and ten across. Its main mast was taller than most trees Ealrin had seen on the island, with two more that rivaled it. Felicia, its captain, had said that once she had been used for war, but now, with the Southern Republic no longer expanding its borders and the goblins fighting among themselves, it was tasked with the more mundane: like transporting cloth and other goods from the mainland to Good Harbor and ferrying back those who could afford the toll.

It was a fine day for sailing, Ealrin thought.

Many of the crew had busied themselves with their tasks. Though they were mostly male and human, there was a large measure of respect, and perhaps a bit of fear, for Felicia Stormchaser.

She was an imposing woman standing a head taller than Ealrin. Her jet-black hair fell down past her waist, tied up in a single braid. Her piercing green eyes surveyed the horizon around her as she steered the ship from its helm. With her rough and salty voice, she barked orders that were obeyed without question. Men flew to follow her command. No one gave her a glance that bespoke of looking down upon her for the gender she had been blessed with. She was the captain of the *White Wind*. The chaser of storms. It was quite the impressive sight to see, Ealrin thought.

Yet for being found shipwrecked, he felt odd. His legs didn't respond well when the boat rocked to one side or the other. The things Felicia would yell to a crewman were foreign to him. Shouldn't he know which side was port and which was starboard? Or how the rudder worked? Or in what fashion the masts were made?

None of these made a path through his fog. Only more questions. If he was a sailor, why had he lost all knowledge of sailing?

It was extremely frustrating. He took his mind off his wonders by getting to know other members of the crew and by practicing his sword skills with Roland. The journey from Good Harbor, which was on an island in the Southern Republic, to Loran, the major port city of the country of Thoran, was four days' worth of sailing with the wind being strong and true.

In the first two days, Ealrin made a point to talk with people aboard the *White Wind* and was never lacking to hear a good story from them. Captain Felicia had with her some of the most traveled sailors in the continent.

There were four dwarves with beards down to their shoes. Admittedly, that meant that their hair was only the span of your arm but still impressive. They hailed from a place they called Dun Gaza. In dwarven tongue, the word before a city tells them how important the city is. It can describe a mining colony or a forge city, where metal is shaped and formed into weapons or other things useful to the mountain dwellers. Apparently, those are the only two types of dwarven cities there are, so Ealrin was informed. "Dun" meant that it was a large forge. If it were a smaller forge city it would be "Cardin", but a "Grandun" would mean it was the biggest forge city on the continent. Grandun Krator was where these dwarves were off to. Apparently, Dun Gaza had completed some great task and they were to inform their masters of it. Grandun Krator rested in the heart of a mountain between Beaton and the Goblin Maw. That mountain range, Ealrin was told, held more dwarves than men in the three countries of Beaton, Thoran, and the Southern Republic combined. Ealrin wasn't sure if this was prideful exaggeration or the truth. Either way, he was interested in the stories these four had about goblin wars, great weapons of war forged in their city, and other topics. Mostly they were about fighting, or weapons they had used in fighting. Or the weapons they had created that were held by some great dwarf or another and used to kill scores of goblins. They took pride in their handiwork, Ealrin could tell, but more pride in what their works accomplished.

Also on board were two elves. It was hard to tell whether they had a dislike for only Ealrin, or a dislike for everyone in general. Granted, these two obeyed their captain without question, but it was obvious that they considered themselves on a higher level than the rest of those aboard the ship. Still, they were glad to share their stories with a captive audience, and Ealrin was more than willing to listen.

As far as they knew, only a handful of elves actually lived on the continent of Ruyn. And those that did were Woodlanders. Long ago in elf history, there was some event that split the elves into three different lines. The Woodlanders lived on both the continent of Ruyn and Redact. They claimed two woods as their home, one in the Southern Republic, and another in what was referred to as "The Northern Wastes." Ealrin didn't think such a place warranted a visit, but he would very much like to meet the elves of the south if he could.

Something happened which had made the Woodlanders move from where they had originated: the faraway continent of Irradan. A second group of elves lived on that continent and claimed it as their home. Some humans lived there, Ealrin was told, but it was predominately an elven land.

When he asked about the third line of elves, Fi-Dash, the older looking of the pair, simply said, "We no longer speak of those who have sold themselves to the flames of darkness." Giri-hon, the other, younger looking elf, simply turned his eyes from Ealrin and looked, instead, at his plate of food.

And that was all they would tell him.

They were all taking a break for a noon meal while Ealrin was hearing about the elves' history. Holve came walking past with his empty plate and kicked at Ealrin.

"That'll do on your history lessons today, young swordsman. It's time to practice again!"

Aboard the *White Wind*, there were three acceptable times to not be waiting for the next command from Felicia: During a meal that Felicia had instructed be given, during weapon's practice which Felicia had advised they do, and whenever Felicia was asleep, which Ealrin had not yet seen her retire to her quarters for the last two days.

And after the noon meal was weapon's practice for those on board. Everyone heartily enjoyed this time of the afternoon, though Ealrin a little less than everyone else.

It was a sight to see all the varied weapons of the different members of the crew, especially between the various races.

The elves fought with two swords, though they both also carried a bow around them as well. The delicate swords were only the length of one's forearm, but the elves struck out at one another with such precision, swiftness, and ferociousness that Ealrin knew better than to doubt their deadliness. He only hoped he would never cross blades with a Woodlander. They were adept fighters.

The dwarves, on the other hand, were not as precise as they were relentless. Instead of fighting with thin and seemingly delicate blades, they preferred anything that was stout, heavy, and most of all, big. Two of the dwarves carried maces with spikes on their heads that were taller than they were. They wielded them with both hands and could easily smash apart a barrel with one solid blow. This only occurred once on this voyage before Felicia came down on them harshly for such waste: the barrel had been filled with provisions and the offender, Farin, had been ordered to clean up the mess and go without the evening meal. Ealrin found out later it was best not to irritate a hungry dwarf.

The other dwarves chose to fight with a giant ax and a formidable looking hammer. Dwarven fighting first involved throwing yourself into your enemy in hopes of knocking them down. Though the average dwarf grew no higher than four feet tall, their girth and muscle gave them plenty of weight to throw around. A head-butt from a dwarf would make anyone's day much worse. If the first blow knocked you down, the second was sure to be the heavy end of whatever weapon they wielded. Your demise would be messy, but swift.

There were two others on board who were neither human, dwarf, nor elf. A curious creature called a Skrilx. For all intents and purposes, it resembled a cat. Not the kind that haunts alleys, however, for it stood on its hind legs and had the very posture of a man. This particular Skrilx indeed had the muscular tone of a very big and well-trained warrior of a man, but its face, its fur, and its tail were all quite animal.

Ealrin was not sure if his kind spoke, for this one didn't say a word. It obeyed Felicia without question or pause. He was her first mate. Roland said that the Skrilx were a proud race, but a dying breed. This was only the second one he had ever seen. Felicia would often say his name: Urt. He carried a giant spear that was three heads taller than Ealrin. Urt was ferocious looking and bested any other living thing in combat on the ship with ease. Ealrin thought better than to offend him.

The last and most curious thing on board was in fact just that, a thing: a suit of armor that moved and walked and fought and talked but contained nothing. Of course, Ealrin had not checked to be sure the thing was empty, but it offered him up the information willingly.

"Fear not me, nor the suit that contains me. I am spirit, though I once had flesh as you have. That was before my body was torn asunder, struck down, and defeated. Instead of passing on, as others do, my spirit lingered here, on this temporal plane. A mighty wizard, who passed on many years previous, bound me to this armor. Though I have not found any method by which to pass from this world to what lies hereafter, I have committed myself to the service of the great country of Thoran, as the wizard who bound me hailed from this land. You may call me Edgar."

Ealrin couldn't imagine which would be odder to a passing stranger: a giant feline walking upright as a man or a suit of armor that contained no body.

This entire crew was a hodgepodge of adventurers. The remaining humans all had stories: some were from Thoran, some from the Republic, and two were from the land of Beaton, which had only one enormous city, resting on the shores of a glimmering sea.

This voyage had done wonders to take Ealrin's mind off his current state and allowed him to learn many different things about the land of which he had no recollection or memory.

And if it were not for the stories, it would be for the practicing fighting techniques. Roland, though he carried several weapons, preferred a one handed short sword to all the various options he carried with him.

"I'd prefer not to run short when the time comes and fight with what is at hand!" said Roland after Ealrin had finally asked him about his collection. "Though, if given the option, I'll use this blade before any other. It's never done me wrong!"

The blade itself was quite beautiful. Inlaid into its steel, which was strong and could cut a cloth in two if it were dropped above it, were various dwarven runes that Roland said were magical. It kept the blade unusually sharp and strong. The handle was meant for one hand and was covered in beautiful black leather. The dwarves on board said it was one of the finest they had seen, though they were unsure of its maker. Roland certainly wasn't going to tell anyone.

"Now, if I told you where I got this sword, you might go get a fancy one yourself!" he had said to the dwarf, Arin, who had asked him where it originated from and got its name. A dwarf could always trace a weapon by its name, for a dwarf would name the weapon after himself, its intended use, and its place of origin.

Ealrin had no weapon of his own, save the small knife Elezar had given him, so Roland allowed him to try out all of the others he had collected. Though Holve proved himself to be adept at handling a spear, the handle of a spear felt odd in Ealrin's hand. He didn't know where the end of it would be at any moment and couldn't get a solid strike with one. He left the spear fighting to Holve. The hammers and maces and axes of the dwarves felt odd. There was too much weight at the end of the weapon for him to handle. He found himself lodging the weapon into the wood of the ship and unable to retrieve it before he was struck by his opponent and on his back.

So Ealrin, instead of trying his luck with a bow from the elves, decided to take up the sword. Of his options from Roland, one in particular stood out to him. It was a sword that could be used with two hands if the bearer so chose, but it's weight was not so much that it could not be used with a single hand either. Ealrin enjoyed being able to switch between the two at a moment's notice, as defending and striking sometimes required one or two hands, depending on the situation or the foe. And instead of a slender blade, this particular sword had a blade that was the span of a hand across. Finally, the blade's end did not have a pointed tip, but instead had a rounded edge. To think that it wasn't sharp was a mistake as Ealrin found out inspecting the weapon. His finger still bled from the cut as he readied himself again to face against Roland. The cloth he had wrapped around it kept the blood at bay while he focused on his foe's attack.

Again and again, Ealrin and Roland sparred with one another. It was easy to see that Ealrin was outclassed in every way by the seasoned swordsman. Whenever Ealrin expected him to swing his blade left, it somehow came from the right. Instead of blocking a blow that was coming from above, all of a sudden, Ealrin found himself being smacked with the flat side of Roland's sword. It was infuriating to him, and so with every blow he demanded another attempt.

On the second day of constant sparring, the crew had gathered around to watch the two facing off against each other. Most were yelling for Roland to teach the young Ealrin a lesson he wouldn't forget. The dwarves had taken sides with Ealrin, grunting out advice or howling whenever they saw an opening in Roland's defense. Seeing as how most of their advice was "Barr! Just tackle him!" they actually weren't very helpful.

Though Ealrin's sides and arms were tired and his legs were sore, after the last meal of the day he finally landed a blow on Roland.

As his blade fell and finally smacked Roland against his exposed ribs, the crew fell silent for a moment, surprised that he had finally scored a hit.

Then the whole crew stood up to cheer for Ealrin. In taking his eyes off Roland for the momentary praise, he found himself knocked to his back and looking up at, once again, the man who had been teaching him hard for the last two days.

"Well done Ealrin, but don't take your eyes off your foe. Otherwise, you'll find yourself on your back!" He let out a hearty laugh and offered out a hand to help Ealrin up.

"I was so surprised I actually landed a blow on you," said Ealrin truthfully, taking Roland's hand and rising to his feet. He was beginning to feel like he would never actually get through Roland's skilled defense.

"That'll do, sailors," said Felicia, who was still at the helm, Urt dutifully standing at her side. "Get the ship ready for the night and the first watch."

The night was divided into two different shifts: sundown to high moon, high moon to first light, and then everyone was expected to be up with the sun. Ealrin's shift wasn't until high moon, so he went to lie down. Only two or three crew members kept watch over the *White Wind* while it sailed at night, so that everyone else could get a decent night's rest. If they could sleep on a boat, that is. The dwarves complained the whole time that sleep was meant to occur on the solid earth, not on the shifting tides. Ealrin had agreed at the beginning, but he was now getting used to the rocking, and the shifts of being at sea.

As he lay in his hammock in the crew's quarters, unable to sleep for the horrible dwarves snoring, he wondered how his slight improvement in swordplay would serve him in the future.

He would learn all too soon.

12: Ceolmaer the Elder

His eyes shot open and he sprung from his bed so fast he felt dizzy. Ceolmaer was old, and the quick movement was unfamiliar to him. It took a minute for him to catch his breath and realize that he was wet with perspiration. He reached to the side of his bed with a groan for a towel to wipe his forehead. Knowing that sleep would not return to him easily, he slowly swung his legs to the edge of his bed. His feet touched the cold tiles of his tower suite in the capital of the Southern Republic. He had to shift over in order to place his feet into the fur-lined slippers.

Being the head elder of the entire country had at least some advantages.

Ceolmaer stood up and wrapped a robe around his frail frame. He was having more and more nightmares recently, and he figured they wouldn't stop until he could somehow convince the three major races of the Southern Republic to find peace between themselves.

Then again...

How in the world was he going to get them to agree to peaceably unite when there continued to be these smaller skirmishes between them? From all over the southern peninsula, reports came of elves being attacked by dwarves after exploring the forests around the dwarven mountains, humans attacking dwarves who they claimed were mining illegally from their surrounding mountains, and elves who were shooting down the caravans of men who came too close to Talgel.

It wasn't always like this.

Ceolmaer was old enough to remember when the three races lived in peace with one another. There were no fights between them. Well, at least not like these brutal ones that were being reported recently. Perhaps there had always been disagreements.

But war?

Surely not, Ceolmaer thought.

He walked past his bed and around to the balcony of his high tower suite. The doors were solid wood and carved with the symbol of the Southern Republic: three triangles facing downward, all supporting the one above it.

The original intent of this design had been to show how each race of the south could learn to depend on one another, as well as a warning. The triangles were precariously placed on top of one another. To move one of them ever so slightly would send the whole thing toppling down. Ceolmaer had always been aware of that balance, and the need to maintain it.

It had been a goblin war that had united the three races against a common enemy and saw the formation of the current country called the Southern Republic. How long could that republic last against senseless violence?

The door opened with great effort. The one-hundred-year-old tower that served as the meeting place for the elders of the south was showing its age. Still, the old elder marveled at the building. It had been a showing of cooperation. No other tower stood as tall on the entire continent. Not even that ruin on Good Harbor, the Tower of Pallum, ancient though it was.

No, dwarf stone had been cut specifically to build this tower. Elven wood had been hewn and carved to make its doors and ceilings, floors and windows. And what had men done? Ceolmaer laughed at the thought. We designed it. We built it. We sit atop it. Our magicians lifted the stones. Our engineers ensured that it would be sound.

Were it not for the brilliance of man, this tower would not have occurred.

"Stop it," he said out loud. It was that type of thinking that would bring down an entire country. It had been an effort shared. A symbol of the unity of the races. Ceolmaer shuffled out to the balcony that overlooked the great city of Conny, capital of the Southern Republic, and breathed the air in deeply. From here he could just barely make out the glittering of the stars along the sea that spanned the horizon. This was the city that had fought the hardest during the goblin invasion, and it was here that the pact of the three was made.

It would be here that they would settle their differences and keep their peace, Ceolmaer thought.

His eyes scanned the city he had lived in all his life. Judging by the position of the moon it was approaching midnight, but from his vantage point he could still hear the activity in the streets below, and see fires and lanterns burning bright despite the late hour.

In a city of over 600,000 souls, there has been rarely a time when everyone slept. Ceolmaer reveled in the buzz of the city. Several buildings stood over four and five stories tall. In the morning their roofs would create a patchwork of color that only those who viewed the city from this great height could truly appreciate.

The streets branched out from the capitol tower like spokes on the wagon wheel. Several towers similar in design to the spiraling capitol tower rose along the city streets. Some were places of study and books. Others were the homes of the nobility, and the second houses of some other elders on the council. Though he knew he lived a soft life in comparison to some of the other residents of Conny, Ceolmaer had never really enjoyed the vanity of any of his fellow elders. Being elected an elder of the Southern Republic was a high honor, but it also came with the possibility of terrible corruption. Many wealthy merchants and landowners would gladly pay to influence your decision on important matters, and several elders had taken advantage of such deals. The two other elders of men, for example, both had at least two other houses in which they lived in the great city. Ceolmaer shook his head just thinking about it. But perhaps this was why he had become head elder. In his many years of service, far too many for him to recount this late night, he had never once accepted payment for decisions made. Perhaps it was his purity in the face of corrupt politics that had enabled him to be the elder of elders for the last 15 years.

Still, there was much to do in order to convince the six other elders to lay aside their differences and focus on the current unrest between the races.

His mind wandered to the council's previous session.

As he sat in his chair at the raised portion of the circle of the council, Ceolmaer was holding his head in his hands. His elbows rested on the armrests of the oaken chair. His eyes focused on the decorative stone table that formed the inside of the circle. Its intricate ruins and carvings of dwarves, elves, and men depicted all the people of the Southern Republic. In the carvings they were living in peace and cooperating. On the table, they were fighting with words like daggers.

"You'll come to find that the ax of a dwarf is much better suited for crushing a skull than some finicky elven blade!" shouted Dollin, one of the dwarven elders that sat around the table. Well, everyone else was sitting. Dollin was in fact standing, but his short stature made it seem like he could be doing either to Ceolmaer. For a dwarf, he was shorter than most. However, he more than made up for it with presence. His red hair flared along with his anger.

"This is not a discussion about weaponry, Dollin, and I'll not have it turn into one. I believe your original point was the elven caravan that traveled to Kaz-Ulum from Ingur," Ceolmaer interjected. It was the first time he had spoken in well over thirty minutes. The bickering between the elves and dwarves was getting worse, and he knew it would soon escalate.

"Now, Dollin, if we are to understand, you are not debating axes and swords, but an elven caravan that intended to travel to Kaz-Ulum?" he said, trying to bring the conversation back to a focus.

"Not only that, but I say there was no caravan!" Dollin shouted at Ceolmaer, who, upon hearing those words put his head back into his hands.

"Dollin of Kaz-Ulum!" shouted one of the elven elders, a tall and brown-haired man named Finasaer. He was younger than Dollin; in fact, he was the youngest of the elders. His youth gave him a pride and arrogance that matched Dollin's rage. The elf was fair and had no beard, for in fact, no elf had ever needed to shave. They never grew facial hair. Ceolmaer's own graying goatee fell into his lap as he continued to listen to the bickering.

"You know full well that the elven caravan came to Conny, resupplied here, and convened with myself and Olweleg before continuing on to Kaz-Ulum. Or have you forgotten that they also spoke with Thrinain, who gave them his blessing to travel to your infernal mountain? If you say there was never a caravan then you are a liar or a fool, perhaps both!"

Shouting on both sides grew so that no words were intelligible, by either party.

Of course, Finasaer was right. The elves had indeed sent a caravan of artisans and craftsmen from Ingur to Conny with the intent of traveling to the dwarven mine in order to learn from the weapon smiths there. It was to be a time of cooperation and learning from one another. The elves had in fact traveled to Conny. Ceolmaer had seen them with his own eyes. The issue was that the caravan never made it to the mountain. Upon searching for the fourteen carts, forty horses, and over two hundred elves that were a part of the traveling group, only a single charred cart was found.

On that cart rested the heads of the lead artisans upon the axes of dwarfs.

Now both sides were furious with the other. The elves naturally assumed that the dwarves had slaughtered the elves for reasons unknown to anyone but themselves. The dwarves claimed no such violence could have taken place. It was during a season of meditation for the dwarves before a concentrated effort to better understand the mountain and its gifts to them. No weapons would be held during the two-week long worship of the mountain. Therefore, the dwarves could not have attacked the elves.

And they said that it damaged the honor of a dwarf to be called liars.

Both sides blamed men for different things at different times. Men should have accompanied the elves to help them travel safely to the mountain. Men should have come to the aid of elves if a battle was to be fought. Men should side with the dwarves because of the weapons forged by them and used in the Southern Republic's army.

And so the argument continued to escalate.

"Peace, my fellow elders!" said a feminine voice finally.

Mara held up her hands to silence the elves and dwarves. Ceolmaer looked up from his hands, hoping that the sole woman elder could grant him respite from this bickering. His headache was worsening by the moment.

Both dwarf and elf resumed their seats, as they looked to the short female who still held her hands high. She looked at both sides of the round table with stern green eyes. Though she was in her sixtieth year, she was still a fiery politician who could easily command a room, as she did currently.

"May we take a moment to discuss a possibility among this tragedy?" Ceolmaer adjusted himself in his rather uncomfortable chair to better look at Mara. He had always admired her for her ability to look at every situation with eyes other than her own. No wonder she had risen to the prominence of an elder. She possessed a wisdom and insight that Ceolmaer envied at times. Should he ever need someone to follow him as head, he would have her be the top candidate.

"Suppose the elven caravan was in fact attacked, and I believe we can assume this report is true. Now, what if what is plain to our sight is not true and, as the dwarves say, the caravan was not attacked by dwarves of the mountain but by another group? We have heard several accounts of a group of raiders harassing smaller villages and communities on the southern side of the peninsula. Could it have been made to look as if the dwarves of the mountain are at fault when truly they are not?"

For a moment, Ceolmaer considered the possibility, that the dwarves of the mountain were honest and had no knowledge of the attack. But then could it be another group of dwarves who led the attack? A rogue group? Perhaps those who would not have observed the Mountain Ritual?

"If one dwarf has killed an elf, then all dwarves are responsible!" roared Finasaer.

The shouting match continued and Mara looked down at the table, shaking her head.

So much for diplomacy.

Ceolmaer brought his thoughts back to the city he watched over from his balcony. He had replayed the scene around the Table of Elders for the last two weeks, during their break from that last terrible session. Could he have led better and helped bring about some peace? Perhaps if he was younger he could have told both sides to quit being foolish and listen to reason. Or at least to Mara.

Tomorrow, during the councils next session, he would ask, no beg, his fellow elders to see the great need of unity. The bickering must stop so that they could address the greater issue at hand. There had been reports of a rogue group of bandits gaining ground among the more unsavory types of man. It sounded like the Merc Rebellion of a generation ago, but surely it was not they who were causing such trouble. Those raiders were smashed against the rocks with the combined might of three races held in unity.

And so it would be again after this tragedy was behind them.

A noise at the door brought him out of his daydream.

"Does my Lord require anything?" inquired a voice from the door. Ceolmaer turned to face the attendant, keeping one hand on the railing of the balcony.

"No, thank you, I'm..." Ceolmaer would not finish that sentence, or any afterward. For the words that he had intended to say were stopped short by a dagger that cut into his throat. The blade was sharper than any he had ever imagined. He swung at his attacker, but his arms were too frail and his frame too weak. The action caused him to lose his balance. Clutching his bleeding wound, head already spinning from the loss of blood from the deep cut, he slipped to the floor. Looking up, he saw the distinct face of a man: bearded and dark. His eyes were narrowed into a grim and satisfied look. A smirk crossed his face. He dropped the blade that had sliced Ceolmaer's neck and turned to leave. He wore the traditional robes of a tower attendant: maroon with a single, golden colored sash and a hood. Ceolmaer wondered where the imposter had stolen his disguise.

The man would undoubtedly leave the tower unnoticed.

The world around Ceolmaer swum and spun. He lay on the cool stone balcony, unable to call out for help. His hand fell limply to his side. With his last moments, Ceolmaer only saw one last detail of his assassination. Left lying on the balcony beside him, it would be heralded up and down the streets of Conny the next day and used to stir hate and unrest. It would be used to ignite a terrible struggle. The dagger that had slit his throat was elven made.

13: The Night Shift

E alrin was awakened with a shake.

"Can't see how you sleep for all the snoring. It's your shift," said a bleary eyed human named Pas.

He had a good point. For all their complaining, once the dwarves were asleep, hardly anyone else could rest with their combined snores. The whole crew cabin shook with their collective breath.

Ealrin thought about reconsidering his desire to visit a dwarven city more than once whilst trying to fall asleep. He removed the bits of cloth he had eventually tied around his ears to help him sleep, and drug himself out of his hammock and into a standing position. He gathered the sword Roland had been allowing him to use, and now had officially given him to keep, and climbed the stairs from the lower deck up to the main deck.

Pas was sent down to wake the next shift and as Ealrin arose, the other three who were on watch gave a sigh of relief and began to file down to their own hammocks. The night was still; a breezy eastern wind was guiding them along to their destination. They would be there after one more day and night of sailing.

Holve rose from the lower deck as well as one of the elves. Ealrin began to look for a fourth, but then realized Urt was at the helm, rounding out the high moon watch.

"Mind if I join you?" said a voice as if spoken inside a vast cavern, with a slight echo behind it. It was never difficult to tell when Edgar was speaking.

"Not at all, Edgar," said a yawning Holve. During this voyage, Ealrin's friend had not been talking much. Instead, he had been pouring over several pages of notes in his own leather-bound journal. Every now and then he would consult a map of Ruyn, make a new note in his journal, grunt a bit, and then go back to reading. His behavior was odd to Ealrin, who had known Holve to be very talkative, despite his bad mood.

When he had inquired about his change in behavior, Holve had only said "It comes from two things, young one: my dislike of traveling by sea, and wishing this voyage to be over quickly, as well as my business in Thoran. Once all my thoughts are gathered I will gladly share what I have been looking over."

Now that he was out under the open sky, Ealrin began to wonder how the first watch had indeed known it was time for their shift to end. The sky was completely overcast with dark clouds. Not a single star could be seen. It made the night eerily dark.

"I fear that easterly winds will bring dark clouds with them. The Dark Comet burns brightly as well. A bad omen," said Edgar, who Ealrin supposed was looking at him. Though how a suit of armor had the sense of sight he wasn't sure.

"It's just so dark tonight," said Ealrin with a yawn of his own. He was trying to think of something to ask Edgar. Surely a spirit encased in ancient armor had stories to tell to help them pass the time. But just as he was about to speak, a light caught his eye.

And then another. And another. Soon the whole western horizon was filled with lights that were level with the sea.

Urt let out a mighty roar that sent chills down Ealrin's spine.

This was no good tiding.

"Goblins," said Holve in a tone of bitter resentment. "To see that many on the horizon spells terrible news for Good Harbor. I had thought their numbers were dwindling."

"As did I," said Roland, rising up from the lower deck, strapping on his weapons. "I spent the last moon before coming to Good Harbor prowling the Maw and I thought their numbers had decreased back down to the days of the Southern Republic's expedition. This can't bode well for the dwarven cities."

Ealrin thought of the dwarves traveling with them from the mountains in-between Beaton and The Goblin Maw. Were their ancient dwarven cities safe, or were thy to be overrun with the gray-skinned, black-haired beasts?

Felicia came flying out of her cabin, fastening a sword in its sheath around her waist. Instead of her typical clothes, she had on the equivalent of a night robe and her captain's jacket. In her eyes, however, was a fierce determination. Urt surrendered the wheel to her as she began barking orders to the crew that was emerging from the lower decks. Sleep was not in their eyes. They had also heard the Skrilx's mighty roar and knew what it meant. They were alert and ready for action.

"Full sail! Prepare the vessel for combat! Every one of you, make ready your weapons! To your stations!" yelled Felicia Stormchaser. A storm had begun to chase her.

Ealrin's post was at the rear of the ship and Roland was at his right, closer to the wheel. This part of the deck was higher up than any other area. The lights that had lit the horizon were coming closer with each passing moment. The *White Wind* was going to be over-run.

"We are using the same wind are we not?" asked Ealrin as the lights began to illuminate their vessels: ships with dark sails that littered the sea like leaves during the harvest.

"Yes, but our wind is a natural one. There's something about this that seems more than unnatural," answered Roland. "Goblins are as inventive as they are cruel. Something drives them other than the winds!"

"I've never yet been overrun by a goblin vessel and I don't intend to be!" barked Felicia in the pair's direction. "If there's anything on the deck that can be lost, throw it over!"

Barrels and boxes and trunks began flying off the *White Wind's* deck. Every piece of cargo that they could afford to do without was tossed.

Several merchants would be disappointed in the fate of their wares, but that was the least of their worries at this moment.

Ealrin glanced back at the approaching menace. There was something odd about the boats. The water they rode on was being stirred with something other than their hulls. They were now close enough to see that their hulls were painted black and that they were crawling with goblins: on the sails, on the rigging, and on the deck. This particular boat carried no less than a hundred. The crew of the White Wind was a scant 30.

"What is that at the bottom of the boat closest to us?" Ealrin asked the closest person to him. It turned out that person was Urt, who was surveying the boats as well.

"Slave oars," said the Skrilx.

So. They do talk, Ealrin thought.

He leapt gracefully to the upper deck and spoke to Felicia, who swore loudly at his news.

"Ready yourselves, crew of the White Wind! We're in for a fight!" she said as she drew her own sword, keeping one hand on the wheel.

"It's not the fight with the goblins that worries me," said Holve who had appeared at Ealrin's side. "It's that I've never known a goblin to go looking for a fight it wasn't totally sure it would win."

Holve had nothing but disgust in his voice. His eyes were narrowed with rage. Ealrin thought about asking him how many times he had to face a horde of goblins that were sure of the results of a battle and won. Obviously, he had dealt with the gray-skinned killers

before. How many of those skirmishes had been won over the bodies
of several defenders who had fought for their lives?

And would Ealrin live long enough to tell the story of his own
encounter with the goblins, or was he living his final moments?

He drew his sword as Roland came to stand next to them.

They would soon know.

THE GOBLIN SHIP WAS now directly behind them, flanked by
two more on either side. Not only was the crew of the *White Wind*
hopelessly outnumbered man to man, they were soon to be surrounded by ships carrying two hundred goblins each.

The blood had drained from Ealrin's hands. He felt numb and
cold. And yet he tried to steel himself with the same gritty determination that his companions had. Those on board had drawn their
weapons. Ten of the crew carried bows with them. They waited for
the ships to come within range so that they could whittle down
the goblin menace before they were boarded and faced the red-eyed
beasts in hand to hand combat.

Ealrin wished now for a bow, instead of simply waiting for the
ships to form a circle and slowly ease towards them, ready to attack.

One goblin ship came close to the rear of the *White Wind*. Close
enough to warrant a volley of arrows from the archers aboard the
hunted vessel.

Several cries from the goblin ships let the crew know that they
had scored at least a few hits. Ealrin could tell from the howls of rage
that the red-eyed goblins were not going to allow those arrows to go
unanswered.

"Goblin arrows!" shouted Roland to the crew behind him and
all of them took cover. Some had shields with which to protect them,
while others dashed behind a mast or behind a door of the lower
deck.

Ealrin and his two companions dropped below the railing of the upper deck. The cover it provided was sufficient enough to shield them from the arrows, but not from the sight of seeing hundreds of arrows scatter the ship around them. A scream from below let them know that one of their crew had been struck with a goblin missile.

"Careful not to touch the things!" Holve shouted over the thud of arrows. "Goblins will poison the tips!"

Getting shot would be bad enough. Being shot and then suffering from poison as well was a terrible thought.

Surely goblins are the worst type of vile creature, Ealrin thought.

The archers on the *White Wind* returned fire as they could. Every now and then a yell from a crew member let Ealrin know that they had lost another good fighter and that their chances of survival were growing slimmer. Not that they were very likely to survive in the first place.

First light broke just as the arrows had stopped raining down on the *White Wind*. It was a sign that the goblins were now close enough to ready their own weapons. Ealrin peered over the decking to see that four goblin ships had now come on either side of their own. Their foes were dressed in dark colors and wielded short, crude looking swords and shields that were also painted black to match the ships. Goblins were truly repulsive creatures and now Ealrin could see their every detail.

Most of them were black-haired and gray-skinned, though some were darker than others. All of them had glistening red eyes that flashed with hate. Their ears sat higher on their heads than a man's and were large and pointed. Unlike the elves, this did nothing to make them seem dignified or proud. It only added to their grotesque image. Their noses were little more than two holes opened above their mouth. Their mouths were also unnaturally large and filled with sharp, pointed teeth. Their howls were deep and long, like a dog who had been maimed and yet was fighting off a vile enemy.

Their voices joined together in a chorus, hundreds strong, that chilled Ealrin far more than the morning mist.

Perhaps he was indeed facing the last moments of his life. Would he face them like a coward, hunkered down behind the decking of a doomed ship, or upright and brave, facing adversity head on?

Ealrin rose, sword held high, and let out the fiercest battle cry he could muster.

He would not die a coward.

14: The Goblin Pusher

S tinkrunt was in a bad mood.

Not that he was ever in a particularly good mood, but this current state of affairs made his demeanor worse than it was typically.

The *Fishbone* rocked back and forth in the sea as scores of goblins sailed east toward human lands. Stinkrunt had never been one for sailing, and now he knew why.

It had been six weeks since they had set out from the beaches of Sharp Claw, and his stomach had yet to adjust to the rolling motion of the sea. Other goblin vessels had been luckier and broken off towards two large islands Stinkrunt knew nothing about. Only that they were ground, and this ship was not.

It didn't help that he had also discovered he had an astute allergy to seafood. Consuming the smallest of fish would cause him to break out in the most horrible of boils. He scratched a place on his leg he was sure would never fully heal. And every time some salt water would spray up from the ocean onto the vessel, it would sting him something awful.

Still, a goblin had to eat. Any bird or fowl that came anywhere near him had a chance of being devoured on sight. Not that he particularly cared for feathers and beaks, but he certainly would rather have indigestion than boils.

An always-empty stomach could put anyone in a bad mood, especially a goblin. Plus, there was the whole being in charge bit that annoyed Stinkrunt to no end.

There were always pesky questions like "When are we going to reach land?" and "Why isn't there enough food for everybody?" and "Why can't I slit his throat, he stole my knife and cut up my best mate?"

Stinkrunt was more than content with pushing them around. He answered their questions with different renditions of "Who cares? I'm in charge!" but that had only lasted for the first week or so of sailing. The crew members were getting restless, and tired of their new captain.

Leadership did not fit Stinkrunt well.

And yet he didn't mind. For once there were goblins who took him seriously when he was looking. He didn't mind so much their shrugs and rolling eyes when they thought he wasn't paying attention. All he really cared about was getting his way when it mattered. Like when another goblin caught a bird and Stinkrunt was hungry.

"Captains rations!" he yelled at the little goblin that had managed to catch his first bird. A phrase he had often repeated whenever he saw food that didn't swim.

Stinkrunt grabbed it away and had swallowed it whole before the goblin had much chance to argue his point.

And then he pushed him overboard for added measure. After all, he was "The Goblin Pusher."

The fleet of goblin ships would soon approach the Southern Republic and instead of fighting each other aboard their boats crammed with goblins, which several of the vessels had turned into near gladiatorial cages, they would begin to take out their aggression on meatier targets.

Stinkrunt was very much looking forward to standing on dry ground again. Much more so than fighting a bunch of humans, elves, and dwarves.

Sleep was something he had given up on also. In the lower part of the ship there were several hammocks strung up for sleeping. The added swaying made him sick when he tried to go to sleep, sicker still while he was sleeping, and downright miserable when he woke up.

So, instead of a hammock, Stinkrunt got away with napping on the deck during the night. But when he wasn't napping at night, like this particular one when the waves were awful and sleep evaded him, he dreamed with his eyes open.

He remembered standing on land in the Goblin Maw. The hard-packed dirt had been so solid. He could walk around without tripping, unless of course a goblin had tripped him on purpose. Then Grayscar would bash that goblin for picking on one of his cronies. Stinkrunt had been practicing bashing a few goblins of his own and working out who would be his cronies. A few had impressed him, mostly because he had seen them fight each other. A good captain needed some cronies to do his heavy lifting.

Or any lifting at all.

Stinkrunt was enjoying thinking about bossing other people around and making them do whatever he wanted. He quite liked being in charge.

In fact, he was daydreaming so hard that he barely noticed that Grayscar had gone to the trouble of having other goblins row a small boat from his own large vessel to the *Fishbone*.

A smack on the back of his head woke him out of his reverie.

"Hey. Stinkrunt."

Had any other goblin aboard the *Fishbone* hit him so, he would have considered actually using the fancy knife he kept attached to his belt, if it hadn't been stolen while he was daydreaming that is. But after being in the service of Grayscar for so many years, Stinkrunt was familiar with the back of his master's hand against his head.

"Got a special job for you. Take five boats and go north. There is a city up there. It's after a ton of mountains. Smash it. Keep all the loot. After the city is smashed, walk south. Meet up with the rest of the Sharp Claws. We'll smash some other cities, too."

Grayscar looked Stinkrunt up-and-down once. Though he was a poor leader, Stinkrunt was enjoying getting to boss other people around. So much so that he had forgotten what it was like to be bossed around himself.

He was sure something on his face communicated that to Grayscar.

He got hit on the head again.

"Got it?" the large and fierce looking goblin asked the smaller and much less intimidating one.

"Got it," Stinkrunt said. "Sail north. Smash the city. Walk south."

Grayscar gave a grunt of approval.

"Make Sharp Claws look good," he said as he climbed an old rope ladder back down to his boat.

As Grayscar was rowing back, a commotion came up from the boats upfront. Stinkrunt looked to the horizon and saw one solitary ship sailing away from them.

And though he really wanted to steer his boats in the direction of that ship and smash it (after all, hundreds of ships versus one was really good odds), he signaled his crew to sail north, and to pass the message along to the other goblins going with him.

Maybe sailing that way, and smashing one city, wouldn't be so bad. One city was less than a lot of cities. Maybe this was his chance to prove to Grayscar that he deserved to be in charge. Maybe this was his big break.

He signaled the goblin to point the ship north.

Of course, his signal was one of his personal favorites: bash the goblin holding the rudder with a stick until he got the direction right.

15: Roland's Fight

The goblins were prepared to board the *White Wind*. They hung from ropes attached to their masts and were getting ready to swing from their ship to Ealrin's. Each and every goblin had a twisted smile on their face, as if they knew the terror they must be instilling.

With howls of rage the goblins made their first boarding attempt. Several of them swung in the direction of Ealrin, Roland, and Holve.

With a sling of his blade, Ealrin dispatched one of them before he touched the deck of the *White Wind*. Holve speared another in his chest and sent him down snarling to the sea. Two more landed to the left of Roland but were dead before they could raise their swords. They turned to face six more goblins who had successfully planted themselves onto the deck around them. With a quick stab from his spear Holve skewered two goblins on the spot. With a powerful kick, Ealrin put the goblin nearest him on his back, and turned to engage another who was swinging his blade across his chest. He quickly made to block the goblin blade with his own. Ealrin pushed hard against the goblin to knock him off balance, swung his blade high, and dealt a fatal blow.

He turned to see that Roland had taken care of another two goblins, and then looked to the ship to see if another wave was coming.

For the three on the upper deck the first wave of goblins had gone well. Ealrin could see that things were not for those on the lower deck.

The second wave of goblins was now boarding the ship. Those on the lower deck had yet to completely deal with the first. Roland bounded down into a pile of no less than seven of the beasts. With his sword flashing in the morning sun, he dispatched one with every swing.

Ealrin felt the hairs on his neck begin to stand up straight, as the air around him charged with energy. He spun around and gazed at the goblin ship directly behind theirs. On its forward mast stood a menacing looking goblin, holding high his staff with a red jewel affixed to its top. The goblin shaman's eyes glowed with an unnatural fire as his mouth moved up and down in silent incantation.

In that moment, he knew he was going to die.

Appearing seemingly out of thin air, Edgar threw both Holve and Ealrin to the ground on the lower deck and out of harm's way. After hitting the deck of the ship, Ealrin looked up to see Edgar's metal suit of armor glowing green with an unnatural energy. And then, with arms spread wide, he burst into thousand tiny smoking pieces.

Ealrin shielded his eyes from the blast with his arm. The spot where Edgar had stood was now a giant hole in the upper deck of the ship. All that was left was now charred and blackened from the blast. Ealrin heard the goblin shaman cackle with the sight of the damage he had caused.

Ealrin stood to his feet, surveying what was around him. The bodies of both goblins and the crew of the *White Wind* were strewn about the lower deck. Still the fighting raged on, and he saw a goblin charging him with his blade held high. Roland came from his left and intercepted the foe, dispatching him with a blow.

"That makes 18 for me! Are you keeping up Holve?" Roland shouted as the goblin fell dead at his feet. "You'll have to do better than that!" He shouted at the goblin ships around him.

And that was when an arrow pierced his heart.

EALRIN HEARD A SCREAM that was loud and long. He could hear the hurt and the pain that was in it, as well as the rage and anger. It took a moment to register what it was that it escaped his own lips.

Roland fell to the deck onto his knees. With one hand he still clutched his sword, the other wrapped around the arrow that had embedded itself into his chest. Arrows now rained down onto the White Wind, and all around them both goblins and crew members fell. Though Ealrin protested with all his might, attempting to stay at Roland's side as he gasped for air, Holve pulled him away and under the eaves of what was left of the upper deck. Then, with what had to have been pure adrenaline, Roland rose to his feet, ran to the side of the ship, and grabbed a rope. He let out a garbled cry of battle as he flung himself onto the enemy vessel.

Roland was too much of a warrior to die by just one arrow. He continued to fight, though now two more arrows pierced him as he swung in the air. He landed on the goblin ship and was instantly surrounded, and nearly covered by gray skinned warriors. Though every swing of his blade killed at least one goblin, it was too much for his poison wracked body. He finally disappeared underneath uncountable goblins.

Roland was defeated.

Ealrin was still trying to come to grips with the indisputable fact that Roland had been slain. He seemed like a warrior who had no limits or weaknesses. Now he lay slain on the ship of his enemies, surrounded by the bodies of those he took with him.

At that moment, the arrows stopped raining down onto the deck. Ealrin saw that he and Holve were the only surviving members of the crew. Then through every crack and crevice in the ship shone the same unnatural green light that had ended Edgar.

The boards of the *White Wind* creaked and moaned under the influence of the dark magic. The last thing Ealrin was aware of before he hit the seawater was being cast into the air by the force of the explosion that split the vessel in two.

EALRIN STRUGGLED FOR not only his life, but for the life of Holve.

The goblins ships had sailed on, which was fortunate for the pair in one sense. Had they been spotted they no doubt would have become target practice for goblin archers. Whether it was fortune or fate, Ealrin was not sure, but as the ship broke to pieces, he was able to grab Holve and hoist him onto a piece of debris. Ealrin had hit the water, but Holve had hit something hard, a piece of the former ship. He was breathing, but unconscious. Then a sail that had broken free from its rigging had fallen over them, covering the two from the view of goblin eyes.

Ealrin hadn't dared to move the sail, though it made holding onto Holve difficult. He was also unable to see the sun, and therefore know the direction they were floating. He only hoped the tide would bring them closer to land, any land.

Before they were attacked it was still a good day's worth of sailing to their intended port in Thoran. Now he wasn't sure what mass of land would be close enough for them to float to. From one of Holve's maps, now lost to the bottom of the sea, Ealrin thought he remembered some cities on the shores of Ruyn.

He prayed they would make land near one of them.

Well, he prayed that they would land somewhere not being raided by goblins.

The sun was well past setting when Ealrin thought he saw the stars disappearing higher over the horizon than they had been before. He hoped that meant land was close and started kicking hard to help them float towards it. The water was cold. Spring had come, but the sea was still recovering from the long winter. It had not yet been warmed long enough by the sunlight to erase the winter cold.

Ealrin swam because he knew that it meant survival. Holve had not woken from his injury. Though he shivered at the coldness of the air, Ealrin had been able to keep him mostly out of the water. It was only the act of swimming that kept Ealrin warm enough to remain alert. His hands and arms ached from holding onto the debris that kept them alive.

There was land ahead of them, Ealrin was sure of it now. He could hear the sound of waves crashing, meaning that the shore was becoming shallower and allowing the crest to break. Though every part of him ached with fatigue, he swam. There would be time for rest after they made land. Now was the time for survival.

When his feet finally touched the sandy bottom of the shore, Ealrin let out a sigh of relief. The threat of death by drowning was over. He continued to push Holve on the floating debris until it began to drag along the bottom of the shore as well. He then picked up his friend as best he could and drug him to shore.

He ensured that Holve was still breathing and went back to where the piece of the *White Wind* was stuck in the sand. He retrieved the large sail, and broke free what pieces of wood he could and brought them back to land.

Crude shelter was better than none.

Further up the shore were trees. They would do for adding shelter from the wind that now bit into Ealrin's flesh. For now, they would give them protection from being seen from the sea. Ealrin didn't know whether or not the goblins would make their way to this stretch of beach.

As Ealrin set up a lean-to of fallen branches and broken pieces of the ship against the trunk of two trees growing close to one another, he wondered what would cause the goblins to raid. He knew, from somewhere in the back of his mind, that goblins were evil creatures, driven to violence by the influence of the dark magic that had created them thousands of years ago. They craved violence as others crave water and food. They had always had to fight. And if no enemy had presented itself to them, they would fight among their own tribes and cities.

Ealrin paused. How could he remember the nature of a goblin, but couldn't recall the nature of himself? He knew a few things from instinct, but nothing that would reveal who he was, or where he had come from. As he surveyed his handiwork, he wondered if, when the sun brought light to the beach, he would recognize the area they now camped at.

Holve stirred inside of the lean-to.

"Ugh. Blasted goblins," said a very weary sounding Holve.

Ealrin had laid him on his back on top of his own jacket. Thankfully, neither had lost their weapon to the sea. Both weapons now lay next to Holve.

Holve raised himself onto his elbow, but immediately clutched his head.

"Gah. My head. I haven't been out like that for a long time," Holve looked up at Ealrin.

"Who are you?" he asked.

The suns! If Holve had lost his memory, too, what in the world were they to do?

A small smile quickly formed on the man's face.

Ealrin made to kick him.

"Don't do that!" he said half angry, half relieved he was alive and alright.

"Ha. Can't have both of us clueless. But, I would venture to ask if you know where we are?" Holve asked as he lay back down. He shut his eyes hard in an apparent attempt to ease the throbbing that must be going on inside his skull.

"Land," replied Ealrin simply and truthfully. That was all he knew. They were no longer floating at sea, but were now on some beach in either Thoran or the Southern Republic. Ealrin wasn't sure which.

"Well, that's a start," said Holve. "We can explore a bit when the sun comes up."

"You mean when your head stops throbbing," replied Ealrin.

Holve let out a mirthless laugh, and then a slight moan. He was obviously in pain.

"Roland..." began Ealrin. Holve cut him off.

"Roland died as he would have wished: bravely and in battle. He never saw himself living past being useful in a fight. He was a good friend and I'm sad to have lost him, but he died a warrior. He wouldn't have wanted anything less."

Still, thought Ealrin, he was gone.

Along with the entire crew of the *White Wind*. Captain Felicia Stormchaser, Urt, the dwarves, the elves, all of them.

Drowned in the sea or speared by a goblin sword or arrow.

The thought sickened Ealrin.

He had only recollection of the last few weeks, and already they bore more pain than he thought he could handle.

He lay down and tried to sleep but was overwhelmed by sorrow and hunger and thirst.

16: Wisym of Talgel

Wisym looked around her. Some of the elven warriors still rushed to put out fires. Others searched the forest floor for goblin attackers. Still others were chasing after those who had fled the battle into the morning. Occasionally the sound of a wounded one meeting its end would rise over the scrambling of feet on the forest floor. Typically, when an elf walked there would be no sound, save for the air that was disrupted from its resting place. Today was not a day for stealth, however. Today was a day of battle. Today was a day for recovering from a goblin raid.

Today was a day of mourning.

A few of her fellow commanders stood around her as she knelt at her fallen general's side. A goblin arrow had struck him in the heart. The cursed thing had punched through his armor, thick and elegant as it was. The poison was claiming his life quickly.

Galebre had walked the continent of Ruyn for twenty generations. He was the finest general the forest elves ever had. And he was taking his last few breaths here at the end of this senseless attack.

Wisym held his hand, knowing that he was too far gone for healing. The poison on this arrow was the strongest she had ever encountered.

Galebre's eyes were fluttering as he attempted to remain conscious. He blinked twice, as if struggling to focus, and then stared hard at Wisym.

"You fought well today, Wisym. The forest elves are safer thanks to you." His voice was barely more than a whisper. His chest heaved up and down with nearly every word as he struggled to breathe.

"Save your strength," Wisym replied. She didn't know what else to say. She knew he was dying. She knew these would be his last words. But she was never good at knowing what to do at the deathbed. So few times had she ever needed to come to this terrible moment for a fellow elf. Blessed with an unusually long life, to see an elf die in battle was much more common than old age. The latter was celebrated as the elf returning to the earth. An elf that died in war was mourned as missing the years they were meant to live. Fate had stolen from them. Fate was now taking away Galebre, the greatest elven general of the last five hundred years. His wounds were too grievous for healing.

Her one hundred years were not enough to make her a seasoned warrior, or an astute leader, or given her the ability to know what to say in the darkest of circumstances like these. So, she did what she knew she could.

She held his hand.

"The goblins didn't attack without purpose. Something is wrong, Wisym. Find out..."

A fit of coughing interrupted his sentence. Wisym held his hand as he struggled for breath. She could hardly conceal her tears from her fellow commanders, who looked down with heavy faces. A scream from a goblin nearby took their gaze for a moment. One had been found alive underneath his comrades. He was not a threat anymore. The elf that had found him withdrew her spear from its chest. She looked over towards the group who surrounded the general at the gates of the city of Talgel. Its beautiful white stone walls and tall spiral towers, however, could not mask the ugliness of battle. The white stones were stained with the black blood of goblins and the bright red of elves.

"Wisym. Wisym." Galebre's green eyes were fixed on the female elf's blue ones. She could see the intensity in his eyes, the same eyes that surveyed countless battlefields, and led the proud elves of Ruyn into battle again and again. Those eyes were slowly losing their light.

"I name you General. Lead them well..."

And with that, Galebre gave his last breath. His eyes still stared at Wisym, but she knew that they no longer saw. She reached up and closed his eyes with her fingers, then placed her fist on her chest, an elven salute of respect. She laid one of his hands on his own chest and finally relinquished her grasp on his other hand.

The other elves around mimicked her salute as she stood, finally taking her eyes off of her defeated leader and letting his last words soak into her mind.

She was now the general of the elves.

WISYM WALKED THE PERIMETER of the city with her four fellow commanders.

No. Not fellow commanders. Her commanders. She was now the general of the combined elven fighting force. She had to both push the thought from her mind, because it meant reliving the death of her general and the closest thing to a father she'd ever known, and to retain the notion because it was pivotal to her next steps.

Though requests for aid had been sent to Ingur and Breyland, neither had been answered. Not only had there been no news from either city, the messengers had not returned at all. Breyland was further away, so she supposed that it was possible the elf who rode on horseback was just delayed. The rider sent to the elven sister city of Ingur, however, could have ridden there and back again twice since leaving.

Surely the elves of their neighbor city would answer their plea for aid?

Unless, of course, they needed aid themselves.

Having swept the battlefield and made sure that there was no longer the threat of a second goblin attack, Wisym made up her mind. She would lead a march to Ingur to find out what had happened to the messenger and the fate of the city. Talgel could not be left undefended, however.

Splitting the elven troops was risky. There have always been so few.

Elves live much longer lives than humans, though similar in span to that of dwarves. To procreate quickly would mean an unstable population. It would mean using far too many of the forest's natural resources and bending it to submit to their wishes, rather than trying to live harmoniously with the woods.

The elves of the woods had always had such a high regard for the forest that they would never ask of it more than they could give back.

And so there have always been a smaller number of elves than of men.

She would split the army. Four hundred would march with her to Ingur and six hundred would stay behind. If Ingur was attacked, but unharmed, she could hope that they could spare enough warriors to bolster her own in case of a second attack. Talgel was easily the most heavily fortified city and would be the natural place Ingur residents would flee in troubled times.

If there was time to flee.

Her head spun.

As a commander she had never truly carried the weight of leading the entire elven army, only her detachment of soldiers. Is this what Galebre had to have done with every decision he made? Galebre.

Wisym shook her head to clear it and turned to her four commanders.

"Egon, Gonaeli. Stay here and ensure that Talgel is safe. Search the woods for any remaining goblins. Burn what bodies you find. We

can't have them spawning in our forest and blighting the woods with
their presence. Celdor, Finwe, you'll accompany me with your de-
tachments to Ingur. I fear for our sister. We will make haste to her to
ensure her safety and return with additional troops and the residents
of Ingur in case of additional goblin invasions. I fear this will not be
an isolated attack, and that more will follow. Egon and Gonaeli, prepare the city for refugees."

"Yes, Sister," came the reply from her four commanders. They
saluted her and departed from her in order to follow her commands.

The feeling was odd to her. She had commanded one hundred
before. Now she was to be in charge of one thousand. Though she
felt in her heart that she was right in her decision, parts of her still
second-guessed what was to come.

She needed to consult one last person.

"Ithrel," she said as she watched the four elves depart. "I need you
to come with me."

Ithrel was her shield maiden, a companion closer than a sister.
Together they had fought in many battles and survived because of
their great bond of friendship and trust.

Ithrel was taller than Wisym. In fact, the two were as opposite
as night and day. Wisym had long flowing blonde hair while Ithrel's
was short and brown. Wisym's eyes were blue and wide, while Ithrel's
were small and green. Wisym could recite poems and ballads from
memory and tell grand stories to friends and strangers alike. Ithrel
talked little. Actually, Wisym wasn't sure if any other elf, other than
herself, had heard her speak more than a few sentences in their entire
lifetime.

But both were bonded to Galebre. Ithrel and Wisym were both
his adopted children, having none of his own. Their parents had perished when they were quite young, only twenty. In elf years, that age
was still considered childlike. Galebre had taken them in and raised
them the only way he knew: as warriors. And yet the elf had been

kind and loving. Surely Ithrel would hurt for the old elf's passing as much as she.

Indeed, for the first time since the sounds of battle had diminished throughout the forest, Wisym looked into the eyes of her sister.

They were reddened and bloodshot. A single tear fell from her face.

Wisym took her by the hands.

"We must be strong, Ithrel. Galebre would desire us to be strong."

Ithrel shook her head to agree. She took back one of her hands and wiped another tear away.

"Come with me, Ithrel. We must beg the Elder's blessing."

EVERY ELVISH CITY HOUSED at least one Elder. An Elder was an elf who managed to outlive all others from his or her generation. The Elder of Talgel was approaching his 900th year. Miranthil sat up in his chair in the ancient elven hall of Elders. The chamber was made with the same white stones as the rest of Talgel and its walls reached higher than most others in the city. The top was opened, so that the stars of the night may be plainly seen. The hall was circular with black tiles as its floor. Several stone chairs lined with furs and pillows stood in a semicircle around the edge of a great raised platform.

Only one was filled, however.

His eyes were closed, whether in meditation or sleep, Wisym wasn't sure. His long white hair reached the floor and blended in with his white robes. Only one purple tree, the symbol of the elves of Talgel, was woven into his garment in its center. Wisym would have been able to see it had his beard not blocked her view. A small wooden wreath crowned his head: the symbol of an Elder of the city. His head rested against the back of his chair, and his mouth hung slightly open.

After walking to the middle of the chamber, atop the platform, she bowed to one knee. Ithrel mimicked her movements.

"Elder Miranthil," she spoke in a voice that she hoped would either wake him from his slumber or arise him from his meditations.

The Elder made a grunting noise. Wisym looked up in time to see him open his eyes. He blinked several times, and then smiled at Wisym.

Wisym stood to attention and spoke loudly, so that his ancient ears might hear her plea.

"Elder, we have been attacked by goblins. The army of Talgel has defeated them, but we are too few in number now to repel any additional attack. Galebre has fallen and named me general. We requested aid from Breyland and Ingur, but our pleas for help have gone unanswered. I seek to take soldiers to our sister city to see how it fares."

Wisym held her breath, hoping the old elf had not only heard her, but understood as well.

Of course, the Elder of an elven city was not the leader of the city. The elven Elders who resided in the capital of the Southern Republic delegated that task to others. Elves who were of younger age and spirit and could handle the daily tasks of running such a large community were given those tasks by the Head Elders.

To achieve such an age and become an Elder of the city meant one's task was simply to meditate and gaze into the future of the elves. Those who had lived so many years had time to study the ancient art of reading the stars for signs and predicting things to come.

Though it was not mandatory, it was customary to ask for the Elder's blessing before embarking on any significant venture, whether an auspicious building project, or the great hunt of a wild animal. To not receive such a blessing would be considered an ill omen, and many would cancel plans laid down for months if it did not carry the Elder's blessing. The blessing normally was a simple yes or no. The slightest nod of the head would be considered a verdict. Every plan of significance was brought before the Elders

Such as marching an army to an unknown fate.

Miranthil blinked several times. Then, with great effort and a wheezing voice that sounded as old as he looked, he spoke.

"Wisym. Adopted daughter of Galebre. I see great sorrow for you. Go, if you deem it wise. But know that you will never again see Talgel."

And with that Miranthil sighed deeply, closed his eyes, and reclined his head back upon his chair.

17: The Shores of the South

Exhaustion must have taken its toll at some point during the night. Though Ealrin had tossed and turned trying not to think about how hungry and how thirsty he was, he now opened his eyes to face the bright light of the morning suns rising.

His dreams had been filled with the howl of goblins, and the scream of friends. It's certainly had not been a restful night. Though his muscles and joints again protested, he rose to walk down the beach a little to stretch himself. Holve was still sound asleep, and Ealrin knew he needed his rest if he was to recover.

The sunlight reflected off the white sands of the beach, forcing Ealrin to squint, even though it was only morning. There were no other signs of debris from the wreckage of the *White Wind*, other than what remain lodged in the sand a few paces from the edge of the shore. Ealrin wondered what port or city would now bear the wrath of the raiding goblins. There didn't seem to be any nearby. Ealrin couldn't see any goblin ships on the horizon.

Slowly Holve walked up beside him. His step was uneven and he covered his eyes with his hand to avoid the bright sun. He wasn't fully well, and if Ealrin's own hunger was any indication of his, he must be starving and in need of water.

"Well," he said. "I've seen enough to know that we aren't in Thoran. At least not close to it. Most of their coastline is high cliff face. These are certainly the beaches of the Southern Republic."

Of course, they didn't end up where they had intended to, thought Ealrin. That would've made their journey too easy. And so far, fate had decided that nothing would be easy for Ealrin.

"Fortunately," Holve continued, "most of the cities of the Southern Republic have a port of some kind. If we head north that would also put us closer to Thoran. What do you think, Ealrin?"

The decision didn't seem like a difficult one, however Ealrin knew that their first priority was to find water. Without it, neither of them would be able to make a journey of any kind.

"I think we ought to head north," he replied. "But not before we find some water."

Holve nodded at him. In that small movement, Ealrin could see his obvious pain.

"I'm glad to see that losing your memory hasn't affected your common sense. You know what you're talking about."

Was Holve really that surprised? Ealrin didn't like being treated like a youth. But seeing as how Holve was injured, he would let it go. This time.

"I'll ask you another question; from where does the sea get its water?"

From the sky when it rains, Ealrin thought, though still a bit annoyed at the young pupil treatment. Then some of it was always there, also. *And from...*

"A river," he said out loud. He looked to his right and his left, north and south on the beach respectively. He couldn't tell if a river was nearby or not. And if one was not nearby, could they indeed walk far enough to find one?

"Exactly," Holve said as he started back to the lean to. Ealrin followed him.

"There are two rivers that feed into the Forean Sea on the west coast of The Southern Republic. And unless I was out cold for a week, and you swam us to the other side of Ruyn, we should be less than a day's journey to either a river or a port. Either way we can restock and resupply, but it's imperative that we continue north to Thoran."

Ealrin realized he hadn't asked Holve the reason they were going there in the first place.

"Blast!" Holve said after Ealrin had asked him why they must get to Thoran. "My notes! My maps! I'd only just now remembered!"

He'd spent the better part of three days writing copious notes in his journal, which now undoubtedly lay at the bottom of the sea.

"Oh well," he said. "Nothing changing that now. Let's get going. I'll explain why to Thoran later."

After they had gathered their weapons, folded the sail, and arranged it so Ealrin could carry it on his back, the two began walking north. It was slow going due to Holve, whose leg had been injured during the battle. Thankfully the cut was not deep, and the blade was not poisoned. Ealrin had cut a piece of the sail off and wrapped the wound sufficiently to stop the bleeding. The sand had gotten the wound infected slightly, but not so bad that it required immediate attention. They washed it with the salt water in order to stop it from spreading.

Perhaps, Ealrin thought, *we were fortunate after all.*

It was indeed half a day's journey to the river. He was thankful for Holve's knowledge of the land. Without him, Ealrin may have decided to head inland in hopes of finding a lake or city without knowing where one might actually be.

They drank from the flowing and fresh water freely, filling their empty bellies. Ealrin was beginning to have headaches of his own. The cool water was refreshing and drove the pain away from his head, as well as his badly chapped mouth.

While they spent time drinking, Holve was able to spear two fish. Being injured had not affected his skill.

Holve, after inspecting his catch, looked at Ealrin, "Gather some of the dryer wood farther away from the river. Leave me your sword."

Holve had gathered some dry brush and cleared a space of grass and weeds until it was mostly bare earth.

Ealrin was staring at him, trying to figure out what he was doing.

"Get us some wood Ealrin, otherwise we'll eat this fish while they are still wiggling!"

That was enough of a thought to turn Ealrin's stomach and cause him to search for wood. He handed Holve his weapon and walked up from the river to where the forest bed was no longer moist from the river. There were enough branches to give him an armful of wood in no time at all.

He returned to Holve and, to his surprise, saw a small fire started in the brush he had collected. He dropped his wood next to Holve, who was busy cleaning the fish. He sat down beside him.

"I'm glad to have you as a traveling companion," Ealrin told him as he put a fish on a smaller branch he had collected in order to cook it over the fire.

Holve just grunted and began to clean another fish.

"It's been a while since I've traveled with anyone honestly," said Holve as he watched his fish begin to steam. The smell of it made Ealrin's mouth water. He had been trying very hard not to think about how hungry he was.

"Roland had mentioned that," Ealrin said, saying the name of Roland with a pang in his voice. He only knew the man for a short time, and yet now it felt odd to be here without him. Why did Holve travel alone so often? Ealrin couldn't bear the idea of dealing with the loss of so many, and the prospect of walking to the next city without being sure of where he was by himself.

"Perhaps it's sufficed to say that several places I travel to are beyond what most would consider dangerous. It has generally been wiser to travel alone than to risk being uncovered by having a large traveling party."

Holve's voice was still normal, but buried within it, Ealrin sensed a grimness he had only heard once before: when he was mentioning the goblins. To where had Holve traveled that required he bring as little attention to himself as possible? He was about to ask when Holve began speaking again, cutting him off.

"You had asked why it was so important that we travel to Thoran. Well, to answer that, I must tell you that I am in the service of King Thoran the IV. He is both a wise and good king. He treats his people as if they were his children. He cares deeply for them. What concerns him is a gang of thieves, robbers, and sell-swords who simply are known as the Mercs. It fits them well as they are primarily a group of hired warriors. The Southern Republic employed their services for a time, in order to put down a rebellion in one of their own cities. Unknown to them, the Mercs were responsible for the rebellion itself. Only with the help of King Thoran were they able to route the bandits and drive them into the Crescent Mountains. At the time, they were crushed beyond survival, so the pursuit of them was halted. Or so it had seemed. That was ten years ago now. Not only have they survived, but also, they have grown in numbers that threaten the lives of many once again. This time they are moving up the eastern coast of the Southern Republic, or so my intelligence says, and are making their way to the Kingdom of Thoran."

Holve gave a great sigh. Ealrin could tell this weighed heavily on him. The sound of their fire and fish cooking intermingled with the occasional sea bird call.

"It would appear that they wish to settle a score with the king himself. I've been gathering as much information about them as possible from those who trust me and know about such matters. That was why I was at Good Harbor. It tends to be an excellent place to garner information about people who are more dubious in nature. I've learned much about their leader and his purposes and intend to report my findings to the king as soon as possible. Unfortunately, I was hoping to sway many of the crew aboard the *White Wind* to join our cause. Captain Stormchaser had been gathering those individuals for that very purpose while I collected information. That part of my mission has failed. I wonder why the goblins went undetected and attacked us so viciously. I assume they mean to raid the Southern Republic, but the ports along the inland are much more guarded than Good Harbor. I suppose time will tell. Now let me eat my fish, as I see you've all but finished yours!"

The fish in Ealrin's stomach was quite satisfying. On top of the water he had consumed, he almost felt full. He sat and watched Holve eat and thought about what he had said.

Mercenary raiders. Goblin ships. Countries dealing with rebellions. A king to whom Holve was in service. And a boat full of warriors meant to repel a threat now dead. It was like a story that meant the continent of Ruyn was a dangerous place for anyone. What part would Ealrin play in it all? He was unsure of any affiliation of his to a country. What would become of him after he arrived in Thoran with Holve? Would he find himself useful to the king as Holve had intended the crew of the *White Wind* to be?

Of his intended recruits for King Thoran, the only one he had managed to bring safely this far was unintentional.

What were the fates doing with Ealrin, he wondered.

AFTER HOLVE HAD EATEN, they again discussed their options.

"If this is the river I believe it is," Holve said, "then there's a city a day's walk upstream. But that will take us further east instead of north. It'll be a little out of our way, but we can restock and resupply there."

"We haven't any money or goods to trade," Ealrin pointed out.

Holve chuckled and replied, "You'll soon learn that I know a great many people who owe me favors or are generally good willed in my direction. In Weyfield, I have both."

And with that, the pair began to follow the river away from the coast and towards the east.

Keeping near the water had plenty of advantages for the traveling pair. It meant that whenever they became thirsty they were able to drink, and the river's water had proved a valuable asset to a great many trees as well. They found a berry bush that sustained them for the better part of the afternoon as they continued to walk. Holve speared a few more fish that they intended to cook once it became too dark to travel safely.

When night fell and the two could no longer see well, they set up the sail by hanging it on some tree branches and then over to another. It wasn't as sturdy as a lean-to, but it would shelter them through the night. It also served a dual role in blocking the fire from any suspicious eyes.

"I learned a long time ago that fires at night on the road attract trouble. You're best to avoid being seen by them if you can," Holve told Ealrin as he cooked his second fish of the day. "And for your future information, Weyfield is certainly up this river. Just a half-day's walk more, I think. The river that runs past it is surrounded by forest like this. The river down south is more of a grassy plains area. We aren't as far off of our course to Thoran as we could have been."

Ealrin was glad for that news. His back was beginning to protest sleeping on the ground. But for now, he was glad to have a belly full of fish, berries, and water. *Perhaps Holve is owed a favor by the owner of a nice inn located in Weyfield?*

With a full stomach and his thirst quenched, Ealrin was able to think about the crew of the *White Wind* without a bitter sorrow this night. Roland's death was easier to handle on a full stomach.

Still.

He wished more of the crew had survived. He knew for sure the dwarves had not. Their bodies were strewn about the deck. They also wanted to go down fighting. Ealrin knew he had seen at least one of the elves dead. The other was sure to have fallen to the goblins as well. And now that he thought about it, he wasn't certain of the fate of Urt or Captain Stormchaser either. He tried to push the thoughts of his fellow shipmates' fallen bodies from his mind.

That night his dreams were painful, but something else also stirred within him.

A desire to fight back.

18: Dwarven Stubbornness

Frerin and Khali stood on the ancient docks of the city of River Head. The stones on which they stood would receive ships sailing from Good Harbor and further locations. Boats both large and small would anchor next to these rocks pulled from the base of the surrounding mountains.

Frerin was fascinated with the architecture and design of the docks, even if they were man-made.

"I'm telling you, Khali," he said as they stood staring off into the horizon. "There's a thing or two a dwarf could learn from the stonework of a man."

"Bah," Khali huffed.

It was plain to Frerin that Khali was not as taken with the design and flow of the ancient harbor as he was.

Yes, dwarves build things that are sturdy and can stand the test of time; it's true, thought Frerin. But as he looked at the intricate designs woven into the top of the surface of the dock, he was more than a little interested in the handiwork that had been done many ages ago by a man.

It was certainly a strange tendency of Frerin to think so highly of anything constructed by a man. Most dwarves held such pride in their work that they saw anything made by the other races as subpar at best. The dwarven halls of the south and the glorious capital of the dwarves to the west certainly out shined the city of River Head in almost every aspect.

Still, Frerin appreciated the work of others not his own race when many dwarves would simply turn up their noses at the notion that someone could create something beautiful out of stone better than they.

Looking behind him, he could see the city of River Head, nestled in between two mountains, and admired the stonework of the city there as well. Like many of the cities in Thoran, this one was made predominantly of stones and rock. Most of the roofs were constructed of wooden planks to be sure, but everyone knew how long the stones would last. If they were well tended to, nice houses that have stood for 100 years could last on for a hundred more.

Frerin turned his attention back to the sea, scanning for the ship they had been waiting on for the last two weeks. Holve was meant to arrive during the first full moon of summer. Frerin looked up to the sky and saw the sinking twin suns on one horizon and the rising half-moon on the other.

For the first time since Frerin had met General Holve, he was late.

"What do you suppose has kept him?" Frerin asked Khali for at least the third time this day. And Khali's reply was the same as it has been for the last two weeks.

"Bah. Don't worry about it, Frerin. We will find out when he gets here."

Khali spat into the ocean.

It was a common thing for him to do, and Frerin had made it a habit of standing far enough away from his older companion to never be hit by stray spittle.

The two dwarves had traveled together for decades. It had been thirty years ago today that they had met when the goblins in the West had sailed to the Southern Republic. Their raids had caused several dwarves to emerge from their mountain homes and defend their country. It had been the first real test of the unity between the races of the Southern Republic since their founding one hundred years ago. Frerin and Khali fought side-by-side against the goblin hordes that threatened their ancient home.

Unfortunately, that same home would eventually fall to the goblins and be crushed underneath the weight of countless thousands of the gray-skinned beasts. Too overcome with grief due to the loss of their ancient home, the pair had traveled north into the mountains of Thoran. It was there that they had met a very young king Thoran, whom they had saved from bandits that had attacked him on one of his early hunting expeditions. After witnessing their fighting prowess, he begged them to join his elite group of fighters as soldiers who could train other dwarves to fight for Thoran. Having no other place to call home, the pair accepted and have been in his service ever since as part of "The King's Swords."

Though, technically, neither of them wielded a sword.

Being dwarves, they preferred the weapons of their race: Frerin a battle hammer, Khali a double-handed long ax, or halberd as they were called. The two would often get into a heated argument about which was the better weapon.

"Since my halberd's forging, it has slain 400 goblins, and I claim at least a third of those," Khali would argue.

"Ah, but my hammer has crushed the walls of several goblin settlements, and not to mention a fair few of their skulls as well. It's obviously the better weapon for ridding the world of that scum," Frerin would counter.

Today, however, there was no talk about which the better weapon was. There was no reminiscing about their old mountain home. The two didn't swap stories of who had drunk the most ale or climbed one of the continent's many mountains.

Today the pair only looked out to sea.

"As far as I'm concerned," Frerin said, "something has happened and we ought to go looking for him."

"Oh sure," Khali replied with a large dose of sarcasm and annoyance. "Let's both jump in the harbor and start swimming. We'll find him in no time." Frerin knew that part of the reason for his friend's hostility was the absence of the general. He paid it no mind.

"And as far as I'm concerned, the both of you are old worrywarts," came a voice from behind them. The elf who had spoken was walking on the dock in her usual light-footed manner. They say that an elf could walk right behind you in a forest, and unless they wanted you to, you would never know you were being trailed. Lote was a fair looking elf with brown hair that flowed down to her waist. Most of the time it was tied up with a ribbon or piece of cloth. Some mistook this for a needless accessory.

Lote wore it in order to keep the hair from her eyes when shooting her bow. Among her own kin, she was a deadly shot.

As she came up behind the dwarves she crossed her arms and looked down at them. She was tall, even for an elf, and had a long way to look.

"Both of you are worried sick about Holve, and there's no denying it."

Khali made to protest and began to point his short finger up at the elf, but she cut across him.

"If you weren't so concerned about him, you wouldn't be standing on this dock along with Frerin, Khali, Son of Karven." Frerin chuckled as he looked at his friend. He knew that Khali despised being addressed as his father's son. There was some bad blood there that, when brought up in conversation, could always get a rise out of Khali.

But then he noticed that the elf also looked out to sea with a hint of worry in her eyes.

"He'll show up," she said. Frerin guessed that it was more to reassure herself than to stop the worry of her two dwarven companions.

"At any rate," she said, returning her glare to the pair of dwarves. "We have been summoned back to the castle. We had better make haste."

With that, she turned around and began to walk back toward the city of River Head. Frerin watched her go for a moment, and then looked back at the horizon. He closed his fist and stuck his hand straight out to sea: a common sailor salute.

"May the wind be at your back, General Holve, and may the bounty of the sea be ahead."

"Bah. Old crusty sailor hogwash," said Khali.

As they went to collect their belongings from the inn they had stayed at for the last two weeks, Frerin couldn't help but notice that Khali turned back for a moment. He quickly mimicked the sailor salute out to the sea before turning to catch up with Frerin.

19: Weyfield's Plight

In the morning, after Holve and Ealrin folded up the sail and cleared away the remains of their fire to make it look like they had never been there. The two continued east in order to make it to the city of Weyfield. The river was their guide. Holve had told Ealrin that ships would travel up the deep river in order to drop off small loads of cargo to the city.

Ealrin was again thankful for the river. Though the spring morning was chilly, he knew that when the noon suns came he would be thirsty again. Holve's leg needed some real medical attention, however. They had been able to wash it, but the redness around the cut was increasing. At this time, it was not a threat, but if they went much longer without at least some medicinal herbs to put on it, Holve might be in real trouble. Ealrin hoped the friends Holve spoke of in Weyfield were gifted healers.

After several hours of walking, the pair finally cleared the forest and were able to see the plains on which Weyfield was built. Ealrin could indeed see the evidence of civilization. Roads of dirt and stone both came out from the city and went south as well as north. There were docks built along the river with houses next to them, possibly the dwelling places of fishermen and farmers. However, the thing that drew their attention the most was the black smoke rising from the area of buildings that Ealrin assumed had once been Weyfield.

Now it was nothing more than charred wood and black dust.

"Raiders," Holve said, quickening his pace. "Mercs. I'd wager anything against it."

At that moment, they saw what looked like six or seven men coming out one of a house. They threw their heads back in laughter as they carried out small chests and other possessions. From here, Ealrin could see the blades of their swords were covered in blood.

Holve swore and broke into a run. Ealrin ran with him, matching him step for step. He unsheathed his sword and prepared himself for the battle ahead. As they were running, Mercs saw them and rushed to engage the two fighters, who were outnumbered three to one.

While they were more than a stone throw away Holve loosed his spear and caught a raider square in the chest. Though the distance the spearhead traveled was great, the force of it knocked him backwards off his feet. Holve's rage was uncontainable. Weaponless, he threw himself into the first man he met, hitting him hard in the chest with his shoulder. Without so much as slowing down, Holve ran to the man his spear had become lodged in, set it free, and turned to face the five remaining men.

Ealrin reached the first and, instead of launching headfirst into combat, he yelled at the men who were now approaching him: three of the five.

"What's the meaning of this? What have you done?" he shouted as they continued their approach, weapons up and ready to strike.

The man who was in the middle of the group wore a smirk on his blackened and bloody face that told Ealrin this would be no time for talk: only battle.

The first sword came from above and Ealrin deftly blocked it, throwing a kick at its bearer to knock him aside. The second blade came from his left. He jumped back, just barely being nicked by the blade across his left shoulder. In retaliation, his own weapon quickly swung around with him, and ended the life of the man who had just wounded him.

Ealrin didn't know these people. He was certain they didn't know him. Yet here they were, trying to kill each other. Why was the world so full of violence and hate? There was no time to think. The man who was in the middle had lost his smirk. Instead, his face was filled with anger, rivaling that of Holve's, who was currently dispatching the second of his assailants.

Ealrin and the man exchanged several blows. This man was no common pillager. He was a skilled warrior. The man who had struck out at Ealrin first was regaining his footing, and making to join the fighting again, when Holve's spear caught him in the side. He let out a howl of pain, and fell to the ground.

After blocking yet another blow from the man, Ealrin charged him like the dwarves had shown him: headfirst and hard. The two fell to the ground, with Ealrin on top. He felt a jab of pain as he was punched in the ribs. He rolled off of the man and stood to his feet, ready to fight again. The man on the ground did not stand. Holve's spear was pointed directly at his throat.

"What is the meaning of this?" Holve asked through bared teeth. "This city had done you no wrong. Why have you burned it to ashes?"

The man's anger ebbed through his voice as he spoke for the first time:

"This city harbored the unclean. We have cleansed it of its filth!"

He attempted to knock aside Holve's spear with his arm. In return, Holve spun his spear around, and ensured that the man would never again rise off the ground where he lay.

Ealrin looked around him and saw the devastation.

People lay slain in the streets: either by the sword or by fire. It was horrible to see. And yet, down the main road another group of three men walked. They stopped abruptly, and then began to run. For some reason, Ealrin began to run, too. Holve followed him closely.

The men overturned an abandoned horse cart. One of them pulled out two small children, no older than twelve Ealrin thought.

Laughing, he threw the girl to one of his companions, who threw her up over his shoulder while she bit, scratched, screamed and fought him. He grabbed the boy by his shirt, and lifted him into the air. The boy kicked out at him, hard enough to make him grunt in pain. Ealrin was yelling at the men now. The one holding the boy turned to look at Holve and Ealrin. In what couldn't have been more than a breath, the man drew his sword and ran the boy through. Throwing him to the ground, he began towards Ealrin and Holve.

Ealrin was sprinting now, running at the men, swearing. He hadn't used these particular words in recent memory. They fell flat as he ran.

What was the purpose of this senseless violence?

"You foul barbarians! Surrender the girl immediately! Drop your weapons!" he yelled.

Two drew their swords and approached him, as the third, which was carrying the girl, ran off in the opposite direction. The young girl was screaming for the boy, who lay dying on the ground,

Before Ealrin realized how he had done it, the two men lay dead at his feet. His sword had been quicker than his thoughts; he had to save the girl. As he sprinted in her direction he felt deeply in his bones that his life depended on hers.

Holve had run ahead of him and had now caught up with the man. He threw the girl aside and scrambled for his weapon. Before he could retrieve it, he was skewered by Holve's spear.

The girl scampered away from Holve, and back to the boy who was under the cart with her.

Ealrin was at his side. His breathing was ragged as he coughed up blood. There were only moments of his life left. The girl was now beside them. Ealrin stood to give them room, and to survey the surrounding area. Were there others, they would soon encounter lurking in the next building?

"Dece! Dece! Don't die, Dece! Stay with me! Who will keep me safe if you die!? Dece! Dece!"

The girl broke down into sobs over the boy. Holve walked up slowly to them.

"With her sobbing like that, we're bound to attract every raider who hasn't heard us already. We've got to get somewhere safe," he said. Rage still burned on his face. Still, Ealrin could see pain in Holve's eyes.

"Dece! Dece!"

The light had gone from the boy's eyes. Ealrin bent down and shut them with his fingers. He then turned to the girl.

"I'm sorry, but we have to leave this place if we are to stay safe. You have to get somewhere safe. Do you have family nearby?"

The girl shook her head.

"Come with us. There's no safety in being out in the street."

She didn't answer.

"You have to come with us," he said, beginning to fear they would be set upon soon if they stayed where they were.

Ealrin wasn't sure his words were registering to her. Her eyes were still full of tears, yet her sobs had abated slightly. She was biting into her knuckles fiercely.

Finally, she nodded her head and stood over the boy. Ealrin took her hand.

Holve needed no further comment. He led the way down a side street, then to another. At every corner, he checked to see if anyone was close by or watching. They moved as quietly and as quickly as they could. Soon they found themselves at a door that was blackened and burned. Holve forced it open, motioned for them to go inside, and then closed the door behind them.

As soon as they were inside, Holve went straight to work. The occupants of the house were either no longer living or had run for it. He managed to find several things those raiders and looters wouldn't have found immediately satisfying: food, herbs, and other things useful for traveling. Apparently Holve knew this house well, for he scoured through cabinets and chests in the wrecked, and already run through, common area that would have gone unseen by someone unfamiliar with the house. Someone had come in through a back entrance, for the door was hanging from its hinges in an odd fashion, suggesting that it too had been forced open and then left hanging. Holve corrected it as best as he could, hiding them from view.

Ealrin turned his attention to the girl. She was shaking as she stared blankly off through a window. He moved her over to a chair and sat her down, then found a blanket and wrapped her in it. The shock was now taking its toll on her. Ealrin tried to get her to talk in order to bring her back to her senses.

"What's your name?" he asked gently.

For a moment, she just continued to stare out the window. A single tear fell from her cheek. After a long time, she answered softly:

"Blume. Blume Dearcrest."

Ealrin repeated the name out loud. It was a beautiful name. In fact, this girl did indeed look like she would blossom into a beautiful young woman. Her hair was long and blonde. Her face was still childlike, but those features were giving way to adulthood. The sadness that she bore now was the only thing keeping her green eyes from shining like Ealrin believed they could.

"Can you tell us what happened here?" He knew she had to keep talking. Something in him told him that she had to talk to stay in reality with Holve and him. Holve was still busying himself around the house. He had procured a pack of some sort and was filling it with the supplies he had laid out on the table beside Ealrin and Blume.

"They came before the suns had risen carrying torches and weapons. My brother and I were out in the streets early getting ready to open the shop our parents own. There were hundreds of them. They kept shouting that we were unclean and that the city had to be cleansed. They set fire to anything that would burn. They killed any who resisted them, but especially the non-humans. One of my friends, a girl elf, tried to run but..."

She paused. Whatever had happened to the girl elf would apparently haunt her for a long time. Tears began to flow again from her eyes, but she pressed on.

"My brother and I hid under a cart. We heard screams. The smoke was awful, but we lay as low as we could to try to avoid breathing it in. We were going to wait until night to sneak away. To find mom and dad. But then those men came and..."

Again, she paused.

Her brother, Ealrin thought.

How horrible to see your own brother killed right before your very eyes.

"As they lifted me into the air, I saw mom and dad's shop. It was burned terribly. I don't know if they were inside or if they made it or..."

Now she began to sob again. Ealrin didn't know what else he could do for her. He got up and searched for a cup. Finding one, he filled it with water. He gave it to her and she drank, though her hiccupping made it difficult for her to swallow.

Holve spoke.

"We haven't seen anyone in this city save for you and the raiders. We didn't pass anyone on our way, and I haven't seen anyone moving about yet either. I doubt you'll be safe if you stay here, but I can't guarantee your safety should you travel either."

"We can't leave her here, Holve," Ealrin said, standing up to face him. "This is no place for a child."

"Nor is the open road, where we'll be vulnerable to attack," Holve replied.

Ealrin looked back at the girl. She couldn't be more than twelve or thirteen. There was no way to ensure that her parents were alive, only to check the ruins of their shop to see if their bodies remained.

"We have to take her somewhere safe, Holve. We have to." Ealrin knew that his voice was pleading. He also knew that he now felt responsible for her, though he hardly knew who she was. A child on any journey would indeed be difficult, not to mention perilous for her. But the ruins of a city were no place for her either.

"We'll check her home for a sign that her parents are alive. If we can't find them, then we'll take her as far as the next city, but we can't risk taking her further than that. Breyland is two days journey from here. That'll be all we can do."

Ealrin was satisfied with that. But then he knew that there was one more thing to do.

"I'm sorry for the loss of your brother," he said as he knelt down to be level with Blume's eyes. He took one hand of hers into his. It was freezing cold and shaking. "Will you come with us? You don't know who we are, but know that while you are with us, no harm will come to you if it is within our power to prevent it."

For the first time, Blume looked Ealrin directly in the eyes. Hurt. Pain. Anger. Sorrow. They were all there in her eyes. But hiding behind all of these was something Ealrin could see quite clearly. A beautiful determination.

She nodded yes, and the pair became a trio.

THE SEARCH FOR HER house took only a few moments. She knew the town very well. Blume showed them the house and Holve checked inside. He returned outside with a grim look on his face and shook his head.

He had found her parents.

She begged him to return inside and retrieve something from the floor underneath her parent's bed: a small chest. While the rest of the house had been sacked, the chest she spoke of should still be intact and hidden. When Holve again emerged from the house, he handed her the chest. She clung to it as if her very life depended on it. It was no larger than Ealrin's two hands.

He offered to go inside to fetch some of her things, but she protested.

"I've nothing of value really. Our shop only sold enough to provide us our needs. My mother was to make me a new dress for the summer but..."

Ealrin understood. Her possessions she wore on her back.

Holve came over to her and looked at her properly. He then handed her a small knife in a sheath.

"Was this your father's knife?" he asked her quietly.

Taking it in one hand, while still clutching the chest with the other, she nodded.

"Take it. Wear it at all times. Whatever you do, don't take it off."

Holve rose and looked off to the east.

"We'll need to get going if we're to make it to Breyland. Nightfall will happen before we are too far down the road. I don't believe staying here will give us any advantages."

And with that, the three of them struck out from the ruins of Weyfield on the road to Breyland.

After they had climbed a hill, the full destruction of the city came into view as they glanced back at it. Blume looked back at what was once her home and stood silently for a moment. She then bowed her head and began to cry. Holve and Ealrin looked at each other. Ealrin bent down to one knee while Holve scanned the country around them.

The plains were beginning to fade and give way to the foothills of a mountain range that rose up from the northeast. The northern border of the Southern Republic was just beyond those mountains and past the next city they intended to leave Blume at. Ealrin had seen this on one of the maps Holve had showed him.

Ealrin took the girl by her shoulders and attempted to look into her eyes that were filled with tears and downcast.

"I can't imagine what this is must be like for you, but you have to understand something: you have nothing left behind you. All that you have is ahead. You could spend every day of the rest of your life looking back and regretting. Or, you could choose to walk forward and live on. Would your parents, or your brother, wish for you to give up and stand on this hill forever, or continue living? I don't know what lies ahead for you, Blume. But I do know that there is nothing back there for you either. There was great evil done today. You could choose to let that evil win by giving in to sadness and despair, or you could choose to fight against it by rising above it and showing the world what one good foot placed in front of the other can accomplish. Okay?"

Ealrin couldn't know whether these were the words she needed to hear or not. It was all he knew to say, though. He knew that some of those words spoke to him as well. Would he bemoan having lost his life before the crash of his ship in Good Harbor and his friend to the vile actions of goblins? Or would he instead keep living day by day in the face of great sadness and look for the one small thing that could sustain him: hope.

Slowly, Blume's tears stopped and she looked up at Ealrin. She whispered something into his ear that was barely audible.

Without hesitating, he complied with her request.

He lifted her off the ground, cradled her against his chest as if carrying his own child, and continued down the path with Holve at his side.

From this moment on, Ealrin felt that his first and most pressing need was to ensure the safety of and care for the little girl from Wey-field.

The one who no longer had a family.

20: A Time to Flee

Wisym stopped short when she crested the hill. Her scouts had confirmed her suspicions and reported to her four hours before; yet as she passed through the ancient trees that stood as sentinels in the forest of Ingur, she could not believe what her eyes were telling her.

Ingur lay in ruins.

The towers of their sister city lay crushed and broken among the ruins of what was once a beautiful elven metropolis. Trees that were older than the Elders lay fallen and burned. These revered forest sentinels would no longer stand to protect the dwellers of the woods.

There had been no answer for their calls to aid because there was no one left to respond.

Wisym gave the command to search the rubble for survivors, sure in her heart that there would be none.

The elves at her command spread out and searched underneath stones, trees, and bodies for any sign of life.

Wisym herself walked through the city with her constant companion, Ithrel, at her side. The words of the Elder still hung in her ears as she made her way to the Elder Tower of Ingur.

As they were sister cities, the towers that held their elders were identical to one another. Therefore, Wisym knew that underneath the great raised platform was a bunker of sorts: the very last line of survival among the residents of an elven city.

When she arrived at the tower, there were hardly any ruins to search.

The massive tower of Ingur that housed no less than seven Elders lay toppled in on itself. If there were survivors underneath the platform, they were beyond reach.

Wisym could imagine their pleas for help in her mind. Screams of desperate elves trapped under a mountain of rubble.

Wait. she thought. That was not made up in her head.

Wisym really did hear someone yelling for help. She turned to her friend to confirm what her ears were telling her, that someone nearby was alive.

"Elves!" Wisym cried out, knowing that some of the warriors she had brought from Talgel were close by. "To me!"

She followed the sounds, first faint and far away. As she ventured away from the Elder Tower and more toward the center of the city, the plea for help grew louder in her ears.

The center of town, as she had remembered it from its previous glory, used to be a beautiful sight. A white stone fountain stood in the middle of a courtyard paved with stones. Twelve beautiful and ancient trees rose up in a circle around the fountain. Around one half of the circle were the shops where elvish craftsmen and artisans could sell their wares. Around the other half stood the homes of ancient and noble families. This was a gathering place of the elves here. This was a place of business and training as well as a place to celebrate and commune with one another.

But the place she remembered in her mind's eye was very far away from the reality she saw when she entered the city center.

All that remained of the once glorious fountain was rubble. The pool that it had fed into it was ruined and, in one section, broken, allowing a steady stream of water to flow out of it.

The bodies of elves, warriors, children, women, and the old lay scattered in and among the city center. No one was spared for mercy or for pity. All were killed.

Save for the one elf that still cried out for help.

Wisym turned from the shops and followed the sounds of the voice in the shadow of one of the homes that surrounded the circular plaza.

And there outside of one of the houses, yet hidden underneath the trunk of one of the great ancient trees that surrounded the old fountain and other debris, lay a young servant elf. He could be no older than thirty, a child by elf reckoning. After clearing away some of the debris, she could see his eyes. He looked terrified. At the same time, as he looked into the eyes of Wisym, she saw a flood of relief wash over his face.

"Quick! Over here!" Wisym called.

Several elves came to aid her. They lifted off the young elf the tree that had trapped his leg to the ground. Wisym looked at the leg and said a silent thanks to her elders; it was not crushed.

Several elves lifted the boy out of the rumble and laid him down close by, not wanting to move him much in case he was injured internally.

"What happened here?" Wisym asked him. "Was it goblins?"

In her heart, she knew the answer. Though throughout the whole city she saw fallen elves, there was not one body of an attacker. No goblin corpse littered the streets. Goblins don't clean up after a battle. Goblins leave their dead in hopes to spawn more of their filth.

The arrows and shields that lay smashed in the streets were not the crude things made by goblin armorers.

These were much better made.

These were too well adorned.

The elf boy shook his head and spoke, though his voice was hoarse from lack of water and weak from lack of food.

"Men."

As the boy spoke the word, Wisym heard the drums of goblins in the forest. Side by side with the trumpets of the armies of men.

It was a deafening sound. As if thousands marched upon them.

She looked desperately for her scouts, who were stationed around the perimeter of the city. Ithrel placed a hand on her shoulder and pointed to the wall of Ingur. A scout was signaling to Wisym with a bow in one hand and an arrow in another. The signals were those used by elves who were great distances away from one another and so could not hear, but with their elven eyes could still see.

As Wisym saw the signs, she spoke them out loud.

"Men. Goblins. Thousand. Thousand. Thousand. Thousand. West. Fire."

Her decision was made as she scooped up the young elf.

"To the harbor. There is nothing left for us to defend here."

She looked down the street that led to the ocean harbor of Ingur and prayed that there would be a ship they could salvage. If they marched from the west, Talgel had fallen as well or was besieged and beyond the help of their small army.

There was nothing to go home to.

"We sail."

21: Holve's Surprises

E alrin carried Blume until the light of day was fading. They decided it would be wiser to make their camp for the night away from the road in case Merc raiders came looting down that road again. The provisions Holve had found made them a decent supper. Their camp was in the valley of two hills providing them cover from the road. No one would be able to see them or their fire, and in the failing light, their smoke would be undetectable.

For a long time, the three sat in silence and ate the small loaves of bread and cooked fowl Holve had managed to kill with his spear. His accuracy with his weapon of choice was incredible to see.

It was Holve who finished his meal first and broke the silence.

"Blume, I know the past day must have been the worst in your life, but do you think you could share with us anything you had heard about the Mercs before they attacked Weyfield?"

Ealrin could tell that Holve was both trying to be gentle in the asking and to also get whatever information from her he could. Perhaps it would help him learn more about the raiders' activities in the Southern Republic. Still, it may be too soon to expect Blume to give them any pertinent information considering the trauma of the day.

To his great surprise, she answered Holve. Her tone was flat and matter of fact, but she began to tell about how she had heard of the events leading up to today.

"The traders who came to my mom and dad's shop had talked about the Mercs making them pay for safe passage through the roads south of Weyfield. They all knew it was a payment to ensure that they would not be harmed by the Mercs themselves. That was what they meant by a 'safe passage.' They were the only bandits on the road to worry about. The merchants kept paying the fees because they knew they could make it back and they valued their necks. It meant that they charged more for their goods. Mom and dad often talked about how unfair it was.

"Then, one day, a shipment of Woodlander elven cloth was supposed to come into town. Instead of cloths, the cart that came into town carried the bodies of the Elven merchants. Scrawled on the cart was the word 'unclean.' My friend, the girl elf, had known many of them personally. She was devastated. Then later, the same thing happened with a dwarven shipment of weapons from the west, except this time it was a ship. All who were on board, men, women, dwarf, and elf, were killed. Again, a word was carved into its hull: 'filth.'

"Two days ago, a man in red robes came through town. His head was shaved, but his beard was long. He had a strange metal collar around his neck, as if he was chained to something. He carried a long pole with a sign on top that simply read: Cleanse the Unclean. He warned us to get rid of all the non-humans in the town or else judgment would come. A couple of the city folk ran him off and called him crazy.

"I guess today was what he warned us about. No one thought that anything would come of it. My family and I have always had a good relationship with anyone who came into our store, human or not. It's so wrong."

At this, she stopped talking and rested her chin on her arms. She had drawn her legs close to her and still huddled under the blanket Ealrin had borrowed from the house of Holve's friend. She stared into the fire, her eyes reflecting the flickering flames.

Ealrin thought for a time. Humans trying to destroy the other races? What was the meaning of this? All the dwarves and elves he had met had been wonderful company. They had the quirks and differences of their race about them of course, but to call them filth?

That was beyond ridiculous. But to kill them just because they were not human? That's insanity. It was unthinkable. Who could stir an army of raiders to believe that killing innocent dwarves and elves as well as other non-humans to be the right course of action? Such a person must truly be evil in their very core.

"Such talk is not unheard of," said Holve as he packed away the remaining food. "There are many who would rather believe that there is someone to blame for their problems."

"What problems could originate with the elves and the dwarves?" Ealrin asked, lost for how such a connection could be made.

"Well," said Holve. "Say for example you had a bad harvest this last fall. In reality it may just be that there was no rain, or it got too hot during the summer, or for a myriad of other reasons. But what if someone convinced you that it was due to dwarven mining."

Ealrin scoffed.

"No, listen," Holve said in answer to Ealrin's frustrated tone. "You could make an argument that their forging and mining had tampered with the minerals in the soil. That if the dwarves stop their mining that your crops would be better. Now, try to convince a dwarf to stop mining. It can't be done! It's their way of life. And so, if you can't convince him to stop, you force him to. By whatever means necessary. It is cruel when you think about it. But what if having those crops means putting food on your table? What if having those crops means your family can live? Do you suppose that someone would do anything to keep his family from starving? Men have gone to war for much less than that."

Ealrin thought about his words. Would he really come to terms with such a violent proposition if it meant that those he loved most dear would survive? Would he allow himself to believe that all of his worries were really caused by an entire race or races?

"Dad didn't believe that," Blume said without taking her eyes off the fire. "He said your problems were your own. That it was foolish to blame others for your own hardships. Some said it was because of the Dark Comet. I don't believe that either. They did this themselves and should be punished. Dad said everyone is responsible for their own life."

Blume was certainly much wiser than her years gave her credit for. Her parents must have truly loved her to instill such wisdom and knowledge into this little girl.

"I hope we encounter more people like your parents, little Blume." Holve said.

Ealrin agreed.

LIGHT BROKE THROUGH the night sky heralding the morning. Ealrin was more than grateful for the coming day.

He had offered to take the second watch of the night and, after being awoken by Holve in the middle of the night, he realized he was more than exhausted. He stoked the fire to provide some extra warmth and sat up as his friend lay down to sleep. They had agreed that they should stay up and look over Blume just in case any raiders or thieves decided to also stay off the beaten path. He watched his two companions, a warrior who had shown himself to be of the highest skill and caliber and a little girl whose family was violently taken from her, and wondered what their dreams were of. Ealrin could not shake from his mind the visions of violence and bloodshed he had witnessed in the past four days. They haunted him while he slept. He saw Roland being overtaken by the goblins. He saw Blume's brother being run through with the raider's sword.

He imagined what it might have been like to arrive in Thoran, surrounded by new companions and friends, as well as both Holve and Roland. Would the violence that haunted him now reach him eventually? Surely the Mercs would still have attacked Weyfield? And if Holve and Ealrin had not been there, would Blume be alive at this moment? Would she have been left to the despicable desires of the Mercs?

He pushed the thought from his mind.

It would be best to take his own advice, move on from what was past him, and seek instead to bring justice to those who had committed the terrible acts of the past week. He would not sit idly by while the innocent suffered. He would do whatever it took to fight back against such terrible evils.

And in his heart, he knew that this feeling was not only familiar, but also right.

AS THE FIST SUN PEAKED over the hill they had camped behind, Ealrin nudged Holve awake.

"Better get a move on, I suppose," he told his groggy companion.

Holve rose to his feet and walked around the camp once, twice, and then a third time. Ealrin supposed this was to get his blood flowing and his mind alert. Waking up was always the hardest part of the day for Ealrin.

"I certainly hope I don't snore as loudly as you do, friend," Holve said, looking down at Ealrin, who was now putting out the fire and attempting to erase the evidence of there ever being one here.

"You both snore and it's quite awful," said Blume, startling both men slightly. She had seemed to be in the deepest of sleep.

Holve let out a grunt, but then bent down to one knee to speak to her.

"Do you think you can walk today, little one?" He asked her.

"I will try. Especially if you stop calling me little one," she replied as she sat up, the blanket still surrounding her. "I'm nearly fourteen years old."

"My apologies, Miss Dearcrest," Holve gave a slight nod of his head, bowing to Blume.

Perhaps Ealrin had misjudged his friend. At first, he thought that Holve would begrudge bringing her to the next village and not treat her well. He was wrong and glad he was. Holve was great with her.

Blume smiled at him and said, "Apology accepted, Mister..."

"Bravestead, milady. Holve Bravestead," he said as he rose to his feet. "And this is the brave Sir Ealrin Bealouve. Or at least, we think he is."

Blume's face showed her confusion at Holve's statement. Ealrin stepped in.

"To take your mind off of walking and other things, let me tell you a story: mine so far," Ealrin said, holding out a hand to help Blume to her feet. She took his hand and got up. He noticed she still clung to the chest that Holve had extracted from her house.

After they had ensured that the roads looked clear, they began walking down the path and west towards Breyland.

Telling his tale indeed took their minds off the current tragedy they were facing. Blume asked some of the same questions Ealrin had already heard but was still unable to answer.

But then, after he finished answering the questions he could, she asked him "Do you think your family misses you?"

Looking down at the little girl by his side, he answered her truthfully, "I hope I have a family at all. And if I do, I don't want them to worry too much. I intend to find them at some point. Finding them, however, will mean that I'll need to remember where I'm from in the first place!"

"I hope you do remember," Blume said, returning his gaze. Her face was sad. It was no small wonder. She had lost everything dear to her. Ealrin had the hope that his family was alive somewhere and searching for him. Blume had no hope for a family. They were gone.

Perhaps she clung to hope for Ealrin because she had none of her own?

Ealrin again turned his attention to the road ahead of them. They hadn't met anyone since beginning their journey and it was nearly midday. Either the Mercs had come this way and it was already too late for Breyland or something else stopped the travelers and merchants from coming south. Ealrin feared they would know soon enough.

"What's in the chest, Blume?" he asked as he walked side by side with her.

She shuffled it in her arms. It was just big enough to be carried under one arm, but she clung to it with both hands and kept it near her chest.

"It's our family treasure," she said warily. Apparently, she did not completely trust them. And perhaps she was right not to. Aside from saving her from the Merc raider who was carrying her away, they were strangers to her. While she might have trusted them to watch over her while she slept, she was not yet willing to tell them what lay inside her chest. And that was okay.

"I don't doubt that it will be safe with you, Blume," Ealrin said. He hoped this conveyed that he had no desire to remove it from her. It was what she desired to remember her family by, he guessed. Let her hold it for as long as she liked.

He desired to change the subject, and asked Holve another question.

"What do you suppose the Merc's are trying to accomplish by raiding cities that harbor nonhuman races?"

"That is a question I've been thinking on since we came to Weyfield. I don't understand their reasoning. When the Elders of the Republic hired the Mercs originally, they were nothing more than a group of mercenaries who sought to make money. The trick was they had incited the rebellion they were meant to crush. No one was sure of their meaning then, and I'm surprised by their resurgence. And I must say that it takes a lot to surprise me when it comes to the goings on of Ruyn. Like the goblins. I can't help but wonder that the two are interconnected in some way that I cannot yet see."

With this, Holve had given Ealrin something to think about. But first...

"What do you mean by Elders?" he questioned him.

"Ah. I forgot that you've no clue what's going on around you," Holve said back to him in a mocking tone. Ealrin didn't mind too much. He was almost certain Holve was joking with him.

"The Southern Republic is made up of three different races: Dwarves, Elves, and Man. By all accounts, men outnumber the dwarves and elves by ten to one. However, the other races were here long before man. It must have been around one hundred years ago that a treaty was made. There was strife between the factions of man as well as the Woodlander Elves and the Dwarves of the Southern Range. A war with the goblins and trolls from the north caused them to unite. Assured that the three races could live in peace, the Southern Republic was formed. For each of the ten settlements, whether man or other race, two representatives are sent to the capital city of Conny. Six of them are the cities of men, two are the forest dwellings of elves, Talgel and Ingur, and the other are the mountain city and forge of dwarves, Cardun-Adush and Kaz-Ulum. Kaz means that it's a dwarven mining city.

"Each of these settlements designates its own elders and they speak for their people. So, on the council there are twenty all together: four dwarf, four elves, and twelve men. By allowing each of these a vote, they are able to keep peace between the two races. Though the men outnumber the other races, it is never wise to always go against them for every decision. For example, say your settlement voted against the dwarven right to mine a new mountain because you feared for damage to your crops? Well, what if that mine would

allow for you to arm the guards meant to protect your city? There
are trade-offs at all levels and that's what has kept the peace between
the races who share the southern peninsula. For the last one hundred
years, it has kept the peace between man and dwarf and elf. Until ten
years ago that is."

Ten years ago. Ealrin remembered that was when the rebellion
first occurred in the Southern Republic. Holve had mentioned that
just the other day.

"One of the Elders of Conny, the capital city, began to make a
case for an entirely human country. In other words, he wanted to either remove the others forcibly or exterminate them. Of course, the
talks didn't start that way. He spoke of better lands for elves and better mines for dwarves. Not all could see through to the end of his
dire plan. Some sided with him. He was removed by the vote of the
council, as well as with the recommendation of the Head Elder, the
closest thing to a single ruler the Southern Republic has. Disgraced,
he fled to Seagate and tried to stir up a coup. The Mercs were sent
in to deal with him but were really sided with him. It was then that
Thoran came to help drive the rebels to the mountains."

"Now they are a threat again. The question is: what is their end
goal this time? And what purpose could be served by burning down
an entire city?"

Holve let out a frustrated sigh. He stretched out his arms and let
them fall to his sides. Apparently, this journey wasn't going how he
had anticipated it either.

"So now we travel to inform the king," he said. "Perhaps the army
of Thoran could be used once again to put down this threat. Crush it
so that the Mercs no longer loot and pillage innocent cities and kill
its citizens."

And what role would he play in it, Ealrin wondered. He had
seen the destruction first-hand. He had witnessed violent acts that
spawned from a senseless hate of other races. This was not the time

to sit idly by, he thought. He would do whatever he could to bring justice to those who had committed these wrongs.

"Yes, I pray that the king will be able to make sense of what is happening here," Holve continued. "And take the necessary action to aid the Southern Republic in resolving it."

Ealrin wanted to know what he meant by "necessary action."

"Twenty years ago, when the Southern Republic called for the king's aid, he quickly and decisively deployed his army," Holve said. "I was one of the generals who helped him fight that battle."

"You? A general?" Ealrin asked, not hiding the surprise his voice.

Holve had been withholding that piece of information from him. Ealrin had assumed that he was a knight of some kind, or perhaps a warrior, or maybe an adviser to the king. But a general? That was a true surprise.

Holve chuckled as he replied, "Do I not seem like a leader of men?"

Ealrin was glad to see that a small smile had returned to Holve's face.

"I suppose now that you tell me it makes sense, but why was the general of an army spending time on the island of Good Harbor?" he asked.

"I told you that I was in service to the king," Holve replied. "But I am not a true citizen of Thoran. The king values my advice and my leadership during times of trial and war. There has not been a war on the continent for the last 10 years, so I was assigned the job of gathering information and bolstering the ranks of the king's personal knights."

"What country are you a citizen of?" Blume asked. She had been quiet for a time, but now that she had spoken, Ealrin was glad for her observation. He had not thought to ask.

Holve chuckled uneasily.

"To tell you the truth," he said, "I am in exile from my own country. I haven't seen it in many years."

Well, isn't Holve full of surprises today?

"Yes, it's been many winters since I've returned to my homeland. It's very far away from here, and not very often visited by those with common sense."

Blume gave him a questioning look that Ealrin interpreted. She wanted to know what country he spoke of.

"I think what lies down the road will be sufficient to take your mind off where I'm from," Holve said.

And he was right. As the three crested the hill they saw before them the city of Breyland. And surrounding it on every side were the tents and makeshift shelters of what was unmistakably Merc raiders.

22: Information

The trio sat around the table of the Gilded Mare eating their food and being thankful that fate had allowed them to arrive at this point unharmed.

They knew they had not been followed. Nor had anyone seen them and run ahead to report to the Merc leaders what had happened to the stragglers at Weyfield. The story of how two men had come and killed several Mercs and rescued a little girl had not yet made its way here.

Holve had to grudgingly agree with Ealrin's plan. If he were to collect information and give it to the king, what better place would he be able to gather it than in the heart of the Merc camp? They had entered the city without being questioned or noticed. Breyland, thankfully, was big enough that any number of passersby and strangers would come in and leave its borders without attracting much attention to themselves.

"Would your daughter like anything else to eat?" the innkeeper asked Ealrin.

"No, thank you. I think we've all about had our fill," he replied to the innkeeper. He huffed and walked away.

The decision was made before they had had a chance to discuss it. There were some strange looks when they came to the inn. Two grown men walking around with a 13-year-old girl unsupervised would certainly bring attention to them, and that was exactly the opposite of what they wanted.

Ealrin had told the innkeeper that he was Blume's father, and that they were traveling north to visit other family. Holve was playing the part of uncle. This had allowed them to be given one room with three beds without any further questions. Though the innkeeper felt shorted in that he had hoped they would take separate rooms.

But there was something about the greedy look in his eyes that unnerved Ealrin. Blume was more than fair looking, and could easily attract most men to her, especially with her striking blonde hair. Ealrin made a mental note to not leave her out of his sight.

"Tell me, Blume. Are you okay?" Ealrin asked her as the innkeeper was off busying himself with another table.

Blume sat quietly for a moment. She put her spoon down and continued to look into the plate she was eating from.

"It doesn't feel real," she said after a few moments.

Ealrin could understand such a feeling. He was still trying to recover from the loss of Roland as well as the crew of the *White Wind*. The action of the past two days had pushed it from his mind, but only when he was active. Sitting or lying alone with his thoughts brought up the images that haunted his sleep.

"Blume, you're still on your feet after losing your family as well as your friends and your whole city. There's much to be admired in a girl with such a high resilience," said Holve.

Ealrin, again, was surprised by how he spoke so well to her. Holve hadn't really shown him a great love for children, even older ones such as Blume. Then again, he had cared for Ealrin when he needed him. Perhaps this was Holve caring for Blume as well?

Blume looked up at the two of them. Fresh tears were rolling down her face now.

"Dad would always sing a song to me when I was scared or afraid or just sad. Would you like to hear it?" she asked them.

"Please," said Ealrin, leaning back in his chair to get a better look at the girl. Perhaps singing was the only thing she knew to do when she was sad or scared. Perhaps it would make her feel better. Either way, whatever would help this little girl cope, Ealrin was going to do.

Her voice was first low and cracked a bit with sadness. As she sang, she became more confident, and with her confidence, the beauty of the song increased.

"Over high mountains,
The sun chases spring.
Over the hilltops,
My love I will bring.
I'll rush through the meadow,
I'll run through the plains,
So that you will feel,
My dear love again.
Over the night sky,
And up with the stars,
My love will be with you,
Where ever you are.
No matter what heartaches,
Or trials that come
My love will come rising,
As sure as the suns."

After she had sung the last note, Ealrin raised a hand to his eye, wiping away a single tear. As he did, he noticed that several had looked over at their table. Perhaps the song had moved them, too.

Only Holve kept his head down, more interested in his food than the attention being put on them.

"That was beautiful, Blume," Ealrin said. "You sing well."

She sniffed.

"Singing is what helps when I don't know what else to do," she replied. "I feel like that now. Where will I go, Ealrin? What will I do?"

He had no answers at the moment. He had been thinking about this for a time. Obviously, she was not meant for battles or long journeys across the continent. Fate had put them together, and he wondered where fate would lead them now.

"I don't know either, Blume," Ealrin said as he put out his hand on the table on top of hers, "but we'll find out. Together if we can."

He gave a smile and then gathered her plate and cutlery up for her. She had finished her whole meal. Ealrin was becoming very fond of his adopted daughter. He wondered if he had children of his own. If he didn't, he made a commitment to have them in the future. He would like to be a dad.

As they sat there, Holve and Ealrin looked around the room to see who would be staying the night in the inn along with them.

Most of the patrons of the inn were a bit rough around the edges. Which is to say that they were an improvement over the raiders who walked the streets. If the Mercs had higher ups, these were them.

A group of four sat at a table and ordered food in such quantities that they kept the innkeeper fairly busy running back-and-forth from their table to the kitchen. They spoke with an air of importance, and so whatever they had to say may well be information Holve could report to the king. As they spoke, Holve and Ealrin did their best to listen in. Blume busied herself with eating everything that was in sight, apparently ravenous from their journey here.

"Do you think he'll make it back tonight?" asked the shortest of the group. He was younger than the rest, but no less muscular and battle hardened. His blonde, rough-cut hair gave him the air of one who either cared little for his looks, or one who tried very hard to achieve an air of indifference.

"Don't know, Xaxes. Better keep it together in case he does, though. He won't be happy about what happened in Sea Gate," replied the robust man sitting to Xaxes' left. He was taller and more muscular than any of his companions. His reddish hair, along with his stout arms and chest, made him stand out from the others. Yet, he was the most reserved and mature of the group.

"Sea Gate was not Xaxes' fault, Verde! And you know it," shot a long, black-haired man from across the table. "That little thief would have escaped us even if he hadn't gotten his prize. He knew the city too well."

This third man was lean and tall. Ealrin thought that there was something about him that resembled a hawk. Maybe it was his angular features or his long, black hair, flowing down to his chest.

"That'll do," replied Verde. "If he does come tonight, and I assume that he will, we will still need to explain how we lost the amulet."

Blume made a small noise, like a hiccup.

The four men turned to glance at Ealrin's table just as the door to the inn opened and they directed their attention to it instead.

In stepped a man who exemplified what it meant to be in order. His jacket was neatly pressed and his brown hair was combed precisely over his head. He wore a handlebar mustache that looked like it had never known a hair out of place. On one eye, he wore a round glass monocle. He stood at an average height, but there was something about him that made his presence larger than anyone else in the room. Like he was more than met the eye. His sword dangled from its sheath at his side.

He starred at the table of four men, and then quietly walked up the stairs to the left of the door that went to the rooms for guests. Silently, and with several glances at each other, the four men rose and followed him.

Ealrin had noticed that several patrons of the inn had nudged each other and nodded to their companions when he entered. Most looked at the man as he entered. Some stared. The only one not looking when he entered was Holve, who had directed his attention at this plate of food instead. It was as if he were trying to avoid being seen by the man.

He raised an eyebrow at Holve, who had resumed a normal posture at this point.

"Ealrin, I think we best retire for the night. What do you think?" There was the slightest hint of a plan in his voice other than sleeping. Ealrin also followed his eyes up the steps that the five men had just walked.

"I believe you're right. Come on, Blume. We ought to get some rest while we can. There's a big day tomorrow."

Ealrin rose and waited for Blume to do so as well. It took her a while, as she had let the chest lay on her lap as she had eaten. She refused to let it out of her possession. Not even for a moment in the room upstairs.

The three thanked the innkeeper for their meal and then walked upstairs to their room. At each door, Holve stopped for half a step to listen.

At the fourth door, he apparently heard what he was listening for, but then sent them on with a wave of his hand to their room, three more doors down. Ealrin and Blume went in quietly and shut the door behind them.

"Who was that man?" Blume asked as Ealrin sat down on his small bed. It was just large enough for his feet to hang off the end of it. They were all this length. Apparently, some beds were reserved for dwarves and halflings, those who were neither men, elves, dwarves nor any other race. Just smaller people. The room was certainly meant for them, as all of the things were a tad smaller than would make sense for a typical person.

It didn't bother Blume any. It meant all of the things were the right size for her.

"I'm not sure," said Ealrin. "I'm betting he's someone of great importance. He definitely had that air about him. Like he was the leader of the Mercs."

Ealrin paused. He didn't know what that would mean for them as they stayed here in the inn. Somehow, he felt like they should put as much distance as they could between themselves and Breyland.

But it had been his idea to gather information, so now they would have more than they had originally hoped.

"We may need to leave quickly if things should not go how we would like, Blume," he told her.

She was sitting on the bed across from him, still holding her chest in both of her hands. It was resting on her lap. She looked up at Ealrin, and then back down at her treasure box. She silently opened it and pulled out a beautiful necklace.

It was a simple silver chain, but on it rested a green jewel that Ealrin didn't recognize. It was about the size of his thumb. Two strands of silver entwined it several times, giving the illusion of growing vines encroaching on the precious stone.

No wonder she had kept it hidden. It must be valuable beyond the comprehension of a girl such as her. Then again, she had already surprised Ealrin by her wisdom. Perhaps she would again.

"That's a beautiful necklace," he told her. He hoped it didn't sound like he wished to have it from her. He wanted her to trust that he would protect her and look out for her, not steal her family's greatest treasure from under her nose.

"Dad owned a jewelry store in Weyfield. This was his favorite piece. It was never on sale in the store, always hidden in our family's house. We kept it safe," she told him as she fastened it to her neck and stuffed it inside her dress.

"If we have to leave quickly I don't want to risk losing it. It'll be safer on me than in a box."

Ealrin agreed and was about to ask more about the necklace when the door opened and they both jumped.

"Holve..."

"We are going to need to be very cautious about how we go about our departure from here," said Holve as he stepped into the room.

He wore a look of both surprise and anger.

"That man is Androlion, a former elder of the Southern Republic and for good reason. He was removed from his post for his radical ideas about racial cleansing, basically what we've just witnessed in Weyfield. This is going to get tricky quickly."

"You mean he's the one telling people to kill other races?" Blume asked him.

"Yes, I believe he is, Blume, but we shouldn't go..."

But before he could finish his sentence, Blume was out the door and back into the hallway.

Quickly the two men followed her. Holve was whispering as loud as he dared, "Blume! Get back here!"

"We need to hear what they're up to if we're going to stop them!" she whispered over her back as she crept down the hallway.

She lowered herself to the ground at the door where Holve had stopped as they made their way to their own room. Holve and Ealrin exchanged a glance, but then positioned themselves next to the door as well.

Ealrin pressed his ear to the door silently.

"...doesn't matter that we are not where we would like to be; the time to act will be very soon. Our friends from the west have begun what I pray will be distraction enough to throw most of the Southern Republic's attention towards the southern part of the peninsula, leaving us to do what must be done in Conny."

There was a general murmur of agreement and then one man spoke up. Ealrin thought it was the long-haired man from below.

"Sir, about the amulet you had requested we look into finding..."

"Yes, I'm aware that you have failed to bring it to me, but it is of little importance now. It will be harder to trace after the rebellion has begun, but I do imagine that it will surface again when the time is right. Believe me, however, I will not be as tolerant should you fail me again in the future, Darius."

There was a moment of quiet. Ealrin could barely make out the shuffling of chairs and bodies. Apparently, it was quite uncomfortable in the room at the moment.

"Sir," said the voice that belonged to Xaxes. "The amulet being lost was my fault. I did not do my due diligence..."

"Enough, Xaxes. I'll not have you taking the blame for what is truly the responsibility of the group."

Ealrin assumed that the one doing most of the talking at that moment belonged to the man who had walked in and was followed by the others into this room. He had no idea who he might be, though he was certain that Holve knew full well who he was. He also knew that they were seeking an amulet and planning something in Conny, the capital of the Southern Republic. Were these men going to attempt to burn down that city as well? And what purpose would that serve?

"Sir, when you have risen to power..."

"There will be no talk of that until all is..."

Blume had made a tiny squeak. A man had just walked up from the stairs below. Ealrin had been so intent on listening to the conversation that he didn't pay attention to the sound of him coming up the stairs.

And there they stood, Holve and Ealrin, ears pressed to the door while Blume kept watch. The man shouted, "Hey! What are you doing there?"

And at that moment, the man named Verde opened the door to the room and stared down at them, for he was taller than Holve by a head.

Ealrin acted without thinking. He kicked as hard as he could, sending Verde back enough steps to allow Holve to close the door. Ealrin grabbed up Blume and ran toward the man who had shouted at him, shoving him down the stairs.

The three of them fell into a heap at the bottom on the floor of the inn. Holve picked up Ealrin by the scruff of his shirt, and Ealrin grabbed Blume.

And with that the three of them raced out of the inn, with the shouts of the group of men following closely behind them.

23: A Quick Getaway

Ealrin held onto Blume's hand tightly as he followed Holve through the streets of Breyland. It was a much larger city than Good Harbor or Weyfield, at least as best as Ealrin could guess Weyfield was.

They darted from one street to the next. The moon had risen enough to light their way through the streets. Every now and then, a city lantern guided their path as well. Sometimes they were forced to hide in an alleyway as someone went past, running in search of them. Each time they did, Ealrin held his breath for fear of being caught. While he and Holve could easily deal with a few raiders, the idea of capture was not appealing. They would escape with what they knew now, rather than risk any more close calls.

It had been some time since they had heard the shouts of those behind them, but they feared staying in the city. Perhaps the trio didn't hear their pursuers because the Mercs had gone back to get more help finding them?

"If we give them time to comb the streets with their thugs, we'll be found out for sure. And Androlion will know who I am," said Holve. "We had better get out of the city and up to Thoran as quickly as possible."

Ealrin agreed, but on foot that would take too long. Then, as they rounded another corner, they came to another inn, a little smaller than the Gilded Mare. The three hid in an alleyway just before it as two men came riding their horses down the opposite end of the street. They talked in loud voices.

"I hope they find us another city to torch soon!"

"Ha! Yeah! That was the most fun I've had in years!"

The Mercs dismounted their horses, led them to the stable beside the inn, and then disappeared.

"Holve, normally I wouldn't suggest what I'm about to," said Ealrin.

"Under the circumstances, I don't think any in this group will disagree with you. Let's go." replied Holve.

Quietly they walked past the inn and into the stable. If there were stable attendants, they weren't around to be seen. The two horses that were just brought in were tied to a post and eating from their bags of grain. Ealrin loosened one and Holve released the other. Holve hopped up onto his stolen horse, while Ealrin helped Blume on top of his.

"I'm not really okay with stealing horses," she said as Ealrin lifted her up.

"Nor am I, but these horses belonged to the people who burned your city to the ground," he replied as he mounted the horse as well, Blume sitting in front of him so she wouldn't fall off easily.

"Does your wrong correct theirs?" she asked him, looking over her shoulder.

Ealrin knew the answer; he just didn't want to give it. Blume was certainly an older soul than her age let on.

"Hiyah!" he and Holve said in unison.

They were out of the city limits without any sound to accompany them save for the clip clop of the hooves of their stolen horses.

THEY RODE FOR HOURS. Stopping only for water at a stream to rest their horses for a moment, they rode by the light of the moon and until the first sun began its slow climb into the morning sky.

Ealrin was certain that Blume had dozed off at least twice. She lay resting now, leaning forward on the neck of their steed. He was weary himself, but he also knew that they must put as much distance as possible between themselves and any potential pursuers. He waited for the second sun to rise to ask his question.

"When will we reach the border that separates the Southern Republic from Thoran?" he asked Holve.

"A river makes the border between the two countries," Holve responded as he looked back at him. His eyes looked just as weary and bloodshot as Ealrin's. They both needed rest, but it would have to wait.

"I hope that we reach it before midday," Holve said as he turned his eyes back to scan the horizon. "It won't make us completely safe from the Mercs, as they have no territory, but I hope it will dissuade them a bit."

And so on they rode. The scenery continued to change. Small rolling hills changed into larger ones, and then in the distance Ealrin could see mountains creating a new horizon. Plains and grassy fields had characterized the Southern Republic. Thoran was to be distinguished by its impressive mountain ranges.

"I hope you know trails that our horses can ride through," said Ealrin, pointing to the mountainous landscape ahead of them.

Holve chuckled a little as he replied, "There is a pass through those mountains as old as the mountains themselves. You are in for a big change of scenery, Ealrin."

A little before midday, they came upon the river Holve talked about. And indeed, the mountains ahead of them rose up from this ancient riverbed. They were about to enter the kingdom of Thoran. The river's waters were beautiful. It was an impressive sight to see.

Presently they came to a mighty looking stone bridge that connected the two countries. On one end stood the flag that must represent the Southern Republic. It was a green flag with a trim of yellow. Inside the flag there were three smaller triangles stacked on top of one another that pointed downward. The triangles were a golden color, like the suns when they crest the horizon in the morning. The top triangle was red, the middle orange, and the bottom yellow. Each one its own color, yet all supporting the other. Ealrin wondered if this was to symbolize the three races living in harmony.

And how long that harmony could last.

As they came to the foot of the bridge, Holve stopped, turned his horse around, and looked back on the path that they had traveled.

"I've been traveling through the Southern Republic now for five years. It's almost become a home to me. It's odd that I'm in service to Thoran but have been so long delayed in returning to it," he spoke as he looked back over the country.

He didn't say it necessarily to Blume or to Ealrin, just out loud so that his head wouldn't trap his thoughts. Ealrin understood, if only just a little, the need to talk in order to clear one's mind. He had done so often himself lately.

Holve then turned and led his horse toward the bridge. The hooves of his steed rang loud and clear over the stonework of the ancient looking bridge. Ealrin led his horse and his fellow rider over as well.

"I've never been this far from home before. I've never left the area surrounding Weyfield, much less the Southern Republic," Blume said.

"How are you holding up?" Ealrin asked her.

He was not yet sure what they were going to do with her. While she slept he and Holve had spoken about her fate. They didn't think they could carry her to the capital. It was much too far: still a week's journey. But Liaf was much closer to them and would potentially have work for her. Maybe a family would take her in. Ealrin knew he would miss her whenever their paths diverged, as they must. He was beginning to enjoy being a father, in a manner of speaking.

"Better than I anticipated, I must say. Still, I miss them so much. Mom, Dad, and Dece. I can't believe they really are..."

She trailed off and Ealrin did his best to console her without words. He didn't have any that seemed appropriate anyway. How could someone say to a child that everything will be all right when they've lost everything?

"If I hadn't come with you, I don't know what would have become of me. Maybe I would have just given up and died myself. This adventure has taken my mind off my tragedy. In a way, it's helping me cope."

Again, Ealrin was surprised by her self-awareness and maturity. She must have been a bit of an enigma to other girls her age in Weyfield. He smiled to himself and cast a casual glance back over his shoulder at The Southern Republic.

It was just long enough to comprehend the ten Merc raiders racing their horses to the bridge with blood in their eyes.

24: The Speaker

"**M**ove, Holve! Quickly!"

Ealrin was shouting as he directed his horse towards Thoran and its mountains. They'd had too easy of an escape from Breyland. Of course, it would be assumed they would take a main road and travel either north to Thoran or south to the capital city of the Southern Republic. Judging by the shouts of the raiders behind them, there was a significant price on their three heads or a promotion in store for their capture or death.

Now was the time for speed.

The horses galloped as quickly as their strong legs would take them. Holve and Ealrin constantly reminded them with their commands how vital it was to race ahead. Ealrin shouted over the stomping of hooves at his fellow rider.

"We'll never outrun them. We're outnumbered. We need a strategy! What do we do?" he yelled desperately to Holve who was keeping side by side with him.

"I'm working that out as we ride. I remember a turn in the path just ahead. Do what I do when we come to it!" Holve shouted back.

The path between the mountains up until this point was straight and surrounded by some trees that provided shade from the hot suns. Now Ealrin could see the turn as they flew down the road. That was when the first arrow zipped by his head. He heard it more than saw it, for he was keeping low and his body spread out wide, protecting Blume, who was holding on to the horse's mane with all her might. It was a bad place for a little girl to be, of that there was no doubt. More arrows flew past them, sticking into trees or falling onto the pathway.

Ealrin prayed fate would spare them from becoming a direct hit. He glanced back to see that the men were still a fair way behind them and were letting arrows fly out of desperation more than assurance of a hit.

As Holve made the turn he had spoken of, he quickly hopped off his horse, took hold of his spear and hit the animal with the end of it to send it galloping down the road without him. He then grabbed on to the lowest tree branch closest to him and began to climb.

Ealrin followed suit. Before he got off his own horse he rode it under a branch and hoisted Blume up first to give her a head start. He then slapped his horse on its rear to send it following after Holve's and began to climb a tree a few paces away from Blume's. He would draw them away from her if need be.

The first four riders sped off down the trail, chasing after the riderless horses, apparently unaware of their trick. The next six, however, slowed down at the command of their leader: the long-haired general from the inn.

"These hoof marks show they got off here!" he shouted over the sound of stampeding horses.

"Look, sir!" A raider called out. "Footprints!"

He was pointing close to the tree that Holve had climbed. As he looked up from the prints he let out a small choke and a gasp as Holve's spear caught him in the chest.

The howl that came from Holve as he jumped from his perch was loud and strong. He collided into another raider and knocked him off his horse. Before any of them could react, he had already grabbed the man's sword and ended him before running to retrieve his spear from the now fallen horseman.

It was time to come to his friend's aid. Ealrin leapt from his own branch, about the height of two men, with his sword swinging high. He wasn't sure if it was fate or skill, but he managed to separate a Merc from his head as he fell from his tree. Holve had let the stolen sword fly and find a new home in the heart of another Merc who had turned to fire an arrow at Ealrin. Being saved in this manner allowed Ealrin to turn and face the general who was still on his own horse with a menacing looking trident at his side, ready to strike. Two other Mercs on their own horses were behind him. One raised his bow. The other raised a dagger high, ready to throw it.

Ealrin took a defensive stance with his sword, unsure if he would be able to block two projectiles and a trident. The Merc with his bow was about to let his arrow fly when a flash of white knocked him off his horse. Blume had jumped from her own tree and tackled the man, saving Ealrin from deflecting two missiles. The pair landed in a tangle on the ground. A spear came whistling through the air and finished off the Merc who was readying to throw his knife. The general was too distracted by the fate of his comrades to fully deflect Ealrin's sword. He had taken advantage of the chaos to run at the man and cut him along his thigh. He jabbed his trident at Ealrin before turning his horse off back towards Breyland.

"You'll not soon forget today!" he yelled as he rode back in the direction he had come from.

Ealrin then turned his attention to the Merc and to Blume, who was now being aided by Holve. He ran up to kill the man before any damage was done to the girl. The man let out a grunt of pain as the point of a sword ended his life. Yet his hand was still clutching the dagger he had pulled from its sheath.

The very same dagger that was now lodged in Blume's shoulder.

BLOOD FREELY SPILT from her wound as Ealrin laid her on her back.

He was terrified.

He had no skill in healing, as poor Holve's leg was still evidence of. He knew only that the blood that poured from her was far too much for someone so small to lose and live. He took off his jacket and did his best to cover the wound and stem the stream of red that was now coming faster from her.

"Holve!" he shouted at his friend. He could hear the terror in his own voice and knew that it must be frightening poor Blume, but he didn't know at this moment how he might conceal his fear. "Holve, what do we do?"

Holve stood above him looking sadly down at Blume. His face was smeared with the blood of the enemies that lay at his feet. He had retrieved the spear that he had used as a weapon of war and now leaned against it. Ealrin knew, at that moment, that Holve was only gifted in ending lives, not saving them.

He shook his head and dropped his gaze.

Blume looked up at Ealrin and smiled a faint and knowing smile. How could she be so calm at this moment? Surely she knew she was dying and that her life would soon be over. The adventure she had taken with them would be over soon. And it had been too short.

By saving his life, she had sacrificed her own.

Slowly, her uninjured arm rose to her neck, lightly pulling at her necklace until she found the jewel that was hidden under her dress. She turned it a few times in her fingers.

Perhaps she wished to hold her family's treasure one last time before she passed?

But then, as the jewel turned in her hands, she began to mutter something that was unintelligible to Ealrin. Words that sounded as if they were made up, or in another language. Ealrin looked back at Holve, who was now staring fixedly at Blume and her necklace.

Then a green light began to illuminate the jewel. Indeed, a light so bright that it stole the suns' rays and made them its own. Ealrin looked back at the jacket that covered her wounded shoulder and noticed another light coming from it. In fact, it the light was coming from the wound itself.

As the light faded, so did Blume. She let out a deep sigh and her head fell to one side. Ealrin was now shouting her name, but Holve took hold of him.

"Our little friend has been hiding a great skill," he said with a calm, steady voice. Apparently, he knew something Ealrin did not. When he saw his confused face, Holve gestured towards Blume's injured shoulder.

"I believe it would be okay to remove your jacket now. You may be surprised at what you see."

Reluctantly, Ealrin removed his jacket that was now stained with Blume's blood. And indeed, he let out a gasp when he saw her shoulder. Her dress was stained a deep maroon, and though it had a hole in it where the dagger had split the cloth, there was no evidence of any injury to her whatsoever. Her skin was soft and smooth and whole. There was not the faintest scar to show where the knife had plunged so deeply into her.

"How is this possible?" Ealrin asked, looking up at Holve.

Holve smiled down at Ealrin, and then looked back to Blume. She was breathing quite regularly and appeared to be asleep.

"We are in the presence of a Speaker."

BLUME SLEPT FOR THE rest of the day, and on into the night. Holve and Ealrin had moved themselves into the protection of a small cave that was far enough from the path to avoid anyone's gaze. The bodies of the fallen Raiders were hidden on the opposite side of the road underneath many tree limbs and leaves. Hopefully their stench would not attract any unwelcome looters to their camp. Not that they had anything on them worth stealing. Holve and Ealrin had relieved them of anything of value. They kept anything they could use for their journey to the next city in Thoran, the mountain town of Loran.

The small fire they had made inside the cave kept away the chill of the night and were just large enough to cook the rabbit that Holve had shot. The bow and arrow had come from a dead Merc. It now served them meat. Holve had figured that the smoke would be hidden by the failing light and the cloudy sky outside their cave.

Ealrin was trying to comprehend what had happened. Blume still slept peacefully, covered in several jackets to keep her warm as she lay next to the fire on the cold stone floor. He was certain he was going to watch her die, and then witnessed her life be spared by the light from the jewel that still hung around her neck. Holve had not spoken much of what he meant by calling her a Speaker. Only that they should protect her while she recovered as whatever she had done apparently drained her of all of her energy. Holve had made very clear that she would probably be ravenous when she woke up.

It did seem like the smell of the fire roasted rabbit was what roused Blume from her sleep. She sat up slowly and licked her lips, apparently also quite thirsty. Ealrin got her a container of water that they had pilfered from one of the Merc's and let her drink as much as she could, which turned out to be the entire thing.

"I hope we have more of that," she said as she let out a satisfied sigh.

Ealrin laughed in reply. "I believe we happen to be close to a certain river where we can get more. Are you hungry?"

"I'm famished," she replied. "Is that rabbit?"

Without much more comment, she began to greedily eat every piece Ealrin handed her. Holve was right. She had developed a bottomless pit of hunger. And just as Ealrin was thinking about him, he appeared at the entrance to the cave with another rabbit and two other containers now filled with water.

"I see our Speaker is awake now," he said as he came and sat next to the fire, preparing the rabbit to be cooked as he did. "And when were you planning on telling us that not only were you skilled in the magical art of healing, but also that you had a near flawless piece of Rimstone?"

Rimstone? The name triggered something in Ealrin, like a memory he could almost recall.

"What's Rimstone?" Ealrin asked. Already he could see the blush on Blume's face as she continued to eat her rabbit.

Holve put the rabbit on the spit he had made from a stick he carved sharp with a stolen knife. He began to spin it over the fire, roasting the meat that would be Blume's second helping. She was almost finished with the first rabbit. Ealrin had taken perhaps two bites; the rest was in her belly.

"Rimstone is found throughout the world. It's a rare stone of differing color and shape. It allows those who have the gift of Speaking to influence and change the elements around them. Those who are able to convince Rimstone to change the elements around them are called Speakers."

"Speak to the elements?" Ealrin asked. None of this sounded familiar.

"Say a Speaker here with us was able to speak to fire. He could easily take the fire and make it bigger, smaller, or give it a shape. But they wouldn't be able to do this through their own willpower or skill. They would need a Rimstone that had the ability to influence the element of fire. Several different Rimstones exist, some that are able to influence the known elements. Others have properties that are still being studied in the College of Magic of Irradan."

Holve paused to check on the meat of the rabbit on the spit. It wasn't done yet, for he returned it over the fire to continue to cook it.

"Then again, we have other Speakers who are able to influence Rimstone to mend wounds and cause bleeding to cease. It would seem that our friend here is able to heal wounds by Speaking through the Rimstone. What I'm lost for, though, and wondering if she'll explain to us, is how did she come to possess such a gift as a Rimstone necklace, and how in the world was she able to heal herself?"

Blume looked up from her rabbit to Holve, with a blush on her face, but Ealrin was more lost than before Holve began talking.

"Why is it such a feat to heal yourself?" Ealrin asked, looking at Blume who was now fiddling with her necklace.

"You see, one of the most advanced forms of Speaking involves convincing the elements to influence the Speaker. For most, causing a fire is easy due to it being outside of you. For a typical healer, convincing the elements to heal others is a much simpler, though still difficult, task than healing yourself. It isn't heard of except in the most skilled and powerful of Speakers."

Holve directed his gaze again towards Blume as he handed her the rabbit.

"How about we start with the easier of my two questions, hmm? How did you come to possess a Rimstone of healing?"

Blume accepted the rabbit and gingerly began cutting small pieces of meat from it, as it was still quite hot. She began speaking in a quiet but matter of fact tone.

"As far as I can remember we have owned the stone. It's been in our family for generations. It was my dad who fashioned it into this necklace."

She said this as she twirled the necklace in her fingers gingerly, as if admiring the handiwork of her father all over again.

"There aren't many known deposits of Rimstone in the Southern Republic," Holve said out loud. It was perhaps just a statement. Or was there something more in his voice, Ealrin wondered.

Blume returned his look.

"I swear our family has always owned the jewel. We're not thieves or crooks," she said as she put the necklace down and went back to her rabbit, still apparently hungry from her previous magical feat.

Holve relented.

"Okay, Blume. So, how did you learn how to heal with the stone?" he asked her.

Blume took a moment to answer because she was chewing a particularly tough piece of meat.

"My father really was a jeweler in the city, but that's not all he could do. He could make the necklace do things also. He had a way of making the precious metals and stones bend into shapes that other artisans just couldn't imitate. He was amazing. My brother could never get the hang of... what did you call it, Holve? Speaking? He could never Speak to the stone like Dad could. I tried to make the metal do what I asked, but it just wouldn't cooperate. Then, one day, Dad had gotten hurt pretty bad working in his shop. He hurt his hand and it looked like he wouldn't be able to make jewels like he used to. I don't know, but it just came to me that I could heal his hand. I saw bones mending and skin returning to its natural smoothness in my mind. So, using the necklace, I was able to mend his bones and repair the damage. It was more from desperation than anything else."

She paused from her story and looked back up at Holve and Ealrin.

"Whenever someone in our family was injured I could heal them, unless it happened in front of a lot of people. Dad never wanted a lot of attention drawn to us. Once my brother broke his arm in the field, but others were with us when it happened. I wanted so badly to fix it for him, but Dad forbid it. He hurt so badly that I healed him when they weren't paying attention and he pretended to have a broken arm for the next few months so that no one would know."

Holve was staring intently into the fire as he listened to Blume's story. Ealrin was speechless. She truly was talented beyond his comprehension. Blushing again, Blume busied herself with getting another bite of rabbit and drinking from the water container.

Then, after a long pause, Holve broke the silence.

"You speak of a natural ability, Blume. There are Speakers who study Rimstone for decades to achieve what you say you learned from just willing yourself to."

Holve studied her for a long time before speaking again.

"Has your family always lived in Weyfield? Or did you move there from somewhere else?" he asked her with a look on his face Ealrin couldn't place. Was it suspicion?

"Our grandfather moved to Weyfield when his father came with their family. I don't know where they moved from, though. Dad never actually told me the exact place. I always assumed it was somewhere else in the Southern Republic."

Holve made a sound that was something like a grunt or a sigh, and then added a log to the dwindling fire. He looked at the pair of them and just simply said, "Loran is the first town we'll encounter in Thoran. I pray that once we reach that small city we will be able to borrow horses to let us reach the king quickly. If Androlion is planning a coup in the Southern Republic, then King Thoran must be warned immediately. It may be too late for the Grand Elder. Perhaps even for the elder council, but that doesn't mean we can't try to prevent the bloodbath that would ensue should a civil war rise up from these seeds of rebellion. We'll need to travel at first light. Hopefully we can reach Loran in two days' walking."

There wasn't much conversation after that. Ealrin volunteered to take the first watch of the night to let Holve and Blume sleep. After hunting all afternoon, Holve was obviously drained. Blume was still recovering from her magical healing and needed rest as well.

Ealrin was happy to guard them as they slept.

There was much more to his adopted daughter than he knew, and more if he was to believe that Holve was suspicious of her. Perhaps she was hiding something from them and didn't completely trust them, even now.

One thing was for sure, though. Ealrin was in the presence of a gifted general, and now a Speaker of great magical power.

As Ealrin began to count the stars he could see through the tree-tops and listen for any signs of movement down on the road below, he felt that he could not ask for better traveling companions.

25: Androlion Fellgate

Androlion Fellgate sat on the armchair that had served as his throne for the past month. Here in Breyland, he was a king. In the inn that was made of wood and nails, he reigned. Men did his bidding without question. Whole cities were raised at his command. He was the ruler of this settlement, without question. He longed for finer things than a musty armchair and creaking floorboards.

Soon, his reign would extend far beyond the simple city.

Who else had been able to unite the warring Mercs under a single banner after they had been so utterly defeated? Who else had given them purpose other than looting and raiding at random? Who had been able to show them a vision of a great future?

It had been he, Androlion Fellgate, a former Elder of the Southern Republic and soon to be ruler of all men.

He was fit to be a king.

Fit to rule those who were lesser than he.

For he alone had been granted the privilege of foresight. He alone had seen what the future held for the continent of Ruyn and indeed, the rest of Gilia if they did not follow him.

After he had been ousted from his position as Elder those many years ago, he had been dejected and broken. His own followers turned him away. Those who claimed to be loyal knew that they could no longer find favor with any in power by befriending him.

With no one to help, he had wandered into the mountains, seeking to perish and be forgotten.

He was a miserable thing.

Yet it was as he stumbled in the darkness, tripping over bramble, brush, rock, and dirt, that he fell. Into the deep pit, he fell. It felt like he had fallen into the very bowels of the planet itself, never to reach to the other side, but rather to fall for an eternity.

There, he heard the voice.

A voice powerful and terrible, wonderful and awful at the same time. Androlion had first feared the voice that sounded like thunder and stone, but soon the voice began to tell him of his reign over men.

And he was no longer afraid but consumed.

Pictures flashed before his mind. Images of himself as a king seated on a throne and exalted.

Men bowed down to him, worshiped him as a god.

But it was only a possibility. One of many futures.

And it would not be unless the other races were subjugated and destroyed.

For a greater threat was coming.

A threat that stood to destroy them all.

The images he saw were terrible. Flame. Ruin. Destruction. He sat not on a throne, but on a pile of the bodies of those who had once worshiped him, now consumed by the demons of his mind.

Two futures, two possibilities. Either Androlion could reign or be ruined along with all other living things.

To cause his future to happen, it was up to him. The vision showed him how he could rule. Where stores of Rimstone could be gathered, harvested, and used to fight back the demons.

And he was shown the key to it all: the Rimstone of Demon Song.

He would control the precious stone and rule upon his throne.

At whatever cost.

When he had awoken from his dream on the mountain, he had been found by the remnants of the Mercs. They bandaged him. They listened to his ramblings in his fever and sickness. And when he had recovered, they followed him.

As it turns out, men are easily swayed to fear the future, to fear that which is unknown. Now that Fellgate knew of the coming darkness he could persuade others to follow him, to rid the continent of the blight of the elves and dwarves who hoarded the stone for themselves.

Unless men used it to stop the tide of what was coming, all would be consumed.

Androlion had learned that he could inspire others to believe that their misfortune was due to others. To begin to hate those who had caused them such hardships. To act upon those feelings of hate.

His thoughts were interrupted by Vyncent, one of his generals whom he had sent to capture the eavesdroppers, the spies.

Androlion leaned upon his arm and looked into the eyes of his general and knew.

He knew he had failed.

"My Lord, we were unable to bring back the..."

Androlion had made eye contact with him, the other general who stood at the door of his chamber. With a simple wave of his hand, a life was ended.

A worthless life of one who was unable to carry out orders.

Two Mercs came in and dragged away the former general.

"My Lord, shall I go and do what he was unable to?"

Androlion looked to Rayg.

Rayg was a man whom he could trust to do whatever he had asked of him, and yet Androlion feared the man's ambition. Oh well. His time would come, as all others who dared defy him.

"Go, Rayg. See that they are destroyed and that no word of our plans reaches the north. We need for our timing to be perfect. Take whatever men you need. I will see to the Speakers in your absence."

Rayg bowed and left the room.

Though he had successfully acquired as much Rimstone as the southern peninsula could offer, there was still more to be found. In the north, on the islands to the west, and the farthest reaches of the continent. More must be added.

In Rayg's absence, Androlion would see to those who were being trained to use the magic stones in battle. Rayg's knowledge of the stones was a boon in this coup, but also a threat to Androlion, who was unable to Speak through the stones.

In his time, Rayg would fall.

As would all of those closest to Androlion who knew too much. Secrets were safer with those whose lips could no longer speak.

Androlion rose from his chair and went to the window.

As Rayg left, another came on a horse. The assassin.

From here Androlion could see the smirk upon his lips.

Good, he thought. *Not all who do my bidding fail me.*

With those who opposed his way of thinking removed from power, it would be easy to march upon Conny and preach to those who were inclined to hear that others were responsible for their suffering. The Mercs readied themselves to move into the city and take what rightfully belonged to man and no other. For months the prophets of Androlion had been sent to preach hate in the chapels of the city. They preached that a better future was upon men.

They preached that an uncertain future awaited them unless they followed him.

Androlion Fellgate, the savior of men.

26: Purpose

In the morning, after Holve had woken both Ealrin and Blume, the three set out on the road again. They had not heard any signs of travelers during the night, or in the early hours of the morning, and didn't fear running into any now. The Mercs were content to let the three go, for now at least.

The day of walking was not a bad one. The spring air was cool and crisp, but warmed gently by the twin suns. There was not much talk as all three of them apparently had thoughts to settle.

Ealrin certainly did.

If Blume really was so talented at such a young age, with little to no training whatsoever, what could she potentially accomplish given the proper education? Could she become a Speaker the likes of which had not been seen before? Could she turn the tide of a battle that she may take part in later by healing the wounds of those who had fallen? Ealrin kept pondering and pondering until, at last, he could not hold his thoughts in his head any longer.

"Holve," he said as Blume was getting a drink of water from a creek, just out of earshot. "Perhaps we should take her all the way to the capital of Thoran. I know we planned to find her a home in a city along the way, but that hasn't quite worked out like we had intended. Not to mention, she'd be useful if we came into any more situations like we did yesterday."

He knew it was a stretch to ask Holve to allow her to come with them. They would travel more quickly without her that was for sure. But then again, she had healed so well back with the raiders that Ealrin was nearly resolved to take her to the capital to receive some type of training, even if he had to do it by himself.

Holve was studying her as she drank from the creek.

"I don't like the idea of bringing her further away from her home, honestly. Plus, we are still putting her in a lot of danger by having her journey with us. The open road is no place for children."

He paused as he spoke, changing his grip on his spear a few times, as if lost in thought.

"Still," he continued. "Her skill in Speaking is unbelievable, considering she has had no formal training. I would like to see what she could accomplish with the proper study."

He glanced up at Ealrin with a look of resolve on his face.

"Let's say this, shall we? We will take her to the capital of Thoran unless we perceive that she is in more danger there than she is here. Such a gift could become useful in the days ahead."

"Agreed," said Ealrin. He was glad Holve had given in so quickly to his idea. Perhaps he had been thinking the same thing? That Blume was useful to them now, and perhaps could become a very skilled Speaker later.

She walked back to where they stood, licking her lips and staring at them both.

"Well, are we going to stand around all day or keep going?" she asked them.

Holve gave Ealrin a look that said, "You wanted her to come," and continued down the road that would take them all the way to Loran, the first mountain town of Thoran.

IN THE CITY OF LORAN, the trio was able to barter for a pair of horses. They hardly dared to sleep at the inn for more than a few hours due to the urgency of their message. Holve not only now needed to inform the king that he was bringing scant few recruits for his order of knights (Ealrin being the sole volunteer to survive thus far), but that there was going to be war in The Southern Republic very soon unless Androlion was stopped.

Rumors of the Mercs' raiding had already reached as far as Loran, and Holve speculated that the king would be aware of their renewed presence as well. Apparently, he made it his business to know everything he possibly could about the entire continent of Ruyn. Because of this, the king could send aid where it was needed and avoid catastrophes where he was able to intervene.

That morning, they saddled up to prepare to depart from Loran. It would take a full week of riding to reach the capital of Thoran. Ealrin gave Blume the news of what they intended for her to do there.

"Holve has told me that in Thoran there is a small school of magic that is a branch of the larger college in Irradan. How would you like to study the craft of Speaking there? It would give you a place to belong, a new home, and maybe friends as well. You'd know your purpose, which is little better than I can say for myself right now," he said as they rode from Loran in the breaking daylight.

"Do you think they'd really allow me to study there, Ealrin?" she asked him hesitantly. "I overheard Holve telling you that they normally only accept students at a very young age."

Ealrin looked down at her as the horse continued to trot towards the edge of town. He could understand her trepidation, but there still remained her unexplained phenomenal talent.

"Blume, Holve also told me that a Speaker of your skill is normally no less than fifty winters. I don't think they'll be too worried about your age when you show them what you are capable of."

She smiled as she looked to the path they planned to travel on. Ealrin hoped that she would join the small school when they arrived in the capital. It would make him feel as if he had helped her find herself. If the girl with no family could not find a purpose, he would feel as if he had failed her.

Then again, over and over Blume had proven herself to be more resilient to tragedy and adversity than even Holve predicted. She had never once complained during their journey about sleeping on the hard ground or eating the rough food on the road. She had traveled very well, all things considered. She had certainly gotten more adventure than she had hoped for.

With her purpose all but resolved, Ealrin began to wonder what would become of him when they reached the capital. Holve had a job to do as a general of the king's army once more with the unrest in the south. Would the king accept Ealrin as a recruit? He had certainly been able to defend himself against Merc and goblin alike since departing from Good Harbor. Somewhere in his past, he must have learned how to handle a sword, for it was easier each time he had needed to use it to fight.

Still.

What would the king say of a man who had no memory and had only just met Holve within the last few weeks? Would he trust Ealrin enough to allow him to stay? Or would he think that the whole thing was a plot by Ealrin to... To what?

Maybe he was worrying too much about nothing. But there was some nagging feeling he had that he would not find his purpose with the King of Thoran.

He prayed he would.

Having no memory had not stopped him from helping those in need. He wanted to continue to help in whatever way he could.

ON THEIR FIFTH NIGHT of traveling, with the capital all but a day and a half away from them, the trio was encouraged that everything had gone as smoothly as it had. The roads had been clear of thieves and troublemakers. The weather had also been on their side. Normally the spring brought rain to the mountain ranges of Thoran, as it was want to cause clouds to form in the bowl of peaks that surrounded the country. No, this trip had gone very well.

So when they set up camp that night, after they had traveled farther than they had managed the day before, the group felt at ease and glad for the respite they would get during a good night's sleep under the protection of the giant tree they had set up camp under.

Ealrin had tried his best to hunt with the stolen bow and arrow, but was a terrible shot, no matter how still he held the bow or how much he tried to compensate for a flying bird or animal that would run away. Holve, on the other hand, was successful in bringing down two fowls and a mountain rabbit. They feasted on the freshly caught game as well as some roots that Blume had dug up from the soil around their camp. She had proven that she was able to identify edible plants from the dangerous ones. This was a very useful skill for anyone in the wild and Holve was impressed with her foraging skills.

"I told Ealrin that I normally don't travel with any companions, but I'm beginning to warm up to you two. The journey has not seemed nearly as long as it normally is. I may begin to travel accompanied from now on," Holve said as he took another bite of the bird he had shot.

"Don't go getting soft on me now, Holve," said Blume through a mouthful of rabbit.

She had definitely acquired a taste for it on this journey, Ealrin thought.

Whenever it was available she was pleased to help herself to it. "I've just now become accustomed to your disapproving glances!"

It started out a low chuckle in Ealrin, which made Holve start laughing in earnest. Before long the three of them were howling with laughter, which echoed throughout the night and into the tree they camped under.

And made the approach of twenty Mercs into the light of their fire that much more difficult to hear.

27: The King's Swords

"Well, if it isn't the trio that escaped Breyland and gave General Vyncent such a hard time outside of Loran," sneered the man who was obviously in charge of the operation. He was not someone Ealrin had seen before.

He held next to him a giant sword whose handle extended to almost as tall as he was. His hair was braided into a single braid that came across his left shoulder. The suit of armor he wore was dotted with small plates of metal that would allow him to move around easily but also deflect blows that were not straight and precise. The smile on his face said that he knew a secret that no one else did, and was loving the fact that he hid it from those present.

His guard of men, the other nineteen or so that now surrounded the group, was armed with swords, spears, axes, and other hand weapons. Ealrin was grateful that none carried bows, however the feeling was short lived, as he knew they were outnumbered six to one and that was taking Blume into account. He had only seen her heal wounds, not use her ability as a Speaker to fight. He hoped she had something up her sleeve; otherwise this would be a short battle.

Both he and Holve were separated from their weapons. Ealrin's was still in its sheath that was resting beside the saddle of the horse. A convenient spot for some time that wasn't this very moment. Holve's spear was sitting next to Blume, who was seated opposite him on the other side of the fire.

They were totally unprepared for this and it was not going to be easy to come out alive.

Holve, as usual, broke the silence that hung in the air after the man's remark.

"Well, I must congratulate you. It's been a long time since someone has been able to sneak up on me without my noticing. Well done."

After saying this, he rose to his feet and stretched, as if the whole affair were quite casual, and twenty men didn't stand poised to strike at him if he made a wrong move. He turned so that he could see the one who had spoken clearly. Meanwhile, Ealrin was trying to judge the distance between himself and his sword, and if he could grab it and be back by Blume's side in time to aid her in any way.

"My master would like to congratulate you for dispatching some of his best scouts. He admires skill when he sees it and would like to recognize you for it," said the man who Ealrin assumed must be a general or other leader in the Merc army.

"Those were some of your best?" Holve asked in mock surprise. "I must say you really need a larger pool to search from if that's all you can come up with. Though with your 'masters' views, I'm not surprised you have such a small range to choose from."

"He offers to you a way to repay him for the loss of his men," the man continued, ignoring Holve's comment for the time being. "Join him and all will be forgiven."

"I think it's safe to assume you know my answer is no, correct?" replied Holve. Was Ealrin imagining this or was he taking a different stance than Ealrin was used to seeing? At the moment he couldn't tell because, out of the corner of his eye, he watched Blume move her hand slowly to the necklace around her neck and begin to mutter a string of words he couldn't understand under her breath.

"If you choose not to come willingly, I have orders to bring you back alive by whatever means necessary so that he might tempt you into his service personally."

The men surrounding their campfire moved in to tighten up their circle. Most hoisted their arms carrying their weapons into a ready-to-strike position. Ealrin had all but decided that he was going to do his best to run for his sword while dragging Blume with him to protect her, when he heard the rustle of the tree above him. And was that Blume whispering to his left as well? Several of the men who surrounded them looked up to see what was causing the disturbance. That was when the very limbs of the tree came crashing down on them, as if they were arms that belonged to a very large giant or troll.

It was all Ealrin needed, he jumped to his feet and grabbed Blume by the scruff of her neck. She gasped quickly as she was pulled from her spot and was now being dragged to the place where Ealrin's sword rested. A Merc jumped out from behind the horse at them and at the same time, two arrows caught him in the chest.

Ealrin didn't take the time to see where the arrows came from or to find out if they were intended for him or the raider. He simply grabbed his sword from its sheath and turned to see that less than six of the original twenty still stood. Some had fallen due to the smashing they had received from the tree and the others were dead from arrows protruding from them in various angles.

There was someone fighting for them from the outside, he was sure of it. But what was causing the tree to come to life and aid them as well? Ealrin looked at Blume, whom he had drug with him to the tree and saw a look of exhaustion in her face. He knew now that the tree had acted based on Blume's wishes and that now she was losing her energy from speaking so mighty an act to occur. She would be defenseless in moments.

Ealrin took up a guarded pose, with his horse and the tree it was tied to behind him. He stood over Blume, who sat at his feet. He would not move from this spot. He would guard Blume with his life.

Holve had acted just as quickly as Ealrin. As the arrows began to fly, he dove for his spear and recovered by rolling in the grass towards a man with a spear of his own. The two exchanged only a few blows before Holve gained the upper hand and turned his attention to a foe that was still living.

The general had watched all this happen with snarling contempt. Ealrin knew that he would not be as easily defeated as his guards were. He took up his giant sword and began his slow and purposeful walk towards Ealrin. The look of loathing in his eyes was evident. Ealrin could tell that he was looking into the eyes of a man who did not like to lose.

Around them men and women were coming into the light of the fire. These were not the raiders who had originally encircled them, but instead these newcomers wore uniform colors and imagery on their clothes. Ealrin hoped he would live long enough to thank them for their rescue and to see what image they wore on their maroon colored garb. Currently, he readied himself to defend Blume from the death gaze of the man who was but a few steps away from him.

"Surrender the girl to me and I'll let you live," he said as he held his sword's handle with both hands. Ealrin was mystified as to how he could lift the massive blade. Why would he want Blume? Had he seen her Speaking to the elements earlier and knew that was how his men were crushed by the limbs of the tree?

"You'll claim her only after my life has spilled from me," Ealrin said with much more confidence than he felt. And yet, as when he had first run to Blume's aid in Weyfield, he knew that he must defend her. That in some way, her life was tied to his. He would not allow her to be taken or killed before he no longer had breath in him to defend her with.

"Fool," was his only response as he lifted his blade and lunged forward to attack.

The brute force of his weapon striking Ealrin's knocked him back against the trunk of the tree. This man was monstrously strong. Ealrin made several attempts to swing his blade at him. All were deflected as easily as one swats at a fly. Ealrin was outclassed and overpowered. Yet he would not give up.

The general made another forceful swing of his blade at Ealrin and again it knocked him back towards his horse. This was not the way to win this battle. He dove quickly to the man's feet and made to kick his legs out from underneath him, yet as he was in the air, the handle of the general's blade knocked him to the ground. Ealrin felt the wind go out of him. He saw the mighty blade rise into the air. He would be dead after the first swing of it.

Then two men came from Ealrin's right and threw themselves into his foe. With his preoccupation with Ealrin, the man was caught off guard and knocked backwards by the force of the two. They quickly regained their footing and raised their swords in preparation to strike.

Outraged that he had been denied his kill, the general let out a fierce howl of rage, and then began chanting in the same language that Blume had when she had healed her wounds by the river. Yet this sounded darker. More like the rumbling of thunder before a storm. And then both his eyes and his blade began to shine with a deep purple light, faintly at first, and then darker. The light rose from its source as if it were smoke from a fire and dissipated into the night sky.

Ealrin had managed to find his breath and his footing and returned to stand over Blume. She was barely holding up her head and breathing heavily, as if she had run a great distance and just now stopped to rest. Sweat poured from her forehead and Ealrin could tell in her eyes that only sheer determination kept her from slipping into the same sleep that had overtaken her before. She knew as Ealrin did that this was no time to lose sense of her surroundings. He stood by her as he watched the general lunge at the two men, both of whom were wearing the same maroon color as the others. They met his attack with full force. And yet every time they struck at him, he was there to block them. He moved with a speed that Ealrin had never encountered before and could only barely watch without becoming dizzy. Every time the glowing blade struck at one of the others wielded by his two defenders, it sparked as if had just been removed from a forger's fire.

And then one man yelled in pain. The general had a satisfied look on his face as his blade split the air across the chest of one of the men and sent him flying backwards. Enraged, the other made good at a chance to strike at his enemy, but a second swing of his sword nearly caught him across the chest as well. And it would have ended him had Holve not shoved him out of harm's way and struck with his own spear. The general let out a cry of pain as the spear pierced his abdomen. Then his blade came crashing down at Holve, who had not yet recovered from the momentum of his attack. In one swift motion, the blade fell and a great purple flame engulfed the man.

He was gone.

And Holve lay on the ground, writhing in pain and clutching his stomach. The purple blade had indeed found its mark.

Holve was going to die.

EALRIN WAS AT HOLVE's side, inspecting the wound. It wasn't bleeding as a normal sword wound would. Instead, it was pulsing with a sickly purple hue. His skin around the cut was turning a crude red and purple mixture. It began seeping into the rest of his body like a poison.

When their leader had departed, the two Merc raiders left threw down their arms and fled. They had been pursued by a handful of the uniformed soldiers, but the rest remained. Two were at the side of the man who had already died from his own run in with the sword of the general. One of them was the man Holve had pushed aside. He was sobbing into the chest that no longer moved up and down with the rhythmic signs of life.

Blume had just now crawled over to Holve and sat next to Ealrin. He could tell she was exhausted from her earlier magic. Still, she grabbed her jewel in one hand and placed another over the wound in Holve's belly. Again, she spoke in words that Ealrin could neither comprehend nor repeat if he tried.

Sweat poured down her brow in earnest as she spoke. Her hand began to shake violently, as a low green light began to shine through the hand clasped over her necklace. Unlike when she had healed herself, no light came from Holve's injuries. Just the spreading of the purple and red poison from his wound. He still writhed in pain on the ground.

"The wound won't... won't let me Speak to it," Blume gasped. "It's fighting me." She leaned to one side and Ealrin had to catch her before she fell over completely.

"I... I don't know if I... if I can help him," she breathed. She was panting hard from exhaustion. "I can try to isolate the damage..." her voice trailed off. She was running out of energy and was fighting to stay sitting up.

Tears began to form in Ealrin's eyes. Was he to lose another friend to senseless violence?

"It's okay, Blume," he choked. "You tried."

It was all he could manage to say. Blume's eyes rolled into the back of her head and she gave in to her desperate need for rest.

Two men came close to them and bent down next to Holve. One with shaggy brown hair spoke to Ealrin.

"If we hurry, we may be able to get him to the healers in Thoran. They may be able to save him. They've seen demon wounds like this before and have treated them with some success."

Ealrin looked the man in the eye. He had no idea who he was, nor why he and his fellow comrades came to their aid. Yet he felt as if he could trust them to care for Holve.

"Do what you can," Ealrin said through his strained voice. He didn't wish to betray his tears as weakness. Holve was the only friend he knew in the world. He didn't want to lose him.

"We will," the man replied, putting a hand on Ealrin's shoulder. "We have to. He's our general."

And with that, the two lifted Holve's body up to a rider on a horse. It wasn't the cries of pain that made the blood run cold in Ealrin. It was how limp his friend looked atop the horse. This was the same man who so skillfully fought with any who had opposed him. Now he was slipping away by the moment. They finally settled him in front of the rider.

"Make haste, Turnin. Tell the king what has happened," said the other man who had bent beside the shaggy brown haired man.

The man named Turnin gave a curt nod and then slapped the sides of his horse with his boots. Ealrin watched them ride into the night.

So, he was now in the presence of the army of Thoran.

THE GROUP BEGAN TO journey north, following behind Holve and Turnin. Ealrin hoisted Blume onto his horse and held the reigns as they walked ahead. There were eight of them in all headed to Thoran's capital, nine if you counted the man whose body they had placed on a horse to carry him back to Thoran to be buried properly, not thrown on the fire and burned like they had the Merc raiders. Including the four who chased after the two runners there were thirteen in all.

It didn't take Ealrin long to see that this was a mixed group, much like those who were aboard the *White Wind*. Elves, dwarves, and men alike wore the maroon colors of Thoran. Among them were two women. Their mood was somber at best. They had hoped to be able to come to their commander's rescue and it had not gone according to their plan.

The brown-haired man came up to Ealrin and walked beside him for a while before he spoke.

"Holve was to bring a host with him. We were meant to meet him at River Head a week ago. When word came of the goblin raiding, we feared the worst, and traveled south to see if he had come by a different route. We saw your fire as well as the Mercs attack. We... We had hoped to route them all and be reunited with Holve as well as the others he was to bring. How long have you traveled with him? What happened to the warriors he was going to bring? And where's Roland?"

A great sadness overcame Ealrin. This was a tale he was not wishing to tell without Holve standing by him. And yet it was all he could give these warriors at the moment.

Tale by tale he related being found by Holve at Good Harbor, encountering Roland, sailing on the *White Wind*, being attacked by goblins, shipwrecked, the destruction of Weyfield, finding and saving Blume, the encounter at Breyland, the subsequent escape that led to the discovering of Blume's ability, and the last few days of camping en route to Thoran's capital.

More than just the man he was walking with were listening. Some conversation had continued when Ealrin first began to retell his story, but by the tale's ending, everyone in the party was listening to him speak.

"And then you came," he concluded. "At every step, one of us should have perished. Yet the fates seem to have a different plan. At least, I hope that fate will continue for Holve. I hope he will live. Holve's been the reason I've gotten this far."

Ealrin fell silent after that, and the rest of the group didn't press him for more information at the moment.

Good, he thought.

He was drained from reliving everything and was glad for the moment's silence to think.

Wherever Ealrin went, destruction followed. What could he have done to prevent this? Was there anything he may have been able to do to save his friend? Though the scene played over and over again in his head, sometimes without his permission, he couldn't think of anything.

Holve's life rested solely in the hands of those healers in Thoran and fate.

"You had said something about a demon wound?" Ealrin said out loud after a long time of hearing nothing but the sound of hooves and boots on the road. "What is a demon wound?"

"General Rayg is no mere man," replied a dwarf carrying a large mace over his shoulder. His red beard was braided elaborately and hung down almost to his knees. "He's a Speaker of great skill, but also a charmer of demons and others from the nether."

The brown-haired man spat.

"Ruyn will be a better land once it's rid of his filth," he said with a tone of hatred and disgust.

"Aye," replied the dwarf. "But you'll soon learn that he can't be bested by any mere man. Most speakers you encounter get incredibly weak after they work their magic, as that little girl did," he said as he pointed a short finger towards Blume, who still lay peacefully asleep on the horse as they walked.

"Not Rayg. He's Speaking the language of demons and shades. He channels their power somehow into his. He's evil in the flesh, he is," said the dwarf. Then he made a huffing sound and added, "Which ought to tell you how good Holve is for wounding him."

Several murmurs of assent went up from those who were traveling with them. Apparently, these warriors held Holve in the highest regard.

Just like Ealrin.

THE GROUP ALTERNATED resting on the horses and walking so that they could reach the capital quickly. There was enough adrenaline rushing through them to make it through two days of constant walking, as long as they could rest on horseback.

Blume was the only one of them who was constantly riding. She was so drained from her two feats of Speaking that she could hardly hold herself up on the horse, let alone walk. Ealrin was her constant companion. The rest of the company took it upon themselves to be their guards. There were always two bows with arrows drawn on them at all times as they continued their journey to Thoran, the capital city.

The state of things must indeed be grim, Ealrin thought.

Though they were in the very heart of the country of Thoran, these soldiers moved as if in enemy territory. They could feel the tension in the air. The Mercs could not have traveled so far into Thoran unless there were others who were sympathetic to them and their cause. It did not bode well for the King.

Ealrin was worried about Holve, so instead of dwelling on the condition of his companion, he busied himself with asking about the new companions he was surrounded by: The King's Swords. The four who chased after the Mercs were elves. They were the quickest on their feet and the most deadly of trackers. The group was quite sure that those who had escaped would either meet a quick end or be brought back to Thoran without much trouble.

Four of the others were men. Well, three if you counted the one woman. Brute was a huge man, easily taller than Roland was and just as strong. He was the quietest of the group after hearing about Roland's passing. The two had shared many an adventure and were training partners. Ealrin knew better than to press him at this point. He was a barbarian of a man who carried a large mace in his hands, and a few small daggers around his waist. He may have a soft spot for a companion, but to cross him on the field of battle would be an entirely a different story.

The woman was a knight. She was dressed head to toe in armor and wielded two blades into battle. Her black hair was cut short but not unattractive. Were it not for her constant scowl as she surveyed the land before her she may have been beautiful. Something about her, however, pushed away all pretenses of worrying about looks. She was concerned with the fight ahead. She was a warrior at heart and had little time for pleasantries. She was also the leader of this group and was addressed only as "Milady." Ealrin didn't think it wise to ask her name.

The two who remained were brothers. Twins in fact. They resembled each other in nearly every way, save that one had brown hair and the other had blonde. They both wielded spears as Holve did and both had a slender but strong build. Cory, the one who had been speaking to Ealrin, was the easiest going, but alert to the situation at hand. Tory, blonde-haired and sullen, was leading the horse carrying the dead man: his best friend other than his brother. Gray was the same age as the twins and apparently bent on convincing those who didn't know them that they were actually triplets split apart at birth. Most believed him. Now he would no longer make the jokes that only the three of them knew. His body would be buried in the soldier's cemetery outside of Thoran. Tory's face was solemn as he led his friend's old horse to its master's grave.

Three dwarves also accompanied them. Two fit the mold of what a dwarf should be; according to those Ealrin had met. Frerin had a red beard that was braided. This was the dwarf who had spoken highly of Holve. The other, Khali, had brown hair that was less braided than his companions but not unkempt. He held a halberd, a long pole that had on its end an ax head larger than both of Ealrin's hands put together.

However, there was something odd about the last dwarf. She, and Ealrin could only guess it was a she for there was no beard on this dwarf, carried two smaller hammers than Ealrin thought a dwarf would carry. She also had affixed to her back a banner of sorts. It blew in the air and bore a black anvil on a maroon background. Ealrin learned that this dwarf, whose name was Narvi, was the forger of Thoran: the master weapon maker of the city, and, in fact, the country. She had come to Thoran to practice her skill because in the dwarven forge cities, the forgers are predominantly male. Ealrin wasn't sure if she had been outlawed from forging or had just wanted to have a better chance to see her skills put to good use. It could have been either way to hear her tell it. She promised to have a good look at Ealrin's sword when they returned to her workshop. Perhaps she could coax it into greater feats in battle.

Dwarves and their weapons, Ealrin thought. *Treating them as if they were living beings.*

As he thought it, his own weapon grew warm in his grasp.

And now I'm imagining it, he thought. That was foolish.

The last living member of the party was a female elf named Lote. She carried a large bow that enabled her to shoot just about anything in sight. Her deadly skill and accuracy ensured that the arrow she launched would hit its target. Her blonde hair was in a bun on the back of her head and her deep green eyes were always darting here and there, looking for the recipient of the arrow she kept continually strung on her bow.

The Southern Republic was not the only country in Ruyn that saw the benefit of using the skills of the three major races. Ealrin was glad of the difference in the company again. Just like on the *White Wind*.

He also hoped that this band would not meet the same fate as the last group he had traveled with.

BY MID-AFTERNOON ON the second day after Holve was injured by the Merc general, the city of Thoran rose up over the horizon. Though he was exhausted from his travels, Ealrin could not help but admire the beauty of the city and its castle. It rose up from the very base of the mountain and indeed, part of the castle must have been hewn from the range itself.

A vast wall rose up to protect its borders from intruders. A giant wooden door, which was strengthened by iron and bronze, guarded the entrance to the city. It was the only way in or out of the stronghold.

The doors were closed tight presently and Ealrin wondered how they might get past them, when a trumpet sounded from the wall and a maroon flag was waved back and forth next to the sound. The same imagery of two swords crossed behind a shield that was emblazoned with a crown was on the uniform of Ealrin's companions.

The soldiers were expected.

As they came closer to the city, Ealrin was able to see more clearly the construction of the wall. The giant blocks that formed the majority of it were taller than him and just as wide. They towered above him. He guessed that if ten men stood on each other's shoulders, they would still not reach the top of the great wall.

A set of smaller doors opened at the base of the large gate and the company filed through. They entered into the structure of the wall and Ealrin was in awe of the vastness of it. Corridors ran to his left and right through the inside of the wall. Eight soldiers could easily walk side by side and march through the inside of the wall itself.

The only thing that prevented any from doing it at the moment were more large doors about a stone's throw away. If the outside wall was ever demolished, the ruined part could be locked down so that no invader could get inside the city. It was brilliantly constructed and would be able to withstand the mightiest of attacks, Ealrin thought.

The party walked another ten paces and then was allowed through a second door, much like the first, on the other end of the wall.

If the wall was awe inspiring, the city itself was magnificent.

What must be the marketplace of Thoran was constructed of the type of rock that the wall was, only the stones were smaller. The shops rose into the air like mighty trees of an ancient forest. Ealrin could see people buying and selling on not only the Main Street that ran in front of him, but also on two streets that were laid over the tops of the shops on the ground level. The city was bustling with activity at the moment, though most who were close to the entrance took notice of the group who had just arrived and parted to make way for them.

Ealrin could see the castle ahead of him, blocked off by yet another wall. As they made their way down the finely stoned road, a knight on a horse rode up to them from that direction.

The man who rode the horse spoke in an official tone of reverence for the soldiers.

"His Majesty, King Thoran IV, wishes to welcome his valiant Swords home and wishes to speak with them as soon as they are rested from their travels. Your quarters are ready and a supper will be served as the sun sets so that you may speak with him. As for your company," the man looked straight at Ealrin and Blume on her horse. She had rested just enough to admire the gates as they were walking in properly and now sat up a little straighter. "He has prepared a set of rooms for them as well and wishes they also join him for supper."

Supper with the king? This was not what Ealrin had expected from his visit to Thoran, especially without Holve's intervention. Perhaps he may have had a quick audience with him, but this was beyond what he had imagined.

And Blume was also to attend?

"If you'll allow me to escort you to the castle."

"As always, Gaflion," said Cory as he gave a deep bow.

The group followed the man as he rode on horseback. Some people stopped what they were doing altogether to watch them pass. Others continued about their business without giving much of a glance towards the company.

When they reached the walls of the castle, two guards wearing maroon came up to assist Tory with his friend's body. They lowered him onto a stretcher of cloth and two wooden handles and carried him away. Tory watched them until they turned a corner and disappeared from sight.

Then he lost control of his emotions and broke down into sobs of crying.

His brother walked back to him and motioned the rest to go on ahead. Then, as if he remembered something, he called back to their host and said "Gaflion! See Ealrin and Blume to their rooms, please. They're unfamiliar with the castle and its rooms."

Gaflion nodded and rode on.

The courtyard of the castle was surrounded by beautiful gardens. It made a large rectangle that could hold several hundred people. Perhaps it could be used as a way to address a large number of people, as a balcony from the castle overlooked the courtyard below.

A man with a trumpet blew a few notes to announce their arrival into the beautiful grounds.

"Your quarters will be this direction," Gaflion said to Ealrin and Blume as he dismounted his horse.

"Can you walk, Blume?" Ealrin asked. He knew that she was still exhausted, as she had not yet had the opportunity to sleep lying down since their confrontation with the Mercs.

She shook her head. Ealrin helped her down off the horse and then lifted her off the ground. He then nodded to Gaflion to say that he was ready to take Blume to wherever she could rest.

Ealrin would be glad for the opportunity himself.

HIS QUARTERS WERE NO less fine than the king's, Ealrin thought to himself as he put on the clothes provided for him: a white linen shirt with black pants and boots. His old clothes lay folded in a pile on the least nice looking chair in the room, which was truly hard to decide upon as all the furniture was ornate and well taken care of.

He had taken a bath and cleaned the dust and dirt off of him from his journey here and already felt better than he had in days. He hoped that Blume was feeling as equally rested in her chambers, or at least had fallen asleep so that she could recover.

After having been cleaned and dressed, Ealrin began to feel anxious again for Holve. He had heard nothing about him since arriving and had not mentioned his name for fear of the news he may receive. Gray was to receive a soldier's funeral the next day at sundown. Would two be buried instead of only one?

His thoughts were racing with worry. He had tried to write in Elezar's journal to pass the time, but he couldn't focus. So instead of pacing his room, Ealrin decided to wander the grounds until he was called to supper with the King and his soldiers.

Long and well-decorated corridors met him at every doorway. Some held ornate tapestries depicting famous battles in the history of Thoran, others displayed past kings and queens with their families. It didn't take long for him to find a portrait of the current nobility.

King Thoran the IV. According to this picture, he was a tall man. His dark black hair matched his well-kept beard perfectly. In the painting, presumably his wife and the queen stood next to him. She was beautiful with her long and golden hair, blue eyes, and winning smile. Their three children stood before them. The oldest, a boy, stood proudly at his father's side, holding a sword and a scepter. His hair matched his father's, black and well combed. The middle, another boy, stood next to his brother and held a bow along with what must have been a kill he was proud of: one of the birds that inhabited the mountains of Thoran. His hair was more like his mother's, golden and longer, flowing almost with the wind in the picture. The third child was a girl, who held a dove with one hand and shield in the other. Her hair was long, but her face was familiar to Ealrin, though he was sure he had not met any royalty thus far. Only the members of the King's Swords.

"Ahem," said a voice that startled Ealrin. He had been so absorbed in the painting that he had not noticed a palace boy standing next to him at attention. The boy may have been standing there several moments before making the sound.

"Sir Ealrin Bealouve, supper is served in the dining hall."

28: Dwarven Aid

Wisym peered off the starboard side of her vessel.

The ship was in good condition considering the fate of the city they had brought it from. Though Ingur lay in ruins, neither the harbor nor any of the three vessels that were currently sailing were sullied by the battle fought next to them. Wisym could see no reason why the ships were left the way that they were. Hardly one stone was left on top another throughout the entire city yet these ships were stocked for a three-week long journey and hardly touched. They had been the only ships in the harbor.

Perhaps there was a great journey to be taken soon by the elves of Ingur that was cut short due to their untimely deaths.

Wisym thanked her Elders that they had been so lucky to find them in such good condition.

Of course, these three ships were stocked and ready for a crew of fifty apiece, though they now held six hundred. The boats were big enough as long as the elves didn't mind being in very close quarters. Even as the general of this army, and the only thing they had close to a leader, Wisym shared her quarters with five other elves.

Being closely packed together was a small price to pay for their current safety. What would become a problem in the near future was a lack of food and drinking water.

Wisym had assigned several elves to fishing duty. Though none she had with them were fishers by trade, most had some experience casting lines off of the harbor docks of Talgel or nets from the nearby beaches.

Unfortunately, fishing from a ship while out at the deep-sea was another issue entirely.

Wisym reminded herself to look over their food stores and do her best to ration what they had. There was no way to tell how long their journey would be, nor where it would take them.

Wisym returned to the main deck of her ship to consult the only map they had. Elves were, as a community, a very close-knit group. Those who would sail far from home or travel by any other means usually had very good reason to do so and were thought of as odd by the elves of Talgel and Ingur. Who would desire to leave the blessed canopy of that great forest of the elves?

Yet the idea pained Wisym, for she knew that the forest was sullied. The goblins had invaded her home and were repelled. Men had invaded Ingur and were victorious.

For what reason? Why were they being attacked? Typically, the land of the Southern Republic, though diverse and compact, was one of peace. She shook the thoughts from her mind so as to address the current question at hand.

To where were they sailing?

The map that Ithrel was considering was laid out on top of a piece of wood laid over a barrel.

All tables were currently serving as beds.

As Wisym stared at the map, she was in awe of its craftsmanship. The ink that covered the well-worn, but still intact, parchment was delicately applied. Each country on the continent of Ruyn was marked, along with each major city and settlement. There were too many smaller villages and towns to be named on a map covering such a large area.

They had sailed west as a start. The beating war drums and trumpets had come so quickly that in their haste, the elves had left with no real desire to know where they were heading. Survival was their goal.

After being at sea for a day, sailing directly west and sure that they were not being followed, Wisym held counsel with her generals and Ithrel about their next actions.

"River Head lies to the north," said Celdor. He was a battle worn elf, with a scar running the length of his face from a goblin's blade several human generations ago. He had fought bravely then and continued to fight well to this day. His brown hair was long and braided and reminded Wisym of the many trunks of a good forest. "Good Harbor to the southwest."

"What about this settlement? Dun-Gaza?" asked Wisym as she looked closer. It was the nearest city that they would see and closer than any other by far. Though sailing to it would put them far from Good Harbor.

"Dwarves. I doubt we'll find much help from them," Celdor said with more than a hint of disgust in his voice.

Among some of the elves there was a disdain for dwarves. Wisym had heard of wars long ago between the two races, long before men walked the earth. Yet now they were a part of the same country, the same republic. Why should they not aid them?

Though, Wisym found herself doubting those from her country now.

Men had attacked. Had they come from Weyfield? Breyland? From Conny itself? She looked over the map and saw that to sail up-river to either of those settlements would take far less time than it would to travel to Dun-Gaza.

And if it were aid they required to reclaim their forest, if indeed that was their purpose, Wisym had heard of no better warrior than a dwarf with a hammer.

Save perhaps for an elf with a bow.

"We sail for Dun-Gaza and beg for aid. Perhaps they will oblige us and put aside feelings from a long distant past," she said with a flick of her eye up to Celdor.

She was grateful for his battle knowledge and the skills he would bring to any fight.

But there could be no room for malice aboard this vessel, of that she was sure.

JUST AS THEY HAD COME within view of the mountain four days later, Wisym knew that something was wrong.

Smoke rose from the mountaintop as well as from many places on the island.

Dun-Gaza was ablaze.

Finwe wanted to sail in to see if they could find survivors. Celdor wanted to sail on and leave the dwarves to their own devices.

The decision was made for them, as two lone dwarves sailed out to the vessel.

"Turn around! Leave! You are not welcome! We'll have no more foreigners on our island! Get out!"

And then, in an old dwarven tongue, they hurled curses at the elven vessels.

Celdor grabbed a bow and strung an arrow.

Wisym quickly put her hand on the weapon.

"They've done nothing to harm us, I'll not have you harm them."

Celdor's eyes were slits of anger. Slowly, however, he obeyed his commander.

Wisym looked back out to the small boat and shouted.

"Master Dwarves! We are refugees from our own homeland! Goblins and men attacked our home! We need supplies and provisions! Let us get fresh water and we'll be on our way!"

More dwarven curses.

"Your trouble is on your own heads! We've been ruined by goblins and man alike! Find somewhere else to steer your pointy ears!"

"Please!" Wisym pleaded. "We are in need!"

"So are many who sail these waters! Good Harbor's been attacked and so has River Head! We've heard of many in need, but our mountain stands because we fought off those who attacked us! We'll not stand to be attacked again by elvish trickery or become victims of a scam! Be off!"

And with that, the dwarves rowed back to land.

"So much for dwarven aid," Celdor grumbled.

Wisym wished he wasn't right.

What had happened here that had caused the dwarves to be so defensive? Not in her lifetime had she been turned away from aid or rescue because of her race.

But the times were changing.

An elf signaled from the front of her ship. Wisym looked off the side to see what had caused the elf to signal danger.

Seven ships approached.

Though they didn't look like goblin ships or those of the dwarves, they did not look friendly.

Black flags flew from their masts.

"Pirates," Ithrel said.

Wisym cursed.

"Prepare for battle!" she called to the wind.

29: Supper with a King

The route the boy took Ealrin wound through the interior of the castle until he was sure that he was lost beyond hope. Then they came to a door that the boy opened for him and motioned that Ealrin should go inside. The view took his breath away.

Before him on the opposite wall rose windows that stood taller than three men and spanned the length of the room, which was more than a stone's throw from wall to wall. Ealrin could see the majority of the city from here and saw that, though the suns were beginning to set, Thoran was still a busy place. People hustled from one part of town to the next.

"I never wish to eat without understanding the effect any indulgence will have on my people," said a deep voice from Ealrin's left.

And standing before him must be King Thoran IV, for he looked every bit like the man who stood in the painting with his wife and three children: tall, dark-haired, and commanding. Yet in his dark eyes there was a gentleness that the painter had not been able to capture. There was a light of the understanding of the common man.

Ealrin bowed deeply before the king, but not for long.

"Rise, Ealrin. You've earned a good supper and a chance to dismiss a few formalities," Thoran spoke as he motioned to the table. Several members of the Swords were already seated, though none had any food on their plates.

How they could resist the spread before them was unimaginable, Ealrin thought.

Meat of all descriptions was laid before them, as well as several fruits and vegetables. Baskets of bread were set between every two chairs and cups, which looked to be made of silver, begged to be filled with the wine that sat in bottles before them.

Ealrin found an empty seat next to Cory and seated himself as well.

As the king came to his seat at the head of the table, the company rose. Ealrin followed suit.

Thoran spoke in a reverent manner.

"We eat in memory of those who gave their lives to ensure that tonight we eat in peace."

He took a cup in front of him and filled it with the wine from a bottle close to him.

"To Gray Furtherland. A Sword for the King!"

"A Sword for the King!" came the response from the rest of the group. As the king sat, so did they. Ealrin noticed that Tory, who sat across the table from his brother, had eyes that were red and swollen. Apparently, he was only just recovered enough from mourning to sit at the king's table tonight.

All the chairs were filled save for three to the left of the king. Ealrin did not see the queen at the table and assumed one of them would be for her. But who would sit in the other four?

The king began speaking to those who had assembled.

"I have heard about your short journey to find Holve and am pleased to let you know that it was not in vain. Thurin arrived a day before you did, and Holve is now in the care of my best healers. I am told he will not only survive but be able to have a speedy recovery."

The collective sigh of relief was felt throughout the room. Ealrin could feel tensions easing away as news of Holve's survival sunk in. He would not need to bury another friend just yet.

"I am also told," the king continued, "that his survival is due to the fact that his wound was contained quickly by a young and yet very gifted healer.

The King looked meaningfully at Ealrin and then around his table.

"And where is our talented Speaker?"

As if she had heard his summons, Blume stepped through a door at the opposite end of the room. Behind her followed the same attendant that had escorted Ealrin here. She looked clean and refreshed, but slightly embarrassed.

"I'm sorry," she spoke timidly. "Apparently I overslept."

The king arose as she took a step toward the table and motioned at a seat next to him.

"My dear, you have nothing to apologize for. It is because of your efforts, I'm told, that Holve still lives. Please come and sit as an honored guest."

When the king had risen, the rest of those seated had also. As Blume walked past Ealrin she gave him a nervous smile. Ealrin returned it with a wink. She would have no trouble asking permission to be accepted into the school of magic here. The king waited for her to take her seat and then he sat down again.

"I have asked you to join me for supper tonight to discuss what I fear are interconnected and disturbing events on the continent of Ruyn. But I have delayed you long enough. We will discuss these matters once you have eaten to regain your strength from your journey. Please, my Swords, eat well."

This was a command Ealrin was glad to obey. He was famished from the week's journey and eating only what they were able to shoot or find. He found himself eating whatever was within his reach. And in that small radius, there was quite the feast. Fruit of all types lay before him as well as a wide spread of other plants and vegetables. There were two types of birds and one other meat that Ealrin didn't recognize but found delicious. Before he had been able to sample everything, he found that his stomach could hold no more and so he simply sat back and took sips of his wine to finish off his meal.

As he observed his supper companions, he noticed that all of them were in better spirits at the news of Holve's survival. All except Tory, who was simply picking at his food. He had eaten a fair bit in order to obey his king, but now food could not satisfy his empty heart.

"I haven't thanked you properly, Tory," Ealrin spoke across the table. His were the first words to rise above smaller conversations going on around the table. "You and Gray saved my life when General Rayg attacked us. Thank you for your bravery and for your defense of Blume and me."

Tory looked up from his picked over plate.

"It's who we are," he said through a constricted throat. "It's what we do."

With this, he dropped his gaze into his plate. And yet, he continued to speak through his constricted throat.

"Gray and I grew up together. He was my second brother. His family was killed by a group of raiding goblins. Out of three other children and his parents, he was the only one to survive. Corey and I begged our father to take him in. We were eight and he was seven. Since then we've done everything together. Laugh. Fight. Grow up. We joined the King's Swords at the same time, though he was a year younger. For six years now we have defended those who were in need. He died doing what we have all sworn to do. I don't suppose he could've asked for more."

Tory then looked up at Ealrin with eyes that were still red, but now shown with determination.

"We are the Swords of the King," he said with a renewed boldness in his voice. "We are the defenders of Ruyn."

The king took notice of Ealrin and Tory's exchange and cleared his throat.

"I believe now is the time to tell you, Ealrin, about the group gathered before you and their purpose. To explain that to you will help you understand why they are gathered here now to hear about these unsettling events happening across our continent."

With this he gave a deep sigh.

"Some believe that their armies should have numbers like the rocks along our mountain ranges: immeasurable. Surely Beaton has always found its strength in numbers. I don't believe in having a military that is all consuming. Instead of using men as hammers and repeatedly banging against an enemy, suffering insurmountable loss and casualty, I use my army as one would delicately use a knife. Precision is what I value. The strength in tactics and advanced planning.

"Those you see gathered here before you," he made a gesture with his hands, indicating that the people seated around the table, "are my Swords, my weapons of choice. They are the leaders of my military. They are my finest knights. If I am able to fight a war using only those you see here before you, I will. They are elite fighters, every one of them.

"Every man in Thoran knows his way around a sword and a bow. We regularly train ordinary citizens, but I don't delight in seeing them arrayed for battle. They are bakers. Farmers. Artisans and craftsmen. I would have them stay that way. We have known peace for years now on the continent of Ruyn. Thoran has not seen war, other than the rebellion in the Southern Republic, for one hundred years. I would prefer it to stay that way. Having a large army means needing to use it. Instead of telling a family that their father is dead because of my actions, I would keep them safe within these walls if it is possible."

"My Swords you see here are a different story." With this statement, the king looked fondly at those gathered around him. Ealrin could tell he was proud of his warriors.

"These Swords know battle. They have fought in hundreds of skirmishes. All of them necessary acts to stave off a greater conflict or war. They are my finest fighters. They are the defenders of those who need it. They are the keepers of peace."

The king rose from the table and walked over to a large map that was hung on the wall opposite of the great windows. Ealrin admired the map in all of its detail and craftsmanship. The top of it rose well above the king's head and went nearly all the way to the floor. It was wider than two men standing with their arms outstretched. It had in detail every city, Mountain range, forest, and country, on the entire south eastern side of the continent of Ruyn. There were several pins of different colors placed around the map. Some of them had pieces of paper with notes written on them hanging from it, while others were simply just round and metallic.

"Unfortunately," he spoke as he viewed the map, his back to the table. "We now know that there is a war brewing in the hearts of our southern neighbors, though perhaps not from their leadership. Ten years ago we helped to put down a rebellion led by a former Elder of the Southern Republic, Androlion Fellgate."

The king shook his head and looked at the floor.

"A madman who quests for power."

The King pointed towards both Weyfield and Breyland as he returned his gaze to the map.

"We know of Merc activity and in both of these cities of the Southern Republic. Holve told me how they burned Weyfield to the ground. They are now camped within the city of Breyland. What worries me is this high concentration of raiders without any response from the army of the Southern Republic. It would seem that he had either stirred the general population to agree with his views or somehow managed to silence his opposition. The latter would be difficult unless..."

Here he paused and again shook his head. After a moment he let out a deep sigh and returned his gaze to the table.

"The Southern Republic is ruled equally by the three major races. If Androlion has quieted the elves and dwarves, I fear that there may no longer be any other race in the Southern Republic other than humans. If that is not the case yet, it is certainly how he would like it to be."

Ealrin looked around the table. Determination showed on every face. Determination and resolve to stop a madman.

"My Swords. It is time to gather our people and go again to aid the Southern Republic. This is not a time for some to fight. Now is the time for all. If Androlion takes control of the south, he will exterminate the other races there and then surely turn his attention here. He must be stopped."

"And yet there are still threats to be dealt with, Your Majesty," said a voice that Ealrin knew well and had not heard in several days.

Holve Bravestead walked slowly from a door on the opposite end of the hall as had the king. Thurin came up behind him. Ealrin could tell that he was readying himself to catch the unsteady Holve if need be. Ealrin was just glad to see his friend alive. He looked at Blume, who looked equally happy.

"The goblins that raided our ship have traveled north and are now attacking River Head as we speak. The message just arrived."

Behind Holve and Thurin walked a man who was breathless and weary looking. He looked as if he had been traveling hard. He bowed to the king.

"It's true, Your Majesty. Goblin ships sail the Crow's Sea. They began their raids just as I was sent to deliver this message. We need aid."

The king looked from messenger, to Holve, to Ealrin, and back. He stroked his beard thoughtfully.

"Goblins raid Thoran. The Mercs burn cities in the south. Could the timing be incidental or perhaps orchestrated?"

"By whom, Your majesty?" Cory raised the question. "Surely not Androlion. He has more disgust for goblins than any other race."

Again, the king thought for a moment.

"We may not know all the details as of yet, but I fear for my people. If the goblins raid, we must defeat them. If the Southern Republic is in danger of collapse, we must come to their aid." His eyes showed a great sadness as Ealrin could tell he was unhappy with what must be done. "We must ready the people for war."

"My Swords." The king walked back to his chair and stood beside it as he spoke. "Each of you is to take ten of your best men to River Head. Intercept the goblins there. Surely they can be defeated by your cunning and skill. I will gather the people and march for Loran. There I will await your return so that we may aid the Southern Republic."

Everyone at the table stood as the king held his cup high again. Ealrin stood with them and took his own cup in hand as did the others.

"For peace on Ruyn!" he called to them.

"We are Swords of the King!" was their reply.

The king excused himself as he went to discuss matters with the messenger who had arrived.

Ealrin walked over to Holve and made to hug him.

"Wait!" Holve said as he raised an arm to block Ealrin "I may be standing, but I'll be bowled over if you aren't careful. General Rayg's sword left me quite wounded. Though I know I have Blume here to thank for my survival."

Blume had also gotten up and walked with Ealrin over to their traveling companion.

"I've heard endless talk about you, little Blume," said Holve with an unusual smile in her direction. "The healers were quite impressed with your ability to contain the damage done."

She blushed at his kind words.

"Do you think they'll take me on at the school of magic here?" she asked through red cheeks.

Holve chuckled lightly but held the spot where Rayg's blade had cut.

"I doubt you have much to worry about there, Speaker."

THE NEXT DAY WAS A flurry of activity. The king sent word that all able-bodied citizens of Thoran were to gather in Loran, ready to march to war and stop the Mercs' pillaging of the south. While the planning was going on, Ealrin received a summons from the king. He walked into the room where he and several advisers, as well as some of the members of the King's Swords and Holve, were gathered. They were planning a strategy for the coming conflict.

"Your Majesty?" he spoke loudly enough to be heard over the general commotion, but still cautious. After all, he was unsure of how to act around a king.

Looking up from various maps and notes laid on a wide wooden table, the king smiled.

"Ah! Ealrin! Come in please."

The king dismissed several advisers to go and attend to other duties. Cory and the woman of the swords were left with Holve, Ealrin, and the king.

"Holve has told me much about you and your fateful journey here. You've no memory of your country, your station, or your past then?"

Ealrin had little time to try to remember who he had been after the encounter in Weyfield. It was strange that it should be brought up here, as he assumed the present was more pressing than his past.

"No, Your Majesty. I cannot recall who I was or where I came from." He felt foolish speaking the truth, but he knew better than to fabricate anything about himself. And why would he? What purpose would it serve?

"I have heard of men who have lost things before, but one who has lost his memory is something that I have not encountered." The king did not speak with a tone of unbelief, but merely one of fact.

"I hear of the good you have done beside Holve," he continued, not allowing Ealrin a chance to explain himself or guess the nature of his circumstances. "He assures me of your heart and your bravery. One such as you would fit well with the rest of my Swords. Would you serve a king and adopt a country, in light of not knowing your own?"

Ealrin stopped short. Become a Sword in the king's army? Hadn't he called them the very best of his soldiers? His elite army leaders? He was sure that he couldn't be anywhere near their caliber. He was nearly going to protest when Holve spoke.

"You see, Ealrin, we are going to head to River Head in the morning. The Swords and 150 soldiers against an armada of goblins. We know that goblins are only sure of an attack as long as their leaders push them to. If we can deliver a death blow to the goblins or trolls who lead them, we are sure the others will flee. Goblins only fight..."

"...when they are sure they can win." Ealrin finished. He remembered all too well the last time Holve told him that statement.

The king looked to Ealrin and grinned. "So you'll become a Sword for my army then?"

Ealrin was still lost for a response. He wanted to aid, to fight. But as an elite?

"I... I uh..." was all that he could muster at the thought.

The king turned and looked Ealrin square in the eye.

"You have nothing to fear. Not all of my soldiers need to be the most skilled of fighters. I also need those who are courageous of heart. From what Holve tells me, that description fits you perfectly."

Ealrin met the king's gaze. His were not the eyes of belittling or babying. He was not trying to convince Ealrin. He believed in him. It was evident in the kindness of his words and the expression on his face.

Ealrin finally found his voice and put words to his thoughts.

"I... I don't know if I am quite the soldier you're looking for. I've survived mostly on instinct and luck so far," he finally said.

The king gave Holve a knowing look and a nod that said that Ealrin's luck so far was just what he was hoping for.

"Sounds like you'll fit in just fine," said Holve with a slap on Ealrin's back. "Welcome to the Swords."

THE REST OF THE AFTERNOON was a blur of activity. Ealrin was fitted with his own suit of armor. It was not a full plate of metal, as Holve explained, that the knights of Beaton wear, but rather a combination of small metal plates that fit together on top of a suit of leather.

"We wear these armored suits so that we are protected, but also so that we are not hindered in movement," Holve explained.

Like all of the other Swords of the King, Ealrin's suit bore the symbol of Thoran.

I may not have had a past that I can remember, Ealrin thought to himself. *But for now, I have a country to call my own. One I will fight for and defend.*

Ealrin was walking around the castle courtyard trying to feel comfortable in his new uniform when Blume came up beside him. The look on her face was, at first, one of happiness. When she saw his armor, however, she began to look worried.

"So, you were going off to fight the goblins raiding River Head, were you?" she asked him with a tone of concern and her voice.

"Yes, Blume," he replied. "I am going to help defend those who are defenseless. This is what I have wanted since seeing so much violence from both the goblins and the Merc raiders."

She placed her hand on his arm and looked into his eyes. Ealrin could have sworn he saw small tears forming in them.

"Promise me you'll be safe, Ealrin. You have to be safe. You saved my life." She hesitated before she spoke her next words. "I don't want to see you die."

"I promise," he said, though inside of him, he knew that in order for him to defend others he must put himself in danger's way. It's what he had done when he had saved her life. It's what he had done when he had fought to defend her and to help Holve. But he knew, that for her sake and perhaps for the sake of others, he would defend; he must not throw his life away needlessly.

"You looked so happy walking up before you saw me in my uniform," he said, attempting to change the subject. "What could make you so glad?"

At this her face brightened, even if only a little. A smile broke out on her face as she blushed.

"I've just spoken with the head Speaker in Thoran's school of magic. They have accepted me and I am to begin training tomorrow."

At that news, Ealrin hugged Blume tightly and then held onto her shoulders as he broke away. He knew the smile on his face must be huge for he saw it reflected in her brightening face.

"That's wonderful news, Blume! Well of course they will accept you! They would be crazy not to. What did you show them that convinced them?"

He let go of her and began to walk around the castle grounds again with her at his side.

"At first all they wanted me to do was to make a small piece of Rimstone glow. It wasn't very difficult, but I may have overdone it. I was blinded for a moment after it shown so brightly."

She giggled.

"I wanted them to know that I could do it. They said that the task of making Rimstone react to your voice was what some Speakers train for years to do. They said that I would be placed in a group of Speakers who are 5 to 10 years older than I am."

The pair climbed a set of stairs that led to a balcony overlooking the castle grounds. There were people running in all directions, preparing for tomorrow when the citizen army would march south to war.

Ealrin was so glad to hear that Blume would be accepted into the school of magic, but he was also hesitant about the role of Speakers in the coming conflict.

"Do any Speakers march off to war?" He asked her as he looked out over the commotion below.

"Yes," she replied, "but only those who are older or much more advanced than I am."

Ealrin gave a sigh of relief. Blume, he thought, had already seen too much war and violence as it was. He didn't want her to be a part of any more.

"I will miss you while you are gone, Ealrin."

Blume turned to him, a small tear actually falling down her cheek.

"You and Holve have been so wonderful. Rescuing me and ensuring that I was kept out of harm's way. I don't know how I could ever repay you."

Ealrin put his arm around her shoulder and gave her a squeeze as he looked out over the clamor below him.

"Become a gifted Speaker and make use of your talents to bring peace to this land," he told her. "And that will be payment enough for me."

Ealrin did not know what would await them in the city of River Head that was under goblin attack. But this one thing he did know: he would miss his adopted daughter.

30: The City Crusher

Stinkrunt was glad that his feet were now on firm ground again. He was glad that there were no more fish to eat and that he could eat whatever berry or squirrel that seemed good to him.

Except whatever Splitear ate. He fell over dead after eating a couple of roots right after they landed. Then again, he could have died because Stinkrunt stabbed him with the knife he found out Splitear had stolen from him.

One of those was definitely to blame.

Stinkrunt held his knife at his side and was pleased that his leadership had helped them get to the right city.

The first three times they had landed when Stinkrunt thought they saw a city didn't count, in his mind. They had found a house or two and smashed them. A city, he reminded himself, had lots of houses.

And a stupid wall.

At the city where they had landed, they were now attempting to smash a big wall built around it, as well as lots of towers.

And the stupid walls just wouldn't smash easily.

Stinkrunt was not a master tactician and he knew it. But what he did know was that this one city was his chance to prove to Grayscar that he was a good boss and that other goblins should fear his name.

Or at least do what he wanted.

And currently, Stinkrunt wanted his goblins to get up the walls.

A couple of the goblins had enough smarts to grab ropes and things from the ship to use to climb up the wall. Stinkrunt thought that was a good idea, so he made all the goblins grab all the ropes they could and rush the wall. Well, he made his cronies make the other goblins do it.

He was far enough back from the wall that he was safe from the arrows that kept getting fired from along the wall.

He had been camped out here for the last week as the goblins tried to smash the city.

So far, it wasn't smashed.

The rope method hadn't really worked out the way he wanted it to, though. He saw that a lot of goblins kept getting smashed with heavy rocks dropped from the wall and stuck with arrows. Neither did they have the ladder strategy, or the throw the rocks back strategy.

He needed a new strategy.

"Hey, you, lazy guts!" he shouted at a goblin who was standing next to him, obviously also trying to avoid being shot with an arrow. He looked around slowly to Stinkrunt.

He wasn't sure if the goblin's name really was lazy guts or not, but it would have fit this particular one. He hadn't done much since getting off of the boat and Stinkrunt was planning on changing that.

"Make some fire, then take it to that big door!"

Stinkrunt pointed at the large wooden door in the middle of the wall.

If the stones wouldn't smash it, maybe the door would burn down. Then the goblins could get inside the city and smash it that way.

Not a bad idea, Stinkrunt thought to himself.

It only took a week.

So, Lazyguts, which incidentally, was actually his name, got the fires ready and led the charge on the door of the city. Stinkrunt was pretty sure this idea might work.

It even had other goblins falling all over him, asking him what they were going to do with all the loot in the city.

Wait, no a goblin really had fallen on him.

Stinkrunt looked at the big underling who hadn't been a part of the charge, but who lay on the ground with an arrow in his back.

Looking in the direction of the fallen goblin, Stinkrunt turned and then did what any great goblin general would.

He ran for it.

31: Strategy

It was early morning and the first sun had barely risen over the horizon. Ealrin stood and watched as an army ten thousand strong marched south. He prayed it would be enough to stop the violence in the Southern Republic and put an end to the Mercs. Still, something inside him doubted that all was right in the leadership of that country. The king's words had troubled him.

Why would the Elders not send aid to the city of Weyfield? Why would they allow the Mercs to camp in another city and stand idly by? Perhaps there was more at work here than he could see with his own eyes.

He turned towards those gathered with the Swords. The thirteen Swords he had traveled with now stood fifteen strong. He had taken Gray's place among them and Holve was on horseback, ready to travel, although Ealrin and the king had tried their best to convince him to rest.

"I was never one for sitting still for long," was his only reply as he began strapping his own armor on. "Besides, Ealrin here won't have a clue what's going on unless I explain it to him!"

Holve now sat on his horse at Ealrin's side.

"I've been in the service of King Thoran for many years now," he said with grimness in his voice. "This is only the second time I've seen him march to war. Both have been south to deal with the Mercs. I think he knows that giving the Southern Republic to them would spell doom for Thoran. We don't have the population of the south to add to our numbers. The mountains give us more protection than the people do. Now with the goblins invading as well, I fear there will be hard times for the people of Thoran in the future if this is not dealt with swiftly."

Ealrin looked at his friend. His eyes were squinted as he surveyed the army marching south. Caravans of supplies followed them, providing them with the necessary food and shelter they would need on their ten-day march to the southern border. If all things went as planned, they would camp at the river and wait for word from the forward scouts sent to entreat the Elders of the Southern Republic on how best to aid them.

If we can just make it past the Mercs in Breyland, Ealrin thought.

He turned his horse toward the west along with his fellow soldiers and rode towards River Head to face the goblins.

Their two-day journey would soon reveal the threat they faced in the city of River Head.

A threat that Ealrin hoped would be dealt with swiftly.

AS THEY RODE IN FORMATION down the road, Ealrin began to understand how the Swords had organized themselves. To each soldier who was a Sword, they had ten warriors underneath them. Each of them in some way reflected the one who trained them. For example, the elves that had returned from chasing down the Mercs now marched with other elves. They all carried bows. The dwarves, whose legs could never dream of reaching the straps of horses, marched diligently with other dwarves. All of them carried the traditional dwarven weapons: things that were heavy and pointed on the end. Men marched with men. Twenty of them were on horses and another forty marched on foot. Most of them were armed with spears and swords.

The whole company, as diverse as they were, was clothed in the maroon and gold of Thoran. How strange, Ealrin thought, that there are some who see such diversity among the races as impure. How well they would complement each other in battle! The elves would fire their arrows at the foe, while the men would rush ahead and form the first striking force. Then the dwarves behind them would form the anvil on which the enemy would be deflected.

It was a strong company that marched west, and for good reason. If the goblins that had sailed from The Maw had kept most of their strength, they would be facing a horde. Fear was what the Swords were banking on. When a goblin became more fearful of the fight than of its master's whip, it would flee the battlefield in a panic. If the Swords could find and defeat the leader of the goblins and his cronies, perhaps a troll or a goblin shaman, the whole army of goblins would falter. Still, Ealrin could not get the sight of countless goblin vessels on the horizon, sailing toward the *White Wind*, out of his mind. Each must have carried a hundred of the beasts. How many would they find at River Head?

River Head was called so because it stood at the mouth of the river that ran throughout the country of Thoran. It was a trading city and would also send goods down river to the smaller cities of Liaf and Loran. It would make a fine prize for any goblin captain looking for things to steal.

The second day of marching brought the company of soldiers to a hill that ran down to the river and overlooked the city.

Ealrin's heart leapt slightly.

Five goblin ships were docked in the river port that served the walled city of River Head. One was burned black and still smoked in the water. Goblins were everywhere. At least six hundred of the short, gray-skinned marauders filled the area just outside the city walls. Thankfully, they had not breached the wall, but they were making a good effort. Three catapults were constructed on the land and were chucking large rocks and pieces of a broken ship at the city.

Thin ladders were attempting to be hoisted to the wall but were constantly pushed down by River Head's defenders. Men, dwarves, and elves stood on the walls and rained down arrows and rocks at the goblins.

Not all of the might of the goblins had sailed here. Still, they outnumbered the Swords four to one.

Should some of the army have marched here instead?

Holve had led the soldiers all the way here. Ealrin spent the second morning familiarizing himself with the horsemen he was now in charge of. Ealrin barely felt capable of leading himself. Then again, there was something natural when he was directing them. Though his group was used to Gray, as they were his men, they responded well to Ealrin. Being a Sword meant leading men.

After two days, he rode up next to Holve. "I don't know if we've enough soldiers to put down this threat, friend," Ealrin said quietly to Holve.

"You've yet to see how we operate," said Holve. "You'd be surprised what can be accomplished with a few soldiers and a lot of strategy."

HOLVE WAS RIGHT. WITHIN three hours, the King's Swords were placed in their positions ready for their precision strike against the goblin board. Forty elven archers stood within bow shot of the goblin leaders' formation. It was easy to tell who was in charge of the battle. Goblins always lead from the back, sending in their cronies to do the dirty work for them. Only when a goblin boss was cornered and trapped would he actually fight the battle himself.

This particular leader stood taller than the goblins he led and was surrounded by tough looking gray skinned warriors and goblin shamans in black hoods.

Ealrin could see the archers moving into position from where he stood with the cavalry and footmen. Once the elves had released their volley of arrows and had taken out the goblin leadership, the men and horse riders would come in from the opposite flank and disrupt the goblin lines more. If the monsters acted according to their nature, once they saw their leaders defeated, fear would take over and the gray warriors would flee back to their boats. If they chose to instead flee south away from the shore, they would find their escape blocked by the most fearsome dwarven warriors Ealrin had ever seen.

Elves on the left flank. Men on the right. Dwarves from behind. Ealrin wondered why anyone would fail to appreciate the diversity of races, especially when they worked as one.

One of the elves reflected the light of the twin suns from his blade in the direction of the horses. It was the signal that they were ready to strike. Holve and the other men emerged from the group of trees they had hidden themselves in and let out a battle cry. Howls of rage came from the goblins outside the city walls of River Head. The goblin boss began pushing his cronies towards the new threat that had risen from hiding.

And just as the full company of goblins had turned to their right, hundreds of arrows rained down from the elven archers. From Ealrin's viewpoint, every arrow claimed the life of a goblin. Truly the elves of Thoran were unparalleled in their deadly accuracy.

Goblins fell in every direction as the missiles rained down on them. As the elves let loose with their tenth volley the men on horseback charged. Boots thudded against the earth as men wielding spears ran behind them. Ealrin was not afraid, but neither was he quite prepared for what happened next. His horse galloped among the leaders, right next to Holve. Goblins were in disarray. Some were standing to receive the charge. Most were fleeing the opposite direction. Only one hundred yards now separated them from the horde. And then fifty. Twenty. Ten.

Ealrin swung his sword just as his horse broke through the goblin line, or what was left of it anyway. With each swing of his blade a goblin fell. Some put up a fight, their eyes filled with hatred. Most, however, began to flee in fear.

The gray-skinned monsters did just as they had anticipated. After being peppered with 400 arrows, there were few goblins left who wished to continue the fight. Some fled for their boats that were down by the river and began to row for their ships out at sea. A large group of them began to run away from the castle walls, knowing that death met them at the left and right.

A mighty shout arose from the dwarves. The goblins soon realized their fate was sealed.

From the walls of River Head came a triumphant cheer as those who stood defending the city realized they had been saved. Ealrin turned his gaze to the walls of the city. They did not stand as high or as impressive as those in the capital, but they had done their job.

As the last of the goblins fell, the gates to the city opened up and a handful of the city's defenders came out to greet their saviors. At their front was a tall, dark-haired man. He stood a head taller than any of those around him and was broader than two of his fellow River Head dwellers put together. Ealrin had always thought Holve was the sourest person he had ever met. This man made Holve look cheery. His brow was creased into a perpetual scowl.

"It's about time you showed up, Holve Bravestead!" he shouted as he walked out with the others. He sneered as he spoke. He stopped beside Holve's horse and stood leaning on the sword he brought with him.

Holve removed himself gingerly from his horse and stood beside the dark-haired man.

"Well, if I had known you would have been able to handle six hundred goblins and five of their crummy excuses for ships I would have stayed back in Thoran where the receptions are more welcoming!"

With that, Holve put a hand on the man's shoulder and smiled at him. Ealrin had dismounted his horse while the two spoke to each other. He could see the last of the goblins being taken care of by elves, men, and dwarves.

More battles fought. More blood spilled.

The Swords had only lost a handful of men, maybe twenty at most. Would this good fortune last?

"Well, Gregory Riverson, it has been too many winters since I've laid eyes on you." Holve said as Ealrin came walking up next to him. "Have you gotten fatter?"

Gregory snorted and looked up and down at Holve.

"I haven't gained as much as you have lost, you twig!" he said as he slapped Holve on the back.

Holve let out a grunt of pain.

"Well, I've seen a lot of action in the last month, Gregory," Holve said as he nursed his back with one hand. "I don't suppose River Head could spare some men who'd like to see some action themselves?"

With this statement, Gregory grunted and scowled at Holve. Ealrin was surprised a man could look so sour.

"Does the king march to war? We had heard rumors of trouble in the south as the goblins sailed toward us. Does Thoran march to the Southern Republic again?"

"That he does," replied Holve. He walked back to his horse and cleaned off his spear on a cloth that he produced from a pack. And as gingerly as he dismounted his horse, he climbed back up as he turned back to Gregory. "We are to meet him as quickly as we can. Round up what men you can spare and march out with us. We go to aid the south."

GREGORY, EALRIN WOULD learn, was not just a large man with a belly that was threatening to betray a formerly fit individual's health, but the mayor of River Head. Once the Swords had gathered outside of the city, Gregory began shouting orders in ten different directions. He was not only commanding men to prepare to march, but also delegating tasks to be done in his absence.

"See that the next shipment from Beaton is ordered properly when it comes. I don't want medicinal herbs being sent off to the kitchens of the inns again!"

"What are you doing, sitting there like a lump? You're marching south with the rest of the men. Get to the city gates now!"

"Someone clean up those goblin bodies outside the walls! See that they are burned! They'll start to wreak by tomorrow and spread disease like wildfire if they aren't taken care of!"

"You there!" Gregory pointed to a man who was shaping a stone outside of his shop. Most of the buildings in River Head were made of stone, due to the proximity of the mountain quarries. Wood was used as a decorative trim around them, but defense was the main reason these houses were built in such a fashion. Barely any of them were scratched after the battle. The shopkeeper looked up from his work, trying to see from which direction the shouting was coming from.

"Yes, you, lazy bones! You're in charge of this section of wall getting repaired while we march! I want those battlements looking superb when we return!"

The bewildered looking shop owner was following the finger Gregory was pointing up to the part of the wall that the goblins had managed to damage with their war machines. Along the wall, every thirty paces rose a tower meant for surveying the outer villages of River Head and helping to defend against enemy attacks. This particular one had collapsed in on itself and was a heap of rubble atop the otherwise untouched wall.

The shop owner was not acknowledging his task swiftly enough for the demanding Gregory, who was now marching closer to him as he continued to gaze upward.

"Do you understand me, Ivan? I want that tower back in pristine condition!"

Though Ealrin didn't think he would enjoy marching south with Gregory because of his countenance, he surely wouldn't mind sharing some of the man's command of people. Whenever Gregory spoke, most people, other than Ivan, who was now taking a beating with a wooden rod that Gregory carried around with him, obeyed without question.

"He's a hard man, but a good mayor," said Holve as he walked up next to Ealrin. He had spent his time since arriving in River Head arranging the weapons from the armory to be sorted between those who were marching. Mostly it was breastplates, shields, spears, and swords. Every other man wore a helmet, but others had deemed them unnecessary. Some had weapons of their own making, but most carried the same steel sword that had been produced here in River Head for occasions such as these.

After men collected their weapons and armor they headed to one of the forgers in the city to have them inspected and sharpened, and then they reported to the city gates to be assigned to one of the captains who were the leaders of the army of River Head.

Again, King Thoran's doctrine of only employing a few men for the army and recruiting his civilians only in the hour of need. There were around twenty captains, each with two hundred men, dwarves, and elves. The army that would march from River Head would be four thousand strong.

Looking out over the men, and then remembering the goblin attack, Ealrin had a thought that weighed heavily on his mind.

"Holve," he asked as the host marched from River Head with the Swords at the lead. "If goblins only fight battles they are sure they will win, why did so few fight against a city as great as River Head? I spoke with Gregory and he believes no more than one thousand originally made landfall to attack the city. It would seem that they were terribly outnumbered."

"I've been thinking the same thought," Holve said with a sigh. "And so far, I'm without an answer. Perhaps they thought the city would not be as well defended. It's been many generations since the goblins have come as far as River Head. Maybe they didn't know how many dwelled there now. Still..."

Holve let his sentence die out as they headed south. His brow was furrowed in such a way that it reminded Ealrin more of Gregory's disposition, not Holve's typical jovial manner.

"Still," he continued, "I've known many a goblin army to turn away from a larger city to lay siege to smaller villages if they believe the pickings are easier. I hope it was nothing more than a goblin leader's lust for blood than anything else."

"But do you remember the armada of goblin ships we saw on the *White Wind*?" Ealrin prodded Holve. "What we saw here could only have been a fraction of the ships we saw that day. Where did the others sail to?"

The female soldier Ealrin only knew as Milady rode up beside them. When she spoke, Ealrin realized it was the first time he had heard her voice. He also noted a small amount of fear in her voice. He looked properly into her face and realized that he recognized some of her features. It was as if he had seen someone else share the same face.

"Commander Holve, I have been listening to your conversation and I fear for the king. We must quicken our pace if we are to meet him and give him aid."

Holve turned in his saddle towards the dark-haired lady in armor. He smiled at her reassuringly and bowed his head as he spoke.

"Milady, we will march as fast as we can. Do not fear, we will see your father soon."

32: The Long March South

E alrin's mind was still uneasy three days after their march for Loran from River Head began. The army marched down the only road that led from the capital city to the border of the Southern Republic. The same road Ealrin and the Swords had traveled north on after being attacked by the raiders. Mountains rose on either side of them, creating the valley path that they now took. The terrain did not hamper the army from marching, but Ealrin was sure they would have made better time over the flat plains of the Southern Republic than the mountains that now surrounded them.

He thought he might be as concerned for the king as Teresa was. Teresa, of course, being the king's daughter and a member of the swords. He could see the resemblance now. How much the two favored each other. The long-haired young and seemingly carefree girl Ealrin had seen in the painting in the halls of castle Thoran, however, was gone.

In her place stood this warrior. A young woman who had seen countless battles and defended her father fervently. Ealrin had watched her fight in the charge of River Head. She was skilled, ruthless, and relentless. Her two swords had flashed before her in a blur as she took to the battlefield on foot rather than on horseback. She was brave beyond comparison. And her soldiers followed her faithfully.

What could have driven a princess to fight instead of keeping court?

These questions and several more tugged at Ealrin's mind as the army marched. Curiosity for how Teresa came to be a member of the Swords could not overtake his concern for King Thoran. Where had the other goblin ships sailed? What would the army find in the south?

"Where has your mind traveled off to?" asked Holve as he butted Ealrin with the blunt end of his spear.

Though Holve had expressed some of the same concerns as Ealrin, his priority at the time was to continue marching the army south. Ealrin could tell that his companion and general was drained by being surrounded with so many people. He spoke in shorter phrases than normal and only dealt with people if it was necessary. He always had time for Ealrin, however, and he was glad for it. Even if it meant getting hit in the back with the shaft of the spear.

"Currently, I'm plotting how to break your weapon in half," Ealrin replied as he rubbed the spot Holve had hit.

"And," he ventured, "I am concerned about the king. Suppose there is something going on that he missed or overlooked?"

"Then I suppose this scout will tell us what it is," replied Holve as he looked ahead of him, squinting into the morning sun.

Ealrin looked in the same direction Holve was, and indeed there rode a man on horseback with the unmistakable colors of Thoran on his chest.

From this distance, Ealrin could see him waving his arm madly and driving his horse ever faster down the hill he rode on. Holve spurred his own horse ahead to meet him. Ealrin followed him and soon found Teresa at his side as well.

"General Holve! General Holve! Raiders! Not two hours behind me!" the young scout was shouting with all his might as he came within earshot of the trio riding toward him.

"Calm down, Cedric. Calm down." Holve was telling the man. "Catch your breath."

Ealrin noticed a twinkle of concern in Holve's eyes. Were the raiders really that close?

"Sir." Cedric said as he regained his breath and could speak without gasping for air. "The raiders are two hours behind me. The other scouts..." He shook his head and looked down.

"They enabled me to escape. We must make ready. They'll be upon us soon."

Holve took a deep breath and looked to Teresa.

"Any word or sight of the king?" she asked Cedric.

"None, Milady," he said, knowing that it meant ill. "But, it did not seem that the Raiders had recently seen battle. It may be that the armies did not meet."

"I don't see how that could be possible Cedric," Holve said. "There's only one road down to the south and we're on it." He looked back to Cedric and away from Teresa. How the king's army had faired would be something to be discovered later. This threat was now what needed to be dealt with.

Ealrin interjected to break the moment's silence.

"How many Mercs approach?"

"Thousands," Cedric answered. "Seven or eight thousand it seemed."

"Not enough to break the army of the king," Holve said, seemingly to relieve Teresa. Ealrin could see that her normal hard face was softening for her father. How terrible it must be not to know.

He had some knowledge of what that was like.

"Hurry," Holve said to them. "We have preparations to make. We'll see to the king after we've death with this army."

"We're outnumbered, Holve," Ealrin said plainly. "Two to one."

Holve looked Ealrin in the eye.

He had that same grin that he had greeted Ealrin with when he awoke from his injuries in Good Harbor, lying on a bed. It was genuine. It was also comforting to Ealrin, who was beginning to feel his hand tremble. He had fought in small skirmishes. The goblins at River Head were insignificant compared to what approached.

"I told you. Strategy."

With that, Holve rode his horse back to the main army, with Teresa, Cedric, and Ealrin following behind.

Ealrin prayed that strategy would work as well this time as it had in the past.

CEDRIC'S ESTIMATE OF the Merc's timing and army had been accurate.

From Ealrin's viewpoint on the eastern cliff, he and a thousand other men could see the approaching army. It was twice as large as the force they came to meet. The banners that they flew were not those of the Mercs that Ealrin had seen before in Breyland. Instead, these banners were gray with a white circle emblazoned on it. Inside the circle was a griffin with its wings and talons out, ready to strike.

"Androlion's own banner. That man has some nerve," said Tory, who stood beside Ealrin. "Does he really think he'll be a ruler of men?"

Tory spat on the ground.

"I've lost one too many to that fiend," he said through gritted teeth. "This army of his will pay for his crimes!"

Ealrin knew that Tory was still hurt from losing Gray. He could hear the sadness turned to anger. He prayed that Tory's passion would guide them well as they attempted to defend the mountain pass.

Again, the forces were split in order to make the best use of the abilities of the races. The elves were camped on the western cliff of the mountains, opposite Ealrin and the men. They were to rain arrows down upon the raiders.

The dwarves were positioned down in the pass. They were preparing to take the full brunt of the initial charge. Just like dwarves liked to battle: charging in, swinging their maces and hammers high.

Holve was betting that the Mercs wouldn't risk climbing the cliffs to face the two forces above them. And so they would be peppered with arrows until they met the dwarves. Then both elves and men would charge down the mountainside to attack either flank. The cliffs were steep enough to prevent the Mercs from climbing up to meet them, but not so much as to prevent the army of Thoran from effectively racing down them.

Ealrin hoped the strategy would work.

As he watched, the army bearing gray standards approached. Unlike every army Ealrin had marched with; this one showed no sign of any race other than man. No graceful elves marched with their bows hanging at their sides. No strong dwarves marched at the front of the army, hungry for the first charge of the battle. This was an army of men.

Each man was decorated in the gray and white of Androlion. A griffin was painted on every shield and some men had them emblazoned on their chests. This army was different than the one that was camped outside of Breyland. They were more organized and better armed.

There was something about it that unsettled Ealrin. It wasn't that their numbers were greater than their own. Ealrin had seen how strategy could overcome numbers alone. It was the large number who walked in the middle of the army wearing red hoods and cloaks that covered their armor. From here, Ealrin could see that some of these carried swords or daggers, but all of them had a staff that was affixed with a red stone at the top of it.

"I've never seen that many Speakers before," Tory said to Ealrin. "There aren't that many in the entire school of magic at Thoran, and that's including the young ones. Where did they acquire so much Rimstone?"

There was no time to discuss the matter. As the army came into the range of elven arrows it began to surge forward. A battle cry rose from the opposite cliff and arrows began to rain down upon the army. Gray shields were hoisted up to deflect the missiles that came raining down.

As the foot soldiers in the army advanced the red robed Speakers stood firm. As one their staffs began to glow bright red and stole the light of the twin suns around them. Just as the first soldiers were about to crash into the dwarves below and Tory was shouting to the soldiers to charge, flames erupted from the group of Speakers and shot to both sides of the mountain pass, covering them in fire.

EALRIN COULD BARELY breathe for all the smoke and flame that surrounded him.

His world had become a swirling mass of black smoke, red flame, and the screams of men on fire. He could barely make out the sound of Tory's voice urging them on higher up the mountain and North, away from the flames of the Speakers. Though he was trying to obey the orders, Ealrin could no longer tell which way was which as he struggled to see the suns in the black smoke.

Holve could not have foreseen this. As he struggled to breathe and escape the blinding fire and smoke, Ealrin feared for the fate of his friend. Holve had insisted on joining the dwarves in receiving the initial charge.

"I don't lead from the sides my friend. I set the example," Holve had told him as the rest of the army split east and west leaving the dwarves to their task. Ealrin had asked to stay and fight beside Holve but was instructed otherwise.

"I need you up there with Tory," Holve had told him. "Learn from him; he directs his men well."

Ealrin could indeed still hear Tory over the shouts around him and the embattled army, directing men to escape the smoke and flame so as to aid the dwarves below. Ealrin hoped that there were still dwarves to help.

ONCE HE WAS FINALLY free from the smoke, Ealrin could see that the dwarves were struggling but still fought. Of the thousand men who would climb the mountain with him, Ealrin could only count three or 400 left standing with him. Many had met their hand in the flames of the Speakers and others had suffocated in the thick smoke. When he looked across the pass to the other cliffs where the elves had gathered, Ealrin could tell that they had fared little better. Perhaps a few more had survived on the opposite side, but they were at half of their previous strength.

Though we have a strategy, Ealrin thought, *what we need now are numbers.*

Tory ran up beside him and looked to the remaining men.

"Men! Men of Thoran! We face an army that invades our proud nation for reasons we don't yet know! Yet I know this: We will not yield! We will not let this army march unhindered! We will stand! We will fight! For Thoran!"

"For Thoran!" came the reply from the men left standing on the hill.

Ealrin took in the absurdity of it all.

King Thoran had said that he kept his army small. These men were not warriors like Tory. They were bakers, craftsmen, traders, potters, fishers, and cloth makers. And yet here they were, prepared to die for the country they loved because it was threatened by outside invaders.

Ealrin rose up his cry with the others.

"For Thoran!"

As their small band raced down the mountain to aid the few dwarf warriors left, Ealrin could come up with one coherent thought as they jumped over rocks and prepared themselves to smash into a wall of shields and raised spear points.

This could have been my home.

33: Surrender and Betrayal

E alrin fought with all his might.

Of those that charged down the mountain, not fifty remained. He could just make out Teresa in the circle that they had formed in order to protect their backs. To his left was Tory, fighting and willing the men around him to not give in, yelling words of encouragement to them. To his right was a dwarf of the Swords. The charge had not gotten the men to the position of the dwarves, but some of the short warriors had fought their way through. They now fought among them.

Bodies lay all around: both those of Thoran and of the Mercs with the gray and white griffin. Ealrin hacked and swung and parried until his arms ached and his shoulders burned. He knew that to lay down his weapon would spell certain death. Yet, as he fought, he saw countless Mercs just watching the battle, ready to take one of their comrades' place should he fall to the army of Thoran.

They were defeated.

A man Ealrin recognized rode up on horseback and held up his hand.

Mercs no longer came to replace their fallen brothers. They simply stood with shields raised and spears pointed, creating a great circle around those who fought under the maroon banner.

Finally, the last Merc who had come out to fight fell at the hands of Teresa. Her double blades had relieved him of his head. She now stood panting and looking around at her comrades and her enemies. For a moment, her eyes met Ealrin's.

"I'm sorry we could not get to your father," Ealrin wished to say. He, too, had desperately wished to return to the king.

It would not be so.

"Warriors of Thoran. You have fought bravely," said General Xaxes. Ealrin recognized him from the inn in Breyland. Though he rode up from behind, Ealrin could see the blood and scars of fresh battle on him.

At least he doesn't lead from behind, thought Ealrin.

"Lay down your arms. Surrender your weapons, and your lives will be spared."

Tory laughed out loud.

"You wish us to believe that you'll spare us? You've invaded our lands, killed our people, and now you are offering mercy? I doubt you'll be true to your word."

A smile crossed Xaxes face.

"Perhaps then you'll agree to different terms?" He gestured to his side and two men came up carrying a third between them.

"Holve," Ealrin breathed.

He was bloody from a wound to his head. His armor was dented and his eyes had rolled to the back of his head. He was completely being supported by the two men. He was unconscious at best.

Xaxes drew his blade and reached it down to Holve's throat. He rested it gently under his chin, bringing Holve's face up to be seen by all around them.

"Lay down your weapons and your commander will live. Lay them down now and I'll spare you the screams of the king's daughter I see fighting among you."

He stared hard at those who stood below him. Ealrin knew that to hope for his life was beyond sanity. They would not truly be spared. Their end would only be delayed. Yet still, to see Holve be finished off because of their defiance was a terrible thought.

In disgust and with a look of pure loathing upon his face, Tory threw down his sword.

Those around him followed suit. The last to lay down their arms was Teresa. Ealrin could tell by the look on her face that she wanted to run headlong into six thousand Mercs and take them all on herself. After a moment, she dropped her swords. Ealrin heard a grunt as her blades plunged downward, ending the life of a Merc who had not yet gone on. Ealrin laid down his own blade, the one Roland had given him and had served him so well, upon the body of a Merc warrior.

Fitting, he thought.

Though next to the Merc he saw the face of a Sword: Brute. Strong, bearlike, and still looking dangerous, even with a spear in his chest.

"Too many have died today," he said out loud as he looked up at Xaxes removing his blade from Holve's throat and signaling the men to take him away.

The Merc army enclosed around them.

They were sat bound hand and foot in rows. The army of Thoran that had marched from River Head, led by the King's Swords was four thousand strong. Now they numbered no more than a hundred.

Ealrin was bound and positioned next to Teresa. She sat steel faced next to him. He was doing his best to read her thoughts. What might she be wondering? How the king faired? Surely her thoughts would be with her father. Had he successfully marched to Loran as they had intended? The city was no more than two days from their current position. And if he had been there, how had these Mercs gotten past the king's army, so much larger than this force that had been defeated. Had the two been able to combine forces, surely this Merc threat would have been defeated.

But then, would the Mercs march north if they felt their rear was vulnerable to attack? Ealrin's head began to ache. He decided that strategy was not his forte. He would leave that to Holve.

Holve.

He sat unconscious across from Ealrin, perhaps less than two steps away. His cut had stopped bleeding. Thankfully the Mercs had tied some sort of cloth around his head to staunch the bleeding. His head drooped down in front of him. Were it not for the steady rise and fall of his chest, Ealrin would fear that he couldn't breathe. For now, though, he was all right.

The dwarves Frerin and Narvi sat on either side of him. Holve had stayed with the dwarves and fought beside them. There was hardly any left. Ealrin couldn't see Khali, the other dwarven King's Sword, anywhere. Perhaps the Mercs had been especially ruthless to the other races. Not one elf was to be seen among those left. Lote. Enlon. Minare. Elel.

Had they been cut down in the fighting? Charged like the men had and now lay slain somewhere along the mountain?

Ealrin banished the picture forming in his head of the faces he had known lying slain with glossy eyes unseeing. What was to be his fate, as well as the fate of the others who sat bound around him? They had been promised life, but for how long?

The Mercs around them gathered around campfires and drank. The suns were beginning to disappear behind the mountains, giving the valley an early night sky. Summer was coming, but there was no warmth in Ealrin's bones.

Only a chill that had nothing to do with the temperature.

NIGHT HAD FALLEN OVER the valley and the drinking and revelry of the Mercs had only increased as the suns set. Most gave little or no regard to the prisoners of war who were aching from being bound for such a long period and starving for food that wouldn't come to them.

Some gloated and held rations just outside of their bite. Others simply kicked them and called them names not worth repeating when one was sober.

Ealrin was concentrating heavily on Holve. He had yet to come out of his sleep or coma or whatever kept his head sunk over his chest. The only relief Ealrin had was the steady up and down movements of Holve's chest, letting him know his friend was alive.

Then a larger group of Mercs sauntered over to them and Ealrin took his eyes off of Holve. Androlion himself came walking up to the prisoners flanked by his generals carrying torches and swords.

Androlion still looked as clean and sharp as he did that night Ealrin first saw him in Breyland. The only exception was that now he wore a breastplate with the white griffin on it and a gray cloak to match it. A sword dangled from the scabbard at his side. Andro-lion had not joined the fight against this army from River Head. His boots were too pristine. Perhaps he had only just gotten off his horse.

A smug look was on his face. He surveyed the prisoners of war with grim satisfaction. The group marched up to Ealrin and stopped. The leader of the Merc army surveyed the fighters bound and arranged in rows.

"Is this the army that King Thoran was to bring to the south? I would have expected better of him. Not here to lead his own troops. A coward."

What? Ealrin thought. *Does Androlion not yet know about the army that marched from Thoran?*

The thought was exhilarating. Perhaps the king had been delayed for some reason. Something may have happened to the eastern pass. It could be possible that still ten thousand marched south to face the threat of the Mercs.

That hope gave him a rush, for a moment. Ealrin realized that even if the king's army was intact, it did nothing for his current state of affairs.

"Ah, but here is Holve Bravestead. The general without a home." Androlion bent down to see Holve's face. He took one hand and tried to bring it up to see his eyes. Ealrin could see that Holve was still mostly unconscious. His eyes still lolled and didn't focus on Androlion, though his face was directed straight at the Merc leader.

"Sad," he said. "Couldn't take the fight without fainting." He let go of Holve who crashed back to the ground in a more awkward position than before. Then Ealrin noticed something. For a split second, Holve's eyes regained their focus, searched around for something, and then shut again.

Was he coming to?

This went outside of the notice of Androlion, who stood straight up and looked around at the others, speaking in a mocking tone.

"I suppose there is another of the King's Swords who can speak for what's left of his army?"

Ealrin held his breath. Did Androlion know about Teresa? Surely the daughter of the king would be the one he would seek? Would he torture her for information? Kill her on the spot? He risked a quick glance at her, hoping not to betray that she was anyone other than a typical soldier. Her brow was furrowed and a single tear ran down her face.

She knew what her position would mean for her if she were discovered or betrayed.

No one spoke.

To Ealrin's horror, Xaxes came forward.

"Perhaps you'll be pleased with this one, My Lord," he said as the tip of his sword found Teresa's neck. There was a rustle amongst the troops in bondage.

Androlion looked over to his commander and at the daughter of King Thoran.

"Ah. What do we have here?" he said as he bent down level with her. "Teresa, is it? Princess Teresa? You're not dressed like any princess I've ever seen sitting on a throne."

He stood and delivered a kick into Teresa's side. Ealrin heard her grunt against the blow. Mercs laughed at her pain as she fell to her side.

"After I'd heard so much about you, wild daughter of the king, I would have thought there'd be more fight in you."

Ealrin could see in Teresa's eyes both pain and intense, soul searing hatred. Her tears mingled with the mud.

Turning to address the rest of the prisoners, Androlion called out with contempt in his voice.

"And do none of you rise to defend your king's own?"

Again, no one spoke.

"Cowards."

"We are no cowards, Androlion Fellgate!"

With that Androlion drew his sword and pointed it directly at Tory, who sat bound a few feet from Holve. Tory looked up at Androlion with a sneer.

"Get that thing out of my face," he said, his voice dripping with revulsion. "I remember you, Androlion. You're a rejected Elder of the south. All you've ever done is try to convince men that the other races are lower than us. We don't believe your bile. You won't find anyone sympathetic to your views here."

Ealrin was sure that at any moment Androlion was going to plunge his sword into Tory and end his speech, but he didn't. Instead, he just glared down at him. From his viewpoint, Androlion's face was hidden from Ealrin, and he could only guess what the leader must be thinking.

He turned around and addressed the prisoners as a group.

"You wear the markings of one of King Thoran's Swords. I ask this of you. Have you ever witnessed the greed of the dwarves? Or the arrogance of the elves?" He then spoke louder so that all those who sat bound could hear him.

"How many of you have seen the viciousness of the goblins or other monstrosities who roam this land?"

"And we have seen those same evils in man. One especially," remarked Tory, who spoke as if he didn't care that a sword's edge was at his neck.

"Yes," spoke Androlion. "Yes, it would be easy to see what I have done thus far as the acts of a madman bent on killing. What you do not understand is what I have seen. I have seen the future. A new age is coming. And that age is either a hell on earth with none but monsters and demons to roam the lands, or one with the human race living at peace, without the other races. And I will gladly sacrifice others in order to save this entire land from flames and preserve the race of man."

"So, I will give this option to you: join me. Trust in my words and the future that I have seen and I will give you a place among my other generals. Give me your allegiance and help us preserve the line of mankind in the age to come. Join me, and I may just spare your princess as well."

Ealrin couldn't believe his ears. Surely Androlion was speaking madness. He spoke as if he could see the future, as if he knew what was going to happen.

No man sees what is going to come! Ealrin thought.

This had to just be something a madman dreamt up to justify his hatred of those who were not like him. Of those who were not men.

And then a voice echoed over the silence of the other prisoners.

"I will fight with you."

Ealrin had been looking at the ground, lost in his thoughts about how Androlion was a man driven to insanity and couldn't be sure who had spoken. He looked to his left and right trying to find who had called out. Surely no one would actually believe these ramblings!

And yet the voice spoke again, one that Ealrin knew well. He could see that he was not the only face that was filled with shock at the owner of the voice.

"I will fight," Cory said again.

Androlion turned to where Cory was sitting, several steps past Holve in the opposite direction of Tory. As he walked from one twin to the other, Ealrin could see the look of surprise that was turning into disgust on Tory's face.

"Ah," said Androlion as he approached Cory. "There are two of you. Brothers no doubt? Twins? How quaint."

At this, Androlion bent and spoke on a face-to-face level with Cory.

"You see that the gods have given me a glimpse into the future and that to preserve our race we must destroy the others that walk this land? Do you agree?"

Again, Androlion blocked Ealrin's view of whom he was speaking to. But the answer was not lost among the stillness of the other prisoners.

"Yes."

Androlion stood and motioned to two of his generals and said simply, "Untie him."

Xaxes and Verde moved forward, each with a dagger in hand and loosened the bonds. Ealrin still couldn't believe what was going on in front of him. Surely this was all a ruse? He half expected Cory to stand to his feet and drive a sword into Androlion's chest. But all he did was stand and massage his wrists. There was no fight in him and his face was expressionless, something that was odd for the typically outspoken twin.

"You will prove to me that you mean to help rid this land of the lesser races. What is your name?"

"Cory. Cory Greenwall."

Androlion stood surveying him for a moment. He then sheathed his sword and drew a dagger from his belt. He marched back a few paces from Cory, stopping right in front of Holve. With one arm he extended the weapon to him and with the other he motioned to Frerin and Narvi.

"Very well, Cory Greenwall. You will show me that you are pure in purpose and that none of the lesser races can be saved. Not even those whom you have called friends. I see that these two dwarves are the last that have survived the battle with my army."

Ealrin could see the twisted smile that lined Androlion's face as he spoke his next words.

"Kill them."

THE SUNS BEGAN TO RISE over the mountain range, but they brought no light with them. None, at least, to Ealrin and the other survivors of the Merc assault.

The survivors were no longer the diverse and complimentary warriors that marched from River Head. Instead, it was a group of only men.

Ealrin was devastated. How could Cory kill his comrades? How could he slit the throats of those with whom he had fought and battled the evils of the realm? Ealrin had listened to countless stories from the dwarves about their adventures as Swords. They always talked so highly of Cory. In his short time of knowing him, Ealrin had thought he was a level-headed soldier. Given over to a little superstition perhaps, but to be so easily swayed?

It was all too terrible to believe.

And yet the missing bodies of the dwarves across from him couldn't be a hallucination. Holve had indeed awoken. He had been able to wiggle into a sitting position from where he had laid previously. When they dragged the dwarves' bleeding bodies away, Holve had fallen into the dirt.

Now he sat up and was trying to ascertain what had happened from Ealrin. With every detail his brow continued to furrow and his eyes more steely than normal. Ealrin finished the story with all the details he knew.

"After Cory... Well, afterwards, Cory left with Androlion and the other generals. I just can't believe he killed Narvi and Frerin. For what? The ramblings of a mad man? I just can't believe it, Holve. He's betrayed us and murdered his friends."

With a moment to think about what was going on around him, Ealrin was beginning to come to terms with all had transpired. Now it was all for naught.

"War is hell, Holve," he finished.

"I've never said it was anything but, Ealrin. War is not what happens when those with level heads can rightly discuss their issues and solve them with peace instead of swords. War is what happens when those who have a need for power or position see no other alternative other than the needless shedding of blood. War is hell. But some wars are fought against those who seek to do a greater evil. And some wars are won when those who seek to do good rally around others who seek to do what is right. This one isn't over, Ealrin. I doubt it's truly begun. We still have a chance to do what is right."

"How? How, Holve?" Ealrin was downcast and desperate. He was bound, hungry, and angry. Angry at Cory for deserting them. Angry at Androlion for starting a war. Angry at war for the bloodshed it caused. He wanted it all to stop. He wanted to stop it himself. But he didn't know how and felt powerless to do anything. "I'm surprised the rest of us have lasted this long. They'll surely kill us before next sunrise."

"Perhaps," said Holve. "But never doubt that there are others around you who seek justice as much as you do."

Ealrin had no other words for Holve. He just sat for a while and stared.

Maybe there are others who would end the war, he thought.

But where were they now? And what good could they do for those whose hands and feet were bound and whose spirits were downcast?

FOR MOST OF THE DAY, the River Head army sat bound and at the mercy of the raiders. Ealrin couldn't tell what they were planning to do. They seemed content to stay in this pass for however long they needed. A few mountain streams were giving them the water they needed to quench the thirst of their army. He feared for the rest of the Swords and those who had marched with him.

He had tried a few times to talk to Teresa, but she only shook her head whenever he had spoken. His attempts to encourage her about the whereabouts of the king went unacknowledged.

Androlion hadn't come back for Teresa yet. Ealrin could only imagine what the enemy had in store for her. So far, however, her treatment had been the same as everyone else's. Maybe he intended to just leave her in the mud with the rest of the prisoners?

Ealrin was starving. His tongue was sticking to the top of his mouth. The heat of the suns above them was blazing down on them. And in the light of the sun on Ealrin, he finally noticed something up on the mountainside. Something gleamed through the trees and shrubs that grew alongside the cliffs that rose to form the mountain. Several things did.

And then came the arrows raining down from above, shooting over those bound and sitting tied up and landing on the raiders who were caught off guard completely by the assault.

Then from all around them, out of the trees and the bushes at the base of the mountain, erupted soldiers wearing the maroon and gold of Thoran.

Ealrin recognized several of the elves that burst forward and began to rain arrows down on the closest raiders. At the same time several others began cutting the prisoners free. As they were cut free of their bonds, the warriors of Thoran began to scramble toward a pile of weapons and grab anything that could be used to defend themselves against the raiders. Slowly, some began to organize and attack the new and unexpected threat. Fortunately, they were still drunk over their victory and from their ale to react quickly, but Ealrin knew that would only give them an advantage for so long.

He was cut free and hastily scrambled to Holve and worked to help him to his feet. Teresa ran to Holve's other side and also began to help escort the general away from the fight and toward the slopes of the mountain.

"Get yourselves a sword and let go of me!" he tried to argue. Ealrin and Teresa exchanged grim looks, knowing that his words had truth to them. Three unarmed and weak prisoners of war would have little chance of surviving any battle. And yet they both knew that Holve was in worse condition than either of them.

The sound of battle horns echoed in the valley as the Merc warriors were alerted to the small skirmish going on. Ealrin knew they were hopelessly outnumbered and could only last several minutes at best.

He looked behind him to see whatever warriors had been able to grab weapons forming a semicircle with the mountain at their back. The last of the army of Thoran that marched from River Head would be crushed against the mountain. He could see that most of the elves were hanging their bows on their backs and drawing their swords. They were running out of arrows.

"I don't know how long we will last here, Holve," Ealrin said as he continued to help Teresa drag him away from the battle.

And then a voice that came from a rock spoke up.

"Bah. A lot longer if you get inside and quit fooling around."

34: Fate

They walked for several minutes through a series of caves and caverns that had Ealrin's head spinning. It was just wide enough for Ealrin and Teresa to stay at Holve's side, continuing to help him walk. The light that contented to lead them through the dizzying maze came from the lantern of a dwarf. Ealrin couldn't see him well enough to know if he was familiar with this dwarf, but he doubted it.

Instead of the maroon and gold of Thoran, this dwarf was wearing brown leather pants and a black shirt. No uniform that Ealrin had seen thus far or could identify. The tunnels they traversed were extensive and reinforced at different parts. Old wooden beams held up certain areas, though some threatened to fall soon if not maintained. Behind him, Ealrin could hear the shouts and boots of several others coming into the underground cave. And then a loud crash echoed throughout the tunnel and a rush of air and dust came down on them. For a moment the light flickered in the dwarf's lamp and Ealrin feared they'd be plunged into darkness, but the darkness passed as soon as it came.

"What was that?" he asked, not truly expecting an answer from Teresa or Holve, who both were looking as puzzled as Ealrin felt. There was also a bit of fear in Ealrin that he didn't want to show at the moment.

"That'll be the entrance we came in collapsing," said the dwarf over his shoulder as he continued to lead the group onward through twisting tunnels. Ealrin's stomach dropped as he realized that this was the thing he feared. Had they been led from their death at the sword to their death underground?

"We're nearly there," the dwarf said as he made a right down a fork. He passed from sight for a brief moment and Ealrin took the opportunity to voice his concerns with Holve.

"Maybe following this dwarf into this cave wasn't the best decision. What if we're no better off under this mountain than out there with the Mercs?" he spoke in a low voice.

"We'd be dead if we weren't under this mountain, Ealrin," said Teresa with a tone of impatience.

"But with no way out..." began Ealrin. He found that he was unable to continue his sentence as he found himself walking into the large cavern that opened up. Giant stalactites hung from the great ceiling of the giant underground room. The light of several lanterns illuminated the room. They were resting on natural rock outcroppings that acted as shelves. It made missing the three hundred dwarves that stood watching the influx of warriors from Thoran impossible.

AS THE COMMOTION SETTLED and the last of the survivors came from the tunnel into the cavern, Holve wrested free of Ealrin and Teresa and stood on his own in order to address the dwarves.

"Well, it looks like we owe you all a great deal, dwarves of Kaz-Ulum," he said with a rare grin. "How in the world did you come to Thoran's mountains from the south without receiving the wrath of the Mercs?"

"If there's a tunnel on the continent of Ruyn, we dwarves put it there!" said the dwarf who led them into the cave originally. A resounding "Aye!" rang up from the other dwarves. Ealrin saw males and females, young and old gathered in the cave. All bore weapons or mining picks or something dwarven made and sharp. Though they looked resolute and smug, they'd been traveling for a long time, and not in the best circumstances. Several had clothes that were tattered or hastily patched. More looked like they hadn't eaten a good meal in a month.

"It'll take them days to dig through that rubble and weeks to find another entrance into these tunnels. These are ancient dwarven paths we're treading, so mind yourselves."

It was then that Ealrin began to see what he had at first missed. Though the cavern was still quite dark and his eyes were still adjusting to the dim light, he was beginning to make out shapes in the stalagmites he was standing close to. In rings around each one were runes that were carved into the rock. Yes, they were certainly runes; similar to the ones Ealrin had seen carved into some of the dwarven weapons.

Then he noticed that some of the rock formations were not natural, as he had first assumed, but rather statues of dwarven kings and nobles, hewn from the rock wall of the giant room. As his eyes lifted, he saw that the darkness of the cave was intermingled with small lights on the ceiling. No lanterns, but rather glowing dwarven runes of light above them. Time had dimmed them, but he was certain that when they were first carved they had lit the cave enough for any who came here.

The dwarf chuckled a bit as he saw several others mimicking Ealrin's glance around the room.

"There's not much time for gawking. Especially if we're to meet up with King Thoran!"

At this declaration, Teresa gasped and stepped forward.

"The king? You know of his whereabouts? Is he alright?"

Ealrin saw emotion in the face of the stout warrior. Though Teresa was a battle-hardened swordswoman, she was still a daughter to a father, Ealrin could see. A small smile creased his lips.

"The King lives or my names not Gorplin of Kaz-Ulum! We saw him not two days ago. He marches south from Liaf. Heard he had a little goblin trouble but took care of it. Nine thousand march south still."

Ealrin took a deep breath. He had been concerned for King Thoran's welfare. His look of relief was nothing compared to that of Teresa's, however. She looked years younger as she turned back to him.

And twice as beautiful with a smile on her face.

Of course, when she saw Ealrin smiling at her, she quickly resumed her usual hard glare.

Oh well, Ealrin thought, chuckling in his head. *At least she does have some emotion.*

"We'll march south in these tunnels and then come out close to Loran. The woods conceal our gate into the mountain, so we ought not to have any trouble getting to the king. Then we can sort out these Mercs!"

A cheer came from the survivors of Thoran, though they were bruised and battered.

"General Rayg has much to answer for the atrocities he committed at Kaz-Ulum and Cardun-Adush. Androlion, too, for that matter," the dwarf continued. "As far as we know, we're the only survivors of that mountain..."

The dwarf coughed into his hand and looked at his feet. Several other of the dwarves also cast their eyes down. Ealrin couldn't imagine what they must have been through. Escaping the carnage of the Mercs. Leaving behind family, friends, leaders, mentors, and others. What a terrible loss.

He clenched his fist. Such evil. And for what? To forestall some insane vision a man had of a coming calamity?

"He'll pay," Ealrin said under his breath. But apparently it was loud enough for some to hear standing next to him. Holve especially.

He placed a hand on Ealrin's shoulder and spoke again to the dwarf.

"We owe you our lives. Lead the way, Dwarves of Kaz-Ulum!"

Gorplin looked up from the dust. A tear stained his cheek and dripped down his beard.

"Bah. Were it not for the courage of your elves and the strength of your men, we wouldn't have been able to get you this far. Unlike Androlion, we're not so daft as to believe there's one race who can survive without the other. We have some weapons from the battlefield we stole in the night. Grab what you can. Warriors of Thoran, we march as one."

He bowed deeply to the crowd before him and his fellow dwarves copied his action.

Ealrin and the others from River Head returned the bow and began to walk forward to where the weapons were. The dwarves stood up and began putting whatever they could carry onto their backs. They looked determined and battle ready, despite their apparent lack of sleep and meals. Ealrin admired the fight in these dwarves.

And then he spotted it, among the other weapons purloined from the battlefield.

A certain sword, with a gap at the base of the blade and without a point at the end.

ACCORDING TO THE DWARVES, the march through these tunnels would take two days. After that, the company would emerge in a forest west of the city of Loran, where the King was supposed to be camping at this point. Though they were few in number, they would add something to the King's forces. Information, if nothing else.

The timing of the marching raiders from the south had helped the king's forces. Had they been late in coming, the two armies would have clashed at the border of Thoran and the Southern Republic.

Hopefully they were not in the midst of a battle yet.

For hours upon hours, they marched through tunnels. Ealrin couldn't help but marvel at the coolness of the caves. Though the heat of the summer suns had been nearly unbearable, it was cool and damp in these twisting tunnels.

On some occasions, they could march ten wide through the underground passage. At other moments the openings were barely wide enough for two. There was no stopping for meals. There was hardly anything to eat anyway. And so they marched on.

Holve was still beat up from the previous battle. He walked with a slight limp, and often needed to stop to rest. Though, he never made it obvious that it was he that needed to stop. He would stoop to help someone who had stumbled, only to linger himself. Or otherwise he would admire something carved into the wall as his breathing got back to normal. Still, the old man continued to walk as the rest of the company did. Ealrin was concerned for him.

Too often on this adventure Holve had been injured, not least of all by Rayg's blade. Whenever Ealrin asked Holve about the scar and the healing, he would just shrug him off and say,

"Nothing for a young buck like you to worry about. Keep marching."

Keep marching. That was the mantra.

It was hard to tell the passage of time in this cave. No sun guided their direction, nor did a moon rise to warn of impending nighttime. There was only the light of lanterns and the dim glow of dwarven runes.

After what felt like two days already, the command was given to halt and find a place to rest. Fortunately, they had stopped in a wider section of the tunnel. Nearly twenty souls could stand next to each other and still have to reach to touch the sides of the tunnel they now walked in.

Dwarves, elves, and men began to search around for a spot to lay themselves down. Comfort was not available, only rocks and dust.

The tunnel smelled damp and musty. The addition of several bodies that had not bathed in many days did not help the aroma of the cave. Ealrin's stomach began to turn due to lack of food and a nose that was too sensitive to the dank air.

"You're looking pale," said Teresa as she laid down her two swords on a natural stone shelf. She then found a place to sit and leaned up against the wall.

Ealrin was preparing a smart comment to fire back, but then he looked to see her face. Though her face was typically stout and showed great concentration, she now showed an emotion Ealrin had yet to see on her: fear.

Her eyes looked in all directions, up and down, left and right. She kept her arms close to her as she sat down, rubbing her arms with her hands. A bead of sweat came down her face, though the temperature in the cave was very cool.

Ealrin had been so focused on Holve today that he hadn't noticed Teresa. Had she been this scared all day?

"Are... are you ok, Teresa?" he asked her tentatively.

"Yes," she shot back at him. "I'm fine. Why?"

She glared at Ealrin with a somewhat normal expression for her, except that instead of keeping her eyes fixed on him, she kept glancing about the cave.

"I'm just not good underground," she said, more to herself than to Ealrin. "Are the dwarves sure this cave is safe?"

Holve chuckled as he too sat down and leaned his back against the cavern tunnel wall. The brown rock wall was smooth, as years of water trickling down the sides of the tunnel wall had worn it smooth.

Holve grunted as he seated himself, obviously still in pain but too proud to say he was hurting.

"They certainly wouldn't be here with us if it wasn't, Teresa. Try to rest."

Ealrin had a sudden urge, so he stood up.

"I'll go speak to Gorplin to check, Teresa. Be right back."

He turned to go and find the dwarf, probably towards the front of the company. As he walked, he glanced back at Holve and Teresa. Holve had a wry smile on his face, a knowing look on his face. Teresa cocked an eyebrow at Ealrin, then shook her head and looked down at her own boots.

Ealrin grabbed the hilt of his sword. It felt good to be reunited with the weapon Roland had given him. He had regretted leaving it behind on the battlefield. It was comforting to hold its handle. And despite the coolness of the cave, the blade and handle were warm to the touch. Ealrin was too glad to have it back to think much about this strange phenomenon.

Gorplin was indeed at the front of the group, discussing something with a group of other dwarves, some elves, and two men.

One of those men was Tory.

THE GROUP WAS DISCUSSING the next day's journey. Gorplin was leading the conversation, the new leader of the dwarves from Kaz-Ulum.

"By tomorrow noon, we'll follow this stream out of the mountain and to where it flows to the sea. Good thing it's a fresh water spring. We'll rest here tonight, where we can eat up some fish and drink plenty. That ought to give us all enough strength to march on tomorrow. If this spring weren't here, it'd be a different story. Let your crews know we leave in the morning."

Gorplin, though he was young for a dwarf, was quite in charge of the situation. He smiled at himself and seemed content with the progress of the day's march.

Then a question arose from the troops.

"And how will we know when it's morning in this blasted darkness?" asked an elf who looked as queasy as Teresa did.

Ealrin looked around and saw that not everyone was excited about being in a dark tunnel. The elves especially looked uncomfortable. Their homes generally were in the light of forests and trees, not the darkness of caves.

"Ah, I forgot!" said Gorplin as he reached into the pouch at his belt.

"At Kaz-Ulum we have reflectors of the suns that tell us the time of day. No such luck in this tunnel. So, we'll use this."

With that Gorplin pulled out an odd shaped object. It was metal on its top and base, but glass in-between. It was like someone had taken a tube of glass and pinched it in the middle. Something filled the top of the glass tube and was falling to the bottom half.

"It's called an hourglass," Gorplin said as he chuckled. "Or in our case, it's a half a day glass. It's filled with sand that flows from the top to the bottom. We'll rest until all the sand reaches the bottom of the glass. I'll have some dwarves take the first watch."

"I and some of the elves will watch as well. I doubt we'll be able to sleep underground anyway," said Lote from behind Ealrin. He jumped at her voice. He hadn't noticed her standing next to him or walking up to him. As all elves were, she was especially light on her feet.

"Not a fan of the dark?" Ealrin asked her.

"The dark I can handle. It's this rock roof I wish to be done with. It just feels like it'll crush us at any moment," she said as she looked towards the ceiling.

Several elves and a few men looked up with wary eyes at the dark brown ceiling of the cave.

Gorplin let out another chuckle.

"I wouldn't worry yourselves much," he said as he put a hand to the wall of the cave.

Gorplin's glove glowed with a dim and gentle green light.

Then Ealrin gasped, as did several others.

Spreading out from the point where Gorplin touched the wall, several dwarven runes began to emit the same green glow as his glove. All over the tunnel cavern similar runes also glowed green.

"This whole tunnel system has been reinforced by dwarven runes, and some dwarven engineering as well. This tunnel won't be coming down in this generation or the next! Now, go make sure everyone's drinking plenty and eating. We march at the turn of the hourglass."

Ealrin smiled to himself and to Lote. Being in a cave wasn't a bad thing, as long as it was with a dwarf who knew what he was doing.

"Go settle the elves, Lote. And thanks for your bravery today," Ealrin put a hand on the elf's shoulder. Without the dwarves and elves, Ealrin would surely still be tied up and a prisoner of the Mercs.

Or dead.

The group began to disperse, and Ealrin looked around. There was still one person he wanted to talk to.

"TORY!" HE CALLED AS he watched the twin walk away from the group. He noticed that Tory's shoulders drooped. It was certainly not how he carried himself normally. But then again, this was not a normal day.

Ealrin wanted to know how Tory was handling his brother's betrayal. Not only had he deserted the king, but he had also killed his fellow soldiers. Dwarves Ealrin had seen him talk with, laugh with, and fight with. Perhaps his brother could make sense of the situation when Ealrin could not.

"How are you doing?" Ealrin asked hesitantly. He really didn't know how else to bring up the topic.

"The march today has been alright, but I'm looking forward to seeing the sun again," he replied without looking at Ealrin. Without seeing directly into the man's eyes, Ealrin could tell that they were red and puffy. Were those tears of mourning or of anger?

"Tory," Ealrin said, trying to figure out how to best approach the subject he was most curious about. He attempted to put a hand on Tory's shoulder, but Tory knocked it away with his own.

"Look," Tory said, taking a step back and looking directly at Ealrin's face. "I don't want to talk about Cory. I don't know why he did what he did. I don't know why he would kill his own people. All I know is that now Androlion has stolen from me not only a friend, but also a brother." His voice was rising as he spoke and several turned to look at him now shouting at Ealrin.

Ealrin was now wishing he had not brought it up.

"When next we see Androlion Fellgate, it'll be his head or mine."

And with that, Tory stalked off into a part of the tunnel where no others were. Ealrin knew that this was something Tory Greenwall, perhaps for the first time in his life, would face by himself.

EALRIN WALKED BACK to where Holve and Teresa were carrying his collected provisions: five fish and two containers of fresh spring water.

Fishing had given Ealrin some time to think. It had also given Teresa and Holve the opportunity to build a small fire out of some moss and ribs throughout the cave. Others had done the same, causing the roof of the tunnel to become filled with smoke, but due to its height and an outlet somewhere unseen by Ealrin's eyes, the smoke did not stay in the cave or come down low enough to bother its occupants.

"I didn't think you were coming back," Teresa said, looking up at Ealrin with a scolding look on her face.

She was never one to begin conversations, or to throw needless words about. Ealrin looked at Holve questioningly.

"She talks when she's nervous, compounded with the fact that we are both hungry. Hand over the fish," Holve said, answering Ealrin's unspoken question.

Teresa gave Holve a mean look but said nothing more. She accepted the fish from Ealrin and began to cook it over the fire, using her sword as a spit.

After eating and drinking Ealrin's stomach felt better, but his mind was still a whirlwind.

What effect was the treason of Cory going to have on the King when he saw him? How was the king faring, and had he met the raiders on the battlefield yet? How was Holve, who was now snoring away beside him, going to handle the next day's march?

Why did Teresa look more beautiful when she slept than when she was awake?

And if fate had intended for Ealrin to survive the dangers he had faced so far, what else was in store for him, the man with no past and a bleak future?

35: The Use of Lesser Races

The company was awake and moving at the turn of Gorplin's hourglass. True to their word, the elves had not slept much at all, but rather spent their time keeping watch, replenishing containers of water, and fishing in order to have food on hand for the next day.

No one was sad for their efforts. Not even the elves.

"You snore," Teresa said as she woke from her sleep. It took a moment for her to stretch and stand up. Ealrin knew why.

Sleeping on a cave floor was perhaps the least comfortable bed he could remember. And that included Soltack's books. His back ached, his legs were still tired from the previous day's journey, not to mention his entire body still hurt from the stress and fatigue of the battle he fought just two days ago. He was unsure of when he would get any real respite.

Twin suns, has it only been two days? Ealrin thought. It felt like he had lived a lifetime in those short cycles of the sun.

After cleaning up to care for the ancient dwarven caves, the group marched on.

Without giving it anymore thought, due to the prodding of the dwarves up front and the goading of the elves behind, Ealrin collected his few things and began marching alongside Holve and Teresa again.

By afternoon they would see the sun.

THE STREAM THAT BEGAN in the cavern where they rested continued on throughout the tunnel they walked in. Perhaps at one time it had filled this tunnel with water and formed it out. That may also have been why the dwarves left the tunnel unused. Knowing nothing about tunnels or caves or rivers and not wanting to frighten Teresa any more than she already was, Ealrin decided to bring up a different topic.

One he was still curious about.

The ground was damper here, possibly due to the presence of the underground stream. There were times when they marched alongside it on rocky paths covered in some type of slimy plant that could thrive in such an environment. Other times the stream widened and they were forced to march through it, soaking their boots and marching as deep as their knees in the cold water.

As they marched through the brown tunnels of rock and earth, ducking under rock formations, Ealrin voiced his question to Holve.

"What are we going to do about Cory?" he asked his friend who, despite his obvious pain and tiredness, was determined to doggedly trudge through the cave. Holve would not take rests today.

"Nothing, Ealrin. Cory has chosen his own path. Fate will deal with him now," was the answer he gave back. He walked in front of Ealrin due to the slimness of their current tunnel and so his face was hidden. What emotion was playing over it right now? Was there any?

"I think fate has little to do with justice," Ealrin said back, hoping to elicit some type of response more than what he had already received.

Holve did indeed look back as he kept walking, shin deep in the stream.

"You think so?"

Ealrin was about to push for more, getting a little upset that Holve had nothing to say on the matter, but was surprised when Holve continued.

"It's true that I've seen good people go to jail or worse for crimes they were falsely accused of. I've seen criminals and murderers live out their lives without ever having to face trial for their crimes or see the faces of those who were most affected by their evil. I've seen kings push their countries to war for little more than a stone's throw of territory and cause thousands to march to their deaths. They win a war and then sign over that same land later to another country just because it would benefit them more."

He paused as he walked. He considered several different ways to say what was to come out of his mouth next. The bubbling of the stream, the splashing of hundreds of feet through water, and the murmur of those around him filled Ealrin's ears for a moment before he began to speak again.

"The difference between a good man and an evil one is how at peace with themselves they are. There's a reason a thief sleeps with a knife. His rest is never rest. He's tortured by his deeds. He may try to convince himself that he's done nothing wrong, but his heart knows better. The one who does well may not get ahead, but he'll be at peace with himself."

Again, Holve looked back at Ealrin. It wasn't anger that filled his face, like Tory had the day before. Instead, there was something else there. Was it sadness?

"Fate will deal with Cory. It may not be today, but later we'll know the extent of the harm he's caused himself."

Ealrin simply nodded and continued onward, thinking on what Holve had said. Would time really be the true teller of the consequence of Cory's decision to abandon his people, kill his friends, and betray his king? Ealrin didn't quite feel like that was sufficient.

"If fate leaves out justice, my swords will not," Teresa said from behind Ealrin as they marched on.

Neither, apparently, did Teresa.

AFTER MARCHING FOR what felt like days through dwarven rune lit tunnels, admiring large caverns, and once being forced down to hands and knees through the underground stream to fit through a very tiny opening, Ealrin could see a trace of sunlight up ahead.

The warm air was markedly different than the cool dampness that he had been breathing all morning. He took a deep breath of the summer breeze that was blowing into the tunnel and sighed.

"I think I agree with the elves," Ealrin said as he took a second, deep breath of the warm air. "I prefer the sky over my head rather than rocks."

"Then don't just stand here breathing in the breeze," Teresa said as she shoved Ealrin aside in an effort to get out of the cave as quickly as possible.

Ealrin smiled at Holve. He knew Teresa had endured the march this morning with gritted teeth and a warrior's determination. The promise of sunshine was all that had kept her from losing her grip and giving into her fear of this cave.

As everyone pushed forward towards the entrance of the cave, they began to bottleneck at the opening. Apparently they weren't quite ready for everyone to leave the cave for some reason. Ealrin could see Teresa making a concentrated effort to leave, pushing her way past several men of Thoran and stepping around several dwarves.

Ealrin put aside what he normally thought a princess would be like: prim and proper, dainty and ladylike. Teresa was a different type of princess.

Holve sat down, winded after a long morning of marching without rest. He breathed heavily and wiped perspiration from his brow.

"Not sure why we've stopped when we're so close to the exit," Ealrin said out loud, more to himself than to Holve. He was really looking forward to seeing the sun and figuring out where they actually had walked to. He couldn't picture in his mind the map of Ruyn that Holve tried to describe to him. He was better at seeing with his own eyes.

In no time at all Teresa had returned. She was no longer wearing a relieved look that promised sunshine, nor was she looking afraid of the cave either. Instead, she wore the look of determination that creased her brow and made her eyes glow.

Something was wrong.

"Holve, Gorplin wants you up at the mouth of the cave. You may as well come, too, Ealrin. Goblins."

EALRIN, GORPLIN, HOLVE, Teresa, and Lote all lay on their bellies as they looked out of the mouth of the cave. What looked like five hundred goblins had made camp within a stone's throw of where the survivors lay watching them. The sunlight filtered down from the tops of the trees that covered the base of the mountain they had traveled under and stretched all the way to the edge of the ocean. From this distance, Ealrin could smell the sea. Gorplin and Holve estimated they were somewhere in-between Liaf and Loran on the southern coast of Thoran.

The coast that was covered in goblins.

Most had made some type of lean-to out of fallen branches and strips of raggedy cloth. Others had simply passed out underneath bushes and other shrubs. There was a lot of commotion going on in the camp, however, and it wasn't because a group of humans, elves, and dwarves were all within reach. Four or five fights had broken out between goblins and around each were fifty or so others egging them on.

They insulted the fighters and encouraged those they had placed bets on. From here Ealrin could see pots that goblins kept chucking gold bits into. Every now and then one of the spectators got drug into the fighting. Whether it was for a particularly nasty insult or betting against a fighter who took it personally, the fights continued to grow and became even rowdier.

Ealrin wondered how any goblin general could convince another goblin to do anything.

These were the strangest beasts, he thought.

"Bah. Nothing to stop us from ridding this forest of their ilk," said Gorplin as he began to rise from his position of observing, using his battle hammer to push himself up.

"Hold on there, friend," Holve said as he put a hand on Gorplin's shoulder, urging him back down. "I'm sure that with your courage and skill we could rid ourselves of these pests, but I'm more curious about what these goblins are doing here, on the eastern side of Ruyn. They would have either had to sail all around the Southern Republic unhindered or marched here without meeting any resistance. And I find it odd that they are positioned outside the very tunnel we traveled through."

Ealrin began to think on Holve's words. It was odd that such a large group of goblins would end up here. It was almost as if...

"Do you suppose they are not acting on their own whims?" Teresa asked Holve, finishing Ealrin's thoughts for him. "But who would a goblin listen to? I'm surprised they listen to their own leaders."

It was true. The scene in front of Ealrin was chaos.

"I'm unsure, Teresa. I wonder, if we may be able to get a closer look at them and find out a bit more about what they are doing here?"

Holve turned his attention from Teresa to Lote. She nodded at Holve's unasked question, understanding her role in this.

Ealrin, though, had a thought.

"I'm going with her, Holve," he said, unsheathing his sword. "If things get crazy, she'll need a helping hand."

Holve looked at Lote, who shrugged as she drew her bow and notched an arrow into it.

"Follow closely and keep quiet," she said in response. Of course she would be able to get close enough to listen in on the goblins. Such was the skill of her race. Whereas Ealrin would only be a hindrance. He was surprised she agreed to his suggestion.

Holve chuckled softly and looked at Ealrin.

"I'd do as you're told," he said. Then turning back to Lote, he continued.

"Look for the biggest one pushing everyone else around. He ought to be the leader, or at least know something about why they camped out here. If you need help, signal and we'll be ready from the cave."

"I'm going, too," Teresa said as she drew her own two blades.

"With hundreds of goblins out there, if you're discovered you'll need more than a bow and a blunt sword."

FORTUNATELY, THE RUCKUS from the goblins fighting and their generally loud stomping and crushing through the woods while trying to find food and pick on other goblins made sneaking around the edge of their camp quite easy.

Ealrin knew that Lote could have tiptoed her way right through the middle of the goblin camp without being detected. Such was her skill as an elf. But Ealrin wanted to know and hear for himself what the goblins were doing here. Plus, he had to admit, the risk and adventure of it allured him.

Maybe, in his life before being shipwrecked at Good Harbor, he had been a little more reckless than he ought to have been.

The trees and undergrowth of the forest grew thickly here. Gorplin and Holve had guessed that they had emerged from the tunnel at the southern end of Thoran and therefore a road that connected the two cities of Liaf and Loran should be close by. If the king was going to march from one to the other, he would have to use this road.

Which could explain the presence of the goblins.

THE TRIO TOOK SPECIAL care to crouch below the bushes and undergrowth of the forest so as not to be easily spotted. Ealrin was beginning to feel like this was an unnecessary precaution, as any goblin who would want to pick a fight was preoccupied with the squabbles taking place deep in the camp.

Other goblins, who were perhaps lazier, simply slept in their tents or out in the open ground. One in particular was much more ornately decorated. Unlike the other tents that were blankets thrown over branches, this one was actually constructed out of tent poles and yellow colored canvas. A goblin banner hung outside of it. Three red stripes ran down a yellow background looking like something with claws had made the design.

Several skulls hung from the ends of the banners as well as adorned the top of the tent pegs. The tent stood taller than Ealrin could reach, which was huge for the shorter goblins.

Around the tent, several taller and more muscular goblins stood guard while others simply ran around the camp.

Ealrin tapped Lote's shoulder and pointed to it. She nodded silently and gestured for him and Teresa to follow her so they could get closer to it.

And so, the three crept closer toward the tent while staying out of sight of any goblins that were close or could see them. They weaved in and out of other makeshift tents and lean twos and bushes before coming within a few steps of the tent.

As they approached it, one of the fights in the goblin camp took a more violent turn. Ealrin could see the head of a defeated goblin being lifted up into the air by his opponent. The goblins surrounding the victorious one began pressing in on him. Some of the larger ones outside the tent huffed and marched toward the commotion. Whether to break it up or join the fight Ealrin didn't know.

Now they were right next to the tent and could distinctly hear voices inside of it. They listened through the canvas to better hear the conversation.

What they heard next sent Ealrin's mind racing.

"...Androlion's original promise to you still stands. The goblins have done well, but you have yet to completely fulfill my master's wishes," said a voice that Ealrin had heard before. One that reminded him of an inn, Blume, and escaping Breyland on stolen horses.

Verde. One of the Merc generals.

"It's not my fault you were late. It's not my fault Grayscar lost. He was dumb. Not strong enough. You promised goblins the mountains. You promised more shock rock," said the voice of a goblin. Ealrin remembered how much he disliked the beasts. Not to mention that this one sounded mad.

"You will keep your promise. Otherwise the goblins might forget their part."

The three heard the sound of scuffling inside and a choking noise. Then came the sound of Verde's harsh words.

"You filth will remember your place. Either bring us the head of the king or forget the bargain. Not only will you not inherit the mountains of Thoran, but you'll forfeit that desert you call home as well."

With that they heard a crash, which to Ealrin sounded like the unfortunate goblin Verde had just reprimanded had been thrown into a pile of wood. Or a table.

The sound of several boots moving at once came to their ears along with the call from Verde, which sounded further away, suggesting he was leaving the other side of the tent.

"The king marches from Liaf to Loran. See that he doesn't make it."

There was the sound of moving fabric on the other side as well as calls of "Get out-of-the-way!" and "Move it!"

Verde and some other soldiers were making their way out of the goblin camp.

From inside the tent there came a groan and a disgruntled voice.

"Stupid humans. Bossing goblins around. We'll teach them. Stinkrunt'll show them all."

The sound of bits of wood being thrown to the side and the goblin scrambling to his feet filled the tent. Ealrin looked to Teresa and Lote.

Androlion was in league with the gray-skinned beasts.

"I'M NOT SAYING I DON'T believe. I'm just saying it doesn't make sense."

Holve was responding to the story Ealrin was relating to him after they had successfully navigated back to the mouth of the cave. Well, mostly successfully. The goblin camp would be missing one nosey goblin tonight, but with the ruckus that was still going on, he probably wouldn't be missed terribly.

"Does it matter if they're in league with the rat or not? We still can't leave this cave until we've gotten rid of the vermin," said Gorplin. Of those gathered around the mouth of the cave discussing their next steps after finding out this new bit of information, his opinion of what to do hadn't changed.

Fight the goblins.

Ealrin was beginning to think there might not be any other options. King Thoran was planning on marching this way. If his numbers hadn't been affected by the march or the struggle with, who was it again? Grayscar? Then he should have no problem with this ragtag bunch of goblins.

Ten thousand versus five hundred was laughable.

But what in the world was shock rock?

"What we still don't know is if there are any more of them," reminded Holve. He was convinced that, for the goblins to think they could take on the King and his army, they must either have been lied to grievously by Verde or have other goblin clans waiting in a part of the forest nearby or on ships out at sea.

He seemed more cautious than Ealrin could remember in recent past.

Lote hadn't said much since coming back and reporting. She instead sat and stared up at the night sky without adding any commentary to the meeting.

Teresa, on the other hand, was beginning to get irritated with Holve and his cautious attitude.

"If the king marches and there are more of them, then all the better for us to deal with the ones we see in front of us," she said, raising her voice a little too loudly for Holve's taste.

He shushed her with a hand.

She was ready to march off fuming when Holve looked to Lote. She had signaled to the group quietly.

Something was happening out in the goblin camp.

Something that involved a whole lot of goblins yelling.

IT DIDN'T TAKE LONG for the survivors in the cave to see what the fuss was all about.

The night sky had begun to turn a deep orange through the forest trees, though the morning light was not due for at least half of Gorplin's hourglass.

All of the goblins were running away from the base of the mountain and towards the sea. Whether it was to escape the light or to get a better look, Ealrin couldn't tell.

All he knew was that their escape was now possible, as the forest had been nearly cleared of the gray menace.

It was time to leave.

Looking back to the others, he could tell they were thinking the same thing. Holve spoke to Gorplin first.

"We'll fight goblins again another time, my courageous friend. For now, let us find a king."

Gorplin didn't argue, but he did look a bit downcast at losing the chance to bash some goblins with his hammer.

Word soon got back to the cave that the company would be moving soon and everyone pressed toward the entrance. Teresa and Lote were already outside, surveying the area in order to see if any stragglers had stayed behind.

Ealrin heard the twang of a bowstring and the grunt of a goblin.

Apparently some had.

"I'll amend what I said, Gorplin," Holve said as they began to file out of the cave. "You'll fight goblins today after all."

Ealrin took up his sword next to the dwarf. Teresa drew her blades and Lote strung another arrow to her bow.

Indeed, there were some goblins that ran to them with a fierceness.

Ealrin's brow furrowed.

The night was about to burn red as well.

THE CAVE EMPTIED QUICKLY as a few defended those fleeing.

Granted the dwarves weren't much for stealth compared to the
men and especially the silence of the elves, but since the goblins were
mostly so far off at this point it didn't matter much.

They hugged the base of the mountain, ensuring to keep as many
trees in-between them as possible as they made their way north.

If King Thoran was to march this way, the least they could do was
to meet him en route.

And still the sky burned orange.

"What in the world is that, Holve?" Ealrin asked as they marched
as quickly as they dared through the forest.

Holve was still slow but also stubborn. The few hundred kept a
decent pace as they made their way north to Liaf. Holve wouldn't
slow for anyone. Though he grunted and grimaced, he marched.

"We'll know once we see the sky," he said through gritted teeth.
Ealrin could tell the journey had worn down the soldier. "For the
time being, march."

And so, they marched.

It must have been two hours, maybe three, before they came to
the clearing. A wide circle of trees opened before them. For some reason, no tall pine or oak grew in this ring, only grass.

It would have been time for Ealrin to wonder what would cause
such a thing to occur.

If it were not for the burning orange comet in the sky.

"Not so dark anymore is it?" said Gorplin as the dwarves came
out of the forest last. Their short legs weren't meant for quickness.

"You know about the Dark Comet?" asked Ealrin, only afterwards realizing how foolish a question it had been. Anyone with a
view of the sky in the last two years would have seen the fireball in
the night sky.

But none, until now, had seen it so close.

"Yes," replied Gorplin, ignoring the silliness of Ealrin's question. "Though we dwarves don't pay much attention to the skies. I'd rather be lost in a mine than the stars."

"A fault of your race at times, I think," replied Lote as she gazed up at the sky.

Ealrin thought that might have been a bit harsh on the dwarf. Gorplin agreed, as he gripped his hammer a little tighter and huffed loudly.

Holve placed a hand on Gorplin's shoulder. Perhaps it was to calm the dwarf down. Perhaps also it was to steady himself. His breathing was still heavy from the last hour's march.

"We've been watching the dark one as it approached Gilia," continued Lote, not noticing Gorplin's anger at her statement. "It brings an omen with it. Though what exactly it is, I cannot say. The stars do not tell the future as definitively as the runes set in the stones of dwarves. They more show the path a river could take unimpeded. A possible course. One of many possibilities."

All stood gazing up at the fiery comet. It was, indeed, closer than Ealrin had seen since he could remember. Of course, that was only a short time. But never had it burned this brightly in the night sky. That he knew from Holve and Roland's stories. It had always been a deep purple, thus disappearing in the night sky and earning its name.

There was a moment of silence from those gathering in the clearing.

In the distance, the shouts of goblins rang out over the night noises: the chirping of crickets, the call of night birds, and the babble of a nearby stream.

Ealrin voiced what he imagined others were thinking.

"What possibilities have your people seen in the sky, Lote?"

She broke her gaze with the comet and looked to Ealrin. Her eyes were misty and, could it be, a tear?

She opened her mouth to speak, but before she had time to answer, they heard the peal of a trumpet.

A herald of Thoran.

36: King Thoran

The maroon and gold banners of the army of the king were a welcomed sight to Ealrin. It had been nearly four weeks since he had last seen them march from the capital. Though they looked as if they had recently been in battle, their numbers were still sufficient enough to take the Merc army from the pass on even ground.

Spears stood tall and pierced the night sky. Swords clanged against shields on the backs of eight thousand. Boots marched along the road that split the beach from the forest and mountains. Two thousand horses carried two thousand spears and their holders. In the middle of it all was the king himself. His personal banner to his left, an eagle clutching a sword and wearing a crown, and the banner of Thoran to his right.

Here was hope.

Men, elves, and dwarves cheered as the company began to march through their ranks. Mostly at the sight of Holve and Teresa: the general of Thoran and the daughter of the king.

Perhaps there was hope in them as well.

Yet something was odd to Ealrin.

It was nighttime, yet the army marched as if it were the middle of the day. Could the light of the comet spur them into action? Or was it something else?

They approached the king, who at seeing them, raised his hand to stop the march. Trumpets sounded out again from all around and the army halted.

"My king," Holve said, as he bowed. Those around him, including the dwarves of Kaz-Ulum did likewise. "We are grateful to see you as we have much to say."

Ealrin looked up at the king.

Though he could tell there was relief to see Holve, Teresa, and the others, there was a furrow on his brow and pain in his voice.

"My general, my daughter. It is good to see you safe. But where is the army that marched from River Head?"

Holve stood up and looked around him. As he did, there came the pounding of goblins drums from further south.

"We've much to say, my king. But I fear it must be as we prepare for battle."

AS IT TURNED OUT, HOLVE was right. From their vantage point outside of the forest, it was evident that at least fifty goblin ships floated out at sea.

And from them rowed countless smaller boats, bringing the remainder of the gray horde to shore.

The scouts who were surveying the landing of the boats counted six to eight thousand goblins. This was to be a battle that would be hard fought and sorely won.

If it was to be won at all.

While the preparations were being made, Gorplin, Lote, Teresa, Ealrin, and Holve met with King Thoran to discuss the current standing of the Swords as well as their new-found knowledge of Androlion.

Of those swords who had marched from River Head, only Tory, Teresa, Holve, Lote, and a male elf named Minare remained. Frerin, Khali, and Narvi had perished in the battle with the Mercs. Frerin and Narvi at the hands of Cory. The two other elves, Enlon and Elel, were unaccounted for, as was Brute, the largest and strongest of the human Swords. Some said he was defending the entrance to the cave that collapsed as the survivors escaped from the Mercs through the tunnel. Ealrin knew better but didn't see a need to correct their stories.

Let them remember Brute as a strong defender, he thought.

King Thoran's countenance was sullen. His most elite warriors had fallen to the hands of betrayal and war. Ealrin could tell that this was why the king had not trained other knights and warriors in his domain.

The man hated war as much as Ealrin did.

"As for those lost in battle, we remember their sacrifice and will hereby make it count for something worthwhile. All of them," the king thrust his own spear into the sky as he looked at those who stood in a circle around him. His shout was loud and fierce. "A Sword of the King!"

"A Sword of the King!" came the salute from those who remained.

"And as for Cory. We will not let such betrayal go unpunished. He will find justice, whether by my hand or by that of my allies." At this, the king looked down to Gorplin and put his hand on the dwarf's shoulder.

"I would hope you will find Thoran to be your ally, brave dwarf of Kaz-Ulum. I owe the lives of those who stand before me to you and your people. You are a skilled and able leader. I am sorry to hear of the attack on your mountain, but I hope that our meeting has been determined by fate and that we can become great allies, Gorplin of Kaz-Ulum."

Gorplin's chest swelled with pride at being addressed so. A grim smile pushed at his beard and mustache as he looked up at the king and raised his hammer in salute.

"Bah! You'll find the dwarves of Kaz-Ulum to be strong allies, My Lord! Our allegiance is set!"

The king looked up as the sound of goblin drums began to resonate stronger southwest of them. The horde was approaching.

"See to your people, Gorplin," the king said. "I've assembled the dwarves of Thoran by the forest on the road. My men can handle charging on the beach. I'll not make you suffer by running in the sand for my sake."

"Bah. A strong ally indeed!" said Gorplin, as he hefted his hammer to his shoulder and jogged off to join his companions and the other dwarves in the coming battle.

The king then turned to Teresa and smiled at her. Ealrin saw in his eyes a great sense of relief.

"My daughter," he said as he held his arms out to embrace her.

On the field of battle, Teresa was one of the most intimidating warriors Ealrin had ever seen; in the arms of her father she was the picture of a king's princess.

He held her for several moments and took her shoulders in his hands. He looked at her with great affection and love.

Ealrin wondered if he had a father like that.

"You have never been one for dresses and frilly things, Teresa. I wonder, if your mother were still alive, if you would have preferred a quieter life than the one you have chosen. And yet, I could never be prouder of who you are. You are one fine soldier for your king and your father. You have served me well. I would tell you not to fight in the front ranks, but I know it wouldn't do any good."

At this the king chuckled and held her face with one hand.

"Be brave, my daughter. Lead your people bravely. Attend to the warriors on the beach. Show them that the house of Thoran is a courageous one."

He embraced her once more and then placed his forehead on hers.

"Be safe and return to me when the battle is won."

With that, Teresa saluted her father and King, and made her way to the beach. Ealrin saw that the king's face showed pride and hurt. How it must pain him to send his daughter into battle. And yet, as Ealrin had plainly seen, Teresa was one of his finest warriors.

The king turned his attention back to Ealrin and Holve.

"I had hoped we would meet under better circumstances, but fate would not have it."

He considered them both for a moment.

With a sigh, he said, "Holve, stay at my side in this. I fear what may come after the goblins as well as for your health. You don't look well, my friend. The journey you've taken has been difficult for you, though you try to hide it, I can tell."

Holve grimaced but bowed.

"Yes, My King," he said as he stood straight again, he hefted his spear to his side. It really was such a fine piece of work and only after having seen thousands of spears being carried by other warriors of Thoran did Ealrin really see that it was special.

He grasped his own odd, but plain sword.

"And what would you have of me?" Ealrin asked.

The king's face turned into a weary smile as he looked at Ealrin with his compassionate eyes.

"My general is at my side and yet my daughter goes to the front lines. I wonder if you would serve the king by serving his princess."

Ealrin bowed and said, "I will, King Thoran."

He began to walk off towards the beach, the same direction Teresa had gone only moments ago, but then stopped.

On an impulse, he took the few steps back to Holve and hugged him.

It certainly caught Holve off guard, but then Ealrin felt himself wrapped in the arms of his constant companion since his shipwreck. It felt good.

He let go of Holve and stepped back to look into those same eyes that had watched over him when he was unconscious. The eyes that had guided him to this point. He felt like whenever he was in the sight of Holve, all was well.

Holve spoke.

"Ealrin Bealouve, you've come a long way in a year. For all I know, I still couldn't say where you come from."

And he knew Holve was right.

Looking down Ealrin thought about his journey. Out of all their many travels over Ruyn thus far, Ealrin hadn't recognized a soul, nor had anyone else thought they had seen him before. But then he looked back into Holve's eyes. Something was wrong.

Was that a tear?

Holve took a deep breath through his nose and continued on.

"To hell with who you were, Ealrin. I've been most impressed with who you are becoming!"

Holve slapped his shoulder and shoved him away.

"Now get out there before the goblins get to the front!"

And with that, Ealrin ran towards the beach to join Teresa and fight for the kingdom of Thoran.

For a country he thought he might soon call home.

37: War

E alrin stood on the front line with the rest of the warriors of Thoran. On his right was Teresa. Once again, her face was that of a stout warrior. While she was in the arms of her father, Ealrin had thought that the warrior side of her had vanished completely. Out here on the field of battle, however, Ealrin was sure he had imagined her softer side altogether.

Her blades were drawn and held tightly in her hands. She paced back-and-forth slightly, always keeping an eye on the growing tide of goblins on the horizon.

"You ever fought goblins before?" asked Cedric, one of the human survivors and scouts for the previous battle. He looked younger than Ealrin, and under the certain circumstances of their upcoming fight, a little nervous.

"Once," Ealrin replied, looking over at the young scout. "It was several months ago out at sea. The key is to aim low."

Cedric chuckled a little, the tension in his face easing.

"I'll try to keep that in mind," he said.

Cedric looked back to the horizon and his eyebrows furrowed.

"They're coming," he said.

Ealrin looked and saw that a flood of gray was spilling over the horizon.

"Why do you suppose there's war?" Cedric asked as he unsheathed his sword and readied his shield.

Ealrin's answer was already on his lips.

"As long as there is unchecked evil and hatred, and those who are willing to oppose it have courage, there will be war." He paused for a moment as he took his own sword out of its sheath. He looked back to Cedric.

"A friend told me that."

TERESA STOPPED HER pacing, grimaced at the approaching goblin horde, and then turned to the army of Thoran.

"Warriors of Thoran!"

She raised both her blades high.

"Do not fight these monsters because you relish the chance to swing your sword! Do not fight them because you detest their race! These that charge us have threatened our home! They come to kill and destroy our families, our people!

"Warriors of Thoran, let us show those that would force evil onto a nation that strives for peace and the good of all what will come to it! Your king fights with you! Defend your homes! Protect your king!"

She turned and pointed her blade at the approaching horde. Thousands of goblins now sprinted toward the line of Thoran warriors. Ealrin could see elves standing in the forest, bows strung and ready. Dwarves stood on the road, preparing for a charge of their own.

War had come to Thoran.

"For Thoran! For the king!"

"For Thoran!" came the thunderous reply as four thousand men surged forward, spears out, swords drawn, fire in their hearts.

EALRIN RAN AS HARD as he could on the sandy beach. His hands already ached from gripping his sword and borrowed maroon shield.

It was the third time in two weeks his sword would draw blood.

Above him, a hail of elvish arrows flew. They rained down on the goblins' ranks and peppered the first hundred.

It was no matter.

Thousands more raced over their fallen comrades.

The two lines smashed into one another. Goblins leapt high in the air, throttling some Thoran warriors with their spears. Teresa carved a path through the gray beasts and Ealrin did his best to keep up, to be her defender.

She hardly needed it.

Through the chaos, Ealrin could perceive the dwarves smashing into their section of goblins.

The elves continued the rain of arrows upon the goblins both at close quarters and at those who continued to run forward.

Blood mixed with sand and ocean around Ealrin's feet.

He parried a blow with his sword, then thrust his own into his attacker. He drew it back and swung again at another goblin.

The tide of gray was endless.

All around him warriors of Thoran slew scores of their enemy. And yet more replaced those slain.

Men fell to the ground and were overcome by sheer numbers. Others fought on despite being desperately wounded.

Teresa whirled around in circles, her blades slaying everything they touched.

Four hours the battle raged.

Ealrin knew not whether he trod on sand, earth, or body.

It didn't matter.

There was no time to see the ground, only the enemy.

And yet in all the battling, as the sun began to sink beyond the horizon, the night sky was a bright orange, as the Dark Comet came ever closer to the land of Ruyn.

FINALLY THE CRIES OF war died, replaced by the moans of the wounded and a triumphant cry from the warriors of Thoran.

They were victorious.

What was left of the goblins were running back to their boats and making their way back to the ships still out at sea. Perhaps only a few hundred fled. The rest were slain on the beaches and the road.

Other warriors of Thoran were going through the bodies, easing the passing of the hopelessly wounded and identifying those who may still be helped by the healers. The healers were in white robes, running from wounded to wounded in order to try to save a few.

Ealrin sat on the sand. His body ached in a hundred different places. His arm hung limply at his side, bandaged and still tingling from the healer's Speaking over it just moments ago. The goblin that had cut his arm lay motionless at his feet. It wasn't the beast that Ealrin was looking at, however.

It was Cedric.

The young scout lay dead. The wound in his chest given to him by the goblin Ealrin had been cut by and slain himself.

A long sigh escaped Ealrin.

Here, among the countless dead of goblins, men, dwarves, and elves, Ealrin wondered if war really was the way for good to conquer evil.

Teresa walked up behind him. He recognized her not by her face, for he didn't raise his head to look, but by the armor on her legs and blades that hung at her sides.

"War is hell," she said.

Ealrin wiped his cheek to brush away a pesky tear that had come. Was a warrior supposed to be this heartbroken over one who gave his life defending his home? He didn't know that much about Cedric, yet looking into his youthful face, staring, but unseeing, he felt as if he had lost a brother.

"Agreed," Ealrin replied.

And then the trumpet sounded.

Not of the king, nor from a dwarf or elf.

Ealrin stood and looked south, from where the goblins had come.

Over the horizon marched thousands of soldiers bearing the banners of the Southern Republic and white griffin of Androlion Fellgate.

38: Negotiations

The king, Lote, Gorplin, and Holve rode their horses down the dirt road packed hard by the years of travelers and the battle just fought. All had small injuries from the battle with the goblins. Holve had a bandage over his head, covering a wound that was still bleeding. Lote and Gorplin shared a horse, no doubt because Gorplin's feet would never reach the flanks of the animal. Lote was scratched all over her face and hands, possibly from pursuing goblins through the forest. Gorplin was not bleeding from any place in particular, but rather from several places that revealed how hard fought the victory was. The king's arm was in a sling. No doubt he had been attended to by healers and now was resting the arm.

Rest for a weapon arm would not last long under the current circumstances.

King Thoran looked down to Ealrin and Teresa. His face was hard. In his face, Ealrin saw sadness and rage, weariness and strength, wisdom and daring.

This was a man he would follow.

"Ealrin, ride out with us. A horse comes for you. Carry the banner of Thoran. We will go to meet Androlion and stop this madness."

As he spoke a rider came up behind them, bearing the image of the king as well as the banner of Thoran. A second horse was with him, saddled and ready.

Ealrin was glad to see the rider looking down to him.

"How did you fare in the battle, Tory?" Ealrin asked his fellow Sword of the King as he mounted the horse and relieved Tory of his second banner, the maroon and gold flag of Thoran.

"I claim at least thirty-seven. Though Holve would dispute the last," he replied as he checked the sword at his side.

Tory, too, was bandaged and weary looking. Still, Ealrin could see a grim determination in his eyes and he remembered his last words to Ealrin.

Tory Greenwall wanted Androlion's blood.

"I'll dispute because I claimed the last. I saved your life and you've yet to be grateful," Holve shot at Tory.

Teresa was not amused by the exchange.

"Where is my horse, father? I'm going with you," she said as she sheathed her blades and looked into the eyes of her father.

Ealrin guessed what was about to happen.

"My dearest Teresa," the king began. Ealrin was reminded of the manner one tells a friend of a family member's passing or of the loss of a good friend.

He had heard that tone of voice many times since leaving Good Harbor.

"We cannot win this battle if the Mercs attack us. Our numbers are too few. Four thousand left of what marched here. Androlion has twice as many as we."

With this he gave a great sigh.

"Your brothers are in Beaton with no one to warn them of what is transpiring here. Flee to Castle Thoran and prepare all those who remain for what is to come."

Anger filled Teresa's face. Her fists clenched tightly at her sides. She looked ready to strike her own father for what he was telling her.

To leave him to die and return to a castle and prepare them for death as well.

"My king, please allow me to fight at your side. Goblins, Mercs, they are no different to me."

King Thoran got down from his horse and took hold of Teresa's shoulders. Ealrin could see the hurt in his eyes.

"My daughter, you are a princess of Thoran. If I do not return from this battle, this country will need someone to lead them. There are dark days ahead of us. Do not ask me to send my daughter to her death while I reign on the throne with sadness in my heart."

"And what about my own heart?" Teresa replied.

The king embraced Teresa and then quickly got back on his horse.

"May your heart guide you as you lead our people in your brother's absence. Send for them. Folke is to be king and Alric his regent. I'd have you be Thoran's general."

"Don't give up on hope, my King!" said Holve. "I'll not surrender my position as your general so easily."

The king sighed and nodded. Teresa stood rooted to the spot. Her eyes were glassy and her lip began to tremble. Through all the sand and dirt and blood and sweat from the last battle caking her skin and armor and matting her hair, she looked terrible. Yet, in her eyes, Ealrin saw only the love of a daughter for her father.

"I would rather die by your side than live without you, father," she finally said.

"And I would rather die an old man defending the love of his life than rot away in grief. I command you, daughter, flee to castle Thoran. I love you"

With that, King Thoran spurred his horse forward, leaving his daughter to shed a tear and turn away. Androlion rode out with his generals to meet the riders from Thoran. Rayg was at his side, as well as Verde. The rest rode behind, carrying the banners of Androlion and the Southern Republic.

BOTH PARTIES STOPPED just short of meeting, with the king and Androlion coming out of their parties in order to speak to one another. A third man rode up slightly behind Androlion, one Ealrin didn't recognize.

The man wore robes of deep green. On them were echoed the same pattern as the banner of the Southern Republic, with one addition: a white griffin stitched over his heart. He had a terrible smirk on his face: one that spoke of arrogance and pride as well as bloodlust.

King Thoran began the meeting without any formality.

"You carry the banner of the Southern Republic, and yet I do not see Ceolmaer the Elder. Where is the leader of the Republic that he might attest to this madness? Never have the armies of the south invaded..."

"Ceolmaer died. Poor soul, he was so old. He was defenseless against the elven assassin that killed him. But fear not. The elves have paid dearly for their treachery. Tane Silverthread here is the Head Elder. He speaks for the south."

Androlion spoke as venomously as a snake bite. Ealrin could feel his hatred for the man welling up inside him. How could one encourage so much reckless hate and war?

The man bowed his head slightly in King Thoran's direction. A mockery of a salute, as evidenced by his dark smile. Thoran paid him no attention.

"I fear for justice and for the elves of the Southern Republic. I hear reports that Talgel and Ingur both burned to the ground. What do you hope to accomplish, Androlion? Genocide? Will you stop only when there are none but men on the continent of Ruyn? I doubt greatly that the death of Ceolmaer, a friend to all races, was orchestrated by the elves or dwarves of the south."

King Thoran was enraged. Though he did his best to keep his voice down, Ealrin could perceive that at any moment he would have very much liked to strike at Androlion.

But that would only incur the wrath of his armies.

"If you doubt the truth of Ceolmaer's death, then heed these words of warning. The whole continent of Ruyn will burn unless we purge the land of the filth of the elves and dwarves. A greater threat of fire and star. If you will submit to my rule, we may yet save a few. Defy me and you will condemn your entire country to chaos and death."

Again, Androlion spoke of his vision. Again, Ealrin doubted. The man was evil to his core.

"What kind of foolish babble is this?" was the King's only reply.

Androlion chuckled mirthlessly.

"Not babble. A vision. One granted to me by the Master Speaker of Irradan himself! A man of great wisdom."

Irradan was another continent Ealrin had heard of from Holve. It was said to be the center of the study of magic and Rimstone. A Master Speaker had spurned Androlion to this? Ealrin's mind was weary from battle and exhaustion. He listened again to Androlion.

"I have seen the future of this land. One that is prosperous and blessed by the light of the twin sisters, another that is flame and shadow. Follow me, and we shall have light. Defy me, and subject yourself to death, either by my hand, or that of the Dark One!"

With this, Androlion pointed to the comet in the sky that still burned orange and bright. Ealrin hadn't paid it much heed in the last few hours. His mind had been solely on the battle. Was it a trick of the eyes? Or did the thing seem closer?

Androlion looked up, following the path of his own finger. He soaked in the orange light of the comet.

And there was no denying. The thing was closer than it was last night.

"The time is nearly here. What will your choice be, King Thoran?

Ealrin wasn't sure what to expect. A lengthy discourse? A speech? He could think of several things to say to Androlion. He noticed that Tory was near fuming at his side. What restraint was it taking for him to not strike?

"Androlion, I make no promises that you'll find defeat here at my hand. But whether by my hand or another's, you'll one day find where this path will lead you. Your own hatred will destroy you if your enemies do not. I will not suffer your army to pass."

Without further comment, Thoran turned his horse and spurred it back to the line of soldiers, men, dwarves, and elves, all awaiting his return.

Ealrin followed the king, knowing he may well follow this man to both their deaths.

AS THEY RODE BACK TO the army of Thoran, Ealrin spoke to Holve.

"How did you fare in the last battle?"

He was still concerned for his mentor and friend. During the last few days, Holve's health had been getting worse. Whether it was from the battle with the Mercs, being tied up as a prisoner for days, the march through the mountain, or the last battle with goblins, Ealrin didn't know.

Thinking through the possible things that could have made Holve look so sickly, Ealrin was beginning to think he must look pretty bad himself.

Rest had not been a part of the journey for the last two weeks.

Still, Holve was worse off than any of their other companions. He was breathing heavily, though he was riding.

It worried Ealrin.

"I'll be fine. Stop worrying over me," he glared at Ealrin. "You've been too preoccupied with my health. Look to your own!"

He was irate. Holve had tried to joke with Teresa earlier. Perhaps that was just to ease her suffering at the moment. There was none of that humor now. Not that Holve had much humor to begin with. The cause of his current mood could be several hundred reasons.

None of the ones Ealrin guessed were correct, however.

"I fear I've led you to your death, Ealrin," Holve looked over at Ealrin and in his eyes, the older man showed more than a hint of compassion and sorrow. "Perhaps it would have been better if you had ridden away from here with Teresa. I fear you would face your end."

Ealrin was at a loss for words.

As their horses came near the front line, King Thoran shouted for his army to close ranks and prepare for battle. Dwarves made their way to the front of the line. Elves prepared on the flanks to fire their arrows. Men adjusted spears, swords, and shields as they prepared for the second battle in as many days.

Holve began addressing the soldiers, directing some here and there, preparing for the combined armies of the Southern Republic and the Mercs.

All wore grim expressions. They knew what this battle would mean.

Ealrin found his words in the faces of those he looked at from on top of his horse.

"Holve!"

He directed his horse towards the general.

"Thank you," Ealrin said.

Holve raised an eyebrow at him.

"For what?" he asked.

Ealrin looked over the faces of those who were prepared to fight for their lives. In their eyes was determination, courage, and pride. This was an army that would not back down, even against impossible odds.

"For giving me purpose. A reason to fight. If it weren't for you, I'd be selling fish in Good Harbor. This is where I belong. Fighting against hate for the sake of what is good and decent. So, thank you."

He didn't think there was anything else he could possibly add.

There wasn't time anyway. A chorus of trumpets and shouts arose from the army bearing down on them. The men of the Southern Republic and Mercs charged.

"To the king!" Holve shouted.

39: Routed

Ealrin lifted his shield again to deflect the hundredth blow from Merc soldiers. His horse had long been slain. It was lucky the beast had thrown him off when it died without killing him in the process. He now fought for his life with the rest of the army of Thoran.

Elven arrows still shot overhead, thinning the ranks of soldiers who had yet to meet the front lines. Dwarves and men held that line as best they could.

Ealrin was fighting alongside Tory and Holve. The spear of Holve was keeping most Mercs at bay. Soldiers wearing the green uniform of the Southern Republic kept advancing when they thought they could gain the advantage. For every soldier from Thoran that fell, a dozen Mercs went with him. This invading army lacked two things that Thoran had: a superior understanding of rimstone was the first. Fire burned in the north. Merc Speakers had attempted to burn down the forest in order to flush out the elves from their defensive position. Ealrin perceived a great rumbling under his feet. He spared a second to glance towards the beach and saw the great wave heading for them.

Speakers from Thoran were calling the waves forward to douse the flames. Two great waves struck in succession. Ealrin was astonished, in his quick glance, at the skill of the Speakers.

The first rose unnaturally high as it approached the beach. Ealrin could see the wave taking the shape of a large eagle. The water-shaped bird flew, literally flew over his head and smashed into the forest, dousing the flames and turning the black smoke into steam.

The second wave took the form of a bull, rushing at full strength. As it touched the beach's sand, it leapt high and crashed down into the middle of the Merc and Southern Republic army, drenching the men, knocking them to their feet. As the water receded, hundreds of men were swept back into the ocean.

The second thing the invaders lacked were a dedication to defend their own lands and homes.

For a moment, Ealrin began to hope against hope that they may win this battle. Some of the Mercs began to slow their approach. Instead, they looked to the sea, perhaps fearing another wave would come crashing into them.

Ealrin remembered how exhausted Blume had become after Speaking her magic. The Speakers of Thoran would be tiring soon, but just maybe they had given them enough time to take advantage of their enemy's fear?

That thought only stayed with Ealrin for a moment.

For several began to yell and point upward.

Several tails had split from the Dark Comet. Great tendrils of a light, like small comets in their own right, raced towards Gilia and Ruyn.

And one was speeding towards the battle of Thoran and Androlion.

EALRIN TRIED HIS BEST to raise himself to his feet. His ears rang. His body ached. White light was all he could see through his eyes. He blinked several times just to ensure that he had, in fact, opened them.

The world was on fire.

He looked around and saw several others also recovering from the massive explosion.

Ealrin closed his eyes and remembered what had happened.

The comet had come blazing from the sky. The giant fireball had smashed into the rear of the Southern Republic's army. Ealrin and several others had been blown from their feet by the impact of the small comet. For a moment, the fighting had stopped as everyone directed their attention to the crater made by the projectile.

And the beast that rose from it.

The monster was engulfed in purple flame. It had the body and hind legs of a great bull, the wings of a dragon, and smoking armored arms of a man. Its head was horned, and yet a great armored helmet that it wore hid its face. And in its hand, it wielded a sword larger than the trees in the forest it had crashed beside.

It let out a mighty roar as it spread its arms wide. Leaping from the crater into a group of men, Ealrin could tell that those who stood around it barely came up to its stomach. This beast was enormous.

With another roar it brought its sword down in a sweeping arc and dispatched twenty warriors with that single blow.

Chaos reigned.

Most did their best to flee from the abomination. None could outrun it. Wherever its sword struck, dozens fell.

Terrified, Ealrin was frozen to the spot. He found that he was unable to look away from the carnage that was only a stone's throw away from him. A hand on his shoulder brought him back to his senses and he glanced to his right.

It was Holve.

"As strong and as terrible as it seems, it is not invincible. We must fight it back or we will all perish here."

Ealrin nodded, yet he was confused. How in the world did Holve know that this beast was not invincible? There was no time to deliberate.

Elven archers appeared and began to shoot as many missiles as they had left toward the flaming beast. Though some arrows were engulfed in purple flame and seemed to turn to ash, others pierced its flesh. With a howl of rage, it turned its attention in the direction of the archers and charged them.

A line of dwarven warriors met the beast as it charged, protecting the archers. Their shouts of battle intermingled with cries of pain as an attack from the monstrosity hit them and they were cut down.

Still more arrows peppered the monster at its chest and head. Its helmet was protecting it from fatal shots and across its chest it wore a huge plate of armor. Yet where there were exposed places of its black skin, the shafts of arrows protruded.

A hundred men with spears and swords gathered around Ealrin. Knowing that this would be the greatest test of his bravery and skill as a warrior, as well as the final charge of his life, he lifted his sword high and sounded a battle cry as he ran towards the demon.

When he reached the monster, he did his best to hack at its legs, only to find that its skin and hide was as tough as the trunk of a tree. Several men attempted to stab him with their spears and still more rushed at it in order to bring the beast too its knees.

With a mighty kick it sent several flying twenty feet into the air, including Ealrin.

He landed with a thud on top of several others. Many cried out in pain, but Ealrin felt winded, not wounded.

Spinning around, he tried to see where the battle between the demon and the others was taking place. All he had time to perceive was a warrior with an ornate spear jumping high into the air. From the tip of the spear shone a brilliant white light.

As Holve forced the tip of his spear into the demon a flash of purple fire and white light overtook the battlefield. Shielding his eyes, Ealrin was again knocked back by the force of the explosion. Recovering quickly, he looked up, and saw that where the demon was standing, there remained only a huge crater.

There was no trace of the giant beast.

Or of Holve Bravestead.

The noise of the battle died around him.

As the Merc and Southern Republic armies surged forward to take advantage of the stunned army of Thoran, Ealrin stared at the spot where the demon stood moments ago.

The spot from where Holve leapt.

The crater that remained.

Holve was gone.

Some warriors from Thoran stood to fight. A group of dwarves was stubbornly holding back the tide of men that came upon them. Ealrin saw Tory lead a charge of a hundred men to their deaths. They fought bravely. They fought until their bodies were ruined by battle. They fought until there was nothing left of them.

Androlion and his generals rode on horseback through the crater. Verde signaled from his horse for a soldier to pick something up.

A spear.

Holve's spear was given to Verde, who then passed it back to Androlion.

After examining it for a moment, he lifted it into the air and gave a shout.

He knew whose spear that was.

The army of Thoran was overwhelmed. Sheer numbers crashed into them on all sides. The beast had knocked Ealrin into the cover of the forest. Most men surged past him on the road or the beach. He looked around desperately.

Where was the king?

It didn't take long for him to spot him. He was surrounded by warriors of Thoran. They defended the road and the few Speakers that remained. Pieces of rock flew through the air, crushing men as they fell. But soon the rocks slowed as the Speakers grew weary with their spells. Though the king and his protectors fought with all their might, they soon disappeared underneath uniforms of green and gray.

Ealrin felt someone tugging at his shoulder. It took ages for him to respond. He looked up, almost unaware of his own sense of touch and time.

It was Lote.

———✝✝ɭɭↄↄ———

THEY RAN THROUGH FOREST and mountainside. They ran, knowing that their life depended on it. They ran with singular purpose: Warn the city of Thoran of what had transpired.

There was no rest. Fewer breaks. They stayed as close as they could to fresh water, and then they ran again.

It was a week before they came to Liaf. Ealrin was exhausted. Lote pushed them on each day and night, knowing full well that the joint armies of the Mercs and the Southern Republic may be close behind.

They bartered for horses and asked if any others had come through town. To find if any wearing the maroon and gold of Thoran had come.

None had.

Either we are the first to come, Ealrin thought, *or the last that will.*

By horse they raced to Thoran.

And what would they say when they arrived? How do you deliver the news they had?

Ealrin's heart sank, as his horse galloped desperately onward.

Teresa.

He began to think of the difference between dying on the battlefield alongside those you care about and living on in their absence.

Holve. Tory. Gorplin. Cedric.

The other men, dwarves, and elves from Thoran who lay dead on the beaches outside of Liaf.

They had lost so many.

And for what purpose? Fighting back the hate of a man who drove armies to madness?

Androlion Fellgate had beaten Thoran's armies.

Now, Ealrin feared, he would come for its castle.

40: Verde

General Verde sat comfortably at the table of the Head Elders of the Southern Republic. Banners that no longer had meaning hung from its ceiling, celebrating the diversity of the south and the unity of the races. A unity that no longer existed.

Victory was surely within their grasp.

The south had given in and believed the rhetoric that was being preached from every hastily constructed chapel bearing the mark of the comet that these calamities plaguing their land were the result of the elves meddling with dark magic and the dwarves mining for treasure and jewels.

It was the purity of man that would cleanse this land of the demons that now roamed over it.

Fear was a powerful ally. And as far as general Verde was concerned, there was much for the common man to be afraid of these days.

Those living in rural areas or villages without walls feared an attack from the demons. Beasts cloaked in purple flame that roamed the night, killing all who crossed their path.

Those who lived in the sprawling cities feared those who now had power in the Southern Republic: the Mercs and their general: Androlion. To fall out of grace with them meant being banished from the protection of the city walls and forced out into the plains where demons roamed.

And now that these beasts were not the babbling of a displaced Elder, but rather the prophecies of a general and protector of the

308

people, it was easy to convince lesser men to do whatever it took to retain their safety.

Verde was quite pleased with himself and the part he had played in bringing down the republic.

Until Androlion entered the Elder chamber.

He burst through the doors fuming and threw Xaxes onto the round table that used to serve as the meeting place of the Republic's Elders.

There was now only one Elder, and he was a puppet of Androlion.

Androlion had become irater than Verde had ever seen him before. There was something in his plan to dominate the continent of Ruyn that was not going as he had expected. A very guarded man, he never confided in anyone unless he was absolutely sure he could trust them.

And then once that trust was given, total and complete obedience was expected. Something that apparently Xaxes lacked.

Verde removed his boots from the table as Xaxes groaned from hitting the hard wood.

"You told me that you acquired the amulet!" Androlion shouted at the young general. "This," he shook a fancy and well-polished silver claw grasping at a blue piece of rimstone, "is a worthless trinket!"

Androlion threw the metallic accessory at Xaxes. It struck him and made a gash in his forehead, which began to bleed immediately. Xaxes grasped his head with one hand and howled in pain.

Verde was glad their places were not swapped.

"This is twice you have failed me!"

Androlion drew his sword from its sheath and approached Xaxes. He grabbed his neck and brought the blade to his throat. He looked him in the eye with as much loathing as Verde had ever seen in his general's face.

"I will have no more failures from you."

VERDE AND ANDROLION left the chamber. The latter took a cloth from one of the young servants who cleaned the Elder's tower. With it, he wiped his blade clean until there was no more blood left upon it. He threw the towel back at the servant who grabbed it and scurried away, obviously more afraid of Androlion than he was disgusted by the bloody rag.

"Verde," Androlion said as they walked down a flight of marble stairs. "I have a task that is of the most importance. I will not trust it to anyone else but you, my most faithful general."

Verde was not exactly sure he coveted that title, seeing how well it had served Xaxes.

He handed him a book bound in leather. Verde accepted the tome and examined it. It was as old as the city of Conny itself. Its cover was worn and stained and the pages were brittle and delicate.

"Within this book, you will find a description of an amulet that I seek. You will also find potential locations for this valuable charm. Find it and return it to me so that I might name you as second only to me in rule over this continent."

Verde had never seen this book in his leader's possession before, nor had he ever spoken if it. A locket or amulet he knew his master had sought and had been told several times of his desire for it.

But this book was a new discovery.

"Do not fail me, Verde," Androlion said as he continued to descend the stairs. He turned and looked up at the general. Though he was considerably shorter than Verde from this angle, Verde felt no taller than his superior. Verde was at his command, no matter what it was Androlion asked.

He nodded agreement.

"Follow me," Androlion said, leading the way.

THEY CAME TO AN ARMORY of the Southern Republic. The stores of weapons were used in times of war and strife.

Incidentally, the stone storage facility was quite bare.

They walked past several guards who stood to attention at the sight of them. Passing through several locked portals, they finally came to an iron door at the bottom of two flights of stairs. Androlion waved aside the two guards and removed a key from his own pocket. He unlocked and opened the heavy door. The creak of the heavy and old metal filled the halls of the armory.

The room was no wider than the span of Verde's arms. Inside were several chests, which were also locked. Leaned up against the back wall was a spear Verde recognized. The spear of Holve Bravestead.

Androlion handed it to him.

"Read through the book as you travel to Beaton. You'll find this spear to be very useful in your travels, but not for battle. Do not use it to fight with. Your sword will suffice for any man you encounter. This spear must be returned to me as well as the locket."

Androlion gazed into the eyes of Verde, who took hold of the spear with awe.

It vibrated in his hands with an unknown power.

Androlion spoke again.

"I will suffer no more failed attempts to find that which I seek. Do not return without it."

And with those words, Androlion was gone.

41: Beaton's Governor

T he elven ships sailed up river.

It had been a full month since leaving The Southern Republic and their supplies were running low. Though no more pirates had crossed their paths, they were still sailing slower than they could have due to the damage their ships had sustained.

The *Fair Maiden*'s sails were badly tattered. The *Oak's Envy* needed several holes patched with more than other pieces of the ship. And if Wisym's own ship, the *Bright Blade*, did not soon undergo much needed repairs, her main mast would surely splinter and break off at the bottom. The only thing holding her mast upright now was a splint engineered out of oars and several lengths of rope.

And their creaking didn't give Wisym any confidence that the ship would last much longer.

So naturally they had cheered when they saw land. The river meant that Beaton lay farther north, only a few days' worth of sailing. Surely, they could last that long.

The dwarves of Dun-Gaza had turned them away. The Southern Republic had not answered their pleas. The harbors of River Head were abandoned and blackened. Surely someone in Beaton would have pity and come to the elves' aid.

But what now would be her request? To send an army so that the elves could reclaim their homes? To give food and shelter to four hundred elves who were crammed into three ships? Or to repair the ships they had so that they could sail to another far-off place and find new homes? Even among their ancient ancestors on the continent of Irradan?

She wasn't sure what her request would be, having been gone for so long and unsure of where the elves aboard her vessel might call home in the future. Only that surely, in a city such as Beaton, someone would listen to her pleas.

Wisym had only heard tales of the great city, supposedly larger than two capitals of the Southern Republic placed side by side. The sheer amount of beings living in one space was hard to imagine.

Surely someone would aid the elves of Talgel?

Wisym's hopes were high.

ON THE THIRD MORNING since sailing into the river of Beaton, Wisym caught sight of the City by the Sea.

Beaton was every bit as huge as her stories had said it would be, and more so.

From one side of the horizon to the other, the walls of Beaton rose up around the river. Like the great towers of her homeland, several watch towers and other stone monuments rose over the top of the great city walls. Red flags and banners draped the stone parapets and defenses.

Truly, this was an impressive city, even for an elf who desired to see the forest trees more than stone and mortar.

As they approached the harbor, one of her generals, Finwe, came to her side. Finwe had been a general far longer than Wisym. She had the experience of an additional hundred years under the leadership of Galebre, and for that Wisym was more than willing to listen to whatever advice she might offer.

"Up ahead, Sister," she said as she pointed up river. There were several ships docked at the harbor outside of the city's walls. Several men in armor were signaling to the ships to make their way to three empty places on the docks.

"They don't look particularly pleased to see us."

"Do as they signal, Finwe," Wisym said, though she was able to perceive the look on the guard's faces. Wisym agreed with Finwe. It was not a welcoming smile, but an annoyed indifference that showed on the faces of several of the guards in red.

Perhaps they were unfamiliar with the four golden leaves flown on the banners and flags of their vessel. The symbol of Ingur. Wisym wished they had some banner for Talgel so that they may be rightfully represented but pushed the thought from her mind.

She was now the representative of all the elves of the Southern Republic.

The guards signaled them into the docks and almost immediately lifted up ladders and walkways to the ship. Without any words, several soldiers began to march onto Wisym's ship.

For a moment, she was a little less impressed with this city.

AFTER A FULL TWO HOURS of interrogation and cross questioning, the dock master and Wisym still did not see eye to eye with one another.

"I have no payment for docking and will not be turned away! Our people have fled from war and you demand a fee for our ships to float in your river!"

Wisym's patience was wearing thin.

"Every ship pays to dock, without exception. It's the law of Beaton. Pay the fee or sail back down river, lady elf."

Lady elf.

The dock master was a heavyset soldier with a strong handlebar mustache. His brown hair was peppered with gray ones. The helmet he wore had a red plume that matched the red of his robes and chest plate. A sword was slung at his side, though Wisym was quite sure the man was no swordsman worth crossing blades with. His eyes almost disappeared into his fattened face and he stood a good three heads shorter than Wisym.

A black castle with a shield for its door was embroidered onto the cloth of his robes and etched into his armor: the symbol of Beaton, Wisym guessed.

To have come this far, seeking aid and then to be told that they were going to be turned away for three hundred coins was ridiculous. The money of the Southern Republic was only useable if it was exchanged for the coins of Beaton. The exchange could only be done in the city and yet here they were, outside and still in their boats after several hours of being told the laws of Beaton. What Wisym wanted was aid for her fellow elves from those whom she thought would give it, and yet here he was bullying her into paying a fee she could not unless she was allowed into the city.

Wisym was beginning to consider sailing away after trying to reason with this short and pudgy man when she heard another hailing from a ship just now coming into port.

"Hail! What brings the elves of Ingur to Beaton?"

Wisym turned. Here was someone who knew the banners of the elves!

She saw a ship that was much larger than their own that was also emblazoned with the red banners of Beaton with black castles.

The difference, which was not lost on Wisym, was that this ship's flag bore no shield upon the door.

"Dock Master! Let the elves come to my ship with haste!"

The dock master huffed loudly, then turned and left the ship with the rest of the guards of Beaton.

Perhaps not everyone in the city is as difficult at that pudgy dock master, Wisym thought.

"YOU WILL HAVE TO EXCUSE the Red Guard for how they handle the docks of Beaton," the man who had introduced himself as Governor said as he invited Wisym, Finwe, and Ithrel into the captain's cabin of his ship, the *Heart of Beaton*.

"In fact," he said as he motioned for them to help themselves to refreshments, "You'll have to excuse the Red Guard for many of their activities."

Wisym was less concerned about who the Red Guard might be when she saw the fabulous spread out in front of her.

There were several different types of bread as well as fruits that she recognized and others that were new to her. There was turkey, venison, fish, and other food laid out on a magnificent table. The hungry elves loaded their plates while doing their best to remember their manners. Having nothing for the last two days save for moldy bread, however, can cause one's table manners to be a little less than desirable.

The governor of Beaton was not perturbed by the ravenous sounds the elves made as they ate.

After having taken a dozen bites of whatever food was within reach, Wisym looked to the man who was their host, and apparently the leader of the city of Beaton.

He was an older gentleman with gray hair and beard that was well groomed. His blue eyes were not faded with age and showed the kindness that was inside of him. He was not any taller than Wisym but she knew that he was tall for a man. He was not skinny, nor was he heavyset, but instead his frame showed that he was a man not given into indulgence but also not familiar with the pain of hunger.

Seeing how his guests ate, Wisym saw him signal for a servant who stood nearby.

"If this is any indication as to how hungry the rest of the elves on board their ships are, please send rations to them immediately. I will not have guests of my city going hungry."

The servant nodded and then hurried out of the room.

Turning his attention back to the three elves sitting at his table, he spoke directly to Wisym.

"Tell me your story, Sister of Talgel."

He placed an elbow on the table and his head in one hand as he looked into the eyes of what Wisym knew must be a very tired looking elf.

She sighed deeply and then began to relive the events of the past month that led her to the shores of the Red Sea.

WHEN ALL WAS TOLD, the governor shook his head.

"I have heard of trouble brewing in the goblin lands as well as down in the Southern Republic. But I had no idea that it had come to war."

Finding within herself a renewed strength from the much-needed food and renewed hope from the warm reception she had received from the governor, Wisym made her plea.

"Please, Governor," she begged. "You have heard our tale and so I am sure you know how desperate our situation is. We need aid. Whether it is armies or supplies or a place to call a safe haven, we are at your mercy."

The governor leaned his head back against his chair and took a deep breath. His expression changed from one of sympathy to that of a helpless onlooker.

"My title may be governor, but I'm afraid my powers here in the city are few and limited. Every action I take must be tested against the Red Guard's wishes."

He cast a glance out of the window of the ship towards the walls of the city. He spoke more to himself than to the elves at his table.

"Many years ago, when I was first elected governor, crime and evil were rampant in my city. I was desperate for anything that could rid us of the terrible blight that was plaguing us. When I was promised that justice could be restored if I handed over some of my power to the Red Guard, I was quick to agree. Perhaps I was more concerned with being reelected and pleasing the people than I was about my ability to lead on my own."

He looked back at the elves with a very sad expression on his face.

"I will do what I can to lobby for you so that aid may be sent. But I fear there is much red tape we must pass through before I can get authorization for such a venture."

Wisym felt deflated. At first, she had such high hopes that the governor of the city would be able to help. Now she was being told he was little more than a puppet. Her current experience with the Red Guard and their dock master did not bode well for getting aid quickly.

"What I can offer is rest for you and your people, though I know it is not everything you desire."

As he spoke, the doors of the cabin opened and two young men walked in. Wisym noticed that they were dressed finely in maroon and gold. Neither of them looked to be more than thirty human years.

"Ah," said the governor. "If I am limited, perhaps these men may be able to better assist you, Wisym of Talgel."

He stood to his feet and gestured to the two men with his hand.

"May I introduce to you: the princes of Thoran."

42: The Northern Wastes

E alrin had been walking for a solid week. He had been following General Verde for a month, ever since he had seen him venture into the Northern Wastes from Beaton. Ealrin was also keenly aware that the general was on a mission. He stayed as far back from him as he dared, merely following the tracks and trails of travel, as Holve had nearly a year ago when they tracked a thief together.

Why the general had Holve's spear, Ealrin couldn't be sure. He did know, however, that the necklace he carried looked extremely similar to the one that belonged to Blume. That he intended to get it back and return to its owner. He prayed that Blume had indeed been transferred to the magical college in Irradan and spared the war ravaging the south.

His thoughts lingered on his adopted daughter as he followed Verde. It gave him hope and warmth as he pressed on. To think, though there was a great evil in the world, that there could shine a light of hope as bright as Blume Dearcrest was surely a sign that all was not lost, that evil had not triumphed.

Ealrin also pondered the odd series of events that had led him to the Northern Wastes to follow Verde in the first place. Blume's fate. Thoran's current struggles. He shook his head clear. He needed to focus on tracking Verde, and not on thinking of the past.

As Ealrin followed the general west, he began to wonder what quest he might have been sent on. What would have been so pressing that one of his best generals, and most loyal supporter, should be sent to the Wastes? Perhaps he had somehow fallen out of grace in the last month. Perhaps now that the south lay in his grasp, he sought something to help him acquire Thoran. Though, in reality, with the south under his rule, conquering Thoran should not prove to be difficult. This also drove Ealrin to follow Verde: to see if there was something Androlion sought that he might steal in order to disrupt the Merc leader.

On this day, Ealrin followed Verde closer than he had before, making sure to keep him in his sights. The blizzard was worsening and the wind blew against him. He felt that if he were to lose him in the snow, he might be lost as well. He had not yet made himself as familiar with the territory surrounding the inn, as he would have liked. Unlike Holve, he was not keeping at least a hundred maps in his head at once. Instead of tracking him in the snow, and because he was dangerously close to him, Ealrin kept inside the forest that had appeared around midday. While Verde hugged its border, Ealrin tracked him from within.

As they approached a hill, though it was hard to tell in this blinding snow, Verde stopped suddenly. Ealrin just barely had been able to make out something flying through the air at him. Then, as swiftly as a fox, someone jumped from the woods and wrapped themselves around the general. Ealrin saw the blade drawn from the sheath, and the unmistakable slice of Verde's throat.

Ealrin dropped to the ground in order to not be seen. The killer had crouched down over his body and was now picking through the belongings he had on him.

So, this is how one of the greatest generals is defeated, he thought, *by a simple thief.*

But there was something more to this thief. Something that was both familiar and strange. Ealrin noticed the wolf skin lay on their back and the mask of a white wolf that covered their face. He saw the strikingly silver hair that was long and braided and now fell over their right shoulder. The thief was a woman. And not just any woman, nor truly a thief.

Ealrin had heard the stories of this woman from those who stayed at the inn. She was deadly, swift; a bounty hunter without comparison. She was exactly what Ealrin needed.

A plan was forming in his head as he boldly came into view on purpose and walked toward her. He knew that if she desired him to die, he would be dead within a moment's notice. Ealrin also knew that, somehow, the fates were not done with him yet and that this would not be his last day.

He hoped his feelings were not wrong.

The wind changed and he knew a hunter as skilled as she would detect him. And indeed, she spun on her heel and raised her sword, ready to strike at this newcomer who had invaded her capture of a bounty.

Ealrin was shocked as he approached her at her beauty. The hard life that she must live had not affected her radiance. And though the face that she gave Ealrin surely bespoke of a quick and efficient end, her eyes betrayed something that Ealrin had learned to look for in others:

Beauty.

He made no sudden movements towards his own weapon that remained at his side. She looked as if she could strike at any moment, and indeed, Ealrin may very well have already been dead had her knife not been currently residing in Verde's heart.

He spoke loudly, boldly, and with as much courage as he could find within himself, for he knew that if he were right and the plan he had in his mind would work, that the senseless war in the south could reach an abrupt end. But this would be the first step of many. The first part of a long journey that hinged on the answer he now sought from a skilled assassin and bounty hunter.

He was surprised at the calmness in his voice as he yelled over the blizzard:

"Silverwolf! Hunter of the north! I am Ealrin, knight of the Sword and servant of those who wish to keep the continent of Ruyn in a state of peace."

The assassin hesitated. She lowered her blade a fraction. Yes indeed, the fates were not done with Ealrin. He then said the words he would remember for the rest of his life:

"I have a job for you."

More exciting adventures

Thanks so much for reading Sword of Ruyn! I hope you enjoyed your journey. If you did, please consider leaving an Amazon review by clicking here. Reviews help an author advertise their book and help readers know about the journey they're about to take!

Also, you could share your experience on social media!

Click here[1] to share a Facebook post.

Click here[2] to retweet a tweet.

Click here[3] to follow me on Instagram!

---

1. https://www.facebook.com/rglongauthor/photos/

a.177127219720324.1073741829.174225813343798/

187096585390054/?type=3&permPage=1

2. https://twitter.com/rglongauthor/status/977253509652451328

3. https://www.instagram.com/rglongauthor/

The Story Continues

Click here[1] to start reading "Magic of Ruyn", book two in the Legends of Gilia series.

Want to be the first to know when the next exciting adventure in Ruyn is ready?

Sign-up to my email list by clicking here[2].

Also, if you want to connect with me, I'd love to hear from you! Find me on Facebook[3], Twitter[4], or check out my website[5]!

Thanks for reading.

Enjoy the journey,

RG Long

---

1. https://www.amazon.com/gp/product/B079YXKKX7/

2.   https://rglongauthor.weebly.com/subscribe.html

3.   https://www.facebook.com/rglongauthor/

4.   http://twitter.com/rglongauthor

5.   https://rglongauthor.weebly.com/

Made in the USA
Coppell, TX
25 October 2021

64676097R00194